BREAKING the TONGUE

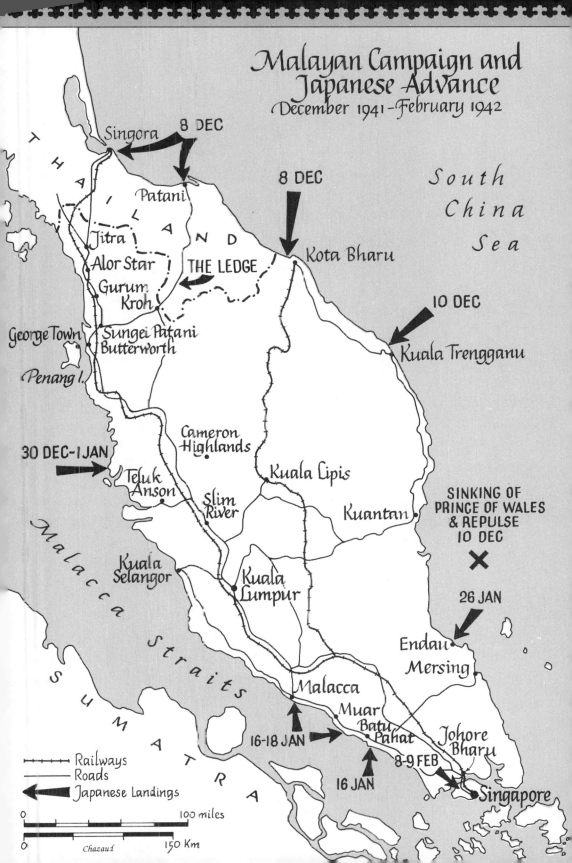

W · W · NORTON & COMPANY · NEW YORK · LONDON

BREAKING the TONGUE

Vyvyane Loh

a Novel

Copyright © 2004 by Vyvyane Loh

Excerpts from *Burmese Days*, copyright 1934 by George Orwell and renewed 1962 by Sonia Pitt-Rivers, reprinted by permission of Harcourt, Inc.

Excerpts from *The Art of War* by Sun Tzu, translated by Samuel B. Griffith, copyright 1963 by Oxford University Press, Inc. Used by permission of Oxford University Press, Inc.

Manufacturing by Quebecor World, Fairfield
Book design by Antonina Krass
Production manager: Amanda Morrison

Library of Congress Cataloging-in-Publication Data

Loh, Vyvyane.
    Breaking the tongue / by Vyvyane Loh.—1st ed.
    p. cm.
Includes bibliographical references (p.   ).
    ISBN 0-393-05792-5
     1. Singapore—History—Japanese occupation, 1942–1945—Fiction.
2. World War, 1939–1945—Singapore—Fiction. I. Title.
    PS3612.O4B74 2004
    813'.6—dc22

                                         2003015870

W. W. Norton & Company, Inc., 500 Fifth Avenue, New York, N.Y. 10110
www.wwnorton.com

W. W. Norton & Company Ltd., Castle House, 75/76 Wells Street, London W1T 3QT

1 2 3 4 5 6 7 8 9 0

To Mauricio, with much love and admiration.
Thank you for all your patience and faith.

Contents

I ❈ Ciphers 15

II ❈ The Employment of Secret Agents 83

III ❈ Generals 141

IV ❈ Civilians 205

V ❈ Terrain 283

VI ❈ Breaking the Tongue 359

Acknowledgments 407

Bibliography 409

BREAKING the TONGUE

A person who gets deculturalised—and I nearly was, so I know this danger—loses his self-confidence. He suffers from a sense of deprivation. For optimum performance a man must know himself and the world. He must know where he stands. I may speak the English language better than the Chinese language because I learnt English early in life. But I will never be an Englishman in a thousand generations and I have not got the Western value system inside; mine is an Eastern value system. Nevertheless, I use Western concepts, Western words because I understand them. But I also have a different system in my mind.

—Lee Kuan Yew
Former Prime Minister of Singapore

O N E

Ciphers

FLOAT, FLY, FLAME UP.

It is a sensation of rising. This is what ether feels like when its vapours flow skyward in wavy rivulets: a lightening of substance. Sublimation. When solid matter becomes gaseous without an intermediate liquid state.

And there is the solid matter below, the huddled shape with its one arm splayed, elbow bent at an impossible obtuse angle. And there are the two interrogators throwing buckets of water over it, turning the white floor brown and briny with sweat, washed-out blood stains, clumps of hair.

They're grunting unintelligible sounds, clipped and staccato as their legs' jabbing and kicking movements into the victim's sides. "Speak! Speak!" one says, his voice shrill, the language suddenly comprehensible: *English*.

They turn him over; his swollen face and split mouth are, for a swift second, unfamiliar. And then the warped features are recognisable: Claude; that's Claude.

You look at yourself, your broken arm, your bloody face, the caved-in ribs, and you almost feel sorry. Almost cry out to them to stop what they're doing, to desist the stomping on your shoulders and chest, to release the broken arm they're now twisting and pulling.

But it is nothing to the scream that suddenly and inexplicably fills the air. No-one else there in the room. Even the interrogators have paused, their ears cocked, and exchanging a glance. The white walls catch your attention. Next door, you tell yourself. The scream came from beyond those concrete walls. Another room, perhaps a hundred other rooms such as this one, but for what purpose? And what is your part in all this? What do they want with *him*? Claude the Body, the solid matter ten feet below, groans and lifts his head, only to be dealt a blow with the horsewhip.

Tell me, you want to say. Tell me why they're doing this, why this urge to hurt, to maim. Why are the walls so white? How many others are suffering? The Body gives no answers.

Then the scream again. A woman's scream, you realise, and this time, you are afraid.

***

Escape to Bukit Timah:

The large colonial bungalow at the end of the lane, its gate and main door facing the slithering tongue of asphalt that ends just before it. The house Claude the Body grew up in, the hiding-place garden of childhood games. The letter-box is marked with his father's name in gold—*Humphrey Lim,* it reads, in a self-important cursive.

Boyhood:

The bungalow has no protection from the path of the sun, so Humphrey Lim has ordered bamboo blinds for the veranda on the first floor, which is open to all the elements. When the family takes tea there each afternoon, the room is a boiling tent of blinds. The family—stiff and formal in buttoned-up frocks; eyes averted; careful gestures. With the blinds firmly rolled down to the floor, no petulant breeze is allowed passageway through the veranda and the family steams in its own sweat like the little Chinese buns they are served along with sandwiches and hard-boiled eggs.

The boy eyes the pot of tea in front of him unhappily. This is a little too much, he wants to say, but remains silent. His mother, Cynthia, pours the tea, leaning across him as she does. He takes in the dampness of her mixed in with her floral perfume; the overall impression is that of a rotting bouquet.

"Why do we have to drink tea when it's so hot?" his sister, Lucy, asks crossly. He can tell she is tired and having a headache from the heat. "Couldn't we have ices instead?"

"It's tea time," says the father, firmly. He is usually indulgent with her but his indulgence is that of an army sergeant allowing the troops to rest in the short moment when he himself drinks some water to lubricate his voice. "Just blow on it and let it cool a little."

"But why do we have to have tea at teatime?" the little girl presses on. "Minah says the English drink beer at their teas. And the children get soft drinks—cold soft drinks."

"Hush," says the mother. She holds her cup to her own lips determinedly and allows herself a small, scorching sip. "Umm. This Assam is quite, quite good, Humphrey. Did you get it at Cold Storage?"

Humphrey nods needlessly. They always get everything at Cold Storage, the European food emporium which caters mainly to the expatriate population. He takes a sip himself. "Yes, first-flush tips. Roger at the office recommended it. Lovely, isn't it?"

The boy, his throat gritty with thirst, can't bear to drink a drop of that livid tea. The bamboo blinds around him are aglow from the sun directly outside; slits of gold pierce the slats like stinging arrows. He feels he is inside a red and angry boil; he feels that in a moment the entire room could burst from the heat and spew sweat and pus all over.

He excuses himself and goes to the kitchen where the cook gives him a glass of cold water. He drinks it and washes his face with a second and third glass. When he returns to the veranda his father has fallen asleep in his chair. The little girl sneaks out to sit under the banyan trees in the neighbours' garden. His mother sits ramrod straight in her chair, shining and still sipping heroically.

He sits with her a long time, until the *amah* comes to clear the trays and his father wakes to go to his study. They say nothing to each other. This is one of the clearest things that you remember about the family.

For whole days, weeks even, nobody notices the boy. When his father gets home from work, he sits himself behind the desk in the study with the newspaper spread out before him like a large mask from which he peers out at the spectacle of the world, a world in which the boy himself is a mere speck. He knows he is invisible to his father until the man wants something from him, and he must obey, hands digging into his pockets, voice low as he mutters, "Yes, sir," even as he wants to say rudely, "No bloody way!" He knows he will never say, "No bloody way" to his father, not out of some sense of what his father might do to him if he did, but because he is too afraid to say no to anyone. For if he ever did say, "No bloody way," he would then have to come up with a sense of indignation and assert his own preferences and he is too unsure of himself to assert anything or, worse, to have anything at all to assert.

This knowledge is a secret shame to the boy: Without his father telling him what to do, without the man informing his choices, he is nothing. He winces whenever he thinks of this and tries, in some way, to remedy it. What he wants more than anything else in the world is to be noticed, to be special; he wants to be like the boys in the Debating Society who argue their points with conviction running like a strong, irresistible current under the river of their rhetoric, using words like "my worthy opponent" and "your esteemed opinion" with open scorn because they *know* that their own opinions and beliefs are superior to those of their adversaries. Their confidence is an elixir to him. He notices how the masters at school laugh at their witty jokes, savour their sarcasms and nod approvingly at the undeniable logic of their arguments. These boys, he tells himself, know how to think. These boys are leaders and heroes who assert themselves regularly with ease, who would, if anyone disagreed with them, laugh and say, "No bloody way!" and know that they were right. He is nothing like them.

He spends hours by himself at the bottom of the garden where a low, dry ditch runs beside their mango tree. The mangoes are always stunted, dropping off while they're still green, giving off sour scents and rotting into pulpy masses that even the flies keep away from at first, because of their acidity. But when the worms have done their job, digesting the green globes and releasing the sugars from the flesh, the flies return, busying themselves with their tiny stick antennae, tonguing the now-sweet juice from their hairy legs. He watches them, wishing he could live like a fly, immune to degradation and disgust, happy to rest and multiply in dung heaps, living a simple, thoughtless life.

Some days he sees his grandmother strolling about in the garden, brusquely clipping the dilapidated roses off the rose bushes. "Rahman," she says, "this is *not* the climate for roses! We should be planting hibiscus or bougainvillea instead." It is true that the roses are closer to a light brown colour than white from the fierce sun. It is true that there are more thorns than roses on the bushes, so that they look like some kind of cactus variant, blooming only occasionally after a wet bout. "Now help me dig these out so we can plant something more suitable."

Rahman, the gardener, shrugs. "But Sir wants roses," he says. "He wants an English rose garden. What can I do?" They stand, looking at the bushes together.

Grandma Siok snorts in disgust but doesn't press Rahman to dig them out. The boy knows they will remain where they are, struggling to survive under the fulminating sun because his father has asserted himself. Grandma Siok will not dig up the rose bushes because they are not hers to dig up; it is not her house or garden.

"They look ridiculous," she sniffs, tossing the wrinkled flower heads into the rubbish heap which Rahman will burn later that day, when the wind is conveniently blowing away from their house and

right into the direction of the Tams' house. But this is only neigh-
bourly justice because the Tams' gardener burns their rubbish in the
morning, when the wind sweeps over the boy's house.

As she passes the boy on her way back to the house she talks to herself. "That fool," she says. "What does he know about gardening? An
English rose garden on the equator indeed!" She too, he knows, is not
afraid to assert herself. Even though nothing will change, she will
tell his father what she thinks of his roses, she will give him a piece
of her mind. The boy himself is unable to decide if the rose bushes
should stay or go. It depends on whom he is with at the moment. If
he is near his grandmother, he is likely to agree with her; if he is
with his father, he is suddenly aware of the charm of roses in a tropical garden. It is this pliancy that he despises in himself.

In the late afternoons, the Tam twins swim laps in their pool on
the other side of their house where he can't see them. On Fridays
they often have guests—English boys who whoop as they plunge into
the pool and then race around the house in their bare feet and
swimming trunks, giggling wildly. Sometimes, peering from his
obscure ditch, he sees them plotting elaborate games under the
banyan tree. "You lot have to take orders from me, because I'm the
captain," the biggest English boy says importantly. "Robin, Robert,
you two are prisoners and after the feast, you'll have to walk the
plank."

"No, I'm the captain," says one of the twins—Robin or Robert,
the boy can never tell—stepping forward firmly. "It's my pool."

"It's *our* pool," the other twin corrects and somehow, the English
boy gives in without demur, letting them both be captains. The boy
marvels at this rapid promotion.

"The ship's on fire," one captain declares. "Everybody into the
water!"

And the horde charges to the pool, the Tam twins leading the
stampede, running faster than all the English boys, yelling directions. Then they are out of sight, hidden by the house, and the boy
hears a succession of splashes, shrieks, watery plops, coalescing into
a cool liquid music which he cannot enter, standing in his dry ditch,
sweat in his armpits, the sun shooting its last rays into his eyes.

Claude the Body is sleeping. His arm is so swollen it has lost its shape; the elbow and wrist have been swallowed into the sausage-like lump that is attached to his shoulder. What was it that they wanted from him? How had this come about?

Something about what he knew, something about the girl. Something about his "close association" with her, and what she might have told him.

But there is something else. Something that has not been mentioned but insinuated in everything that has been said to him in this room. It is the language he speaks.

Claude the Body speaks English as a first language. It is this that his Japanese interrogators can't stand. You sensed it in the dismissive way they tossed the questions at him in his own language. You caught the disdain in the way they tortured the English sounds and threw them at him, the venom in the way they darted the words at him. All this you registered as they probed endlessly into your life, your conversations with the girl, one Han Ling-li, with whom you spent the last days before the Fall in a battered clinic on Serangoon Road.

What for? you had asked, willing the words out of the Body's mouth. Why do you want to know?

To record history, one of them had said with a sudden, unexpected burst of hilarity. We have made history, he said, and now we will write it down.

The year before the war the boy is sitting in the kitchen of his upper-middle-class home in Bukit Timah. Ah Lan, the washerwoman, had quit the week before, claiming that she couldn't continue to work in a house with such bad luck and *feng shui*. It's affected her health, she told her employers, and she's had it.

"Silly superstitious natives!" is all Humphrey says when he hears the news, snapping his wilting newspaper to attention. The *amah* is left to do the laundry.

The boy sits in the corner on a stool, waiting for her to finish ironing his shirt. Rahman the gardener, Phatcharat the old cook and Muthu, the Tams' chauffeur from next door, are having their morning tea break. They eye the spindly figure warily at first but when he keeps his eyes fixed on the book in front of him, they quickly lose interest.

Muthu makes the coffee in the *tarekh* style, "stretching" it by pouring it in a long stream back and forth from pot to mug, then mug back to pot, on and on. The *amah* (simply called Amah by everyone), Rahman and Phatcharat are all talking amongst themselves in Malay. The boy has never spoken to them in anything other than English, the only language he knows. As required by his father, all the servants speak basic, albeit appalling, English.

"Chong's shop burned down yesterday," says Amah, her arm passing rhythmically over his shirt. Watching her from the corner of his eye, he notes the sing-song quality she manages to inject into her Malay.

"Chong? The baldy with the big belly? *Cheh,* where will I get my spices from now on?" Phatcharat asks as she fans herself with a cheap paper fan. The boy hears Chong's name, recognises they are talking about the owner of a sundry shop a mile away from them, where Phatcharat does her shopping every Sunday. Humphrey has always said that many Chinese sundry shops are nothing more than larger versions of the usual squatter's hut, and fire hazards at that, because of their poor construction and store of kerosene, paraffin and other flammable goods. At least one burns down each month, leaving the grumbling customers to seek out another to patronise.

Chong's shop was Phatcharat's favourite because it carried all the Thai spices she needed for her cooking, as well as week-old Thai newspapers which she devoured with a passion. Phatcharat is in a constant state of homesickness, which she propagates with care. She never takes leave and has not been back to Thailand in ten years, because, she says, she enjoys it more from afar. "I like the longing for it," she has said before, "more than I like visiting. Just the deep wanting—it makes me feel more alive."

"I heard," Amah says, dramatically now, "that it was no accident.

Chong is friends with many Japanese—too many." She twists her head about on her neck to survey the effect of her words on the room.

This is greeted by a collective cry of "*wah's*" and "*aiyo's*" to her great satisfaction.

Chong again, the boy thinks. What's he gotten up to?

"So he is a spy?" Rahman says in wonder. "He always looked so simple—who would have thought?" He shakes his head. "You think his whole family too?"

Amah begins talking in rapid Malay, swallowing half her words in her excitement. " . . . getting money for collecting information on traitors . . . book with names of all *towkays* . . . can't trust anyone at all, and things going so badly on the Burma Road . . ." The iron pauses dangerously long on the front of the shirt but just as a very faint whiff of smoke lilts the air, she lifts it off and is cooling it with her breath.

Muthu, the Tams' chauffeur, joining them at the table, lowers his voice and changes the subject. "I was at a meeting last night." The boy can feel the chauffeur's glance on him and forces himself to turn a page casually, uncomfortable with the atmosphere that has suffused the room.

"Mother's boy!" says Rahman and they all laugh.

"Okay, *lah*," Muthu says in English and then lapses back into Malay. "They were talking about India. Home Rule."

"India? Can they do that?" Phatcharat asks.

"*Goondu*, of course they can," Muthu says. "I agree with what they said—India should be ruled by Indians."

"It will never happen in Singapore."

"What do you know, Rahman? You need people like the Indian Independence League—politicians! Everything is talk, you know, even this business of who gets to do what with a country. You just see, if you people get some good local leaders—"

"You people?" asks Rahman, raising his eyebrows. They all stare at Muthu.

The chauffeur draws himself up proudly. "After all, I am Indian."

"Since when?" Rahman asks dryly.

"I—am—Indian."

No-one says anything for a while. The boy looks up from his book, wondering at the sudden strain in the voices around him. Muthu is holding himself in a stiff, slightly defiant pose and Amah has just started on his trousers.

"What else if not Indian?" Muthu asks. "What is this place? It's not India, it's not China, it's not even Malaya. It's nothing."

"Well, I wouldn't say that—"

"No, Phatcharat? Then tell me where you send your money to when you say you send it 'home.' Where does most of your pay go?"

"Thailand, of course. I have family to support there—"

"And Amah sends her money 'home' to China, and I send mine to my relatives in Madurai. You see?" They digest this in silence.

When Muthu speaks again his voice is lowered. "You see, only *his* type will feel this is their country in the end." Again the strange, buried aggression in the tone. The boy senses it, feels the antagonism directed at him, the sly glances burning the top of his head, and forces himself to turn a page.

Encouraged by his ignorance, Muthu continues. "This type will serve the white man to the end, they even think they're white themselves—only speaking English, dressing like English, behaving like them. Let them have Malaya if they want!"

"I think the old man is only *gilah*," says Phatcharat. "This nonsense about being English—I mean, the day he takes a good look in the mirror he'll understand he's been talking rubbish."

"Malaya is my country," says Rahman, his chin tilting. "I don't mind the British. We Malays get along with everybody, but it's true that whenever I pass through the Unfederated Malay States, it feels—different, good. To be able to walk around without the British controlling everything—but realistically Malay cannot have self-rule. Too mixed up—Chinese, Malay, Indian, Eurasian, altogether in one big *rojak*! Only the Malays will want to obey the sultans."

"And who says the sultans will rule if the British leave?" Muthu asks.

"Ah, you! You just go back to India and leave us in peace! What's it to you anyway? After all, India is your country, not Malaya."

Phatcharat smacks the kitchen table with both hands as she gets up from her chair. "Enough talk," she says. "Soon they'll be pestering me for food."

Amah calls the boy's name. He pretends not to hear for a moment, composing his face behind his book after the snarled but incomprehensible words. She raises her voice, practically shouting. "Oh," he says as she hands him his shirt, trousers, handkerchief—all pressed—and a pair of socks.

"This one," she says in Malay to the scattering group. "Always in a daze. Hears nothing except English!"

They snicker as they disband.

To record history, you say with a sudden, unexpected burst of hilarity. You too can make history, write it down. The thought is so clarifying, so renewing that you hardly feel the slap. Too busy with possibilities, too delighted by options.

Give them what they want, tell everything.

They want to know about Ling-li? Tell them how stubborn she is, how maddening. Tell them her past as no-one else would know it. No-one except you, of course, you the sudden Possessor of All Memories. Give them Information.

Let them lunge and hurt with their tools, let them play with their instruments. You too have a creative task; you too have an opportunity to perform.

Sing away, write it down. Make it—

She's always been thin, but lately she has had to pin her clothes every morning to keep them on her. Uncle Hong-Seng, whom she lives with, enjoys teasing her about her stick-like shape. "Just like a *changkol,*" he says in Malay. "Or a chopstick. Which will it be, Ling, *changkol* or chopstick?"

"No time for your jokes, Uncle," she says acidly. Though they speak to each other in Hokkien, her native dialect, she keeps slipping into Mandarin, the language she's used in school and continues to use with friends. "Some of us have things to do. You can keep your jokes for after the war."

"After the war! Everything's after the war for you! You have to enjoy a little now or you'll be a sour old maid after the war!" He wags his finger at her but she knows that underneath all his teasing, he takes the Sino-Japanese war as seriously as she does. But he's right about her weight. She has been looking quite skeletal recently and many people besides her uncle have commented on it. Having lived her whole life in her own body, however, Ling-li is not taken in by the alarmist theories of her friends.

"You must have tapeworms," a colleague at the Youths for China Organization diagnosed a week ago. He's halfway through his first year in medicine at the University. Privately Ling-li thinks he's too much of a sensationalist to make a good doctor.

"Too much heat in your system," another one has told her, sub-scribing to the Chinese belief of "hot" and "cold" imbalances in the body. "You need to eat more cooling foods."

"Blood sickness," says yet another. "My nephew died of it a year ago. Go see a doctor."

But Ling-li knows what's wrong. She just needs to eat more. Ever since her childhood she's had to eat in large amounts just to keep her thin frame from looking malnourished. It was worse when she had to participate in sports. The year she played field hockey in school, she had to consume three bowls of rice at each meal plus extra helpings of meat whenever possible. She also supplemented her diet with chocolates, soya bean milk, fried dough sticks and hard-boiled eggs which she carried around wrapped in a large hand-kerchief during the day, and which she could crack easily and eat in between classes. In the end, the hockey had had to go because her uncle said she would eat him out of everything he owned and ruin him.

Now that she's training to be a nurse, she's had to double the vol-ume of her food to keep her weight stable. All the activity of chang-ing bedpans, making beds, turning obese, moribund patients, lifting heavy boxes of supplies, rolling corpses onto stretchers that would take them to the morgue—all this unceasing running up and down and short sleep hours burn up all the fuel she shovels into her body. At work, she was so hungry that she could not dish out the patients' food from the meal trolley without stuffing a potato or two in her mouth. None of the patients seemed to mind, but the ward sister caught her once, and reprimanded her at the end of the shift. Ling-li was more cautious after that.

But despite the constant eating she's losing flesh fast. Her uncle has been making her his special soup with high-grade ginseng twice a week but it hasn't helped. "How about coconut milk?" he suggests finally. "It usually fills me up. That's why those curries sit like rocks in your stomach afterwards, you know."

Not bad, she thinks, and embarks on her coconut milk spree. She makes herself eat thick curries, rich *nonya* desserts, Malay cakes, anything that contains a substantial amount of coconut milk in it. She also begins frequenting Indian food stalls and buying *murtabak,* the rich Indian pancake made with eggs and plenty of ghee. "More, more," she'd urge the *murtabak* maker in Malay as he ladled the ghee over the cooking pancake. Eating three at a go helps quiet her stomach rumbles and allows her to make it through midmorning before she needs to eat again.

"It's working," she says to her uncle happily. She doesn't gain any weight, but she doesn't lose any either.

When she stands with arms akimbo, she looks like a clothes hanger, her bony arms and elbows forming a triangular shape.

What Ling-li told Claude—"Every Chinese knows this":

Before General Yue Fei rode into his first battle in Southern Song Dynasty China, he went to pay his respects to his mother. His troops unfurled over the landscape at rigid attention, flags fluttering.

Yue Fei's mother told her son to remove his tunic. He knelt, back to her, facing his troops as she'd commanded. He never expected the knife at his back. Eyes closed, he awaited death: My mother—she gave me life, she has the right to take it from me.

But she was carving in his flesh. She was branding him with words. She was scarring him with her sure calligraphy: 精忠报国 . The Ultimate Loyalty Is to Serve Your Country.

When the blood dried he put on his tunic and walked steadily to his horse. Already the scabs were crusting, hardening. He rode off without looking back.

All his life, on the eve of battle, the scar tissue tightened and itched. His first wound inflamed him, kept him up till dawn gazing at the enemy's watch fires, fighting down his fear. On the battlefield it drove him forwards, tormented him with its injunction: to serve his country with his body. Words embodied, become flesh, driven into action.

Ling-li at six years old is General Yue Fei over and over, refusing even to let the boys have a turn at her war games. She has on a shirt with the words 精忠报国 painted on the back. It's dirty because she's never washed it. Her first shirt had made a mess when it was soaked. The ink had run and stained everything else in the wash bucket. Not having access to waterproof ink she has simply resolved never to get her new Yue Fei shirt wet. The sour, oily smell of it is a fair exchange; she even likes it and sniffs at it when no-one is looking. She imagines its sour odour must be like the smell of battle.

Serve Your Country, Yue Fei's mother had written on his back. These same words are now carried on Ling-li's own back. What country? she finds herself wondering. What's my country? she asks her teacher.

Why, China, of course.

But I don't live there.

You're Chinese, aren't you? Then China is your country.

China, the chunky, blunt bulk of it which she caresses on the map. General Yue Fei's country, and hers. It suits her fine.

Strange. For a moment you *were* Ling-li, in her six-year-old body, playing war games. She has never talked about her childhood games to the Body, but just a little while ago, you possessed those memories. Claimed them, relived them as your own.

This confuses you more than the immobile shape on the floor, the way it doesn't react when the Japanese interrogators spit on it. Is he dead? But even as you think this you see the movement of his chest, its stubborn rise, the startling way it seems to collapse as it falls. Must be the broken ribs, you think, relieved he is still alive.

The interrogators have had enough for now, it seems. They leave after a few more half-hearted kicks. Their voices are amused, the short vowel sounds of their speech mocking. The door shuts and their footsteps fade off like ellipses. Claude the Body, sensing this, seems to relax, breathe more slowly.

You might have gone down for a closer look, had it not been for the scream again, a terrible rasping grate on the nerves. You see a girl, a knife carving a back, generals and flags. You see unspeakable things.

Ling-li said that as far back as the 1920s, the British had had warnings from their own kind. Of course they wouldn't listen to us, to the Chinese community leaders, she'd said, but you'd think that they would pay more attention to a fellow countryman.

The situation unfolds before you—General Sir Theodore Fraser, General Officer Commanding, Singapore, is reading his most recent correspondence:

Committee of Imperial Defence
Special Memo to the Ministry of Defence
****January 16th, 1923****

The committee would like to recommend the Royal Navy's proposal to build the Empire's Eastern Naval Base on the north end of Singapore Island. Strategically, this site allows for better sea communications in the Indian Ocean and the South Pacific than the other proposed sites in Sydney, Hong Kong and Trincomalee. Our studies show that the north end of Singapore Island is ideal in that it faces the state of Johore in Malaya and is protected by the impenetrable Malayan jungle. The committee is confident that no enemy force will be able to succeed in passing through this thick and hostile jungle territory. Voyaging time from Home Waters approximates to seventy days (via Suez), as previously reported.

The general throws the report from the military planners onto his desk, watching the papers fan out as they land. "Impenetrable indeed!" he snorts.

The map on the wall winks at him. He takes in the protruding tongue of the peninsula, runs his finger from its northern border down its spine to its southernmost tip. "I tell you what," he says to himself. "I'd hazard a guess that anyone attacking us would land here—" He prods the belly of Thailand. "Yes, quite, and make their way down the roads to Singapore."

But those erstwhile military planners believe the island to be an impregnable fortress. Impregnable. The word makes Fraser think of a city hewn out of rock, an unyielding ground. But when he's walked the island's perimeter, all he's seen is swamp, the mollusc nature of the soil. It is ground that absorbs everything.

Oh dear, he thinks, oh dear.

Is it possible to see so much, to be an entire people all at once? Is it possible to bear such knowledge? Weightless like this, the possibilities are infinite. But most of all, you are drawn to the body below: Claude, clod, clot, cloth, clout, clown; you, light as floating cloud, possessor of a broken arm and cracked ribs, the English-educated boy from Bukit Timah, you the practical, level-headed Ling-li, you the peanut vendor dragging his cart behind him, you the Malay clerk in City Hall, you the Chinese women labourers laying down roads and fearlessly scaling flimsy wooden scaffolding to erect the growing skyline of Shenton Way, you the pommified soul of Humphrey Lim and associates, you the Bengali doormen of vaulted banks and airy hotels, you the tormented psyche of Cynthia Lim, you the satay-seller, you the scrofulous gangsters and clan leaders in the querulous heart of Chinatown, you the sometime Voice of a confused and cantankerous city. More than that, you are witness to all that has brought about the fall of the city, the many and petty English foibles that have changed the course of history. Or obeyed it.

It's a game Grandma Siok has invented. She makes up messages on small strips of paper in code, leaves them scattered through the house, and if Amah hasn't swept them away, the boy finds them eventually and tries to piece together the key. Sometimes there are only numbers and he has to ascribe the letters of the alphabet to them. Other times they are more like riddles and word puzzles. Once he finds strange designs on them, things that look like: 重整旗鼓 and 鞠躬尽瘁. "They're Chinese characters," Grandma Siok tells him but doesn't explain.

"Teach me," he says.

"It's not that easy."

"This one, for example—what does it mean?"

"Heavy, weight, importance."

"And this?"

"To burn to ashes, to exhaust."

"How does it work? Is this a verb? A noun?"

"It's a world, just like every word, every character. An image of the world."

He squints at the neatly brush-painted worlds, turns the paper scraps upside down, then right side up again.

"All depends on Memory," she says. "You start by memorising brush strokes, by memorising stroke combinations, by committing the world to memory and then reproducing it, one word at a time."

"Teach me," he says again.

She shows him to her room, unrolls a scroll of rice paper onto her desk, hands him an inkstick. "You'll have to grind the ink first." She catches his other wrist, slaps a heavy weight into his sweaty hand. He looks down at the purplish stone. "Feel it," she tells him and he rubs his thumb in the carved depression which is shaped like a pond. In the corner of the inkstand, on the rim, is a carved buffalo, his tail draping carelessly into the pond. Indigo swirls in the stone's grain imitate water, miraculously flecked by sunlight. "Gold."

"Gold," he repeats, rubbing at the flecks. "Real gold?"

"This wouldn't have cost me a fortune otherwise," she says, taking the inkstand from him. She pours a few drops of water into the ink-stand from her bedside carafe. "Now this is how you grind the ink." She takes the inkstick and rubs one end in the water.

It takes an hour before the boy manages to grind up ink that meets Grandma Siok's standards. "You press too hard—it makes the ink gritty." So he has to learn to relax his grip, to make even circles with his wrist. When he is done, the ink seeping into the tiny lines on his hands, pooling to a smudge under his nails, she nods at him. "That's it for today."

"And the words? Do I write them now?"

"No. Not until you can grind the ink properly. You're a quick learner, it won't be longer than a few weeks."

"And then?"

"Then you'll learn the basic eight strokes. If you practise every-day, it should take you a few months."

"And then?"

"Then we will combine the strokes to form each word, which you will copy out until it is engraved in your memory."

"And then?"

"And then word by word you will learn Chinese. That is the way it is with our language."

It is strange to hear her say that: "Our language." He finds him-self looking over his shoulder, just in case his father is within earshot. For a whole week he rubs the inkstick until his hand learns its own weight and fills the pond so that the water buffalo stares at its own reflection in the inky depths.

Grandma Siok teaches him to hold the brush the classical way, not allowing him to rest any part of his arm or hand on the paper. When he tires he is supposed to stop and rest, then resume, always with the correct hand position, and over time he will acquire the necessary stamina to write for hours. But just after he has learnt the vertical and horizontal strokes, when he is about to learn the dot stroke, his mother catches them at their lesson. She does not say anything, just leans against the door, smoking and watching, watching and smok-ing, and Grandma Siok does not say anything, just loads the brush and writes, flicking her fingers, controlling her wrist, correcting him when he makes ugly blots on the paper, until they have finished the lesson.

And that is the last lesson. He doesn't hear the heated words between his parents and his grandmother, but he guesses at them. "We will educate our children the way we see fit," his father says.

"It's our duty, and our right," Cynthia adds just before Grandma Siok can open her mouth.

"And what is wrong with them learning their mother tongue?"

"It's archaic," says Humphrey. "A waste of time. It won't get Claude into Oxford."

"Maybe he could teach them something at Oxford."

"Mother."

So the lessons stop, and for several days the boy carries the scraps around in his pocket, makes illegitimate copies of the characters by assembling the strokes clumsily in his coarse hand. Grandma Siok, tired of fighting with his parents, refuses to translate the words. "It's nothing," she says when he appears in her room holding out her enigmatic notes. "Shoo. Go read some Milton or something." She settles her head on her pillow and covers her face with Sun Tzu's two-thousand-year-old treatise, *The Art of War*. "I'm studying Strategy."

The boy places the paper scraps in his clarinet case, in the little section where he keeps his reeds. Sometimes he takes them out, sets them on his music stand and plays them like music. He never deciphers them.

You don't want the Body to tell too much, to say anything that would be misread or jeopardise friends and family, and if anyone had suggested this possibility a mere few days ago, you would have laughed it off. Absurd that he would know anything at all that would be of interest to the Japanese, or implicate anyone. As Ling-li would have scoffed—Claude, of all people!

And yet, these memories come unbidden to you, these revelations and half-dreams that have been lived out by others and the Body. Or made up by you—who knows what the mind can do under pressure? Who suspected you would have such a perverse delight in fictions, versions, variations? History: the Detour. And you, its author.

Air Chief Marshals might be expected to be dashing, energetic, forceful and decisive. But London sends expendable men to the East, men who have grown tired of long meetings, who would like nothing better than a game of chess under palm trees by the Singapore River, whose flat arches ache at night from standing too long at parades and strategic exercises.

Sir Robert Brooke-Popham knows the irony of titles. C-in-C, Far East—the appointment suggests immeasurable power over the sweep of Asia. Yet he has no say in the navy, and shares the army and air force with the General Officer Commanding and the Air Officer Commanding. He is powerless in the civil administration. A younger man might have had more ambitions, but Brooke-Popham, at sixty-two, is rather grateful for the shared responsibilities. It gives him time to breathe, to weigh things carefully. It certainly allows time for golf and tennis, and short naps after lunch. It is not, after all, a far cry from retirement, and he is grateful. The Empire takes care of its old soldiers.

❁

Altar: an arrangement of sacred objects and idols for worship; a platform for ritual, sacrifice, prayer; a place of communion for the family, uniting past generations with the present; where commercial dealings are undertaken with offerings, bribes and bargains struck with the appropriate deities.

There is no family altar in the house. Humphrey disdains the very monumentality of it, for a proper altar would have to have been situated prominently, facing the main door, plumb in the middle of the family hall, recklessly gaudy in its Oriental scarlets and gold. There would have been porcelain gods, brightly robed and wielding swords, hatchets, axes in martial arts poses—"barbaric displays," Humphrey calls them—laughing Buddhas with skin hanging flabbily over large paunches, goddess figurines on ceramic lotus flower bases. And the red candles weeping melodramatically, leaving messy splats of wax everywhere, the joss-sticks burning to a fine powder that would then spray across the room in the slightest breeze, so that everything would be coated with ashes. "So distasteful," Humphrey says of the altars in local homes, laden with colourful figurines. "So loud!" And yet, when his father dies, a temporary one is erected in the garden at the insistence of his sick mother.

The boy has just had his ninth birthday. His grandmother and grandfather had always lived in Holland Village in their own little bungalow, but in the past ten months, due to their collective ailments and frequent falls they have had to move into the guest room in his house. His grandfather had kidney problems and smelled of urine and for the rest of his life, the boy could not hear the word "kidney" without thinking of the frail, constantly embarrassed old man in diapers, whose organs needed to be soaked everyday in a special chemical bath to get rid of the toxins that had accumulated in his blood. He's hardly ever said anything to his grandfather since he moved into the house, and never even thought of him throughout his birthday party, engrossed as he was by the cake and ices and the magic show that Muthu gave. When the old man died, the routine of the boy's day was untouched, and he continued to play with his birthday toys without being disturbed by household events.

Now he has overheard Amah saying that it's very bad luck to have a birthday so near a death but his father has forbidden any further superstitious talk in the house, which frustrates the boy because he likes scaring himself with Amah's stories. When he begs her to say what could happen if one's grandfather dies two days after one's birthday, she refuses with righteous dignity. "No super-sti-tious nonsense in this house," she tells him, imitating Humphrey, spit flying out of her mouth in the effort of getting the four-syllable word out in one breath.

Humphrey makes an initial protest to his mother when the monks arrive with their wooden blocks and sticks. "But he wasn't even a Buddhist! Why would he want all that chanting and toc-tocking at his funeral?"

"He wasn't an *outright* Buddhist," his mother says, her diabetic breath overwhelming him with its fruitiness. "But he believed inside. I know he did. Now tell the child to kowtow at the altar. As the only grandson, he must stand with you to receive the last respects."

And Humphrey gives up because his mother looks so close to passing on herself that he is afraid to upset her any further. "Well, son," he says to the boy who has been waiting outside his grandmother's door. "You can go in and say hello, but just for a moment.

After that . . ." He winces, thinking of what lies ahead. "We'll deal with it later. Go on."

The boy walks into the room with mincing steps because he doesn't really want to see his grandmother. She's been sick his whole life and he is afraid of the gap in her right foot between the big toe and the middle toe which resulted from an amputation years ago, and the strange yellow-chrysanthemum-purple-orchid bruises on her stomach where she has had to have her insulin administered everyday. Although she is usually sweet with him (unlike Grandma Siok), he is nervous and drained in her presence. Maybe it's her way of crushing him to her until he can no longer make out the sour lavender smell of the talc she sprinkles over her creases, or her insistence that he eat all the sweets she offers him. "Another," she would say, when he's managed to suck one into nothingness. Her eyes follow his hands greedily as he undoes the wrappers and pops the sweet into his mouth. It's as if she tastes these forbidden treats through him, savouring the candied flavours as his teeth bite through the hard candy, staining his tongue.

Once, his throat was raw from so much sugar that he almost cried. But there was no water in her room because the doctor had thought her lungs were "wet" and she was to drink only four glasses a day until her swollen legs deflated. "But you can't leave me," she had said when he asked to get some water from the kitchen. "Have another sweet—it'll make you forget you're thirsty and stir up the juices in your mouth." And so he was stuck until Amah rescued him at teatime. When she dies of a diabetic coma five months after his grandfather's death, this is what he remembers of her.

"You remind me so much of Humphrey when he was a child," she says now, not holding out her arms for her usual bone-cracking hug. He can tell she has been crying. "You have to be very well behaved at the altar, do you understand? When people come to pay their respects, you bow back and shake their hands. And you'll be kneeling the whole time—no fidgeting! It's the way your grandfather would have wanted it." She closes her eyes and he can see that her lashes are wet.

He moves to the door. "I'll be good," he says, but she doesn't move, doesn't open her eyes. "I'll do everything you've told me." Still nothing. "I'll be off now."

He closes the door and hurries to find his father, eager to get to the altar for a closer look. Amah has spent the entire day setting it up and he has not been allowed near it because she has complained that he distracts her by asking too many questions. There is no-one but Grandma Siok in the living room and he has to bite his lip to hold in his frustrated sigh. To go from one grandmother to another—what bad luck! He bends low, hoping to slip out of view behind the sofa, but Grandma Siok has always had the sharpest eyes in the family.

"Ho! There you are! Your father wants you to change—he's in his room and wants to see you when you're done." He starts to leave but she hasn't finished. "White—top and bottom. You know that, don't you? I fancy Siew Lian told you." His other grandmother has mentioned no such thing, but he pretends that she has, and nods before retreating hastily.

When he goes to his father, Humphrey is having a hard time finding his clothes. Usually, Cynthia lays them out for him, but since the old man's death, she has moved into a hotel for a few days. "Being pregnant is awful enough," she said. "I'm not sitting through such an uncivilised funeral! You deal with it, Humphrey!"

"Aren't you dressed yet?" Humphrey asks sharply when the boy enters after a dutiful knock. "I thought I told Siok to tell you."

"She did. These are all my white clothes. Socks as well."

"Did she tell you to dress like this?"

The boy hesitates before replying. "Grandma Siew Lian did."

"Oh." Humphrey moves around the bed and places his hands on the boy's shoulders. "I think a suit would be better. I've told Amah we'll receive the guests in the sitting room and the monks can do their bit out in the garden. I just hope they won't go on for too long."

"But I thought . . . Grandma Siew Lian said—"

"She's a very sick woman, and we mustn't always take her so literally." Humphrey bends down to tie the boy's laces. "One of these days you'll trip . . . Your grandfather was a very modern man, you know. He wouldn't have tolerated all that nonsense with the monks." His face is so close that the boy can see the sheen of oil on his nose and cheeks. "We can't embarrass him now, can we? Cynthia was right—we'll conduct this in a civilised manner and let the poor man lie in peace. So—you'll change into your suit, won't you, like a good boy?" He straightens, his fingers quiet after the busy-ness of knots. "I'll come check in a moment." His thumb sweeps over the boy's head several times, as if strumming the prickly bristles of hair.

"You know it's what I would want as well—if the situation were to arise one day," Humphrey's voice comes drifting over his head. "You know that, don't you, son?"

"Yes," the boy replies, his heart suddenly racing at the thought of his father dead.

That afternoon, he shakes hands with all the guests who have come to pay their last respects to his grandfather. With Amah's help, he serves them tea and bars of coconut candy, soda biscuits slathered with coconut jam, savoury prawn paste sandwiches and fat samosas bursting out of their skins. The windows are closed to keep out the chanting in the garden and fans are brought in to help them all breathe. He sits on one of the dining chairs and doesn't kneel even once. And when the last guests have gone, the altar has already been dismantled and the monks seen to the gate. When his father calls him, the boy refuses to go into the dining room to see the waxy body of his grandfather. He is afraid to, feeling as if he has let the old man down.

And besides, though he doesn't show it, he's a little angry he never got to see the altar. "He's had a hard day." Hearing his father say this, he drags his feet deliberately as he climbs the stairs to his room. His grandfather will be cremated the next day, and there will be nothing left but some long bones and ashes. Grandma Siok told him. "He'll never forgive you," she added. But he's known that already, on his own, deep inside. Because he himself can never really forgive his father.

This is what it means to be Family.

For some reason they are interested in these stories. As if their own pasts and boyhoods are revived in your remembering through the Body, as if these experiences bolster theirs, even though you have never been to Japan, nor do you have any understanding of how they might have grown up. The thing is, with Japanese storytelling, truth is mostly irrelevant, save for *emotional* truth. That the story renders closely the interior state of the protagonist, reproduces his inner turmoil—that is how they judge their stories. How do you know this? Perhaps you read it somewhere, or overheard a particularly impressive scholarly lecture on the subject. Perhaps they simply told you. An invention, perhaps. You could have made it all up.

Jack Winchester arrives to torpor and tortoise time. He has never met such heat; it wraps itself around him in a boa grip and squeezes till he is almost lifeless. Every second is magnified, stretched out, warped. The Indian and Chinese stevedores slouch and lumber along with their burdens. He sees his burnt shape at his feet, shrunk to a quarter of his size, for it is only a little past noon. By the time his brother, George, and the chauffeur get his luggage into the car, he is hardly able to speak. "Short shadows," he keeps muttering.

"I think we'd better get you something to drink at once," says George. "Hussein, take us to the Cricket Club."

The rooms of the Cricket Club are cool and dark, like a wet towel thrown over the face. Jack revives somewhat under the army of ceiling fans. "Well," he says, that being all he can manage for the time being.

"I don't suppose you'll be up to the dinner that Janet has planned for you tonight," says George. He has sweat stains at his armpits but otherwise looks quite comfortable. Jack wonders how he manages to stay so unruffled.

"Only five or six people, really—friends, neighbours, that sort of thing," George goes on. "She's gone to so much trouble, I would hate to disappoint her."

"No, no, of course not," says the wilting Jack.

"She wanted to surprise you, have you try something different.

She's had the cook concoct some splendid sort of curry and mango chutney to go with it. Oh, and there's a fantastic bread these Indian fellows have—absolutely superb—cooked in lard, you know."

Jack's stomach unfolds, quivers, undulates. He is back at sea again and he is ready to throw up.

The unobtrusive Punjabi waiter appears with a small metal bucket. He swoops it under Jack's face just in time. George looks away and lights a cigarette. The Punjabi never wavers in his duty, even when the smell from the bucket wafts upwards into his impassive, slightly bulgy face.

"Will that be all, sir?" he asks when Jack flops back against his chair.

"Well, let's see—that was my breakfast all right, and I haven't had anything else yet today," he says, hazarding a peek at the mushy contents of the bucket. "Yes, that will be all for now."

The Punjabi disappears into the dim passages of the Cricket Club.

"Well, Jack," says George. "Regretting it already?"

"Quite the opposite," says Jack, feeling much better. He is even almost eager to try the curry dinner, lard notwithstanding.

✺

Two weeks later, Jack's biological rhythms are finally in tune with Singaporean time. He is hungry when everyone else is eating and sleeps when everyone else turns in at night. Even his digestive tract seems to have settled down and he is beginning to savour the complicated layers of taste in the food he encounters. And yet he is still disturbed by something.

Is it sunstroke, is it fatigue, is it delirium or just plain madness that makes him hear this eternal singing? It is everywhere he goes, everywhere he sits; it fills his eyes and stomach, it tickles his ear and confuses his mind. Since he's arrived on the island there's been no quiet at all. Always the singing until it wears him out.

George and Janet don't hear it. When he mentioned it once they looked at him queerly and began asking rather personal questions. Was he adjusting to the food? Were his bowels all right? Did he feel feverish? Was he, well, had he been indulging in drink too freely?

Many chaps who were new to the Colonies did that, did he know? It took him two days to shake loose of them and he learned to keep such things to himself after that.

Children, though, are another thing. His niece, Katherine, is five, and one year away from boarding school back in England, where her older sister studies. She is as cinnamon-coloured as a Malay from playing in the sun and has a keen sense of observation that often startles her parents. She's overheard all the commotion about Jack's hearing and when he's finally done with her parents, she waits for him by the fish-pond in the garden where they spend afternoons watching tadpoles with flowery gills sprout hind legs and white carp move through the dark waters like beacons.

"I know why you hear the singing," she says seriously as he hands her bread crumbs to throw to the carp.

"Oh?" He wonders how much she's heard, whether her parents' interrogation has gotten to her.

"It's all those other people talking all those languages." She flings a handful of crumbs which falls disappointingly close to the edge of the pond. "It happens to me sometimes, but I'm more used to it than you are, and more sensible. Mother says you're just like *your* mother—not too stable in the head." She throws him a brilliant smile as if being considered soft in the head is a point in his favour.

"So you're sensible, are you?" he asks, lazily stirring the water with a leaf.

"Oh yes," she replies. "And I hear the singing too, but I can make it stop."

"How?"

"I shut out all the voices around and I sing my own song louder and louder in my head until it's the loudest thing around. Try it!" She bounces around excitedly, dropping bread crumbs all over him.

"Help me understand this. The singing comes from other people?"

"All those other languages. You know—Chinese, Malay, Indian, Thai," she recites. "They sound like singing. They go up and down and wind about, like this." And she launches into a strange, yodelling noise.

"Well, yes, rather," he admits after a bit. It does sound familiar.

"You have to learn to shut it out or it sticks in your head and gets tiresome after a while," she insists. "Close your eyes and find a real song—I use 'Sing-a-Song-of-Sixpence'—and make it really loud in your head."

He tries it, using, for lack of any inspiration, "Sing-a-Song-of-Sixpence"—it has the advantage, he figures, of having worked for her. For a few moments, the hum fades and he's baking four-and-twenty blackbirds in a pie, but this soon degenerates into the hum. "It takes practice," Katherine says reassuringly. "Soon you'll be able to push the other singing away, most of the time, unless there's a wedding or a Chinese funeral—" She sighs knowingly. "You'll just have to put up with those."

"Well," says Jack, getting to his feet. "Now that I'm on my way to a cure, I think this warrants some ice-cream at the very least, don't you think?"

Young Katherine has no objections.

❀

At age thirteen the boy squirms at the thought of being seen too often with his parents, but somehow he doesn't mind traipsing around town with Grandma Siok on her shopping trips. On many afternoons she likes to stroll the breezy, quiet avenues of the Botanic Gardens, and if ever they meet a schoolmate of his who might find it funny to see him spending his afternoons with her, she is apt to point her umbrella at the unfortunate child and pronounce a curse that will have the latter gulping furiously, trying to hold back panic. The fact that her curses are always delivered in a friendly, almost sweet manner only increases the victim's terror. "A painful and bloody fate awaits you the next time you have a seaside holiday, young man. A catastrophe with tentacles, but your poor parents will get over it," she ends with an enigmatic wink as the poor child backs out of her reach.

"You're very good at making things up, Grandma," the boy says uncertainly, watching his classmate run out the main gates of the Botanic Gardens.

"Who's making things up?" she says, walking over to feed the swans.

One day she tells him they are going to another type of garden. "What types are there?" the boy wants to know.

"Well, there are botanic types like the one we usually go to, and there are those that are less so," she says evasively. But she gives it away when she tells the taxi-driver to take them to the "Haw Par place."

The boy has heard of Haw Par Villa from fragments of conversation between his parents. "Such vulgarity," Humphrey said when the Aw brothers first opened its grounds to the public.

Cynthia was just as disparaging. "The worst kind of taste, what with all those unbearable tableaux of mythological rubbish! Where do they come up with these stupid ideas?"

"There's a zoo in there, isn't there?" the boy asks.

"There was one, but the Aw brothers had to close it down when they couldn't get a licence for it from the British. But never mind," she says, shrugging. "This will be better than a zoo."

The taxi draws up in front of a large, ornate Chinese gateway with a leaping tiger spanning its width. The boy recognises it as the Tiger Balm label. The Aw brothers' father invented Tiger Balm, which even the British use to soothe their mosquito bites and to cool their necks on windless evenings. For this reason, Tiger Balm is grudgingly allowed in the house by his parents. He likes the smell of it, and the fact that, according to Amah, its healing powers are due to the ground tiger bones it contains.

They have to walk uphill, puffing and sweating, to reach the garden proper. Along the way, he sees a few Chinese families, smartly dressed, having their photographs taken, the children in their bright, fussy frocks, licking their ices. There are also European couples holding hands, giggling as if sharing a private joke, gobbling little sing-song chants that he knows to be made-up Chinese. At the top of the hill, there is a large Laughing Buddha, his flesh undulating with endless jollity. They stop to stare at it.

"I like it," Grandma Siok says. "There's something earthy about this fellow."

The boy can't see what's earthy about it. The statue's exposed nipples and belly button make him uncomfortable. "I think he should

have more clothes," he says, touching the swath of cloth at the Buddha's base. His entire hand is smaller than each laughing slit eye on
the Buddha's face.

Grandma Siok considers this. "You're quite a prude, aren't you?"
she says at last. She walks on ahead of him, not waiting for his
answer. He is *not* a prude, he thinks, only a person with good taste,
as his parents would no doubt agree. Why does she have to compli-
cate his life when it is already hard enough to be the kind of boy his
parents expect him to be?

They wander the gardens on their own, each keeping the other in
view, studiously staying apart yet drawn together by familial obligation, circling each other in elaborate, odd-shaped orbits. There are
statues everywhere, dotting the landscape like large and unusually
gaudy flowers. He likes the little ones best, the ones which are
grouped together to tell fantastical stories or allegories that he can't
quite grasp. He spends a long time looking at a scene in which tiny
mermen are battling crabs double their size, slyly sticking their
miniature tridents under the crustacean shells. The water swirls
furiously around the battle scene, and red splashes here and there
suggest blood and a terrible death between the fearsome pincers of
the crab enemies.

When he finally drags his eyes from the scene, he can't see his
grandmother and for a brief moment, he worries. Then he feels her
hand on his shoulder and when he turns around, she holds out a
bottle of cold orange squash. He takes it and clamps his lips around
the straw, surprised at his own thirst. When he finishes his drink,
she takes the bottle from him and removes the straw. Then, holding
the neck, she places her lips close to the mouth and blows. An airy,
raspy note emerges. He takes the bottle back from her and, with his
lips pursed expertly, he too blows over the rim. This time there is a
low moan, strong, unwavering, sonorous. Grandma Siok raises her
eyebrows, for it is a beautiful sound. He sees the admiration in her
eyes and is satisfied. When they start walking again, he allows her to
take his elbow.

Now when he looks at a tableau, she is there to explain it to him.
"This one is of the adventures of the Monkey God," she says, pointing out a hairy figure garbed in lemon-coloured robes.

"How do you know?" he asks, warily assessing the pointed spear the Monkey God carries.

"I read the signs," she says. He hasn't noticed them till now. There are signs in front of each tableau, written in Chinese characters. He reflects on how lucky he is to have come with Grandma Siok instead of his parents who cannot read a word of Chinese.

"This one," Grandma Siok says, peering at the sign. "Let me see— ah yes! The Bad Father." She points to a tiny man sitting cross-legged on the floor, playing cards. "He's too busy gambling and pursuing his vices to think about his family. Behind him on the street is his son." A small boy lies with his eyes closed beatifically in the middle of the road. "The boy was out looking for his father whom he had not seen for days, when he was hit by a car and killed." In the background is a blue car. The driver is talking to a policeman and looking for something in his wallet. The father's eyes are focused on his cards. The boy likes the dead boy best. There is a quiet resignation about him that is almost saintly and yet melodramatic at the same time.

"Confucianism," Grandma Siok is muttering. "They don't teach you that at Littleton, that much I know! Respect towards your elders, the role of the father, duty to country. Vital stuff."

He imagines what it would be like to be the dead boy. The best part is still to come. The father, staggering home after his game, will see his son lying in a pool of blood and will then begin to wail and cry, but it will be too late. The son will stubbornly remain dead and the father, repenting, will swear off cards and drink forever, but no matter what he does, he can never make it up to his son; he can never be forgiven.

"Let's go," his grandmother says, tugging on his arm impatiently. There is a sudden gleam in her eyes. "We're coming to my favourite part—the Ten Courts of Hell. This should give you a nightmare or two!" She laughs, giving him a slightly malicious look.

He wants to stay with the tableau of the Bad Father a little longer, to linger on the innocent, patient goodness of the dead son and the heartless neglect of the father, but when she tugs his arm again, he shuffles his feet and follows her.

At first glance, the Ten Courts of Hell seem much like the other small tableaux in the Tiger Balm Gardens. The boy, his mind still lingering on the Bad Father, only half takes in the stream of characters making their descent to hell. But then he shuffles four more steps after his grandmother and stops.

"Each court is under the charge of a 'yama,' or demon king," Grandma Siok says, relishing the look on his face. She squints at the first sign and then translates it for him. "Here we are—the First Court. For Robbing and Causing Pain to Others, and for the vices of Gambling and Prostitution, the punishment is to be flung into a volcano or onto blocks of ice; or one could be drowned in pools of blood." And before them, the little people in the tableau have their faces fixed in painted terror. The boy's insides writhe but he can't take his eyes away.

"Over here, let's see—for Evasion of Taxes and Lack of Filial Piety, you get your body ground to dust between two boulders. Quite appropriate," she adds in approval. "Oh, and for Money-lending and Usury, for Cheating People Out of Their Property, the punishment is to be thrown onto a hill of knives." There is a little figure impaled on several blades, blood oozing out of his body as he screams in pain. The boy leans closer, even as he starts to sweat.

"Body sawn in half for Wasting Food and Misuse of Books," Grandma Siok intones cheerily. "You see, Claude, this is how the real Chinese bring up their children. They scare their little souls into being good and moral citizens when they grow up. I'm just doing your parents' job because they're too full of British airs to do it themselves!" She throws him a dark look. "If they don't watch out, you'll grow into a soppy, pathetic creature who can't think for himself and, worse, who'll eventually end up under the charge of one of these 'yamas.' "

He doesn't know if he is supposed to be grateful to her for this particular excursion; he is too busy staring at a man who is having his stomach slashed and his intestines ripped out. "Cheating in Exams," Grandma Siok supplies, following his gaze. There is a sickly greenish hue about the intestines and he is awed by the lengths of rubbery viscera uncoiling on the floor. An acidic lump dislodges from his own stomach and rises to his throat where it burns and hardens but refuses to be ejected from his body. He moves, pivoting on one foot, so that the disembowelment scene is out of view, only to come face to face with yet another tableau.

This shows a man struggling in the grip of two others who are in the process of tearing out his tongue. The boy freezes. The man, his face contorted and his neck muscles straining with fear and pain, lets out an endless, silent scream. His tongue bleeds profusely as it is being severed, a long cord-like appendage that will soon lie quivering and useless in the dust.

For an unbearable moment that seems to stretch with elastic ease, he just stands there staring at the tongue, horror and something else, something even worse, claiming him. It is the unexpected sheer familiarity of it that he cannot tolerate. Something in the boy slackens suddenly—a liquefying of his guts, a kind of dissolution. Lysis, he thinks blankly, a word he remembers from science class: disintegration, decomposition. From *lusis,* the Greek for loosening. Everything that has kept him in one piece, now coming apart.

He sees his grandmother turn and open her mouth. She is saying his name, and it comes out like a lie, a lie of existence he cannot deny as he loosens his hold on the world and falls.

⬦

Consider this: knife, poised, over heart.

Ling-li, drawing knife: 刀. A threat, perhaps? The lingering death of sharp edges?

Ling-li, revealing heart: 心.

Ling-li: For what is endurance but the strength of the heart under knife-blade?

Pronounced like a growl held back in the throat, dipping first downwards in despair, then upwards in challenge. Ren 忍.

⬦

On the journey home he counts the beggars on the street to distract himself.

"Are you all right?" Grandma Siok asks. He has given her a fright, he knows, because she is quiet and almost soft when she speaks to him.

"I'm fine," he says, keeping his eyes on the beggars as their taxi picks its way through a crowded square. He likes the mad ones the most, the ones who walk with their heads between their legs or skip about, weaving in and out of traffic, singing and shouting. In their silliness, they seem serenely happy, for all their problems.

"Perhaps," Grandma Siok says slowly, "perhaps we could go to Fort Canning Park next week." It's his favourite place. In the middle of the park is the aquarium, a large room covered in black cloth and lined with brightly lit tanks. There is one of clown fish, stroked by jellied anemone, and a sleepy eel whose flat face fascinates him, but mostly the tanks are filled with guppies, caught from drains and canals by gangs of young native boys or scooped up from someone's well. The *pièce de résistance,* a six-foot-long crocodile, sits uncomfortably in its tank just outside the room, its snout squashed against the glass. Grandma Siok detests the place.

"Perhaps," he says with deliberate nonchalance, unwilling to help her out. They sit out the rest of the journey home in silence, and afterwards are careful never to mention the trip to each other or anyone else in the house. When Amah happens to bring out her Tiger Balm ointment to rub her rheumatic knees, he turns away, unable to look at the blue label with its leaping tiger.

And though he never asks for anything, for the next six weeks Grandma Siok indulges him with ices, chocolates and visits to the crocodile. On the first day of the seventh week when he has come to expect these treats she tells him, "My conscience has finally shut up, so the debt's all paid. You can buy your own ices." So he counts out his hoarded allowance and even treats her to one.

It's not a matter of being unsympathetic to his own kind, Humphrey Lim tells himself as he turns away yet more zealous nuts seeking donations for the Singapore China Relief Fund. It's a matter of openly declaring one's position and loyalties, a question of deciding with clear, firm, unflinching logic who has (a) more power and (b) is the future of the colony.

He is walking back to his office in Collyer Quay, having just lunched at a small establishment near the Grand Market. Pride wells up in him as he surveys the hazel-hued river, sampan filled and bustling. Prosperity! The swelling, belching, fat feel of it. This is what it's come to, this diamond-shaped jewel of the Far East. A stone in the rough when the British first landed, but since then they've been grinding and polishing and this, this shining, sun-catching, flint-sparking city is what it's come to.

Humphrey believes in progress. He believes in science, logic, the granite of knowledge over the clay of superstition. But he is also a romantic. He craves tradition, ceremony, flourishes, titles and aristocracy. He is grateful to the British for their unfailing leadership, their unflappable disposition. He is infatuated with the idea of Empire. Humphrey is a man born to serve. Rather than deeming it unseemly he is proud to think of himself as a model subject, a contributing member of this vast, successful enterprise. Had he been English he would undoubtedly have made an excellent butler. In military terms he is first-rate support staff.

He watches the coolies eat their midday meal of rice and fish on the docks with misgivings. One twists his neck to look up at him and Humphrey, receiving the full blast of the man's rotting teeth and puggish nose, increases his pace.

His own father also admired the English but by the time he recognised their superiority it was already too late for him. He could never conquer the consonants of the language, the precise, full vowels, and his English was mocked. Humphrey, however, went to an English school, and now his own son has been raised at home in the English language. With each succeeding generation the family will become more Anglicised, Humphrey believes, and with luck and diligence, they will eventually be accepted by the British themselves as their equals.

The trick, Humphrey knows, is to avoid any contamination from the "hard-core" Chinese—especially the flag-touting, fund-raising ones with Communist leanings, he thinks as he sees yet another batch of these zealots singing and selling flowers at the corner of his office building.

A boy not much older than his son hands him a pamphlet with the lyrics in Chinese and English.

"No, thank you," he says, trying to hand it back. "I don't read Chinese."

"You're not Chinese?" the boy asks, scanning his features. "Sorry, I thought you were. Are you Peranakan?" He speaks in clear, carefully drilled Chinese-school English.

"No! I mean, of course I'm . . . Well, yes." The boy's pitying look catches him off-guard and embarrasses him. Worse, the boy's colleagues in the flower-selling group are shaking their heads and nudging each other. Humphrey collects himself, taking two steps up the stairs leading into the office building so that the boy has to look up to him. "I'm Chinese, but I don't speak the language."

"That's okay." The boy has misread everything and tries to be sympathetic. "It's hard if you went to a foreign school, but you can always learn. There are classes—"

"I have no intention of learning the language at all!"

"This one's in English," the boy says, thrusting another pamphlet into Humphrey's hands. Insolent little devil! The song grows louder as people begin to clap and join in.

"What a bloody din," mutters Humphrey moodily as he enters his building. His eyes skim the pamphlet.

> *Sir, buy a flower, buy a flower*
> *The flower of freedom*
> *Buy one and save your country.*
> *You don't have to love the flower*
> *You don't have to buy it*
> *But if you do, you'll save your country.*

What rubbish! Save your country indeed! This is Malaya and they'd better remember that! He hurries up the stairs to his office. If they love China so much, they should just go back there, he thinks. We don't need that lot here anyway.

And when he reaches his desk, he closes his window despite the heat, to shut out that infernal singing.

This is how it is: as usual, no invitations for the Indian officers on weekends. Lieutenant Mohammed Zahir-ud-Din decides to take his sepoys out in defiance. "Let the bloody English have their parties," he growls. "We'll dine in style on our own."

"Where will we go?" Amir asks him.

"I said 'in style,' " the lieutenant says, "so 'in style' it shall be!"

"The Raffles then!" says a jubilant sepoy. A gutsy pick.

"The Raffles!" echo the men. This is a treat. There is usually nothing for them to do in their off-hours.

Out of the corner of his eye, Lieutenant Zahir sees a trio of English officers entering the mess, gleaming with polish and anticipation of the night's events. "Bah!" he says, nodding curtly as they pass. What is the difference? he wonders. King's Commissioned Officers from Sandhurst and Indian Commissioned Officers from Dehra Dun like himself. Why aren't they equal in the army's eyes? The Indian Independence League is right—if one is to fight at all, why do it for the British? Why not fight instead for Home Rule?

He goes to join the waiting sepoys. He listens to their jokes, their silly name-calling, he listens to the simpletons sing. He'll listen for now and get them relaxed. And when they get thrown out of the Raffles later as they surely will, he'll start his talk. He plans to talk all night. After all, there is nothing else for Indian Commissioned Officers to do on weekends.

❖

Hugh Chung, the boy's Eurasian classmate, is short, pugnacious and hates the local Chinese. His mother is Australian and his father is also Eurasian—half-Portuguese—so he himself has only a quarter Chinese blood in him.

Hugh's favourite after-school activity is to have his chauffeur drive him to Orchard Road for tea at Robinson's and to pick out the Chinese-educated students thronging the streets from the English-educated ones, an activity that requires minimal skill. But Hugh does it mainly because he enjoys making disparaging remarks about the "locals," as he calls them. He does not include himself or his own classmates in this category because they are all at Littleton, the top school for English-educated students, and almost everyone to a boy speaks the language without an accent. To possess one would have meant instant ostracism by one's peers, all of whom regard themselves, as Hugh does, "Anglicised." The boy avoids Hugh mostly, because he is too loud for his taste, and because he has a bullying way about him with the younger boys. Still, the Eurasian is head prefect in the final year at Littleton and the boy realizes he's not one to cross. Trouble is, he seems to like the boy and to seek him out at recess. Hugh has told him he doesn't really consider him Chinese because, well, the boy and his family are different. His father has such an English spirit about him, Hugh says every time he comes over for dinner on those occasions when the boy's father expects him to produce a "friend" from Littleton to show off to his assorted acquaintances.

"Look at them," Hugh says as they watch the Hwa Ming students spill out of their school a block away from the Littleton gates. "Look at their hair," he says with a snicker. The Hwa Ming boys all have crew cuts and they're dressed entirely in white. Actually, to the boy they look like a disciplined lot, rather like army fellows with their way of standing at attention whenever a teacher approaches.

"Thank God we're nothing like them," says Hugh, a look of disgust on his face. "They're a disgrace—the way they speak, the way they dress."

The boy has heard all of this before from his own father, and it has always disturbed him a little. Surely there is nothing wrong with talking a different way, living differently? The Indians and Malays are different, he's mused, but they are better tolerated by Hugh and his father than the Chinese are.

All the masters at Littleton are English except for two. One is the French teacher, Madam Low, and the other is Mr. Kirpal Singh, chemistry teacher for the Lower Forms. Both speak impeccable English except for Mr. Singh's faint accent. Most Littleton boys are Asiatic or Eurasian and share Hugh's sentiments.

Yet the boy is uncomfortable. He sees something in the Hwa Ming boys that he cannot name, something he vaguely wants, admires perhaps. Certainly it's not their way of talking; it's not their shabbiness, their stiff mannerisms.

"Listen," says Hugh. "They're squawking!"

And sure enough they're going at the top of their voices, laughing and making funny grimaces. There they are, all gangly and awkward, some voices cracking into squeals, the one-inch channels between their ears and hairlines distinct even from this distance. Who would want to be them? And yet—

Suddenly he knows what it is about them that he envies. It's their spontaneity, their way of yelling at each other and making a god-awful row and not caring. Littleton boys are always on their guard and at their best—there is always the feeling of being watched, of being afraid to be disgraced with a mispronounced word or gauche behaviour. The boy almost wishes he were one of them, but then they walk by Littleton's gates and he realizes they are speaking to each other, not in Chinese, but in patois.

"*Alamak!* How can?" one says.

"Can-can, *lah*. After all, he total *bodoh!*" replies his friend.

Hugh turns to the boy and mimes a gagging gesture, and he laughs back loudly, almost meanly. His father and Hugh are right; he doesn't envy them at all, no matter how carefree they may seem.

Then the Tams' chauffeur drives through the gates to pick up the Tam twins and, since he is their neighbour and their parents are cordial, he gets a lift from them everyday.

"Home, Muthu," the Tam twins say in unison, ignoring the boy even though he is their senior. They never say anything to the boy except in school where junior students are expected to pay their dues to seniors. Grandma Siok would have had something to say about their rudeness but Humphrey thinks the world of the Tams and will not allow a word against them.

Muthu pulls out of the Littleton gates and through River Valley Road littered with *kampongs* and squatters' huts. The smell from the open sewers hangs in the unmoving air and the boy catches sight of some Hwa Ming students returning to their squalid huts. One picks up a baby who has been crawling in the dirt while his mother hangs washing on a line. He sees the familiar self-imposed uniform of a troupe of Red Hat Soldiers—women labourers from China who live with their peers in dormitories and who are doomed to die alone in Chinatown's death houses—bent at road works in the noonday sun.

A legless beggar sits by the side of the road, eyes downcast, his raw stumps oozing a salmon-coloured liquid and vulgarly exposed to curious passers-by who ogle and then give nothing except expressions of pity and revulsion.

And then, blessedly, the car is coming upon Orchard Road from Patterson Road. The bustle of shops and offices reassures him with their glinting and white paint and European fronts. Civilisation, flush toilets, cinemas, taxis, banks, parks, yes, even those blasted afternoon teas—he sees it all with his father's eyes. None of this would have been possible without the British.

His father is right—there is nothing glorious about being "local."

Mute: condition of deliberate resistance and lack of cooperation, making it necessary for the interrogators to

Mutilate: one way would be to clamp the victim's nails, exert pressure, *squeeze*. Joints are to be manipulated, organs intentionally distended and stomped upon. The orifices are lined by the most tender surfaces. Familiarity with the vagaries of the body is crucial, and an instinctive feel for vulnerabilities and soft spots can be most productive, causing the victim to cooperate by providing the necessary information—

Mutatis mutandis, of course. Covert mutiny.

All stories are corruptible.

The boy's life has been cloistered, to say the least.

After school he reads, studies, plays the clarinet. Sometimes he is invited by his classmates to join them at the cinema or in a game of tennis. If it's at the Tams' court next door, he goes half-heartedly. It's obvious he's not the athletic type and will never grow hair on his chest and therefore he sees no need to exert himself in the heat. When he plays, he looks as if he's dangling from the end of his racquet, holding on for dear life, and may just fall flat on his face if he lets go.

Mostly, though, he stays home, partly because he prefers it and partly because he knows his mother prefers it. She doesn't say so but he knows she hates it when she is left alone in the house with his sister and the servants.

It's not his conversation she seeks, for she often sits in perfect silence with him on the veranda before the sun turns and hits that side of the house. She's done this ever since he was twelve. At first he had sat awkwardly trying to keep his hands from fidgeting and waiting for her to speak, to interrogate him on his day at school as Grandma Siok often did. But when, day after day, she sat looking unhappily into the brown and scorched garden, he began to engage himself in other activities. He read, he did his homework, he sharpened his pencils with a pen-knife and cut himself. She just sat there, looking at his bleeding finger until he went to get Amah himself. The old servant cleaned his wound, painted mercury solution on it and took away his pen-knife. When he got back to the veranda his mother was still sitting there, staring at the garden in her unseeing way.

Another time he experimented with smoking right there on the veranda in front of her. Boldly he took out the pack of cigarettes that Hugh had sold him during recess and a box of matches from the kitchen. He sat striking match after match, spark and flare, spark and flare, letting each one burn down till the flame almost ate his fingers. The truth was, he wasn't all too clear how a cigarette was lit (which end? In the mouth or out?).

Finally, his mother broke the silence. "Oh, Claude, you're always seesawing like that, you've never been able to make up your mind." She took the matches and cigarettes from him, perched one on her lip and expertly lit it. Then she handed over the cigarette, now alive and spewing tendrils of smoke like a dragon.

She sucked in her cheeks, then blew. "Like that," she said.

He put the cigarette in his mouth, tasted the sour nicotine of it, sucked at it like a straw and burnt his lungs. He held his breath as long as he could, which wasn't very long at all, and then coughed out a seething ball of smoke. He tried again and choked, his nose and throat tingling.

"Practise," she said, so he took yet another puff.

His eyes smarted and he began to wheeze. She reached over and took the cigarette from him. "Enough? Satisfied?" She sounded amused.

And he was. He had gotten her attention.

"Good," she said when he nodded, drawing a long breath on the cigarette and veiling her face with smoke. "Good." And to his horror, she laid the glowing tip onto her left wrist beside the jumping of her pulse.

Her eyes closed, her jaw tightened and behind the smoke cover her face took on a vicious appearance. He counted, starting randomly—he didn't know why—at eight: eight, nine, ten, eleven . . .

And then with a grinding motion of her wrist she stubbed the cigarette out and flung it over the banisters into the garden below. She got up and went downstairs. He sat with his matches and cigarettes until Amah came to let down the bamboo blinds and cool the veranda in time for tea.

After that day he is afraid to let her sit alone. So he brings a book, thumbs it, sketches her profile in secret. He sees the deep wanting in her face. What is it for? he wonders, drawing the half-a-face mystery that is his mother.

One of the things that amuses Grandma Siok, though the family has never been able to figure out why, is to seek out and attack ants' nests. It's no easy task, for she tracks down each anthill from scratch and this entails an elaborate process that she's created and mastered.

First, she mixes up a small jar of sugar solution, and then, with a dropper, she plants several glistening, irresistible single-drop domes of sweetness on the footpath in the garden. A few minutes later, the ants come calling. The key, Grandma Siok has discovered, is to pick your ant and keep an eye on it, a task which requires excellent eyesight, the ability to tell one ant from another at a fair distance, and great perseverance. All this Grandma Siok has in abundance, so she is usually very successful at this stage.

After much crawling in the grass, the targeted ant inevitably returns to its nest. Sometimes, on a lucky day it's an anthill, other times, it's tightly and snugly packed in the soil. She marks the spot and returns to the house to gather up the rest of her paraphernalia and to plan her attack. For this she consults General Sun Tzu's *Art of War*.

It's a book she reads every morning when she takes tea in her room and before going to bed at night, and, of course, before an attack on an ants' nest. Sometimes, when Humphrey isn't around, she'll translate for the boy and his sister: *All warfare is based on deception. Therefore, when capable, feign incapacity; when active, inactivity. When near, make it appear that you are far away; when far away, that you are near. Offer the enemy a bait to lure him; feign disorder and strike him.*

The boy usually responds with a scandalised expression that he knows is most gratifying to Grandma Siok, while Lucy, wide-eyed, tells her she is better than the witch in Hansel and Gretel. "She just eats children," she says dismissively. "But Grandma, you kill armies!" Sometimes, on a cool day, the two of them are persuaded to hunt along with her.

She makes them stand over the ants' nest while she reads: *There are five methods of attacking with fire. The first is to burn personnel; the second, to burn stores; the third, to burn equipment; the fourth, to burn arsenals; and the fifth, to use incendiary missiles. To use fire, some medium must be relied upon. Equipment for setting fires must always be on hand.*

"General Lucy!" she bellows.

"Here!" Little Lucy's feet snap together as she salutes.

"The equipment?"

Lucy holds out a box of matches, pilfered from Phatcharat while the cook was in the toilet, and an old newspaper. The boy carries a bucket of sand and drags a hose with him. He loves his grandmother dearly but finds her irresponsible at times. Really! Teaching Lucy to play with matches, and invoking some ancient general in the process! His father would have a lot to say about that if he knew.

Rahman, the gardener, is instructed to dig, fast. "Really quick, Rahman—the idea is to catch them unawares." The old woman is fairly bouncing up and down. Strange woman, thinks Rahman, not for the first time, strange family. Too much time and money on their hands. In his own family, all the children, including Rosniah, who is eight and takes care of his chickens, work. On a day off or a holiday they'd pray and then visit their cousins and fly their kites. None of this crazy ant-hunting business! And to think it's at the old lady's instigation too! Bah! You'd never see his own mother behaving like that. He sticks his *changkol* into the soft loamy soil and rapidly unearths the colony.

Lucy starts squealing. "Here they come, here they come!" And sure enough, the ground is swarming the streaming lava of startled ants.

"Newspaper, matches! General Lucy, to your station please!" Grandma Siok commands. She can't abide any lack of discipline or loss of control and is displeased that Lucy is not already in position, ready for the attack. Lucy throws the newspaper at her and drops the box of matches, all in one movement. Swiftly—so swiftly that not even the boy can believe it—Grandma Siok retrieves the box, lights a match, sets the newspaper on fire, waves it in the air to stoke the flames and then drops it on the chaos of the nest. "Air attack by fire," she announces solemnly.

The ants seek refuge on the boy's foot and sandal straps and tickle his toes. Then they begin to bite. He flies about, hot-footed, stinging, smacking the bolder ones that are already scaling his shin. Lucy too howls from being bitten. Only Grandma Siok and Rahman stand grinning, Rahman because he has prudently retreated, and Grandma Siok because she is wearing, the boy notices now, a pair of thick Wellingtons. "I've been doing this a long time, boy," she says with a chuckle, following his glance.

In the end it's a failed attack because Grandma Siok is certain she didn't get the queen. "Scuttled away before I could do anything about it," she says. "You have to get the queen to kill the colony— otherwise, it doesn't matter how many commoners you get, it still doesn't count."

"Workers," the boy says automatically, "I think they're called workers."

"Right," she says, ignoring him, "now come take a look at these commoners." She finds a spot where there are few ants and gets on her knees. Cautiously, one eye looking out for stray attackers, he and his sister follow suit. They find themselves peering at a line of ants with what look like rice grains clamped between their jaws.

"They're running away with the food," says Lucy, but he sees an eerie pair of red dots at one end of each rice grain.

"They're pupae," he says, spooked by the staring red dots.

"Smart one, aren't you?" His grandmother reaches for a clump of soil in the side of the nest and teases out the earth to reveal several pupae sleeping in her palm. "Don't poke too hard," she says when Lucy tries to stroke one. "You'll end up squashing them. Gets messy."

"What will they grow up to be?" Lucy asks.

"These won't. Grow up, I mean. They need to be coddled by the adult commoners. But under regular circumstances, well, it depends on what they're fed. If they're given special rich foods, they end up being little queens, otherwise they're more slaves for the big queen."

The fire has burnt down and all the ants have scattered. "I work better alone," says Grandma Siok, surveying the deserted nest. "Come along, now. The ice-cream man usually makes his appearance around this time and I'm hot and hungry."

The boy stays behind to dump his bucket of sand. He picks up a handful of earth like his grandmother did and ends up with five comatose pupae in his hand. They have a slight curve to their cylindrical shapes, and their red eyes shine dully like unpolished rubies, unmistakable amidst their whiteness. Something about them, their milky paleness, makes him uneasy and yet attracts him at the same time.

"You coming?" Grandma Siok calls.

He slices each one neatly in half with a fingernail, flicks their mutilated bodies back into the smoking nest and runs to catch up with Lucy and Grandma Siok.

In Chinese Opera, the role of *Xiao Sheng* is the Junior Male role, the part of a young man, a late adolescent. To the untrained ear, his singing is offensive, or at least hair-raising. The voice is high and shrill, a penetrating falsetto that plunges downwards over the end of spoken phrases to signify the child's voice breaking into early manhood. Physically, he is fine-boned, clean-shaven, unassuming—perhaps even effeminate. He is either falling in love or lunging towards war.

The hard thing is not to make a sound, not to wake anyone with an inadvertent cry or moan. For the boy knows he is dreaming, knows that elsewhere in the house, everyone is fast asleep and would be annoyed to be awakened by his nocturnal encounters. Thus, even in his fear, he suppresses any sound that might pass his lips, and resolutely endures the dream.

It starts with the man being held down by others. A knife is produced. Sometimes it is a pair of scissors, like the black-handled ones from China that Amah is fond of. Suddenly he is all the people in his dream at once. He pins down the victim, feeling him wriggle like a dying carp as it's scooped out of water. He is the one holding the scissors, its steadfast weight in his hand like a heavy stone one might use to stun the carp with a blow to the head. When he cuts, the tough, fibrous tongue surprises him with its resistance, but when he squeezes the handles of his scissors together, closing its open blades, there is a soft springiness to the muscle that both fascinates and repulses him.

And then most of all, he is the man ululating in pain as his tongue is cut, the organ thrashing on the floor of his mouth, cringing at the saltiness of its own blood.

When it is over, when his tongue is finally severed from its root, he is reduced to grunting and howling, a primeval language in which he contorts his face, the muscles of his mouth, his whole being, in order to be understood.

When he awakes, he is speechless, his throat tightened in spasms so gripping that if he does not pant to force air into his lungs, he is sure he will die of suffocation. The condition lasts until dawn and the stirrings of the Tams' gardener outside, sweeping dead leaves into a pile, gathering the rubbish and then setting fire to it.

He watches the smoke drift lazily in the morning air, hears the crackling of burning leaves and feels the constriction in his throat

relax slowly until he can breathe normally again, until he tests himself with a word, any word, just to be sure he can speak. Sometimes
it is "reckless," or "palindrome," or "curtsey"—any word, as long as
he feels his tongue sweep up to his palate or flatten in his mouth as
he enunciates each syllable, unsure if it is an indication of health or
disease.

Then he sleeps restfully for about an hour, until Amah wakes him
with a shake to his shoulders and a hissing noise, not unlike that of
a snake.

Is it sunstroke, is it fatigue, is it delirium or just plain madness
that makes for this eternal singing? It is everywhere; it fills your eyes
and stomach, it tickles your ear and confuses. No quiet. Singing
until it wears you out:

Dai Toa Kessen-No-Uta. Song of the Decisive War of Greater
East Asia. Aikoku Koshinkyoku. Patriotic March.

Buy a flower, sir, save your country.

When the boy is fifteen, a family moves into the drain that runs
along the street where he lives. He is sitting on the veranda with his
mother one afternoon, doing his homework, which in those days
involves memorising almost entire Shakespearean plays, and when
he looks out, there they are, squatting in the drain, arranging their
little bundles of possessions. It hasn't rained in weeks, and there is
only scattered rubbish in the large gutter, which, thanks to the Tams'
influence in local government, has been constructed in concrete,
like the grander canals in town.

Over the next hour, the squatters erect a roof of flattened cardboard boxes to shield them from the sun. When this is done, the
father rolls a cigarette, leans back against the sloping wall of the
drain and lights it, working his thin cheeks like bellows as he sucks
in, then puffs out the smoke in an unhurried manner. The mother
hops in and out of the drain gathering bits of dried twigs and leaves
in her arms. There are sweat stains on her *samfoo* and she stops

repeatedly to wipe her face with a handkerchief tucked into her open collar.

Two boys, both younger than Lucy, crawl about in the drain, stopping occasionally to smack each other indiscriminately. When one starts crying after being hit on the head, they are both made to help their mother and run about quite happily, picking up bits of coloured paper and fistfuls of dried grass to add to the mother's pile.

A little while later the boy sees them waving to a girl who is coming down the street. She looks about his age, and her long hair is done in a tight plait down her back, like the Indian girls he sees around Serangoon Road. She is carrying a pail of water which she is very careful not to spill. When she arrives at the spot where they are, the father reaches up to take the pail and sets it under the shade of the cardboard roof.

The boy hears Amah coming up the stairs. Across from him, Cynthia is dozing off lightly, a smear of lipstick at the corner of her mouth. He runs to the top of the stairs. "I'll put the blinds down, Amah," he says, leaning over the banister. "You don't have to come up."

"Okay," she says, panting, relieved. "I bring tea up when your father come."

He heads back to the veranda where Cynthia has shifted slightly in her chair. She has kicked off one shoe, revealing a surprisingly ugly foot. The nail of her big toe is thickened and deformed, bulging upwards like the cap of a toadstool. Where the shiny red polish has chipped off, the nail is a dull, uneven yellow. All her toes are bunched together, taking the shape of her pointy, pinched pumps, and the skin on the sole of the foot is peeling in places. He marvels at this unexpected contamination of his mother's beauty, dragging his eyes away only when he hears his father's car at the gate, and runs to look outside again.

Rahman has opened the gate and his father's car is already in the driveway. As Rahman closes the gate, the boy sees the younger children of the squatter family peer up curiously at the house. The father continues to smoke indifferently; the mother and the girl are fanning themselves under the cardboard roof. Rahman glares at them, snapping the padlock shut. They ignore him.

Humphrey is already in the house. "What are those tramps doing outside in that drain?" the boy hears him asking Amah. "Do the Tams know about this?" The telephone rings then, and it is a call for Humphrey, which he takes in his study.

Cynthia yawns. "Is he home already?" she mumbles.

Quickly, the boy lets down the blinds, shutting out the family in the drain. "Did Amah forget?" his mother asks, watching him work the pulleys, but she is not really interested. She slips her foot back into her shoe and gets up. "I'll go freshen up."

At teatime, Humphrey talks about his work. Apparently, some people are being transferred from the bank's Shanghai branch because of growing tensions there with the Japanese. "Renata is from Shanghai," says Lucy, who has just started school. Renata is a classmate. "She lived in a big house there, with lots and lots of servants. She says the Chinese are stupid and poor, and very dirty. She says they can't read and they eat dogs, and the children are all beggars and lepers."

"Well, that just about describes you," says Grandma Siok caustically. Humphrey's cup pauses midway to his half-open mouth, making him look rather oafish. Cynthia glowers at her mother.

"Me!" cries Lucy indignantly. "I'm not Chinese!"

"Oh, you're not, are you?" says Grandma Siok, biting into a biscuit.

"She's not a 'local' Chinese," Humphrey says. "Stop confusing the poor child, Siok."

"Hmmm," says Grandma Siok noncommittally.

The boy finishes his tea, glad that no-one has brought up the family in the drain. He wonders where they were living before they moved here. Although he has seen many squatter families in the past and has shuddered at the filth that surrounds them, there is something about the cardboard roof and the sheer cockiness of just setting up house in someone's drain that appeals to him. When he watched them that afternoon, it was like watching a group of people play house. He has developed a strange fondness for them and, despite his parents' feelings, hopes they will stay.

It rains the next week, and the cardboard boxes are soaked through. The drain fills up quickly, and the boy watches the family straddle it at first, and then scramble out when the water rises to cover their feet. They have bundles on their backs, and he wonders if they always keep everything packed like that so they can move with a minimum of fuss.

They huddle in the Tams' empty guardhouse, just outside their main gate. The *jagar* sits there at night reading his newspaper, getting up every half-hour or so to walk around with his truncheon, which, when the boy looked closely once, turned out to be an old cricket bat. The family packs into the little guardhouse so tightly that they can't close the door and the father's back sticks out of the doorway, no doubt shielding the rest of them from the rain. The glass-louvered windows on one side reveal the faces of the two boys as they stare solemnly at their flooded home and the cardboard roof being swept away in the current. The glass and the rain warp their faces so they seem to be underwater, bobbing and undulating with the waves.

Muthu, the Tams' chauffeur, comes out holding a deformed golf umbrella. He is in his rubber slippers so his toes are wet and he walks with a curious shuffling-waddling motion to avoid splashing water onto his trousers. When he gets to the guardhouse, he waves his free arm crossly at the family, and the father slowly turns around so that he is facing the chauffeur in the doorway. Muthu launches into his speech and after listening a while the father points to the drain and both he and Muthu stand watching the rising water level.

They stand there, mesmerized by the flow of water for perhaps a full five minutes, before Muthu seems to give himself a shake and order the family out of the guardhouse, his finger indicating some indefinite point on the road. The family troops out, glaring at Muthu. In the Tams' house, the boy sees a flicker behind the jalousies upstairs, the whiteness of a sleeve and the flash of a face, and he knows Mr. Tam must be watching.

The family stands in the middle of the empty street as Muthu picks his way carefully back to the Tams' house. The girl with the plait throws a rock at Muthu's retreating back, but he is too far away and it bounces harmlessly, skidding across the wet concrete before coming to rest in one of the cracks that split the driveway like a river on a map.

It rains for two more hours, but the family never moves from its spot in the middle of the road, all of them defiantly facing the Tams' house. Later, when the boy goes to the open front porch to flick stranded earthworms back into the soil before Rahman comes to squash them heartlessly under his galoshes, he sees the two boys splashing in the drain. The mother, father and the older girl are nowhere in sight.

That night, the boy leans out from the veranda to see a makeshift hut with a corrugated zinc roof erected by the Tams' gate, on the other side of the guardhouse. The *jagar* watches the family from his little room, unsure of what to do, and they ignore him, drying themselves in front of a fire. When he circles them, swinging his cricket bat suggestively, they calmly roast their yams over the fire and eat, the whites of their eyes shiny and glinting with orange lights.

The hard thing is not to make a sound, not to give out any inadvertent information. This excessive knowledge—how to contain it all without any of it spilling out, how to know for sure when Claude the Body speaks, or when you're remembering, or imagining, or witnessing? Pain has erased those boundaries and recast the terrain. Trouble is, you have no map and can only grope your way through, leading them with you on some trail—the wrong one, you hope. Trouble is, you won't know for sure . . .

The boy has had the dream again, though this time, the spasms in his throat have not lasted as long as usual. But he is thirsty, the insides of his mouth coated with a slurry of chalk that he longs to wash out. In the kitchen, he fills his glass from the terracotta urn that contains the water Amah boiled the night before. The hum of the refrigerator masks the little sounds he makes in his slippers, rinsing out his mouth at the sink, drinking his water, then refilling his glass and drinking some more. He has kept the lights off, because

Amah and Phatcharat sleep in the room next door, where light from the kitchen floods in through gaping cracks at the top of their doorway.

He finishes his drink and starts to go back to his room but stops, sensing another sound under the mechanical surf of the refrigerator. He holds his breath, thinking he must have awakened Amah and Phatcharat, but the sound that seeps in is silvery, musical, like rain. He creeps round to the back door and the window beside it. The slatted shutter has been pushed outwards and he stands to one side, hiding his face behind it.

The tap outside, on the other side of the kitchen wall, is running. This is where Amah does the laundry and Phatcharat cleans the chickens she has slaughtered for their meals. He has seen the strong, clean cord of water from the spout and has felt the slapping force of it by placing his hand in mid-stream and seeing the tube of water splay furiously into a million threads. Kneeling beside the tap, her head ducked under the cold water, is the girl from the drain, her long black hair released from its plait and running like another kind of liquid down her neck and back.

She has taken off her *samfoo* blouse, and is rubbing herself with Amah's mud-coloured laundry soap, her face coated in lather, her eyes closed against the alkaline sting of it. His eyes follow her hand as she works the soap in small, brisk circles that grow larger and lazier as she moves down her body. He has seen breasts before— Amah's which look just like more folds of loose skin on her wrinkled body, the swollen teats that women on the streets hold their babies to, a girlie magazine that Hugh showed him once, where the women wore grass skirts and flower garlands that did nothing to conceal their bare chests—but he is fascinated now by the girl's pointed nipples in profile, the skin tag that clings to one nipple like a dark bud, the glisten of wet on her curves like circles of ringworm in the pre-dawn light.

He must have breathed in audibly, or made a sound, for she has stopped and is looking behind her quickly, water spraying off her hair as she whips her head around. Soap smarts her eyes and she turns back to wash the lather off her face. When she is done, she stares, red-eyed, at the shutter and he knows she sees him, revealed in the horizontal strips between the slats. Her expression is openly hostile and challenging at the same time. She continues to soap herself slowly—on her chest, under her armpits, behind her ears—never taking her eyes off him.

Then, with a quick, defiant movement, she slips the *samfoo* trousers off her hips and down to her ankles. His heart tingles in his chest, the warmth spreading down to his stomach, along with a feeling of nausea that comes with the anticipation of pleasure. Her hand makes foamy circles on her flat belly, then slides to her tight curl of pubic hair, her surprisingly full thighs. He is not sure if he is blushing, but even in the poor light, he knows she is not. There is nothing rushed about her movements—just a deliberateness that makes tiny incisions in his groin, little stabs that send the blood rushing between his legs.

She lets the oval bar slip from her fingers and tilts her head back, easing into the full stream of the tap. The water makes little stutters on her shoulders, pommels the space between her breasts. The white lather slides off like an old skin. She stands up, turns the tap off, dries herself with little more than a rag and slips on a tattered housedress with big patch pockets at the hips. She wrings out her clothes and her heavy hair. He watches this as though it is a film at the cinema, bathed in near darkness and held by a breathless feeling at the enlarged world before him. Here she is on the screen and then she is gone, and a dim light in his startled brain tells him that time has passed. He shakes himself out of his half-trance and walks to the window by the sink. From there he can see her scaling the lattice ironwork of the gate with more strength than grace, her foot resting at one point on the padlock. Then she is over and walking back to the makeshift shack with the three walls, and the bodies of the rest of her sleeping family piled up like rocks.

He makes his way back to his room, unnerved, after the reassuring one-note silence of the refrigerator, by the enlarged, exaggerated soundlessness in the corridor.

Ling-li has heard the rumour that Sister Regina Underwood douses in Dettol every morning and polishes her silver fillings once a week on her day off. Not surprising that such things should be said of her, exaggerated as they are, for the English ward sister is relentless. At the Singapore General Hospital, she has all her charges changing bedpans for the better part of the morning and even assigns two to scrubbing the floor in the surgical theatre.

From the very first day Ling-li has been a target and Sister Regina's dislike is also not surprising. Ling-li, after all, is not easily likable. There is something about the insolence in the girl's posture and her severe, ascetic figure that naturally offends the sister's cream-puff rotundity. She finds herself double-checking everything Ling-li does and posing the most difficult questions to her just to have the satisfaction of taking the smirk off the girl's face. Not that it's easy to fault her work. The irritating trainee is a skilled and efficient juggler; she charges at her chores and assignments like a tractor and manages somehow to complete her work in good time and with very few mistakes. No question about it, she's bright, that one, but a self-sufficient one-man band. She never asks for help and on joint assignments, takes over the entire project without seeking anyone else's approval. Good Lord, the next thing you know, she'd be telling the patients how they should be breathing.

Sister Regina carefully observes her now as she stuffs a dead body. End-stage cirrhosis, yellow as a lemon and the lumpy hardened shape of his liver bulging under his ribs. All the holes plugged up nice and tight, skin smelling fresh after the Dettol sponge-bath, shaved and combed fit for church, which is his next stop after a day in the mortuary with the resident entrails reader, Marty the pathologist—Ling-li's hands never stop. She'll make a good nurse, Sister Regina admits. Why, if she wasn't so annoying she'd remind me of myself, she thinks. Just a little . . .

How could it have happened? She might have been prompted to join by her classmates, or by some mentor, or out of a sense of youthful rebellion, she might have liked the social aspects of it all. How to tell what really made Ling-li join the Singapore China Relief Fund? How to explain her association with the group's anti-

Japanese activities, her participation in rallies, fund-raising events, morale-raising concerts? Maybe it was another woman altogether. Maybe they have the wrong person. Maybe she was forced.

None of this seems to make any difference to them. A finger can be bent back only so far—

One version:

Ling-li is late for the rally at the Ee Hoe Hean Club on Bukit Pasoh Road, but it can't be helped. Sister Bernadette had insisted that she clean out the supplies cupboard before leaving for the day and she had spent an extra hour rolling bandages and refilling bottles with iodine and mercurochrome.

She is surrounded before she can get close to the entrance. "Ling-li! Did you hear? The Wuhan Choir tour has been a wonderful success. They're making a record to commemorate the trip and they've already promised that we can use the profits for the war effort."

"Where is Hong-Seng? He was supposed to do factory visits with me yesterday, but I haven't heard from him in days."

"Tan Kah Kee wants to see you after the rally—don't forget."

Ling-li smiles off the waves, the pats on the shoulder, the rush of words—part greeting, part news, part gossip. She wriggles through the crowd and ends up near the front of the hall, right beside a large standing fan, which makes it difficult for her to hear even as the rally leaders shout into their megaphones. After several minutes she realises that the fan is the least of her problems—all that shouting blurs the diction of the speakers and not much can be caught above a general howl.

But it is a speech that she and the crowd know well. They have heard it so many times they could recite it in their sleep, and when the three tag-team speakers get to the Compatriot's Pledge, they do indeed all recite it: *We will not engage in trade with the enemy, we will not spread or read their propaganda, we will not communicate with the enemy or traitors . . .*

The fan turns left-right, whirring and clanking in its slow sweep.

Ling-li closes her eyes as its draught blows over her, first as a small tickle that teases the tendrils at her temples, and then as a gratifying blast that warps her voice as she mouths the words, so that it sounds as if she is gargling as she speaks. The pressure builds up in her ears as the fan blows directly in her face—*my family and I will support the relief work with our savings, I will encourage my employees to pledge monthly contributions and I myself shall do so*—and just as her ears begin to ring, she stretches her mouth wide into a forced yawn. The fan swivels and her ears pop, and there's a curious deflating sensation in her head. The final words of the pledge shouted over the megaphones and blending in with the crowd's voice become more distinct, crisp—*I am strong and will give much help to the relief effort, I am a Relief Fund worker and will do my best.*

There is a lull after the pledge during which most people fan themselves and undo their top buttons. The room smells of sweat, hair cream and cologne. Ling-li tries to breathe through her mouth as the committee leaders read off a list of the largest donors to the fund. People cheer as the donations become more and more extravagant, stamping their feet in approval and thumping the donors on their backs. This could be a hockey match, Ling-li thinks. Secretly she disapproves of this reading of names. It reminds her of temple pledges, with each rich *towkay* in the city trying to up the other with his donations, and the temple monks trying to keep them all happy by erecting prominent plaques in the worship halls declaring their acts of charity. Still, it has to be done. "People love hearing their own names," Ng Aik Huan, one of the committee's "Three Tiger Generals," once said. "They hear their names and the next thing you know, they want to make another donation. What's wrong with reading out a few names? It costs us nothing." So far, the money has been pouring in, and not just from the rich. Every Chinese worker in the city, every student and household has contributed monthly to the fund, punctually and without complaint.

A square-faced gentlemen picks up the megaphone. Tan Kah Kee, the head of the Singapore China Relief Fund. Ling-li has only met with him three times, in conjunction with other youth leaders, to discuss the flag day sales and recruitment concerts at Boat Quay.

Why does he want to see her today? There are no youth events scheduled for the rest of the month and she hasn't even been attending meetings very regularly these past weeks because of her work at the hospital. She scans his face but finds no answers, only a bland little smile half-hidden by his moustache. He holds one finger at the bridge of his spectacles as he speaks to keep them from sliding off his nose. "I would like to thank the donors for their generous contributions tonight." His Hokkien is genteel, scholarly. "Thank you all for coming and for your hard work. It's clear to me why we are the centre of relief activities amongst overseas Chinese in South-East Asia. Our plan for the next few months involves coordinating a dependable flow of supplies to the Yunnan-Burma Road and for this I have asked—"

"Tan Kah Kee!" All heads turn towards the voice in the middle of the room. "Why are you taking orders and collaborating with the British?" The young man smacks his left fist into his right palm as he speaks. The fan, blowing in Ling-li's face again, dries her eyes and makes it hard for her to see him clearly. She blinks several times but the crowd has closed in around him and some members are already muttering his question among themselves.

Tan Kah Kee raises his hand and the spectacles slip onto his cheekbones, causing him to look, for a moment, like a slightly demented old man. "Compatriots," he begins and the room hushes. The finger goes back to the spectacles. "I was appointed to this position by the British Colonial Government. It's only natural that I should report to the British regularly. They have not issued any specific orders, have only charged me with coordinating relief for China in this war against the Japanese. And as for collaborating with the British . . . we should make every effort to do so—it's our duty."

The room erupts into an angry buzz. "Damn the Colonial Government! This has nothing to do with them—we're for China, and China only!" the young man shouts, and this time he is backed by many others in the room. A chant picks up: "Serve our nation, our nation is China! Serve our nation, our nation is China!"

Amazingly, Tan Kah Kee does nothing. He takes off his spectacles and tucks them in his breast pocket, puts down the megaphone, folds his hands and stares straight ahead, waiting. Defiantly, the chant continues for another minute and then loses steam. The crowd fidgets as Tan Kah Kee continues staring at some faraway point in the distance. One or two try to resurrect the chant but there's no interest and most people begin to look down at their feet while Tan Kah Kee, unmoving on the platform with his neatly folded hands, ignores them. Ling-li marvels at his composure, so well complemented by the staid, grey folds of his suit with its severe black necktie, but even she begins to grow impatient at his lack of action.

Finally, the entire room is silent, save for the fan's unceasing mechanical breaths, and finally, Tan Kah Kee replaces his spectacles and addresses the assembly. "Compatriots," he says and there is a soft pinging sound from the megaphone. "This is something you might as well understand now—the British have no love for the Japanese. For now, they are the rulers and administrators of this island, and they have helped us set up the Singapore China Relief Fund. Any cooperation we can get from them—from any race or nationality—to fight Japan should be welcome to us all."

He allows his gaze to sweep the room. "I too am for our nation. Everything I do here, every sacrifice I have made is for China. And I will continue to do everything possible to secure our country's liberation from the Japanese imperialists—even if that means collaborating with British imperialists! That," he concludes, "is a battle for another day."

The crowd murmurs and a scatter of applause follows this speech, but Ling-li can tell they are not entirely convinced. Still, she realises, no-one is challenging the head of the Relief Fund anymore, and those who have gathered into small clusters are looking thoughtful and more subdued. Ng Aik Huan has taken hold of the megaphone and is hastily reading the calendar of events for the week—usually the last item at every meeting—but hardly anyone is listening. Ling-li savours one last blast from the fan before making her way to the platform where Tan Kah Kee has just dismounted.

"Mr. Tan," she says and he nods.

"Yes, yes." He gestures at the people swarming around him. "I have a few things to take care of. Be in my office in fifteen minutes."

She bows automatically, as every Chinese-educated child has been drilled to do in school, and almost catches herself saying, Yes, Teacher Tan. But he would not have noticed, surrounded as he is now by Relief Fund members. She moves towards the flight of stairs at the end of the hall. His office, she remembers, is on the second floor.

The Fifth Columnist is constantly noting faces, names, ranks. She gets paid for every name she hands in, and though this might spur others to dishonesty, she appreciates the respect the Japanese accord her and is careful to maintain her reputation. So she takes scrupulous notes, verifies everything, documents meetings, protests and speeches. There is a polish and efficiency to her reports; her files are the most detailed among South-East Asian Fifth Columnists.

It's a job that she has slipped into effortlessly. Her plainness and uninspiring dress are assets; her speech is dull and eagerly over-looked; her movements are uncoordinated and slow. No-one ever notices her. She volunteers willingly but never takes the lead, and she bears the blame for any failure or incompetence without com-plaint, even when she has had no hand in it. This has led to her being everyone's favourite helper, a half-sister who could never threaten to steal the show, popular in her own harmless, unassum-ing, unremarkable way. She enjoys her role, laughing at them all behind their pathetic, unsuspecting backs, confident of her covert superiority.

And yet she has a vulnerable side. She has a secret passion for one of the Youth Leaders of the Relief Fund. He is only two years younger than she is, and reminds her of her father with his hand-some face and athletic build. He is surrounded by young women, all of them eager to receive his attentions and each praying that she would be his girlfriend. For weeks, the Fifth Columnist has dreamed of dancing with him at the Great World, watching the British at their polo matches together from secluded *kampongs*, taking long walks hand in hand at Seletar where the reservoir-fattened vegetation has pro-vided a convenient lush jungle screen for more intimate moments.

He doesn't even suspect, she muses whenever he passes her; he has no idea who she is, what she is capable of. If he did, he'd see her differently—he might actually *see* her. This thought is what keeps her hope alive and helps her endure his blindness.

But one day it is clear he is smitten with somebody else, and is moping over her unbearably. The gossip is that she is a great beauty with strong ties in the organisation, outspoken and chillingly competent for her age. For the Fifth Columnist this is what stings the most, this widely acknowledged competence. Brilliance she might have forgiven, and certainly beauty she would have allowed, but competence is *her* special domain and one in which she resents being challenged, even indirectly.

So she sets out to take notes on this usurper, tailing her back and forth through the city, doing all she can to keep up with the paragon's quick march. Luckily there are the frequent stops at food-stalls along the way where the target wolfs down obscene amounts of food without any of it seeming to make a difference to her spare frame. One day the Youth Leader tries to walk her home after a meeting. "Do you need help with your bag?" he asks with a faint blush that the Fifth Columnist notes with approval.

"No thanks."

"Are you going to the bus stop? I'll walk you."

"No need."

"Oh." He falls behind a little, then catches up with her. "I'm going that way myself. I may as well walk with you."

"Suit yourself."

"How are the school parades coming along? I saw the flags you made—they're very striking."

No response.

"If you ever need any help with the fund-raising drives at the schools—"

"I had everything worked out a month ago. I've done these drives a thousand times. What makes you think I would need help?"

"Of course, yes." Quick march uphill as he trails after her. "Would you like to go to the cinema?"

"No."

"Oh."

"Goodbye."

He watches her run for her bus. In the next few weeks he tries again, many times, but Miss Competence always brushes him off—she has too many things to do, *competently*, of course, and doesn't want the complication of romance.

The Fifth Columnist falls behind in her work for the first time. She has missed tailing two suspects in a week and lost a page of notes because she has been distracted. Her superiors are concerned. Is she feeling well? Maybe she's been overdoing it, her case load is too heavy . . .

Insult! She who has always been the Sure Thing . . . *Doesn't want the complication of romance*—the arrogance! She begins to re-focus her energies on her work, typing into the night, bright with insomnia. She'll show them just how much she can overdo it. After all, a name is a name; a life can be assembled, a version offered or selected.

❁

Maybe:

Ling-li reaches Tan Kah Kee's office and stands outside pinching her lips with her index finger and thumb, her shoulders hunched as she leans against the wall. This is how he finds her when he appears five minutes later, his black shoes tapping on the wooden floor.

"Miss Han! Come in," he says, unlocking his door. She follows him into the dark room, noticing the neat but endless piles of paper along one wall, the collection boxes along another and the flash of window along the far wall. His desk is positioned in front of this window and when she takes her seat her eyes tear from the glare. "Oh, let me . . ." He draws the shutters and turns on his lamp so it's suddenly twilight in the room.

"How have you been, Miss Han? How have the youth groups been?" he says, letting himself into his chair carefully, one hand on the small of his back as if he is an old man. She wonders how old he is. She knows he's married, has children who haven't seen him in a while—rumour has it that they had to come to the Ee Hoe Hean Club to pay their New Year respects last year because he was too busy to go home—and has left all family matters to his wife and his mother. He has been known to spend weeks working, eating, sleeping in his office, and the fold-up cot in the corner attests to this.

"Quite well. The youth activities are going well and we've made a lot of progress in the secondary schools. We've got plans to start going to the primary schools and forming some groups there as well. Goh Sim Hock says it's never too early to start saving, and even children can donate to the cause—" She is aware that he is not really listening. What does he want with her?

"Yes, yes—very good." He waves vaguely and leans back in his chair. "Would you like some tea?"

"No, thank you." But he is already up and reaching for the teapot on a small table in the corner. He pours out the tea into two glasses and hands her one. Ling-li tries not to notice the packet of water biscuits and the plate of buns next to the teapot. The tea is Tik Kuan Yin, a strong oolong known for its appetite-stimulating effects, much to her distress. She merely wets her lips with it—the last thing she needs now is to feel even hungrier than she already is.

"So." He catches her eye. "What did you think of the meeting? Do you think I'm a British underling, ready to kowtow to their smallest wishes?"

"Er—" He's asking *her,* of all people? She's only a Youth Leader, one of many. Why should her opinion matter to him?

"It is vital that we collaborate with the British. Our own resources are limited. We have money, sure," he says with an off-handed shrug, and Ling-li's eye rests for a moment on the collection boxes. "But we can't do much on our own to contain Japanese activities here."

"The British—"

"Can't do much on their own either. They're not the most organised, as I'm sure you know. Drink—there's plenty more tea here," he says, mistaking her glance at the table in the corner.

Ling-li has heard that he often skips his midday meal and works on into the night with only a banana or a few cups of Horlicks to kill the rumblings in his stomach. Someone must have brought the biscuits and buns to add to his dietary stockpile—she shouldn't think about taking a bite, even if he were to offer her a biscuit out of politeness.

"I don't know how much you know, but Japanese surveillance

activities have swelled in Malaya in the last year. The peninsula is totally infiltrated with their agents, and they have begun operations in Thailand already."

"Oh," she says, feeling stupid. He's obviously waiting for her to respond in some more appropriate manner, but she is completely unsure of what that might be. "Oh," she says again, her sense of inadequacy pervading the word.

"You speak English well, I've heard." This change in topic takes her off-guard and she blinks at him. "I mean, my reports . . . you attended an English school—"

"Only till Primary Six."

"—and you've been training as a nurse, working on the European wards. You shouldn't be modest, Miss Han." He throws her an encouraging smile.

"Well, I—I read and write it well enough." What does it matter?

"Top in English, according to your teachers at school."

She can't help feeling a little churlish. Top in my class, she wants to say—in everything. But it would be childish, she knows, and besides she is curious as to where he is going with this English business.

He pushes a large envelope towards her. "You could be very helpful, you know—to China." She stares down at it, at its smooth brown unlabelled front and at his fingers tapping along one edge. "You speak English fluently, and Chinese, of course. And I believe you also know Malay."

She nods. Her Malay is a little rough but serviceable—an expressive, only occasionally eyebrow-raising Peranakan Malay that she has picked up over time from shopkeepers, hawkers, civil clerks and Straits-born Chinese classmates.

"The British, you know, have had their secret agents here for years. They've been keeping tabs on the Chinese community here, and other local groups, and now, more recently, they've been taking notice of the Japanese community as well." He ignores her sharp glance. "Trouble is, British agents are easy to spot. They need to train more dependable, talented local agents to do the job."

Ling-li gulps, her hunger suddenly sharpened by her nervousness. "I—?"

"Your language skills are certainly a great advantage. We have reviewed your case very, very carefully. You should think about it."

She looks down at the envelope again, this time noticing the bulge of it. "Will I report to you?"

"Once you accept this position, you will no longer deal with us. You will report directly to the British." He clasps his hands on the table and leans forward. "We cannot, you understand, be involved in any formal way, but if there is anything we can do that will be of assistance to you, you will let me know." He edges the envelope closer to her. "Go through these papers, think about it. Tell me your answer next week."

Realising she is being dismissed, Ling-li gets to her feet and bows, holding out both hands to receive the envelope. As she turns to go, he stops her. "Wait." His voice is lower, more urgent now, and she frowns slightly as she strains to catch his words. "You surely understand that the Japanese are watching us as closely as we are watching them. Their agents are everywhere, and the Relief Fund is no exception."

Tan Kah Kee stands and tosses her the packet of biscuits. "Here, take this."

She blushes, cursing herself for having stared so hard at his food. Mumbling her thanks, she hurries to the door, doing her best not to trip in her haste. When she closes the door behind her, she waits a full minute trying to steady her breath. A week, she says to herself. The packet of biscuits crackles in her hand and she looks down at the label: Ingram's Best Quality Water Biscuits for Energy and Well-Being. The first-floor conference rooms begin to fill up as the Relief Fund members go about their usual business. She rips open the packet of biscuits and begins demolishing the whole lot while sitting on the top stair.

Decisions, she tells herself, should never be made on an empty stomach. The crumbs collect on the envelope on her lap.

The Fifth Columnist writes on, her handsome Youth Leader long forgotten. The report is going very well and she has not felt so optimistic and inspired in days. Miss Competence was right after all, damn her—the complications of romance aren't very stimulating.

Certainly not compared to the complications of fictional histories, historical fictions.

⁂

All warfare is based on deception, reads Grandma Siok. It's her favourite quotation from Sun Tzu. She's had a calligrapher copy the characters onto a scroll, along with another quotation:

He who knows the art of the direct and the indirect approach will be victorious. Such is the art of manoeuvering.

TWO

The Employment of
Secret Agents

用間

PATRICK HEENAN WAS GLAD TO turn his back on England as his ship pulled out of the harbour. Born in a mining town in New Zealand, his dusky colour had at first startled the doctor and nurses at the local hospital. They had held him by the legs under a stream of warm water, rubbed him with towels and swathed him in blankets and hot water bottles in order to "bring out the pink in his cheeks," but the pink never appeared, buried as it was under the coppery glaze of his skin. He grew up fatherless for two years, an unexplained, undiscussed fact that his mother bore with inscrutable cheeriness. His Indian-born Irish stepfather furnished him with a baptism certificate bearing his surname, moved the family to Burma and then died six months later of unknown circumstances. Patrick and his mother stayed on in Burma until Patrick was twelve years old. His mother finally took a job in England as a governess, and young Patrick followed, straggling through school with lacklustre grades and a penchant for fighting. It was a relief, finally, to join the army and to be sent off to India.

But now in India he has gotten everyone mad—a predictable trait in the man. This time, it is over the two Muslims and fourteen Hindu officers in the mess the weekend after successfully warding off the Pathans. Wine and champagne, cigars all round, and on the menu: a choice of pork chops or roast beef. An officer can almost forget he's in India (that being the whole point) unless, of course, he *is* Indian.

"We're in their country after all, damn it! We should have some respect for their ways," Heenan announces, standing on a chair. "Could we not have seen to it that the kitchen prepare a vegetarian meal for these fellows?"

The sad thing is that after this incident, he's a pariah to all, including the Indian Commissioned Officers, who prefer handling their own battles. There are outcasts even among mongrels, and Patrick Heenan, hero in the charge into Ahmedzai Salient territory on the north-west Indian frontier five days before that February of 1940, is the most mixed-up, incomprehensible breed of all.

In the end, it is a relief to be transferred, finally, and closer to Japan. In Heenan's years in India—between 1936 and 1940—his most memorable period was the time of his six-month leave in Japan. He has never talked much about it, but he dreams of it every night. In his dreams, the autumn of 1938 is serene with paper umbrellas and demure Japanese ladies gliding by in their clogs. He remembers his last day there the following spring, his hand resting on a smooth thigh, the cherry blossoms waving outside in the breeze. These memories have lifted his spirits on his remaining isolated days in India, waiting, hoping for a transfer. And now that he has been sent to Malaya—where there are Japanese communities in every town—he looks forward to renewing his Nippon ties.

If it is natural for a man to prefer his own kind, what would make one go the opposite route? What is that mysterious magnet that draws a man to another culture, a whole different way of living? Could it be that never having really lived in his own world, never having been fully alive, he jumps at the chance of a fresh start?

Could it be that the exotic is far more vivid and therefore stimulating to the senses, a drug of sorts, one that intensifies the world? For, as much as you have been brought up to dislike your own race, there are others who, incredible as it seems, have fallen in love with it, others who are drawn to "local" life as much as you resent it.

Patrick Heenan has always been an outsider. He understands his place in the pack, he knows the role of the underdog. Oversensitive and humourless, he has never been tolerated long enough to be considered sociable, much less popular.

But in the East, when he's moving among the squabbling, spitting, raucous, sun-toasted, earth-toned rabble he feels uncommonly at home. They're marginal, misunderstood, just like him. In India he was always close to the Indian officers, could talk to those chaps on just about anything. They had an instinct, these Eastern peoples, for standing back and giving a man room. A notable feat, considering most of them live like rabbits in a narrow burrow, without any real privacy or an unobserved moment. Perhaps it's this circumstance that has cultivated their ability to erect mental walls and put on blinders whenever it's appropriate. They can discuss a man's most private and delicate matters with him and then back off at those blurry, indistinct borderlands of impropriety.

During his assignment in Malaya, he is assigned to Singapore Island for an Air Ground Liaison Course. The training is relatively easy, and Patrick is most carefree these days when he is playing golf in his ample spare time with his newfound Japanese friends. So different from the Indians, but again with that sure instinct for distance within intimacy. Akito and his wife are charming hosts, and after eighteen holes in the placid dusk, walking too briskly for the mosquitoes to land and settle with any accuracy, it's a treat to eat Kano's sushi in their immaculate, screened home.

Ah, why question it? These Asiatics believe in past lives—well, he might've been one of them in his last life, which might be why he's so uncomfortable among whites in this one. The thing is, he's happy, truly happy for the first time since his childhood, and that's what's important. Drinking saké, listening to Akito's drunken singing, staring at Kano's floral print kimono and losing himself in a vertigo of swirling pink flowers—

That's life, Patrick tells himself: This is living.

During his leave in Japan, he had barely managed to learn a few Japanese words, but now Patrick Heenan picks up Japanese with ease, drinks green tea, eats Japanese food whenever he can, chewing noisily and belching as they do in appreciation of a good meal. He receives presents of beautiful teapots, lacquer bowls, roasted seaweed, saké, cognac, paintings, silk. At night he receives the favours of Kano, hair falling over him like a black spray, eyes cold as dark river stones, ears like labyrinths his tongue travels.

He wakes to the scent of jasmine, frangipani, saffron, cumin, coconut oil, tangerine, joss-stick incense, wafting up from under his window, the dawn light still diaphanous and diffuse. How the East can overwhelm a man's senses, how it seeps in, like music, or perfume, like mysterious signals to migrating birds chumming the air, beating out "home, home" across the spread of sky.

※

A means of persuasion, they say, when they display the thin supple rattan switch. When it lashes skin, tiny blood vessels coursing the surface rupture, nerve endings are activated. "My worthy opponents . . . your esteemed opinion"—Counter persuasion with Persuasion. All depends on Rhetoric.

※

Ling-li is working in the Class A wards now, where the European patients are treated. She is among the first batch of new trainees to be sent there and she knows the inner struggle Sister Regina went through before recommending her. The old tigress must've wanted so badly to send someone else instead, but at least she recognised Ling-li's competence and diligence. Ling-li felt the vague and reluctant stirrings of admiration for her instructor when she first learnt that she would be starting in Class A but she's gotten over it by now. At Morning Report, the tigress hardly looks her way and Ling-li is only too glad to return the lack of attention.

Class A is run by Sister Bernardette Richards who talks in whispers. It's hard to hear anything she tells the trainees, even when they beg her pardon and ask her to repeat, so Ling-li has taken to smiling and nodding brightly and then going about doing things her own way. Common sense is what you mostly need anyway, she reckons.

But common sense can only get you so far, Ling-li finds out when, in her first week, one of her patients vomits blood—buckets of it onto the pristine sheets and sanitized floors. Ling-li stares at the scarlet stains setting into the sheets. She stares for so long that the smaller spots begin to brown and the man gives a pathetic groan, and then something clicks in her. Haemorrhage, she thinks, seeing the word in her head—bleeding. The connection pleases her. That's right—bleeding: haemorrhage.

Maintain blood pressure and circulation to the brain, she can almost see the words from her textbook in front of her. *Place the patient in Trendelenburg position.* She cranks the shaft on the side of the hospital bed so that it tilts and the man's legs are elevated, his head is not more than a foot off the floor. SEND FOR A DOCTOR.

She goes running.

By the time she returns with the doctor and Sister Bernardette things have gone downhill. Her patient is drowning in his own blood, he makes an awful gurgling and his face is a mess. The doctor is furious. "You put him in Trendelenburg position? The easier for him to choke on his vomitus and blood?"

"Aspiration," Sister Bernadette whispers piously in Ling-li's ear. "One must always protect the patient's airway against the risk of aspiration. Never put a vomiting man on his head."

"Get his head back up," snaps the doctor. "Get me blood for a transfusion, and a surgeon! Now!"

Ling-li grabs the crank and works it with everything she has. The man's head rises, his feet descend. She runs to the blood bank for blood, leaving Sister Bernardette to hunt down a surgeon. But it's all a wasted exercise—the man is dead before she even makes it back to the ward. The doctor, a white-headed, dog-faced fellow, can scarcely look at her.

"She's only a trainee," Sister Bernardette is whispering. "She just started in Class A this week."

"God save us from these dim-witted natives," the doctor says heartily.

Ling-li, failed general, hangs her head for the first time in the presence of a white man.

❁

Chinese is a language that floats. No tenses, no moods, no declensions or inflexions, syntax malleable. Read left to right it can mean one thing, right to left another. A Chinese character is flexible—now a verb, now a noun, an adjective, an adverb—an actor comfortable in all parts. Its nature is architectural; meaning is designed by relative position, by auxiliary words, parallel beams, juxtaposed elements. Tone is critical, as is perspective. A word is not just a word—it is a made image of the world, an idol to be venerated. Chinese is often spoken with the index finger painting strokes in the air, pictures that reveal all and nothing: the perfect vehicle for poets, historians, rulers and spies.

❁

For weeks, Humphrey and Mr. Tam have been engaged in a battle with the family camped outside their homes. Bullying has not worked, neither has bribery. Cynthia caught the two boys stealing mangoes from her tree one evening and when she shouted at them, they had merely chanted senseless imitations of her English rant back at her, infuriating her all the more. When pushed, something of Grandma Siok surfaces in Cynthia, and she has actively joined the plotting against the squatter family.

"Well, that's that," she announces at dinner one day.

"What?" Humphrey asks irritably. He has just had a yelling match with the father of the family because they have been cooking over an open fire inside the three-walled shack. "It's a fire hazard," he had shouted at the man who had merely yelled back something in Chinese and sealed his pronouncement with a spit that landed an inch short of Humphrey's polished oxfords. Remembering this, Humphrey raises his voice. "What?" he says again.

"That family," Cynthia replies. "I've taken care of it. With a little help from Mr. Tam, of course."

Even as she speaks, there is a commotion outside. Lucy runs to the window where she has to jump up and down to get a view. "Oh," she says, "there's a fire! Someone's pouring petrol on their hut!" She makes another leap. "Oh, there's Mr. Tam! He's yelling at the family." Jump, jump. "Oh, and he's got his dogs with him." There is a shine of efficiency and competence to Cynthia's face. Leave it to a woman to get things done.

They all rush to the window, obscuring what little view poor Lucy had. "Hey!" she protests, but is ignored. The family is standing outside their burning shack. Amazingly there is a ring of men standing around them, armed with buckets of water and sand, watching the flames with interest. As soon as the makeshift building crumbles, they spring into action, dowsing the fire, sending greasy smoke clouds into the air. Two of the men chop up the charred wood with axes, and flakes of cinders flurry over them, landing on their perspiring faces and dissolving into smudges. The family watches in stillness, heads down.

When it is over, Humphrey has joined Mr. Tam outside, both of them yelling from their respective driveways. "Scum! Pests! Get the hell out of here!"

"Come on, Claude, Lucy," Grandma Siok says and scurries out with them. The men with the axes are turning their attention to the family, swinging the axes in lazy loops just out of reach of an ear or a nose.

"Tell them if they ever come back here, they'll be buried here," Mr. Tam says, his face an ugly purple from all his yelling. His dogs prance excitedly at the gate, flinging themselves at the iron grills. The men with the axes translate, turning Mr. Tam's words into a violent spew of Chinese. The family stares back wordlessly, their faces blank. From where he stands, the boy is close enough to see the jutting collarbones on the girl's chest, the angry heave of her chest, the tight strap of neck muscles that reminds him of racehorses as she turns her head a little to one side. He wills her to look up, to see that he is not responsible for this. He doesn't know why, but this is important to him. She keeps her eyes averted. The dogs leap and paw the air, whining for Mr. Tam to open the gate.

The family starts walking. The girl has not acknowledged him at all. "Bums," mutters Humphrey. "Vagabonds." The boy is ashamed of his father, overwhelmingly and furiously ashamed. He wants the girl to see this in his eyes but she will not. "Bastards, hooligans."

The boy picks up a stone and flings it at the girl, hitting her on the right shoulder. She keeps walking. He clenches his fist in a sudden rage. "That's it, son," Humphrey encourages. The boy represses the urge to stamp his feet at his father. He keeps quiet.

When his grandmother catches his eye she is disapproving. "Coward," she says.

And then they all go indoors, back to the dining table, where Cynthia is waiting. It is the end of his boyhood.

Humphrey has always felt inadequate in her presence. Even on their wedding day, when he caught Cynthia looking at him from behind her veil, he knew he was not what she had expected of a groom. No matter how many fittings he had had, his wedding suit had not sat well on his barrel-chested body, and he had stumbled over his vows. More than anything else, he realises now, this had gained her disapproval, for it had embarrassed her in front of her friends and relatives. His slight hesitation and confused mumbling of the words had made him appear somewhat less enthusiastic than he should have, almost as if he were forcing down some unpleasant medicine, she told him later.

No amount of apology could quite remove the rancour she felt at his feeble performance during the wedding, and ever since then, Humphrey has found himself trying unsuccessfully to make up for it. Her unpredictable mood swings and strange temper tantrums have puzzled him since their marriage. She was never so tempestuous when they were courting. His father, in fact, had commented upon how sweet-natured she appeared, and had been thrilled when Humphrey announced their engagement. Raised in a respectable family and beautiful too, she seemed the ideal woman to help Humphrey succeed in his career. Indeed, in their public life together, Cynthia never faltered, charming his bosses at work with her lovely face and gracious manners and the praises for his choice continued to pour in, swelling him with pride. But in private, they never again exchanged the tender moments they had shared as sweethearts and he was saddened and often disturbed by her deliberate distance.

"Why did you marry Father?" he overheard Lucy asking when she was five, and Cynthia had paused an inordinately long time before she answered.

"We were a good match," she said coolly.

"What's a good match?" Lucy pressed, never one to be put off easily.

"Oh, I suppose it's when the man has money and the woman has the looks," she replied and Humphrey had been shocked by the harshness of her tone.

For weeks afterwards, he tried to recall a time, even in their courtship, when she had said outright that she loved him. The realisation had depressed him, but he had taken it in stride, reassuring himself with the adage he had heard so many times before, that love would grow in time. He himself became more unapproachable, having somehow gotten it in his head that the more unavailable he was, the more she would want him. The Theory of the Irresistible Challenge that women were apparently drawn to. But Cynthia, it became clear, was not one to take up that challenge. And then over time it had become a kind of stupid pride, not wanting to show her that he was in the least bit affected by her disinterest, determined to match her apathy with his.

Somehow, despite all this, their partnership as parents and song-and-dance team on the social scene had flourished. They seldom argued over their public roles; they painstakingly avoided personal and matrimonial issues. It was, it could be said, a peaceful life.

At dinner, George Winchester does all the talking, Humphrey all the agreeing and the "ahh"-ing, Janet the tittering and Cynthia the critiquing: Diamond ring, but those pearls aren't real, that dress is too tight for her, she really looks porcine in it. Dinner with the Winchesters at last, to Humphrey's triumph—the first of several to come, and, to Claude, the most painful.

He sits in shy silence beside Jack, trying to think up something to say. *How are you adapting to the climate, Jack?* Too hackneyed. *So, when do you start at the office? I heard you're working for a tea agent here.* Too abrupt. *More potatoes?*

This is finally what he ends up blurting out, to his own disgust, but Jack merely says, "Yes, please," and carries on with his meal. He's not even trying, Claude realises, and suddenly he's embarrassed and clams up.

"You're very quiet," George says to him across the table.

Can't win, Claude thinks, and mentally gives himself a little shake. "I was just enjoying your story about your trip to—" *Where?* "Your trip."

"Always in his own head, our Claude," says Humphrey, filling in the long pause that follows. "Always thinking, always observing. When he was in primary school his teachers used to call him Professor because he was such a serious little fellow. 'Look at the size of that head,' our gardener said the day we brought him back from the hospital, 'he's a brainy one!' I know all babies tend to be a bit egg-shaped on top, but Claude's never really outgrown that, and his performance at school has been quite brilliant, so I'm inclined to believe our simple gardener."

All heads at the table swivel to examine Claude's marvellous cephalos. He turns a beefy red, stares self-consciously at his peas and wishes he were one of them. He imagines himself being swallowed by a gigantic mouth and pestle-like teeth crushing him into oblivion.

"Oh, it's not as bad as mine," says Jack. "The hair helps. Mine definitely looks, well, odd and knobbly. The shine accentuates it, I think."

Attention is now diverted to Jack's bald pate, ringed by a thin hedge of hair that flops meekly against his skull. Claude is grateful for the distraction. Cynthia gives an uncertain laugh and looks uneasily at Humphrey. From the top of the stairs they can all hear a stifled giggling. "Lucy!" says Cynthia.

The giggling ceases and there is a faint rustle. "She's supposed to be in bed," says Cynthia, getting up. "Excuse me, I'll just have a few words with her."

From upstairs they hear the muffled scolding voice of Cynthia as she upbraids Lucy for not being in bed. "But Mother, he does have a funny head, and when the light shines on it, you can see the bumps on the top." More muffled scolding.

"So, have you started work yet?" Claude says.

"In another two weeks. My firm was kind enough to insist that I acclimatise myself before starting work." Jack smiles around the table. "And so, Claude, perhaps I could persuade you to do a little sight-seeing with me? I need someone who's familiar with the island and knows all the 'in'-spots."

"Oh, he'll be happy to," says Humphrey, a warning glint in his eye at his son.

"Mmm, happy to." Where in heaven's name are the 'in'-spots?

"Show him a good time," booms George across the table. "You should know, eh, boy?"

Why? he wonders. Why should he know?

"You Asiatics can get pretty randy at times, eh?" George continues, as if to answer Claude's unspoken question. There is an awkward silence around the table. While Humphrey forces a laugh, Claude stares down at the napkin on his lap, his mind unexpectedly filled with the memory of the girl bathing behind his kitchen. He has a sudden panic that they all know what he is thinking as they lean across the table to look at him.

"Dessert, anyone?" Cynthia's voice rings out as she returns to the dining room. "Dessert, yes?"

"Good idea," Claude says, not thinking of food. Abscond, desert the dinner table—yes, that's what he'd like to do right now.

✷

Some would have thought the assignment to Asia a penalty, but Jack Winchester had waited months for it, and had asked his brother, George, to send letters and telegrams to all his influential contacts when it had seemed at one point that the position would go to another man. On the sea voyage to Singapore, still a little stunned by his good fortune, Jack had kept to himself, and ate alone in his room each night. He avoided the tiresome dances and varied amusements that the ladies arranged after dinner and napped until the voices subsided and the deck cleared out. Then, at about two in the morning, he smoked his cigarette on the east deck, reading under a paraffin lamp borrowed from the crew. His favourite passages were from Conrad, passages he had read through weeks of winter damp, staring out at skies that bore the dirty colours of newsprint:

> And this is how I see the East. I have seen its secret places and have looked into its very soul; but now I see it always from a small boat, a high outline of mountains, blue and afar in the morning; like faint mist at noon; a jagged wall of purple at sunset. I have the feel of the oar in my hand, the vision of the scorching blue sea in my eyes. And I see a bay, a wide bay, smooth as glass and polished like ice, shimmering in the dark. A red light burns far off upon the gloom of the land, and the night is soft and warm. We drag at the oars with aching arms, and suddenly a puff of wind, a puff faint and tepid and laden with strange odours of blossoms, of aromatic wood, comes out of the still night—the first sight of the East on my face. That I can never forget. It was impalpable and enslaving, like a charm, like a whispered promise of mysterious delight.

On board the *Gentleman's Folly*, the smell of prawns and menthol salve drifting up from the hold below and the East nothing but an uncompromising stretch of black in front of him, it had seemed to Jack like a time just before creation. He was certain he would never want to go back to the other known world.

Among his other books was a treatise on Chinese customs, as well as a complicated primer on the Chinese language. He flipped through its pages often but could never make himself focus on the lessons. For the moment it was enough to conjure up the language, its exotic sounds and strange locutions. For the moment it was enough to read and to believe everything he read, to listen and be engulfed by the tale.

Claude faces his father in his study. Humphrey is still in his pyjamas. "Morning, son."

"Mother said you wanted to talk to me." He is uncomfortable in his father's presence. He always has the sense that Humphrey expects things from him—success, accomplishments, the right qualifications.

"Come and have breakfast with me. We haven't done that in such a long time," says Humphrey, spreading his hands to offer the array of fruits set on his long reading table. In fact, Claude has never had breakfast alone with his father but decides not to comment on this. Instead he sits down and starts working diligently on a slice of watermelon.

"What did you think of Jack?" asks Humphrey in between chunks of pineapple and papaya.

He nods, hoping it will suffice. What can he say? What does he want to say? The same old problem. He doesn't know himself, not because he hasn't thought of it but because he's thought too much. The trouble with him is that he doesn't very often come to conclusions. There's something in his father's constitution that ends up making him nervous. It seems to affect everyone else in the household except Grandma Siok. It's his way of making others feel that they don't measure up, that they're not good enough. But lately Claude has noticed that Humphrey is never like this in front of Europeans. When he's in their presence he's always pleasant and effusive—he acts like the people who kowtow to him.

"I'd like you to comply with his request, you know."

Claude sits up straighter, begins to search his brains. What request? "I mean, it would be so nice if you could indulge him by taking him sight-seeing. It'd be a good opportunity for you to have a—another friend."

A white friend, you mean, Claude thinks and wonders why it annoys him. After all, it would be to his own advantage, since having white friends automatically accords more social mobility. *Get to know him,* is what he knows Humphrey really wants to say—*insinuate yourself into his company, and that will be one step closer to George Winchester for me, one step higher up the ladder.* He spits out the watermelon seeds into his napkin, trying not to be too noisy about it. "But Father, what is there to see?"

"Well," begins Humphrey and then pauses. He hasn't really considered this. "How about the financial district? The river would be nice, the, er, *kampongs* perhaps—it might interest him to see how the natives live. Oh, and take him to the beach somewhere—Changi or Punggol Point where he can look across to the mainland. Anything will do—I'm sure he just wants a bit of local colour."

And what about me? the thought creeps in unexpectedly as Claude listens to his father, am I "local colour" too? A native guide?

He's confused by those thoughts, struggles to keep them from showing.

"Don't," says Humphrey, startling him.

"Sir?" He pauses between bites, a frosty slice of watermelon hovering near his mouth.

"Don't think too much, son. It's not necessary."

Claude bites into the foamy melon. It's tasteless but juicy. "Yes, Father," he says. "I'll give Jack a ring after school this Friday."

❀

Grandma Siok reads.

Sun Tzu said:

Now the reason the enlightened prince and the wise general conquer the enemy whenever they move and their achievements surpass those of ordinary men is foreknowledge.

What is called "foreknowledge" cannot be elicited from spirits, nor from gods, nor by analogy with past events, nor from calculations. It must be obtained from men who know the enemy situation.

❀

On one of his Sundays off, Captain Patrick Heenan gets up before dawn and heads for Geylang on Singapore Island. He uses a borrowed bicycle because he is loath to spoil the bristling, tinnitic peace of the city. It's not a silent, dead quiet, but one that crackles

with static as wash water swooshes and throats are cleared and joss-
sticks are lit. The muezzin calls a nasal, spiralling drone from his
tower and holy ash is distributed at the temples to Indian coolies
before breakfast. The city tingles.

In the peeling alleyways of Geylang, Patrick finds the birdcages.
Two long rows of domed bamboo birdcages covered with dark cloth
and strung out along wire down the length of an alley. Underneath
are Chinese men in fresh white singlets and shorts. laying out tea
sets from wicker baskets. They steal glances at Patrick even as they
pretend not to notice him, grunting cordially to each other and
pouring hot water from their thermos flasks to make tea, but he has
been there often enough and has been unobtrusive enough on previous occasions to warrant their general acceptance. They exchange
news in low voices, light up cigarettes or do stretching exercises for
a few more moments until the sun, wobbling like jelly, rises.

The men pick up their long poles and line up, each facing his
birdcage and then, just as the giant solar yolk cracks on the horizon
and runs over the steely sky, they lift the covers off the birdcages and
the contest begins.

Birdsong trickles, then floods the alleyway, twitter and chirp,
twitter-chirp, until the sound rises and takes flight over the yawning
zinc roofs and washing-lines fluttering awake. Patrick's ears are
inundated with it, it throngs over him like a shoving marketplace
crowd, shrill, dense, frenzied, it unravels something in his spleen
that rises and twists and sends the blood shuttling through his heart.

He remembers the gracious men from the Japanese Intelligence
Service who had visited him several times when he was on leave in
Japan over a year ago. "Asia in the hands of Asiatics," they had said,
"set free like songbirds finally united with their soaring voices."

One bird chirps louder than all the rest, its notes domineering,
higher, piercing. Patrick cannot single it out from the rows of swinging birdcages, but a man is pointing at his bird and babbling to his
friends. Patrick looks up. From where he stands it looks like a
nightingale. It is a clear winner, and its voice mesmerises Patrick
with its loud, mellifluous insistence. Already its owner is acknowl-
edging his bird's superiority, already he is boasting.

Patrick watches as the old man is toasted by the others, the way his left hand covers his right fist in a gesture of thanks. The birds are covered up again, the birdcages lifted off the hanging wire with the long poles and carefully lowered to the ground by the owners. More tea is drunk, jokes circulate. After the contest, joviality and human speech prevail.

Patrick is startled by a polite cough over his shoulder. He turns to see the owner of the winning nightingale. The man holds up his birdcage. "*Gong hei,*" Patrick says clumsily in Cantonese, congratulating the old man. He points to the bird and says, "*Ho!*"—good. It is all the Chinese he knows.

The man nods briefly. "It's yours," he says unexpectedly in English. Patrick stares. "Don't you want it?" the bird-owner asks.

"Yes, but he must be worth a fortune," says Patrick.

The old man smiles a waxy smile—slippery, polished, flammable. "A fortune, no—just a few secrets here and there, a price that surely you can afford."

❁

—Who gave you this information? How did you come by this?

A blank, even though you are trying.

—Name your sources, why did you ask for this information? Who are you?

Whispering through the Body's lips, you give your name, but it doesn't satisfy them. You make yourself search your memory, wanting the answer almost as much as they do, but there is nothing. Nothing but a certain knowing, a fluid omniscience that you're not sure you want.

Everything you have told them seems to drive them into a frenzy. There is an intense discussion, more cold water thrown over the Body, lights that throb behind its eye sockets. A man shouts and the spittle from his mouth settles on the Body's shirtfront, but it doesn't matter, it can't get any wetter. It's his voice you don't like. High-pitched, snipping off consonants with a brittleness that makes you flinch, it wears down the ear and brings you precariously close to hysteria. If you cried now, it would be the Body screeching, and you wouldn't know how to stop it.

The sudden relief of a baritone. The dark low notes are a balm to your twisted nerves, catch you just before that point of no return, anchor you to their reassuring cadence, their almost gentle rise and fall. "Don't worry about him," they say, so human that you want to cry, this time like a baby, willing someone to understand what you are trying to communicate, the warped magnification of your world that is beyond your own comprehension. Through the Body's hiccoughs, you tell him you don't know what is required of you, why they won't believe you. He tells you never mind, has someone prop the Body up on a chair, turns off the painful lights. *He* knows you are doing your best, assures you he doesn't doubt your sincerity in the least. You are spinning alarmingly in your weightlessness, but the Body's feet and the chair feel solid enough so you try to lean back and rest a little. He says something in Japanese and though his voice is still soothingly low, there is something of a snarl in it that chokes the Body's gullet and it holds its breath, steeling itself against the next blow.

But it is only a glass thrust to its lips, the wet burning through the cuts. The Body drinks greedily. The liquid tastes like water at the dentist's when one is told to rinse out one's mouth, salty with blood and the faint metallic burr of the drill. You know this is only a short reprieve before the drill starts up again, and it won't stop until it exposes the tender root.

Amazingly, a blanket is thrown over the Body.

—Better now? asks the voice, all concern and kindness, the accent flawless. Good. You see, we don't want to—inconvenience you in any way. We want nothing more than to talk to you, to understand you.

—Talk? What is there to talk about?

The voice laughs pleasantly.

—Oh, I'm sure we'll find something, it says jovially. Let's start, let's see—tell us something about yourself. Tell us about your life.

—My life? But there is nothing that would interest anyone, surely, nothing remarkable.

—Come now, the voice coaxes. Every life is interesting, every life has its secrets. Perhaps you'd like to share one with us. Come on, Claude Lim, tell me a secret. Tell it as if you were telling a—friend.

Friend? How quickly Ling-li springs to mind at the word. What secrets would you tell her?

—Claude. We're waiting.

Even in your disoriented state, you hear the command in the rich baritone. Without thinking, the Body opens its mouth and in the darkened room, you spill out the nebulous shape of narrative . . .

※

As Defence Security Officer, Hayley Bell spends weeks travelling up and down the peninsula, sometimes in the company of his daughters, more often alone, gathering information for British Intelligence. He startles and disarms people when he speaks, drawing disbelieving stares and strange looks from all corners of the room. Many sidle up closer to get a better listen in on his conversation. They exchange glances, they shrug, they nudge each other.

The man and his two daughters make a handsome trio. His voice has the deep ring of a well, his gestures are graceful and his Cantonese is fluent, old-fashioned even. More than that, he is white! No matter how long the natives spend in his presence, they can never get over this incongruity.

Hayley Bell loves the first blank look of shock on their faces when he makes small talk in Hokkien or Cantonese. On a rare day he'll even flaunt the dicier Hainanese just to watch them gawk. But just as much as it's gratifying to him that they have no problem understanding his diction—he has been told numerous times that his pronunciation is flawless—he is appalled that among his own kind he is a minority.

"How can we rule effectively when we don't even bother to learn the languages of our subjects?" he's been heard to say over and over at the various clubs in town. His compatriots merely smile and move on, bemoaning once again amongst themselves their poor luck at being stationed in this far-flung outpost. They compare endlessly between the colony and England, languishing on homesickness until their chauffeurs come to ferry them to their spacious homes in Tanglin—chauffeurs and homes they would never have in England but which are cheap enough here.

Hayley is meticulous and patient, an astute man. For years he has been sifting and sniffing, drafting report after report on the situation in the Far East. He knows the Foreign Office barely reads them, he knows they think them sensationalist, but he keeps digging and sleuthing. He does not trust the Thais and gives warning. Unlike Cassandra he does not merely prophesy; he has facts and documents, he has evidence.

But he shares Cassandra's fate. No one wants to hear bad news, no matter how well researched.

—Bad news, the baritone says brightly. You know all about bad news, don't you, Claude? Why don't you tell me some of what you've heard?

It is hard to focus on that voice when you are straining against the solidity and weight of the Body, but you force yourself, knowing he will not understand if you try to explain. You tell him you don't know what news he means, what he wants out of you.

—Ah, but it's simple, he says. It's not a lot to ask. I want to know about your friend, the Englishman. Jack, I believe, is his name. Tell me what you were doing with him before the war. Tell me what he wanted to know. Tell me how you became friends.

—He was a friend of the family

—Ah, yes. Very interesting, your family. Admirers of the Empire, I've heard.

You say nothing.

—You had a servant, a Chinese national, the baritone says, clasping his hands.

—Amah.

He inclines his head. There is the sound of furniture being dragged around in the adjacent room, the shuffle of feet, a cough.

—Who is there? you ask impulsively. He frowns, not understanding. Who is there, you insist, next door?

—Not your concern, he sniffs.

It suddenly occurs to you that you, of all people, should know the answer. There are no walls for you. All you need to do is to look.

But you don't. You don't want to. You can't. It is the last thing you have, this one piece of wilful unseeing. Too much light can blind you.

He is staring at the Body and you try once more to focus.

—Yes, you say, not my concern.

Now Amah. What do you know of her? That she has taken care of the boy since he was born, that she was sternly warned not to speak Chinese to him, that the plaited bun affixed to her nape is her own hair, but from thirty years ago. When the boy found the thick, shiny black coif bundled neatly in a hairnet years ago and teased her about it, throwing it into the air and feeling the springy weight of it in his hand as he caught it, he glimpsed a look—just for one moment—on her face that made him put it back down soberly. It was a look of helpless anger, as if she wanted to hit him but could not and was almost bursting from her restraint.

She is sitting alone in the room she shares with Phatcharat behind the kitchen and through her eyes you can see the window louvres, painted red on the inside, unbeknownst to Humphrey, who would have forbidden it. ("Red! Too damn local!") There is a calendar on the wall, the dates boxed off and marked with little horses to indicate race days, variously shaded circles to indicate the lunar cycle, and Chinese characters to indicate special festivals and auspicious days. "What's that day?" the boy asked her when he was young enough still to be playing in her room.

"That one dumpling festival," she replied. This lost child, her face read.

"And that one?"

"Oh, that to look at moon."

"And that?"

"That for—long story." She waved her hands, trying to find the right words. "Young people in love, you know? Bridge with birds?" But of course he didn't know, because it was a Chinese story and no-one had ever told him one.

She has just turned sixty-three, and her outward manner is calm, collected, as befitting an old woman, but the inside of her head, you are amazed to find, is blistered with burning for her home village in

Guilin, China. She has not seen it since she left as a little girl of nine, first for Hong Kong, and then, seven years later, for Singapore. Coarse-faced and clumsy, she has worked as a maid since she left home. Dutifully, she has sent half her earnings to her parents and sisters, and ever since, she has talked about saving for her return to China.

She has seldom talked about her home, but now, in her head, you see it with all the haziness of her childhood eyes. The hills are vibrant with green and the tall, peaked chalk formations that lean over small fishing boats in the rivers cast a magical quality to the landscape. When Amah hears the lap-lapping waters and the rustle of twisted scrub trees perched precariously on one of the natural menhirs that rise out of the depths, she almost cries with longing. There is a sudden expansiveness of space in her old mind, as if her world has grown infinitely large and distant as the sky overhead, as she thinks aloud, "Jia," a word the boy would not have understood because it is Chinese, but inside Amah's head, you do. "Jia," she says over and over, and it is a kind of intense singing: Home.

***

—China. The baritone's voice is softer now. What do you know of China?

You don't answer because there is nothing to say.

—What do you know of China? There is a blow between the Body's shoulder blades and it falls forwards, almost off its seat.

The baritone speaks sharply to his men and they back off, bowing deeply. You register fear on their faces and are alert. This voice of civility and reason is far more dangerous than all the other brusque, coarse ones in the room. Tread carefully, you warn, but the Body can only respond physiologically, its heart thumping away. You will have to handle this.

—Have you ever been there? he asks.

The Body almost smiles. Humphrey would rather spend whole years covered to his neck in mud and red ants than spend a day in China.

—My father would never agree to such a trip.

—Why not?

—He says that it's a primitive country. He wouldn't even let us learn Chinese.

—But the English? They are acceptable?

Eyes turn down. Careful, you think, noting the blood that pounds in the Body's temples.

—Now, now. You see, we are only trying to understand your kind. How you could stand to be slaves of Western pigs, why you've accepted their language . . . We come as liberators, but first we must liberate your minds and the sick attitudes you've imbibed from your former rulers. Help us understand this. Give us some clues. History must not be repeated.

Ah yes, history again. Chosen frames of descriptive interpretations or interpreted descriptions. By now you know the game. This much you can do for them.

The rules of English society outside the motherland are stringent even for home-grown lads like Jack. For one thing, there is the impractical dress code, an absurdly formal, glamorous injunction upon members of the expatriate community. Jack discovers this first-hand when he tries to dine at the modest Yarmouth Club in a plain linen shirt and freshly pressed trousers. He is duly informed that his dress is inappropriate, that a dinner jacket and tie are mandatory for dining despite the ninety-five-degree temperature, and that his shoes lack the proper shine and smartness.

When he complains to Janet, she brings him the club's rule book. Under "Dress Code" there is a prominent epigraph by a woman called Charlotte Cameron who had visited the colony in the 1920s: "In the evening, both men and women are more particular than we are in England to don dinner-jackets and décolleté gowns. I presume this is with the idea of setting an example to the natives and to proclaim our caste."

Jack is uncomfortable with the word "caste," even given the context that the quote is at least twenty years old. His way of dealing with it is to avoid dining at the clubs and to patronise native establishments instead, where he is fussed and fawned over so much that he feels a little guilty. Do they know he's just a junior clerk at his office and not some bigwig *ma'salleh*? And yet the attention is addictive, and he finds himself a regular at the local eating houses, chugging down Chinese beer and strange, delicious dishes (he never asks what they are) that are usually presented with solemn ceremony before him.

And the women! He has never been so admired! Eurasians, Chinese, White Russian girls—he knows it's his position as a single white man in the colony rather than his looks or charms that attract them. His salary, unassuming as it is, overshoots the average educated local's income at least six- to eightfold and doubtless adds to his popularity. Nevertheless, he enjoys their attentions and allows himself to be fawned over and seduced.

The funny thing is that their dress is quite a few times more flamboyant and intimidating than that of the Europeans and when he begins to frequent local casinos, fine restaurants and dance clubs, he is required to be as spruced up as the Yarmouth Club's dress code demands. Yet this time he's eagerly shopping for new clothes and grooming himself meticulously for his nightly pursuits. He even engages an *amah*—something he has resisted since his first day on the island out of a sense of moral enlightenment—to wash, iron, lay out his clothes and polish his shoes. She needs the money, he tells himself, so what is wrong with helping her out?

The Europeans, his compatriots, drift out of his life. After all, he is in Singapore, and he has no intention of taking up with his own kind when there is so much more to discover.

✦

She runs her hand over the rows of dresses in her wardrobe as if scanning them to decide what she wants when, in fact, she already knows exactly what she will wear. Still acting, Cynthia, she addresses herself cattily, even to yourself when you're alone, you poor dear!

She pulls out the red cheongsam she's had in mind all along, flings it onto her mahogany bed. Amah slips in, bringing tea. "I'll need a taxi," Cynthia says without looking at her. "In an hour. Is the bath full yet?"

Amah, her teeth out today because of a gum infection, manages a choppy "Yeth" and goes downstairs to find Rahman. "Madam needs a taxi in an hour," she tells him in her colloquial Malay. She adds, "She's got a cheongsam out again."

Rahman raises his eyebrows. "Why does she do this?" he asks, but goes outside to hail a taxi without waiting for Amah's reply.

"I stopped wondering years ago why this family does the things it does," she says to herself in her native Cantonese and retreats to the kitchen to beg Phatcharat for some ice for her gums.

Cynthia spoons the lukewarm bath water over herself. A part of her wishes she could just stay where she is until Humphrey comes home and they can all take tea together on the veranda. Another part knows she won't, that she'll finish preparing herself in exactly an hour and stride into a dank-smelling taxi, that she'll miss tea as she has been doing once a week for the past year, that Humphrey will believe that she is at her Young Orphans Committee meeting with Isobel Tam and ask her eagerly afterwards if she has been invited to any parties with the committee ladies.

She's long stopped asking herself why she continues to give in to her impulses. It's a magnetic force she can't refuse, she's polarised and drawn to it, even though she secretly hates herself for it. Well, perhaps not so secretly. Cynthia spends hours torturing herself to pay for her sins. The trouble is, even her penance disturbs her. She sneaks out to a small, decrepit Chinese temple in Chinatown, lights a forest of joss-sticks, kneels in a smoke-blackened and windowless room for whole mornings, until Amah comes to fetch her and they go home together, ostensibly returning from doing the marketing and shopping.

Humphrey, she thinks as she's watching the golden tips of the joss-sticks burn down to ashy stubs, he'd die of shame if he saw me here, praying with the heathens and indulging in superstitious practises.

And yet, though she knows that he'd feel shame at her visits to the temple, she's unsure what he'd feel about her visits to her lovers. Her white lovers. Ha! she thinks, that should throw a wrench in his well-formed opinions of everything. Adultery—hideous, but to have your wife sleep with a white man, well, things get muddied here. Sometimes her curiosity as to Humphrey's reaction has been so strong that she has teetered on the brink of revealing all, but that two-timing double pull-push of the magnet holds her, shoving and pressing until she's a wreck and has one of her nervous fits, for which Amah has to dose her with a sedative from a silver-plated dropper, each drowsy fat drop plopping into her half-open mouth.

She lifts herself from the tub, scrubs herself vigorously with her towel as if trying to slake off her skin. Wouldn't that be nice, she thinks, to shed your shell every couple of years, step out a brand-new person? Why don't we all get second chances like that?

The comb leaves neat tracks in her hair. She gathers the ends into a chignon and teases a strand so that it falls in an exaggerated curl just off the middle of her forehead. She puts on the red cheongsam, flinching as she sees herself in the full-length mirror. She looks like a Chinese floozy.

No point hiding it, she tells herself, steel glinting in her eyes. A spade's a spade. "Finish it," she says through clenched teeth to the mirror. She paints her lips vermilion and tucks a red carnation in her hair. The vision stares back at her, inviting and familiarly exotic. It sickens and excites her. She bares her teeth suddenly and the face crumbles to a snarl. "Bitch," she spits out.

And somewhere inside, a calm voice is saying, Exactly, exactly.

⁂

As part of his tour-guide duties, Humphrey has told his son that he should take Jack to the Victoria Theatre. The Royal Glasgow Symphony is on a month's tour of the Far East and he is to procure tickets for the event. "Shouldn't I check with him first to see if he wants to go?" Claude asks with a sinking heart. He loves the symphony but can't stand the dressing-up and pomp involved. Better the gramophone, comfortably ensconced in his own room, pyjamas and pillows, no fuss.

"It'll be a nice surprise," says Humphrey. "Here, take what you need and see if you can get a lift from your mother tomorrow to get the tickets. She's got a Young Orphans meeting."

He removes a suitable number of notes from his father's wallet and goes to look for his mother. He is surprised to find her in the kitchen with Amah, folding paper ingots out of gold paper. "Mother?" he asks in mild wonder. He has never seen her so focused, so fervent.

She doesn't seem to hear him. Amah looks up, clears her throat, puts her hand on Cynthia's agitated paper-folding ones. His mother stops uncomprehendingly. "Hummm?"

"Mum, will you give me a lift tomorrow to the Victoria Theatre on your way to Young Orphans?" He can't take his eyes off her hands, which even now are folding crisp edges, shaping ingots.

"All right," she says and forgets about him.

"Mum?" One ingot, two ingots. "Mum?"

"What, Claude? I said okay! A lift tomorrow!"

"What are you doing, Mum?" he asks in awe. Her fingers are flying. He has never seen anyone fold so quickly in his life. She's an alchemist, shaping gold with her hands.

"Penance," she replies sharply. "Any more questions?"

He can't quite meet her eyes. "Er, no, Mum. Good night."

In Amah's face he sees a queer mixture of pity and tenderness for Cynthia and, unaccountably, it frightens him.

Her liveliness and flirtatiousness in the presence of white men has made Humphrey uneasy, but characteristically, he has said nothing to her. It's always hard to know how she would react. What he's afraid of is that she might have a fit or create a scene at one of the functions they attend, just to spite him—he wouldn't put it past her. It would be hard to live down anything like that, so he endures her over-bright smile, the attention she dotes on the Europeans at their office parties, or at Anglo-Chinese socials organised by upper-crust locals, such as the dinner and dance benefit they are attending tonight for the Deaf, Dumb and Blind Association.

To all other eyes Cynthia is as poised, effervescent, witty and as attractive as any Eurasian; to Humphrey she is uncomfortably on the edge of scandal. He wonders why no-one else seems to notice the way her eyes follow the white men around, the strange feverish gleam in them as she casually drapes an arm over undistinguished fellows from the office who then puff up suddenly and strut around her dripping compliments, their accents plummier than he remembers. At such times, a crazy, involuntary tongue of anger flames up in him, causing him to break into a sweat and clench his fists. He recoils from his own irrational behaviour even as he stuffs his hands into his pockets to keep them from doing any harm.

She's just doing her duty, he tells himself as he tries to unlock his tight jaw and smile at the matrons who nod at him in passing. He has told her countless times that they needed to expand their social circles—he can hardly blame her now for trying.

When their paths cross on the periphery of the dance floor, he catches her waist on impulse, spinning her round to face him. "You always said you would teach me the cha-cha," he says with a forced smile, squashing his natural aversion to dance. Her hand reaches for his chest, and for a second he is happy to feel the warmth in its well-shaped palm, the slight scrape of her nails through his cotton shirt.

"Do you want to make a fool of yourself?" she hisses and the hand hardens into a wall, a barrier between them. When he lets her go, they both stumble backwards, causing people to turn and stare. "Oh Humphrey! You've always had two left feet! It's a wonder I don't break something dancing with you," she declares gaily. Humphrey marvels at her quick transformation from resisting partner to endearing wife. Or perhaps not quite so endearing—

"Come, Peter—dance with me before Humphrey causes any real damage," she says, resting her hand on one of Humphrey's office acquaintances, an Englishman whose position is below Humphrey's at work and whose lacklustre job performance would no doubt ensure that he stay there.

Across the dance floor her eyes catch his like silk against a splinter. Humphrey barely has the presence of mind to look away first, so that he's not left standing there feeling pathetically abandoned. When he does manage to disengage his gaze a second before she does, it's a bitter triumph.

Claude has always wondered why his mother wears a cheongsam on most of the days she goes to Young Orphans. Sometimes, though, to his added bafflement she has gone in a *sarong kebaya* like the *nonyas*. But it's no use asking her anything, so he merely tells the taxi driver to stop at Victoria Theatre before taking her to her destination, and settles down to watch the scenery blur past him.

"Do you have a girlfriend, Claude?" Cynthia asks abruptly.

"Er, no, Mother," he mutters, hoping she'll let it rest. There are some things that get her going on and he hopes this isn't one of them.

"Why not? Don't you like girls?"

He swallows hard, hoping to God that the taxi driver doesn't understand much English. "Really, Mother," he says.

"Well? Yes or no? Speak up," she says, looking straight ahead. At times like these he sees the resemblance between her and Grandma Siok.

"Mother—I, well, I suppose I do. I just haven't had the time for—you know, girls, girlfriends, that sort of thing." He finishes in a rush.

"Why not?"

"I have my studies, and Father's always said I should lay off . . . girls . . . until I get through university, so I don't get distracted. There's plenty of time later," he says, echoing Humphrey. Though it's more than that, he knows. It's also the matter of not being sure of himself, of never knowing what to say. In his eyes, a man has to be a leader, an independent spirit, larger-than-life, for a woman to look up to him. He remembers, from a few years ago, the girl washing herself outside the kitchen, the look of scorn in her eyes and her absolute indifference to his presence. Running that memory over and over in his mind, he has often wished he had been able to banish that indifference, to inspire, instead, some sort of admiration.

"Your father—" Cynthia stops short, takes a deep breath. "Sometimes his beliefs can be so, so—Eastern. That's just the sort of thing they teach in those dreadful Chinese schools—I should know. I was in one for two years until my father put his foot down and made your Grandma Siok transfer me to an English one. Everything was so goddamn puritanical—all that bullshit about purity, duty, duty, duty before everything, boys on this side, girls on that, and absolutely no mixing without a scandal!"

It sounds exactly like Littleton, he thinks, but he says nothing to her. It shocks him a little that his school is not too different from the Chinese schools. Girls attending Littleton (like Lucy) are in separate classes, aren't even on the same campus. They are taught in a small house off of Clemenceau Boulevard and he never sees them except on Sports Day or during Parents' Week.

"Some things you can't change," Cynthia continues with a sigh. "I mean, he has the accent, the right job, the right contacts. We live in an upper-middle-class, English-educated neighbourhood, you and Lucy are in a top-notch school and yet underneath it all, he is still so Chinese himself. Or, as your friend Hugh would say, *Cina*." She smiles bitterly.

He steels himself for more, but she suddenly decides she's had enough and retreats into her own little dream world. She does that often, particularly when she's bored. He spends the rest of the ride trying to be as uninteresting as possible, so as not to rouse her from her reverie.

At the Victoria Theatre he waits until his mother's taxi is out of sight—as if to assure himself that she's truly out of his hair for now—before he goes inside. Once the big wooden doors close behind him, he is enveloped by a sensation that has a sound of its own—a muffled feeling, as if the world has suddenly been muted with a heavy blanket.

He follows signs to the box office. There's no-one queuing at this hour and he pulls out his Straits dollars. "Two tickets for the Royal Glasgow on Saturday night, please."

The cashier, an elderly Eurasian, shakes his head. "Wrong counter, sonny," he says. "First-class tickets only, see?" He points to the sign above him.

"Well, yes," he says, not sure what to do. "Two tickets," he repeats, holding out his money so the man can see that he has enough for them. A white couple comes up behind him.

"First-class only," says the Eurasian firmly. "Over there for second-class." He leans over the counter and points behind his shoulder to another counter farther back on his left where there's a small queue.

"Right," he mumbles, heading off for the other counter. The one for non-whites. Of course, he tells himself, but then he's never bought tickets here. Usually the Tams give his family their spare tickets, for matinees and second-rate companies not attended by the European community.

"Colour-blind, is he?" he hears the white woman say to her companion—one of the White Russians. He forces himself to stand in line and get his tickets. Only when he is outside does he realise that Jack will be sitting with him in the section for non-whites. He has half a mind to go back and change one ticket for a first-class one but then something in him hardens. "So what?" he says to himself. "I'm the one buying the tickets, after all!" He refuses to admit to himself that he can't return to the ticket counter again, the eyes of the White Russian woman and her companions on him as he tries to explain why he needs one first-class ticket.

Some people turn around and look at him strangely, and he wonders if he's been talking to himself. A hawker has set up her assorted knick-knacks on two straw mats just outside the theatre. There are earthenware pots, spittoons, pans and pails in one corner, hair accessories, re-bottled fragrant water, tortoiseshell-backed mirrors and canvas shoes in another. On one mat, arranged on neat trays, are Malay *kuehs,* glutinous rice balls and sesame buns all topped by flies. No-one in his right mind would eat any of it, Claude thinks, and for no reason, he is enraged at the woman for setting up store in the European plaza, disgracing him and all other natives. He sticks out his foot as he walks by and knocks over one of the trays. The flies wobble in the air as they look for new scavenging spots. The woman hawker starts to shout, but he looks about and says, "Police," and she shuts up immediately. In her perpetual squat, she waddles from place to place to gather up the food, and then dusts the rice balls and buns with her hand before rearranging them on the tray. As she does so, she comes very close to where he is standing.

It happens all at once: she spits on his shoes and in a violent reflex action, his right leg slips out from under him and he kicks her. He feels his foot stub her under the armpit, throwing her off her feet and causing her to roll several yards away from him. "*Aiyo, aiyo,*" she screams, though no-one pays any attention. Hurriedly he crosses the street to the Esplanade. By the time he is on the other side the hawker has picked herself up again and is tidying up her display.

No harm done, he tells himself, unable to believe he has just kicked a woman. His hands are shaking and he is feeling cold in full sunlight. When he replays the incident in his mind, he can't even recall the woman's face. There is a reason after all, he thinks, for second- and even third-class tickets.

It's the one book in his collection that he doesn't enjoy reading, and yet Jack finds himself taking it out more often than the others, reading through the troublesome sections like a man tonguing a sore tooth. Always the same questions. Would he, put in the same position, have been a stronger man than Flory and insisted that Veraswami be admitted into the European Club? Or would he have suffered from the same moral cowardice and weakness in the end and put a bullet in his own heart?

Orwell was brutal with the English:

> "Sit down, old chap, sit down," Westfield said. "Forget it. Have a drink on it. Not worth while quarrelling. Too hot."
>
> "My God," said Ellis a little more calmly, taking a pace or two up and down, "my God, I don't understand you chaps. I simply don't. Here's that old fool Macgregor wanting to bring a nigger into this Club for no reason whatever, and you all sit down under it without a word. Good God, what are we supposed to be doing in this country? If we aren't going to rule, why the devil don't we clear out? Here we are, supposed to be governing a set of damn black swine who've been slaves since the beginning of history, and instead of ruling them in the only way they understand, we go and treat them as equals. And all you silly b——s take it for granted. There's Flory, makes his best pal of a black babu who calls himself a doctor because he's done two years at an Indian so-called university. And you, Westfield, proud as Punch of your knock-kneed, bribe-taking policemen. And there's Maxwell, spends his time running after Eurasian tarts. Yes, you do, Maxwell; I heard about your goings-on in Mandalay with some smelly little bitch called Molly Pereira. I suppose you'd have gone

and married her if they hadn't transferred you up here? You all seem to like the dirty black brutes. Christ, I don't know what's come over us all. I really don't."

"Come on, have another drink," said Westfield. "Hey, butler! Spot of beer before the ice goes, eh? Beer, butler!"

Jack turns red every time he reads these passages. He tries to speed past them and when he catches himself doing so, he forces himself to linger, to take in every painful word. Of course he would have voted to accept Veraswami, he tells himself—it would have been the only decent thing to do. One can't take fiction too seriously. All writers are known to exaggerate. In real life, people are generally more sensible and humane.

Of course he doesn't quite believe it, or it would not continue to trouble him so.

※

As far as Claude is concerned, there is nothing to see in Chinatown, but Jack has insisted on going. When they arrive, there is a Chinese funeral occupying two full streets and a babble of chants as the procession of monks makes its way through the crowd. Jack tries to say something above the din but all he can hear is " . . . way . . . exciting . . . often?" In any case Claude is not eager to respond to any questions Jack may have because he does not want to be here at all. The noise and smells, the overflowing drains with their rubbish of paper wrappers, burnt-out firecrackers, torn gunnysacks, broken furniture. He is ashamed.

But Jack is striding further into the crowd, oblivious to the stares he is getting. The crowd parts naturally wherever he goes; he carries with him an automatic authority that requires no questioning. Even though he is a stranger intruding upon a private funeral, no-one seems offended. In fact, the relatives, dressed in sackcloth, seem to regard this as a point of prestige, that a white man should be present. They crowd around Jack, offering him food and drink, and someone brings a stool to set down in the shade where he might be more comfortable.

Claude stands, shifting his weight from one leg to the other, outside the circle that has gathered around Jack. "Here, try some of these buns—they're wonderful!" Jack says, holding out a vivid pink bun. The crowd hushes a little and people throw them cautious, curious sidelong looks, which Claude tries to ignore.

"No thanks," he says, noticing the way his pitch is higher, almost shrill, and he coughs to loosen up his throat. "I ate a little while ago."

"I'll save one for you for later," says Jack and then is distracted by a man pulling on his sleeve and showing him some strange herbal concoction in a bottle. The man rubs his head and then points to Jack's shining top. Jack laughs. "There may be hope for me, Claude. Should I buy a bottle?"

A young street urchin, not more than five or six, tugs on Claude's trousers and asks him something in Chinese. He shrugs uneasily in reply. The urchin tugs harder on his trousers, pulling at strategic points and causing his knees to buckle. "Stop that," he says, almost shouting. "I don't understand what you're saying. Go away."

A voice in the crowd says something loud and mockingly in Chinese and everyone starts laughing and pointing at Claude. Must they point like that? he thinks angrily. But he is embarrassed as well, and wishing he were home, away from this strangely foreign, chattering crowd, away from Jack, away from the discordant gongs and smashing cymbals.

The noise grows louder. The professional mourners lined up behind the deceased's relatives are in full swing, wailing and beating their breasts. One falls to her knees and bangs her head against the grimy road. Not to be outdone, a chorus of shrieking picks up behind her as the other mourners hide their faces in their roomy sleeves and hold onions to their eyes. Unbelievably, while this is going on, the relatives have set up a small table by the side of the road and are beginning a game of mahjong.

Jack is everywhere, miming his questions, tasting everything, taking pictures of the elaborate trays of food, the barrel-like drums. Claude plants himself by paper models of houses, clothes, money and even servants. The models are constructed of metal frames covered in glittery coloured paper. A woman in sackcloth tosses each

paper figure into a bonfire in a large metal barrel. A man who had
been fawning over Jack with drink and coconut candy earlier,
approaches Claude. When he is an arm's length away, he spits at
him, and utters an incomprehensible stream of sound while pointing at Jack. Claude is too shocked to do anything. He feels the heat
of the fire nearby, and the man's humid breath as his guttural words
pour out. Finally the man jabs Claude in the chest a few times, all
the while making threatening noises and punching the air with his
other fist.

Claude takes an instinctive step backwards but the man is gone
before he can push the jabbing finger away. Several people on the
sidelines clap and glare at Claude. They too had been all over Jack
only a few minutes ago. These are the people his father had always
warned him to avoid. For a wild moment he wonders if they are jealous because he is friendly with a white man. But even now, behind
his back, they are sending Jack venomous looks.

Hypocrites! Claude thinks, flaming hypocrites, every single one
of them! But at the same time he can't quite raise the contempt he
wants to feel. Instead he is filled with a heaviness he can't explain,
and a sense of guilt that he doesn't want to probe. He looks
around at the peeling, yellowing building and takes in the trishaws
swerving to avoid the funeral crowd. He takes in the women pouring dirty wash water from their windows and the haphazard shrine
boxes beside the drains and electric poles. Father's right, he tells
himself, we can't possibly make any progress if we behave like these
people here.

He sees the dried old men and women in their hip-length tunics
and loose trousers. Even the younger ones are flat-faced, limp-
haired and coarse in their speech and gestures. They may be Chinese but he has nothing in common with them. At that moment he
wants more than anything to be white, and English, and yet something
inside him prevents him from admitting it, from wanting it even.

Stop it, stop brooding, he reminds himself, taking in a deep
breath, leaning back against a telephone pole.

The mahjong game is going fast and furiously, with the players
building long walls along the table's edges with their thumb-sized

green and white bricks, and then sporadically casting away an unsuitable brick into the pile at the centre. Jack is fiddling with some buttons on his camera and blowing at the lens. Up till now, he has not taken any pictures of people. Claude sucks in another deep breath, knowing what is to come, knowing he should, as a good guide, run over to Jack, prevent him from doing what he is about to do. He feels his weight shift, that almost imperceptible moment before the body begins to walk and then, deliberately, he leans on the telephone pole again, and settles back to watch.

Jack, satisfied with his fiddling, walks over and aims his camera at the mahjong party. The players freeze and then, in one unchoreographed motion, they all duck under the table just as Jack's magnesium flash fires. Jack, unsure of what is happening, but following a photographer's instinct to keep shooting, bends down and takes a picture of the huddled group under the table. The paid mourners hurl themselves at him, wrestling the camera from his hand, kicking and punching at the same time. Jack staggers back, both hands half-raised, and one of the players, a woman, emerges from under the table and orders the mourners to stop. The woman, her front row of gold teeth bared in a snarl, takes the camera and rips the film out. She throws it to the ground and stomps on it. Then she faces Jack, holding out his camera in a gesture that is half-challenge, half-disgust. Jack, his hands still in the air, takes a step back. "Who you think you are?" she demands in her cracked, shrill English.

Jack begins to explain.

Claude turns his head away, his heart thudding. He looks for something to distract him. The woman in sackcloth is still throwing paper figures into the fire—a car, a whole set of furniture, a radio, a gramophone set. He remembers Amah telling him that these are for the dead, burnt to send them into the afterlife so that they can continue to live there in luxury. Now the woman starts on the half-sized human figures, the servants, hands clasped in front of them and heads bowed.

With a deft fling, she tosses them into the fire. The lazy flames flicker and climb up the arms and backs of the figures. The colourful paper servants brown, then blacken to ashes that flake off their

metal frames and fly into the air. Later, the ashes will settle, contributing to the dust and grime that covers the mangy streets of Chinatown and the people who live there.

⚜

—*The Art of War,* sighs the baritone. The venerable, incalculably
devious Master Sun Tzu. Genius. Have you read it?

The Body shakes its head. And yet, there is Grandma Siok again,
intoning: *All warfare is based on deception.*

The yellow man, sly, cunning, full of delaying tactics, indirect—the memory of
a crude flyer pasted on the Littleton gates several years ago just
before students were let out for the day—*can he ever be taught the
demeanour of an English gentleman? Is such a sort capable of honesty, character,
loyalty?* Mr. Hawthorne, the principal, had ordered an investigation,
but it had fizzled out over the week and no-one had pushed for it to
continue. Was that because everyone including masters and students
had secretly agreed with the flyer?

Deceit, cunning, evasion. Now a yellow man of the Japanese
Imperial Guard is speaking, and they have become words of praise.
All warfare is based on deception.

—Tell me, young man, what you know of deceit, the art of the
counterfeit. What do you know of lies, illusions and half-truths?

⚜

SunTzu:
*Now there are five sorts of secret agents to be employed. These are native, inside,
doubled, expendable, and living.*

A pity, thinks Grandma Siok, they don't pay more attention to
this at Sandhurst. The Japanese, now—she pauses in her thoughts—
whatever else they feel about the Chinese, they respect Chinese military strategy.

But no one listens to an old woman anyway, so she takes her usual
nap.

⚜

At Alor Star airfield on the Malayan peninsula, Captain Patrick
Heenan, while unpopular, is nonetheless enthusiastic and curious

about all operational systems. He has taken to missing evening socials with his peers and reading in his room. He even borrowed a manual for the Smoke Curtain Installation on planes carrying it and is known to have an interest in weapon loads.

"Should've trained to be a pilot," the flight sergeant armourer at the airfield says of him after a particularly intense flurry of questions. "Not that he would've inspired much confidence in the air. He'd need a better personality for that."

Major James France, Captain Heenan's superior, keeps a tight rein on him. Besides having a talent for irking all his colleagues, Heenan is too curious for his own good. For the Forces' good. For anyone's good, for that matter, except, the major appends sombrely, possibly the Japanese.

Patrick Heenan types a letter to his mother.

> *Dear Mother,*
>
> *I have never felt more at home. Everything's changed for me, everything's finally going right. I have friends, I have started photography and develop my own pictures. Last week I took some of two water buffaloes in a paddy field. You remember them from Burma. The light wasn't as good as I'd hoped; it was changing so quickly as the sun set. The nights are deep purple here, the colour of royalty, which is just right. There's something regal about the East, I've always felt.*
>
> *One more thing—I've learned to fly a Malayan kite. It's not too difficult at all. The winds are predictable, the best times being around eight in the morning and about three-fifteen in the afternoon. Everything goes up in the air at those times, I've found, and it's impossible to fail.*
>
> *I'll send some pictures soon.*
>
> > *Love,*
> > *Patrick*

The man died two hours ago. He had virulent pneumonia; the entire ward realised he was dead when he stopped hacking and rasping. Ling-li, gowned and masked because of the infectious nature of his illness, dips her towel in the milky Dettol solution and feels it sag in her hands when she lifts it again. She wrings it out, relishing the strong disinfectant smell of the solution—it makes her feel somehow immune to the germs she imagines swarming about the dead man.

She rubs the towel briskly over his face and neck, toning it down as she wipes the corners of his eyes and the cold, rubbery flaps of his ears. There's a blister on his lower lip, a boiling, vehement purple bubble. It pops when she runs the towel over it and leaks a thin, runny pus which she mops up.

She doesn't mind working on dead bodies. This is her first white one. She surveys the corpse's long, solemn face. Thirty-six, and so, so remote somehow. There's a strange, unworldly glow to his pallor, like a pearl illuminated from within, the last embers of life burning out perhaps. Is this what the Christian Jesus looked like when he died? Did that glow never go out but rekindle itself into a living flame when he was resurrected? Did the women laying out his body see it, that strange luminescence, and know before any of the disciples what was to come? From Primary Three to Six, Ling-li had studied in a Catholic school, where English was the medium of instruction. By day she had read and listened to all the Bible stories, by night she had listened to her parents caution her against being taken in by Christian fairy tales.

She rinses the wash-towel in more Dettol and lifts the sheet covering the corpse, noting how the chest curves slightly inwards so that it looks like it's caving in. She scrubs it and the arms, the armpits with their tangled anemone of hair. She traces his ribs and cleans the shallow bowl of his abdomen. There is no fat on him—the pneumonia's taken every inch of it. With her free hand she lowers the sheet even further and the smell of urine lurches into the air. He'd wet himself before he died.

She studies his shrivelled genitals lying crinkled and mottled between his legs. When she lifts the scrotal sacs to wipe off the urine they are cold and almost weightless.

So this is a white man, she thinks. Unremarkable, and a little sad. Then she sets about stuffing his orifices.

Cynthia regards her white man, this one very much alive but asleep beside her. His mouth is open and there is a faintly oafish look about him even though when he is awake he is beautiful. His arms and legs are splayed and he has heat rash in the folds of his groin, his armpits. She blows on his skin to cool it. She fans him with a piece of paper and somehow has a view of herself from the ceiling, as if she's watching another woman. One who looks like an Eastern slave in her golden nudity, a fantasy slave-girl.

It nauseates her and she bites herself, leaving tooth marks in her arm which are still visible when she gets dressed and goes home.

Victoria Theatre is small, chanderliered and velvet-covered, but nothing can detract from the fact that it's a second-rate theatre set up in the colony to appease the expatriate community. The humidity breeds a mustard-smelling fungus on the heavy drapes and the padded seats and makes tuning the instruments a frustratingly daunting feat.

Claude is standing with Jack outside the theatre while the Englishman smokes a cigarette. He can smell his own sweat swilling about him whenever a transient breeze lifts and flows by. Even though it's hot outside it's preferable to standing in the boggish foyer and bumping into oily, sticky, drenched bodies while waiting for the bell. The ladies, in particular, seem to have the notion that liberal dabs of perfume to their wrists and necks would somehow mask the scent of their acidic sweat, but this only serves to make the air around them a cloying and unbearable mixture of sweet and sour.

Jack has appeared enthusiastic from the start, though Claude suspects it's more from politeness than any real desire to attend the symphony. This must be a joke to him, he thinks, taking in the Englishman's bald, wet head, the way he tugs at his collar. "I hear you play clarinet," Jack says, smoke escaping through the grates between his teeth.

"A little." In two hours it should be over. Thank goodness when the concert is in progress there'll be no need to make conversation.

"I got some very good pictures," Jack says. "From the first roll of film I used in Chinatown—before they grabbed my camera and gave it a good battering."

Claude watches the sampans in the distance.

"Anyway, I'll show you the photographs sometime, if you're interested."

Interested? In Chinatown and its surrounding filth? Claude throws him a weak smile, not exactly looking at the Englishman's face.

"I say, it's never happened to you, has it?" Jack asks. "That sort of thing with the camera—I mean, I never expected it."

Claude shifts his weight, scratches his neck, tries to look unperturbed. "Yes, funny how upset they got! But Father's always said the locals are too superstitious." He hopes he sounds convincing. Jack looks at him in a piercing way, starts to say something, then smokes on in silence, allowing his gaze to fall, neutrally, on the brown river.

The last bell sounds and they turn towards the theatre, entering the large wooden doors into an unbearable tomb of thick carpeting and windowless gloom. Jack begins to queue behind the last of the European concertgoers. "This way," Claude says, following signs for the second-class seats. "You're sitting with the coloureds." His tone is gruff, angry. He can't help it.

"Oh," says Jack, taken aback by the sudden change in mood. "Great."

They climb up the wide curl of stairs and find their seats in silence. Claude notes the turbans and saris around them, plus a scattering of Chinese in Western evening dress. They eye Jack with suspicion. "Trying to take over our section as well, are they?" he hears a Sikh say in his distinctive accent. "It's hard enough to get seats here without them invading our area as well."

A flurry of "shh's" ripples through the section at this. Claude gazes straight ahead, struggling to keep his thoughts at bay.

"These are comfortable," Jack says, leaning back heavily in his seat. "And there's even air-conditioning, isn't there?"

Not in this section, Claude mouths, even though the cooled air from below circulates quite comfortably through the second-class seats.

The music starts at last, and it is Mozart's Clarinet Concerto in A, to Claude's surprise. He hadn't even checked the programme. He waits for the orchestra to declare the first exposition and then, with the repeat, plunges in with the clarinet, and thankfully, for the rest of the evening, stops thinking.

⚙

—But that's why we're here, the voice is saying. To free you from such shames.

There is such persuasion in that voice and you are almost lulled, grateful, until you register again the trickle of blood from the Body's nose, a timely reminder.

—I am hardly free, you say bitterly. The words are slurred through the Body's lips, but comprehensible. The voice laughs.

—I meant on a larger scale, he says. That's the trouble. All you think about is the self, the individual, your petty day-to-day problems. I'm talking about nations, young man, and sometimes we have to make individual sacrifices for the larger good. But here, let me read you something. You might know it. From Sun Tzu:

And therefore only the enlightened sovereign and the worthy general who are able to use the most intelligent people as agents are certain to achieve great things. Secret operations are essential in war; upon them the army relies to make its every move.

He watches the Body closely.

—I have heard my grandmother reading that.

He leans so close to the Body that his teeth take up most of its view.

—I am very keen on finding out everything I can on "secret agents." You wouldn't happen to be able to help me, would you? The voice like velvet, tactile, a rough smoothness.

Steady, you instruct the Body, willing it to take as deep a breath as it can take without incurring too much pain from the ribs. You count down the relative moments of comfort.

—I don't know what you're talking about, you say, and watch the truncheon descend.

⚙

Domicile: Flat 12, Block B, Hwa Lin Gardens, Katong (next to Hock
Lim Market)
Suspect's daily route to the bus depot includes a stop at corner
murtabak store where she is extremely friendly with the owner, Salleh
Acher, and sometimes sits for thirty minutes or more conversing
with him. Last Friday, she accepted a parcel from him, wrapped in
newspaper. This same Salleh Acher was involved with last month's
burning of Japanese rice merchants' homes in Telok Ayer.

The Fifth Columnist stretches out her fingers after that flurry of
typing. A stroke of luck that Salleh Acher's store is down the street
from Miss Competence. The building blocks of fiction are always
more satisfying when cemented with facts.

❀

Han Hong-Seng hears Ling-li enter and head for her bedroom,
followed by the bathroom in the corridor between the kitchen and
the cramped living room. He is lying on his cot in the tiny storage
room next to the kitchen, a space just long enough for him to fit in
horizontally, nursing the remains of his cold. He hears the water
run as his niece washes her face and waits impatiently for her to finish. He's missed the last two meetings of the Singapore China Relief
Fund Committee.

"Going out again?" he asks, sticking his head out the door of his
room. "Aren't you at least going to eat with me once this week?"

Ling-li, face and hair damp, emerges with a towel draped about
her shoulders. "Your lucky day," she says, padding into the kitchen
in her slippered feet. "Noodles?"

"We never have anything else in the house," he says good-
naturedly. "Maybe we should go marketing more often. You could
teach me to cook—I'd be willing to learn."

She snorts. "Uncle," she says mildly, "you're so full of shit. I'd
end up 'teaching' you every night and you'd never learn, conveniently enough. Meanwhile there'd be a hot meal for you each
evening after the 'lesson.' I'm not such a fool!"

"That you never were," he agrees with a smile. After a short pause he gets up and shuffles into the kitchen. "Any news?"

Ling-li's eyes roll quickly upwards to the ceiling, indicating the floor above them. "They're out," says Hong-Seng. "Some relative or other has a birthday and they're having a banquet at the White Jade Restaurant. I still don't know why you worry about them, Ling. They've been checked out as harmless."

She heats up a pot of water and scavenges the cupboards for some seasoning—any kind, she's not particular. "They may be harmless," she says, her voice muffled as she sticks half her body into the cupboard, "but they're still supporters of Wang Ching-Wei, which means they support Japan. Which makes them, in my eyes, traitors, whether or not they're actively engaged in helping the Japanese."

The water boils and she throws in two handfuls of soft egg noodles. In one minute, they're ready. Ling-li adds some fish-balls to the water, salt, white pepper, and tastes the soup. "See? You don't need cooking lessons. It's just a matter of throwing things in, heating them up."

"How are things going in the committee?" Hong-Seng asks as he sets the table with bowls, chopsticks and porcelain soup spoons.

"The fund-raising is going well," she hedges.

"The rest?"

Ling-li carefully ladles soup and noodles into the bowls. "Not too good." She pauses. "You know I don't like repeating hearsay. I haven't heard anything directly myself, but the rumours are that Japan is gearing up for war and will probably land in Thailand. Of course, the British can't believe it. Or—" She stops.

Hong-Seng looks up from his soup. "What?"

"I just thought of something. Maybe it's us they don't believe." She stirs her bowl abstractedly.

"What?"

"We've been supplying the British with information regarding Japanese Fifth Column activities for years. They appear grateful enough, but they never take action on any of the information we give them. Maybe they don't trust us—for some reason I never thought of that."

Hong-Seng chews on his noodles thoughtfully. "I don't know, Ling-li. I've never understood the English, what they want out of us. You should know better, you speak their language."

"So do you, even if you don't let on."

"But you're fluent, much more so than most of us. What do you think, Ling? Would they ever pack up one day, leaving this piece of rock to ourselves?"

His niece stops eating and leans back in her chair. "No," she says. "Unless we—or the Japanese—insist on it."

At Jack's insistence and Humphrey's prodding, Claude goes to Changi Beach to sunbathe. It is absolutely true what they say about mad dogs and Englishmen; they adore the sun. More than that, they seem to have an immense tolerance for the tropical midday sun boring into the skin. They may turn purple, red and, ember-like, emit glow and heat, but they'll not budge from the unshaded beaches, relying only on a limp cotton hat on their pink heads, as Jack does that day.

Cynthia would be appalled. The years she's spent keeping the entire family out of the direct rays of the sun, the thick kaolin pastes to block out its effects, the bleaching creams slathered on the body at the least hint of melanin. All come to waste at the hands of that ignorant Englishman. For exposure to the sun and the subsequent tan signify a life spent toiling in the open, a sure sign that one is a labourer, of the lower class, peon. Only the rich, like their precious orchids and songbirds, can afford to idle away indoors, cultivating paleness and delicate hands.

On the beach Claude notices the bold stares of the Chinese and Eurasian women. They are drawn to Jack, deliberately parading their bare legs in front of him, giggling and whispering among themselves all the while. Often, one or two of them would get up the nerve to come over and start a conversation with him. "Where you from? Australia? England?" they ask, mangling the word so that it sounds like "Ang-land." "First time here? We show you around, we be your tour-guides."

"I've got one already, thank you very much," Jack replies sweeping his arm towards Claude. The women sweep their eyes over their competition dismissively.

"You from Changi?" one asks abruptly.

"No, I live in Bukit Timah," Claude tells her.

"How old you are? You know Bugis Street?" she presses. He shakes his head at the name—sounds shady, unlikely he'd ever have gone there.

"So you useless as guide," the same woman says with glee. "Come on, sir. We know Singapore town better. We show you around, why not?" She flings herself onto the sand beside Jack and takes hold of his arm.

"No, no, no, you're too kind, but Claude has been marvellous, and we have plans already." He smiles at Claude, makes no attempt to shake off her hand.

"*Wah*, you all hear that?" the woman says to her companions. "This boy here *made plans* with the Sir. What you do, you going to the zoo?" Her friends burst out laughing and Claude joins in uneasily, not knowing what else to do.

"Now don't tease him too much. He's a good friend of mine." There is an underlying warning in Jack's lazy voice and the women pick up on it straightaway. The one who has been hardest on Claude links her arm with his.

"You know we just joking, *yah*?" Her hair is curled in the latest style and her lips are scarlet, not from lipstick, he realises with revulsion, but from betel nut juice. Her tongue gives it away; somehow she has managed to keep her teeth unstained, but just the thought of her chewing those leaves and spitting them out causes him to shake off her arm and to shift his body away in the pretence of dusting off some sand.

The woman's friends kneel in a semi-circle around them, chattering as if they've been invited to a picnic. Mostly they focus on

Jack, but as his friend, Claude finds himself getting a fair share of attention as well. "Bukit Timah," says a woman with chestnut-coloured hair loosened about her shoulders. "You must be rich."

"Not really," he says, liking the way the wind brushes her hair across her face.

"You ever been to England?" Again that awful "Ang-land," but this time it doesn't bother him as much. It's almost charming when she says it, especially with that smile.

"No." The smile fades a little. "But I will. I'll be at Oxford next year." He can hardly believe he has said that. Nothing's official yet, of course, but there's a good chance . . . a very good chance. "I'll be reading law," he adds, throwing caution to the winds.

"Oxford. Maybe I come visit you when you there," she says, surprising him.

"Of course. Yes, of course you must. You'll be my guest." There is an ease and lightness, he realises, to just responding to the moment and giving in to her relaxed manner. His father was right—not everything needs to be analysed and sorted out. It feels good to be so carefree and to have her curvy body so close to his that strands of her hair whisk over his neck, shoulders, arms.

But he stiffens when he catches the curly-haired woman looking at his hairless chest and bony arms. She holds his eye for a moment and then deliberately turns to Jack. The implication is clear. If he wasn't with Jack, he'd have been dismissed long ago.

Claude's hand touches Jack's folded trousers and reaches into his pocket for his pack of cigarettes. He draws one out of the box, hands it over to Jack and leans across to light it for him. "Thanks."

Claude's message is just as clear. He is Jack's friend, and if she wants to stay, she should remember that. She looks away as if she's been distracted by something else, but he knows she's understood. Satisfied, he stretches out, one hand boldly touching the chestnut-haired woman's arm. Her eyes are closed and she doesn't move. His fingers find their way up her arm and to her nape and play with the soft hairs on her neck.

As Claude lies on the sand next to Jack, belly exposed to the full blast of sun, he notes that he is as pale as the Englishman. And even then there is a difference: In the clear light the translucent pink flush under Jack's skin is like a baby gecko's, so new to light that its gut radiates a pearlish sheen. By comparison, his own skin is sandy, with faint yellow grains flaring under an intransigent white. He understands then, as never before, the different whites that are sold in paint shops, the spectrum that encompasses dazzling cloud, fish-belly and weak tea.

More sight-seeing, more "show him some local flavour" and "quaint places," as Janet Winchester put it. This time Claude agrees to go to Penang with Jack during the school holidays, and finds himself sitting awkwardly beside the Englishman on the train and tossing pennies into the sea as the ferry putt-putts self-consciously across the Straits of Malacca from Butterworth. But at least there is the anonymity and bustle of the Golden Straits Hotel where they will stay that week.

During the trip, he envies the way Jack slings his camera round his neck and secretly admires the debonair image Jack cultivates while sight-seeing. Once, as he waits in the hotel lobby for Jack to make a phone call at the reception desk, he picks up the camera from the side table where Jack has left it. He sticks his head through the loop of strap and wears the camera dangling down the front of his chest as if it were a trophy. It feels heavy, important. He lifts it and positions his eye over the glass window and his world narrows to a stage framed by the hotel entrance. Just beyond the doors is the street, muddled and noisy with traffic and pedestrians. A car is parked on the far side. A white man and his female companion stand beside it, leaning on the bonnet and looking down at the front wheel on the driver's side where some Chinese coolies are changing a flat. The man's suit is so white that it makes everything else appear flat and muddy. Even the woman's cream-coloured linen blouse and long skirt look wilted by comparison. They are a handsome couple, and there is a regal quality to the way they lean on the car or swat away the flies. Once the man reaches out with his handkerchief and pats at her temples. His thumb strokes across her brow and she smiles.

"See anything unusual?" Jack asks, making Claude jump.

"No," he says, lifting the camera strap up and above his head, the woman's smile reflected on his own lips. Nothing unusual at all, he thinks. The world is as it should be.

Claude has only been to Penang twice before—brief weekend stays each time—and has no idea where the natives go. In fact, the whole point of the previous trips had been to avoid the "natives." His mother had been determined to stay at the rakish Dunbar Hotel, which was the only white hotel that had a separate section for coloureds. It was considered by the Europeans to be a third-rate hotel—one for sailors, those with native wives and half-caste children and other dubious characters—but Cynthia had insisted on going there because it was better then the hotels for "locals." They spent their time taking tea in the gloomy sitting-room of the Dunbar, walking the shabby stretch of beach in front of the hotel in the late evenings and avoiding the sun because Cynthia didn't want her family to get too dark.

In Penang with Jack Winchester now, Claude is as much the tourist as he, and once he's boldly commandeered the guidebook and flicked through its pages, he flags down a taxi. "Snake Temple," he says.

"Hah?" the taxi-diver grunts, leaning backwards to hear better. He's a leathery man in a sweat-stained singlet, a jade fish amulet dangling on a red thread around his neck.

"Snake Temple," Claude says slowly, knowing it will do no good. It's clear the man does not understand English.

"Hah?" he says again, launching into virulent Chinese, which ends with him spitting expertly out the window.

"What did he say?" Jack asks.

"I don't know," Claude replies, looking at his hands. "I don't speak any Chinese."

"Nothing? Cantonese? Hokkien? Hainanese? Teochew, maybe?"

"Ah—maybe some Cantonese. I can manage 'hello,' 'goodbye,' that sort of thing, but I don't know how to say 'Snake Temple' in Cantonese."

"Well."

Finally, Claude resorts to the humiliating trick of hissing furiously for several long moments, while Jack obliges with a sinuous movement of his arms and trunk until the astonished taxi-driver understands and chuckles all the way to the Snake Temple.

After the driver's been paid and they're both standing at the entrance to the temple, Jack asks, "What do you speak at home? When there's no-one else around but your family?"

"English."

"Only English?"

Claude doesn't reply.

The steps leading to the temple lie like vertebrae in the sun, stacked one on top of the other, curving upwards. Snakes coil sleepily on the banisters on either side. Claude makes sure to stay in the middle of the steps while Jack bends down in front of several snakes, marvelling at their individual markings and lidless eyes. "Gleaming with intelligence," he says.

In the main hall of the temple, incense greys the air. Snakes lie muscled against each other, in neat quoits on the floor, hanging with lascivious abandon over the altar, drugged by the dense, interlooping curlicues of smoke from joss-sticks stuck in tubs of sand. A saffron-draped monk, the excess material of his robe trailing casually over one arm, adds new joss-sticks to the altar and removes the burnt-out stubs. The smooth baldness of the monk's head reminds Claude somehow of the snakes that encircle him in the room. Something about the head's pure shape, nothing superfluous or extraneous, an efficiency of form like the rippling cylindrical bodies, which could at one moment be linear, or circular, or spiral, could undulate in waves. The way the light falls and changes on the polished baldness of the monk reveals infinite surfaces, a complexity based on its very simplicity.

"I'm getting a little groggy," Jack says, rubbing his smoke-stung eyes. "It must be all that incense. I heard it makes the snakes drowsy so they don't attack."

Sleep or trance. What is the difference?

In the end, Penang brings Claude no closer to Jack than the previous partnered hikes to "quaint places" in Singapore. He learns that Jack loves roast duck, sings unsteadily—unable to hold each note's centre, wobbling on the periphery—sends a lot of postcards to a friend named Hillary in London, is slow in doing sums in his head. It's a relief to say goodbye to the Englishman at the train station in Singapore when it's all over, a lightness to catch a taxi home alone. No need to double-check his grammar before speaking, to pronounce each word in his head first so that when he finally speaks, it seems like an echo of his own ghostly voice.

Revelation: It's not that she doesn't love him. It's just that she feels as if she's missing something in her life. Humphrey is handsome, for a Chinaman—even she will concede that. But when he puts on his puppy face and eagerly flies about trying to please his British superiors, she has to look away. He is a willing and reliable follower, but it's a leader that Cynthia wants.

You catch her bent over an unassuming notebook, the kind that has *Exercise Book* printed across its brown paper cover, one that the boy and his sister used in school everyday. In fact, when you look closer, it turns out to be one of the boy's exercise books, filled about halfway through with maths problems from Primary Four. He was nine then.

Where the sums and problem sets end, Cynthia's writing begins. She writes in a heavy, angular scrawl that leaves indentations in the underlying pages, so that the book is scarred through with her words. Sometimes there are places where she has completely blacked out passages, as if she couldn't bear to read them herself; in other places she has starred and circled key phrases as if they were to be memorised for an exam. You bend over the book and her words pour like whole images.

This is how you come to learn about the boy's mother. How she fell in love with an Englishman at the age of eighteen—a colleague of her father's and ten years older than she—and had become his lover, sneaking out of her house to be with him at night. She loved the way people stared at her with awe and envy when they were together, respecting her ability to capture and hold a man who represented authority and privilege in their world. She did not fail to notice the deference with which he was treated, and the aura of power that he held and, by extension, which she held too. This is what a man can do for a woman, she thought. Make her a princess and imbue her life with glamour and excitement. How they had talked archly of children and a married life together, but how, when the time came, he chose to marry a woman of his own kind, pale as wedding cake frosting, blonde, thick-boned, whose parents could meet his, and be sincerely civil to each other.

And ever since then, with each one—tall, thick-waisted, scrawny, effeminate, hearty, cruel, amusing, useful, adventurous—Cynthia says to herself, I am beautiful, I can hold your attention, I can drive you crazy. Poor Humphrey is totally unaware of his wife's infidelity, but the saddest, strangest part is what Cynthia imagines would happen if he ever finds out. "Oh, he'll sulk and mope, to be sure, maybe throw a tantrum or two in his best Royal Theatre voice, but underneath it all, we are more alike than he knows," she writes. "In spite of himself, he would feel pleased, proud, that he has a wife whom white men covet. In this way he is truly even sicker than myself, but it is also a great relief and consolation to me and I don't feel quite as bad about what I've done."

January monsoons, 1941, the rain like a distant waterfall in the lushly carpeted Thai state room. The British Minister in Bangkok, Sir Josiah "Bing" Crosby, is having tea with the Thai Prime Minister, Field Marshal Luang Pibul. The Prime Minister takes his tea English-style, lightening it with milk, but the pastries are all Thai, rich in coconut milk or battered and lightly fried.

Sir Josiah allows the last bit of his *Tod Mun* to disappear down his gullet before speaking. "Prime Minister," he says, putting on his "official" voice. "I've been meaning to discuss with you the inappropriate numbers of Japanese agents you've allowed into the country. I've been receiving a lot of pressure from London about this and I must say I'm inclined to agree that this extraordinary permissiveness on your part may be sending out the wrong signals regarding your allegiances."

Pibul bites into a delicate spring roll. His face is serene. "Well then," he says, "might I suggest that the British step up the number of their own agents in Thailand? I, for one, would not object to however many agents your country deems fit to send in order to counter any perceived imbalances."

These Orientals, sighs Sir Josiah. No telling how they will respond to things. They're like children, trying to deal with the world with their naïve understanding of fair play. He chuckles to himself. How much they need a fatherly hand to lead them through the intricacies of politics and intrigue in the modern world.

And, popping another *Tod Mun* into his mouth, Sir Josiah proposes to do just that.

❁

"Three, Prime Minister, three clearly pro-Japanese deputy Foreign Ministers! I must protest!"

"Then my Foreign Minister will definitely be pro-British, Sir Josiah, I assure you. Three pro-Japanese deputies to one pro-British minister. That should even things out, don't you think?"

Damnably unfathomable, these Orientals, and quite maddening.

❁

No, reading it over and over, wincing over passages and struggling to see them in a different, kinder light does not give him any solutions:

> "The old type of servant is disappearing," agreed Mr. Macgregor. "In my young days, when one's butler was disrespectful, one sent him along to the jail with a chit saying 'Please give the bearer fifteen lashes'. Ah well, *eheu fugaces*! Those days are gone forever, I am afraid."
>
> "Ah, you're about right there," said Westfield in his gloomy way.

"This country'll never be fit to live in again. British Raj is finished if you ask me. Lost Dominion and all that. Time we cleared out of it."

The burden is on him, Jack decides, to prove Orwell wrong.

Amah sits sorting out the grains of glutinous rice at the kitchen table. Phatcharat gets headaches from this task and has traded it with Amah for dusting duties.

The old house-servant flattens the mound of rice with a chopstick, divides it into quadrants. She picks through each of these with the tip of the chopstick. The white, pearly grains she keeps; the yellowed, browned, blackened ones she discards—sweeps them off the table onto the floor where her toes roll over them. Later, Phatcharat will sweep them into the drain outside.

Upstairs, Madam has flung herself at her wardrobe and, she is sure, has taken the scissors to all her clothes. It's not the first time.

Poor Madam, caught like a fly in honey in her own desires and inferiorities. She doesn't understand her own preferences. It's simple, really, Amah thinks. It's like sorting this rice—white, not-white, white, not-white. There is no incongruence here—even the most Chinese of Chinese has preferred for countless ages the paler shades over darker ones. As basic as sorting rice, she repeats to herself, rocking slightly in her seat.

If only poor Madam could understand that. Amah pats the letter in her trouser pocket. It is from an old friend from China who asks for money and tells of desolation that Amah herself cannot believe, fixed as she is, on her old memories of home. The letter speaks of battered fields, blackened villages, a landscape fetid with corpses from the war with the Japanese. *Do not come back,* the letter says. *You have a new home now, and a good life. There is nothing here for you at all except death and misery. You can't believe how much happiness can be had with a full stomach, and a house to live in, where you can leave your doors unlocked in peace.*

Is it true? Amah asks herself. Is it really enough? Or has her friend never witnessed this:

The boy sitting in his room preparing a set of reeds for his clarinet, scraping down the thin end of each reed rhythmically with his penknife—the one she had to confiscate from him once—paring it to a translucent sheet, down to the edge of nothingness, all the while listening to the sound of clothes ripping from his parents' room. His door is open, and so is his mother's door. His sister squats in the corridor, watching her mother's sure hand as it slashes yards and yards of iridescent fabric, her young eyes unblinking and solemn in the cool dimness. His grandmother's door is also open for cross-ventilation, revealing the old woman splayed star-like in sleep, limbs outstretched, fists clenched, her noisy alarm clock ticking doggedly towards the hour when it will clang her awake from her nap.

A house of opened doors and uncrossed thresholds. A home of an uneasy, teetering peace.

MOST SECRET. WAR CABINET. TO BE KEPT
UNDER LOCK AND KEY.
DIRECTIVE BY PRIME MINISTER AND
MINISTER OF DEFENCE
28th April 1941

Japan is unlikely to enter the war unless the Germans make a successful invasion of Great Britain, and even a major disaster like the loss of the Middle East would not necessarily make her come in, because the liberation of the British Mediterranean Fleet which might be expected, and also any troops evacuated from the Middle East to Singapore would not weaken the British war-making strength in Malaya. It is very unlikely, moreover, that Japan will enter the war either if the United States have come in, or if Japan thinks that they would come in consequent upon a declaration of war. Finally, it may be taken as almost certain that the entry of Japan into the war would be followed by the immediate entry of the United States on our side . . .

There is no need at the present time to make any further dispositions for the defence of Malaya and Singapore, beyond those modest arrangements which are in progress, until or unless the conditions set out are modified.

❁

Grandma Siok spits melon-seed husks at the wastepaper basket strategically placed three feet from her bed. She has not missed yet. Lucy is enthralled. Her own efforts have only resulted in large globs of saliva landing on Grandma Siok's bed. "Sorry, Grandma," she says, mouth full of melon seeds.

"What can you do?" Grandma Siok shrugs. "One has to practise."

She brings out the manual and reads aloud.

Sun Tzu said:

Anciently the skilful warriors first made themselves invincible and awaited the enemy's moment of vulnerability.

Invincibility depends on one's self; the enemy's vulnerability on him.

"Do they ever teach you this in school, Claude?" she asks.

He shakes his head. "Too bad," she says. "You could have learned something useful."

THREE

Generals

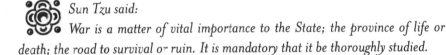 Sun Tzu said:

War is a matter of vital importance to the State; the province of life or death; the road to survival or ruin. It is mandatory that it be thoroughly studied.

Therefore appraise it in terms of the five fundamental factors and make comparisons of the seven elements later named. So you may assess its essentials.

The first of these factors is moral influence; the second, weather; the third, terrain; the fourth, command; and the fifth, doctrine.

By moral influence I mean that which causes the people to be in harmony with their leaders, so that they will accompany them in life and death without fear of mortal peril.

By weather I mean the interaction of natural forces; the effects of winter's cold and summer's heat and the conduct of military operations in accordance with the seasons.

By terrain I mean distances, whether the ground is traversed with ease or difficulty, whether it is open or constricted, and the chances of life or death.

By command I mean the general's qualities of wisdom, sincerity, humanity, courage, and strictness.

By doctrine I mean organisation, control, assignment of appropriate ranks to officers, regulation of supply routes, and the provision of principal items used by the army.

There is no general who has not heard of these five matters. Those who master them win.

✹

8th December 1941:

It is clear now, how it could all have ended so quickly, so breathlessly, like a screen siren blowing out the candles in her bedroom. It is blisteringly clear from the moment Chief Operations Officer Major Angus Rose of the Argyll and Sutherland Highlanders bellows into the telephone receiver in the War Room of HQ Malaya Command. "Go for the transports, you bloody fools," he says, unable to believe he has to tell them even this. "Knock out the transports with everything you've got. Whatever happens, don't let them land."

There are the crucial days before—the Japanese signals picked up in Hong Kong and inexplicably hushed by London; the sighting of Japanese transports and escorts trudging pugnaciously 185 miles north of Kota Bahru; Air Chief Marshal Sir Robert Brooke-Popham's quandary: to launch or not to launch Operation Matador, an invasion of Thailand under threat of Japanese attack? Sir Josiah Crosby's pleading, almost hysterical telegram to let Thailand alone until the Japanese touch her first. All logically and inevitably leading to the landings at Singora and Patani in Thailand, Kota Bahru in Malaya.

Bone-hammering rain. Needles pelting eyelids, obscuring whatever light is left past midnight. The struggling beacons of a Chinese Fifth Columnist on shore guides in 5,500 Japanese men. Ling-li, had she been given vision, would have cried out in anger. "We've known about him for over a year, and we've reported his spying activities to the British, but they never took us seriously, those useless idiots!"

The sea unfurling its many tentacles, lassoing in a full fifth of the salt-pickled Japanese—but no matter, their tattered rafts leap over waves and they keep coming.

Australian pilots, their fierce charge dissolving into hesitancy and confusion at the "K" flashed from the Japanese escort ships. "K"—the British recognition signal for the day, coming from . . . the enemy? Well done, Patrick Heenan, competent traitor.

The British Brigadier Billy-the-Bulldog Key holding the beaches, 35 miles between two battalions: the 3/17th Dogra and the 2/10th Baluch. See how his valiant Dogras fight, hastily dug-in, spitting bullets, clambering over their dead brothers in the brackish black swamps backing the beaches. Rain, rain, bone-hammering, eye-piercing, boot-squelching rain. Nothing holds the Japanese back. As their feet strike sand and they roll off their rafts, the whole inglorious, ignoble, ignominious end is in sight.

Claude is in his room, unable to sleep from the strange humming that has permeated his hearing. He is unable to shake it—wonders briefly, even, if he has caught it from Jack. But there are no voices; it does not resemble singing in the least. The volume increases through the night, layers of un-deciphered sound vibrating in the air. Several times he glances out his window, unsure of what to look for. The whiskered roots of the Tams' banyan tree flap listlessly in the tepid breeze. He throws them suspicious glances, remembering childhood stories of *pontianaks,* female vampires who live in banyans. Could the humming be coming from them?

Perhaps Amah's cooking is affecting him finally, brewing nightmares. Phatcharat is due back tomorrow, having visited a friend in Johore for a week. In the meanwhile, Amah has made do—in fact, the whole family has made do, with Amah's making do. She has been steaming everything, even meat. Perhaps the humming is really the magnified rumbling of his stomach, disgruntled with last night's steamed tripe and beef.

Just before dawn the humming reaches its peak. It is almost unbearable and Claude has already decided to see a doctor in the morning—to check out his ears—when the boom occurs, bursting across the sky and splitting the dark with a vicious orange streak. Before he can react, it happens again. The hint of smoke rises from somewhere far beyond the Tams' banyan. He hears Lucy's excited scamper of feet in the corridor, his parents' shuffle. Even Amah is awake. He opens his door to see them heading for the veranda.

When he joins them, the booms are reverberating regularly throughout the island and Humphrey is rubbing his head, trying to make sense of what is happening. "Might be some kind of celebration," he says, doubt heavy in his voice.

"We are being bombed," Grandma Siok says from the shadows behind Claude. "We should probably go downstairs. They might head this way next." Everyone stares at her, unable to speak.

"Bombed, Grandma?" Lucy says at last. "Air attack by fire? Are we going to be killed like the ants?"

This moves Humphrey to action. "Downstairs!" he orders. "At once!" There is an immediate rush for the stairs. Claude has never seen Amah move so quickly. Only Grandma Siok, he notes, is walking.

"Hurry up, Grandma!" he says. Fiercely, she clicks her tongue at him and he backs down. As usual she will move at her own pace, bombs notwithstanding.

Down in the living room, Amah turns on the lights, stinging everyone's eyes. Grandma Siok reacts sharply. "Oh, you fool, turn that off! You don't want to advertise that we're home, a shining target for the bombers, do you?"

"Yes, turn the lights off, Amah," Humphrey says unnecessarily, after the lights have been shut off by a terrified Amah. All have their eyes on the ceiling, as if tracking the movements of the bombers overhead.

Claude is the first to realise when it is over; the humming, so loud and insistent just moments ago, has begun to subside. The vibrations lessen and are damped in the air, giving way to an uneasy quiet. The world seems to open and enlarge in that new silence. "They're gone," he says.

"What does this mean?" Cynthia asks. In the garden the bougainvillea bushes begin to emerge from the dark, their red florets like chocolate berries in the dawn light.

"War," says Amah, surprising everyone. "Very bad sign. It means war."

"What do we do now?" asks Lucy, eyes on the ceiling. Claude knows she is scared and thinking about her only experience with war—her forages with ants as Grandma Siok's ruthless general.

"Well," says Grandma Siok, "I've always found that the best thing to do in a war is to have a good breakfast. Amah, why don't you see what Phatcharat has in her pantry? She's coming in a little later, I know, but I think we need some sustenance right away."

Ling-li, out of bed at the first blast of bombs, slides into an old pair of slacks and a blouse and heads for the door where she meets the sleep-furrowed face of her uncle. "It's happened," she says sombrely.

"We knew it was coming," says Hong-Seng, but there is mild disbelief in his voice. "Where are you going?"

"I think they're hitting the harbour," she says, flinching as another bomb explodes.

Hong-Seng peers cautiously out the window. "Can't tell from here," he says. "We need a window that faces south-west." He trots over to the kitchen as the sky flashes overhead. "Same general direction as the harbour, but I think it's really the mouth of the river they're bombing."

"Chinatown," Ling-li says, thinking of their friends.

"I'll make some tea," says Hong-Seng, "maybe some toast." He catches sight of Ling-li's face and shrugs. "You know, niece, as well as I do, that this is no time to go running out into the streets. There'll be plenty to do once the bombing stops and we might as well eat and rest up now to get ready."

Ling-li backs away from the door, feeling as if she has just been saved from doing something as foolish as, say, positioning a vomiting man with his head down. Before the water begins to boil the phone is ringing: reports are pouring in. Yes, the planes are Japanese and yes, Chinatown is the target. Also, apparently the Japanese have landed on the north-east coast of Malaya though the report can't be confirmed yet.

How anyone would ever think Ling-li could be afraid, and yet, here she is—heart thumping, stomach rolling, throat tightening— embodying all the familiar symptoms of fear.

But of course, she doesn't show it. She just allows herself to stand in the semi-darkness, listening as the symphonic beginnings of war rise up around her. She closes her eyes and though she doesn't actually pray, it's the closest she has come to it. And then—

"That water should be boiling by now, Uncle," she says briskly. "And forget about the toast. Just cut up the loaf and toss it over here. If this is really war, we won't have time for leisurely teas."

"You young people are always so impatient," grumbles Hong-Seng, digging his knife into a brittle loaf of bread. "Impatient for everything, even a war."

❋

Lights on in the flat. *Her* room and then a few minutes later, the kitchen. This should keep her busy, that Miss No-Time-for-the-Complications-of-Romance. Does she have time in her ambitious little schedule for a war?

The Fifth Columnist suppresses a sneeze. The night air can be chilly in December and she must not catch cold now. There is not much to do really—all the important work was done months ago, in her case even years ago, but she has been told to be on general alert until the city is taken. She can catch up on some of her paperwork, review her Japanese. All her reports have been typed in English and handed over that way. She assumes they have their own translator for sensitive documents.

It's a nice time for a lull. She'll have plenty of time for inventing, a task she has come to enjoy.

❋

Despite the declaration of war, the city continues as jauntily as before, crowds jostling in the open markets, sampans plying the river, labourers laying roads. Jack comes over to see if Claude would accompany him to the Great World. This is Claude's favourite place in the evenings, despite Cynthia's disapproval. "A waste of time," she says every time she knows he's headed there. "You won't meet anyone decent in a dance hall. Why don't you go out with the D'Almeida girl or Mrs. Simpson's daughter?"

"But lots of Europeans go to the Great World," he'd protest, tactfully saying nothing about the young women his mother has suggested. Tonight she is even more unwilling to let him go.

"What if there are more bombs?" she says.

In the end Jack wins her over. He tells her he can hardly be in Singapore and not visit the Great World, that it's been highly recommended by friends and his guidebook, that he's dying to soak in the "atmosphere" of what he calls "The Real East," that the Japanese are undoubtedly paying the price for their folly last night. "Our lads will wipe them out of the sky for their cheek," he says. He flashes her a boyish grin and looks earnestly into her eyes as he speaks. So in two hours the two of them are at the gates getting their tickets, the Great World stretched in front of them, winking and beckoning.

"How are you taking to the weather?" Claude asks, wishing he could be more original.

"It's the humidity that's killing me," Jack replies. "I'm sweating like a pig, aren't I? Sorry." He pats his handkerchief over his face. His shirt is wet at the armpits. "I say, aren't we going to have some supper and a beer, perhaps?"

Maybe the heat is making him thirsty, Claude tells himself, trying not to think of the three beers the Englishman has already had with Cynthia that evening. "Let's eat here," he says when they reach the Thong Huang Pork Ribs stand. Around the hawker's cart are a cluster of tables and stools. A woman sidles by, eyes fixed on Jack. Claude sits down at the furthest table, trying to ignore her as he places his order.

"Nice," says Jack, looking back at the woman. Claude looks at his feet. Size forty-two, left foot, forty-one on the right. Bunion on left, etc., etc. He sneaks a glance upwards. Jack and the woman are making eyes at each other.

"Er, Jack," he says, clearing your throat. As Jack's tour-guide, he is duty-bound to explain things. "I think she's, er, you know, er— lives in a brothel."

Jack laughs so loudly that heads swivel to look at him. "I figured that out myself," he says, "but thank you all the same." It's so funny that he keeps making little explosive noises and Claude is annoyed. It had taken a lot for him to say what he did, *and* he had said it in Jack's best interest, for God's sake.

"Look," says Jack, mirth frothing over again. "Sorry, didn't mean to laugh. Thank you for the, er, warning, but I've been here before, you know."

"But I thought—you said to my mother . . . I see."

The woman is trying to re-capture Jack's interest, smiling at him alluringly, but he is distracted now and good-naturedly waves her away. "I was just trying to get her to let you out of the house," he says, a beer moustache glinting and popping tiny bubbles above his upper lip. Then, unexpectedly, "I say, do you have a girlfriend?"

"No!" It almost comes out as a shout. "No time," he adds, not wanting to be thought a prude.

"Ah yes, all that studying!" Jack nods, his serious look exaggerated. Then, unable to hold back, he breaks into a broad smile.

"Yes, studying." More annoyed than ever, Claude does not smile back. There is an awkward pause that lengthens and thins out, like taffy being stretched. A snake charmer displays his de-fanged serpent to an amused crowd. A medicine man is having his sidekick break bricks on his compact back to half-hearted applause.

Jack taps the tabletop with his fingers, hums a few tuneless bars, then turns to his companion. "Have you ever—?" A nod towards the woman who has, by now, moved on to the next table. "You know!"

How could an Englishman be so vulgar? Humphrey would not have believed his ears.

"A girlfriend can be demanding on your time," Jack continues, oblivious of Claude's discomfort. "But there are other—arrangements, that can be so much more convenient. Many people I know have a woman friend tucked away in a modest but comfortable flat on Beach Road or Bugis Street. A small allowance, an occasional dress or trinket, that sort of thing, and some kind of agreed-upon schedule. It's all very civilised and hardly any trouble at all. Quite conducive to studying, if you know what I mean—relieves excessive late-night worrying, eliminates distractions.

"There's the question of how much one can afford, of course," Jack goes on shamelessly. "But even that problem can be surmounted. I know four army chaps who couldn't afford the expenses individually, so they split it four ways. It works out pretty well—once a week each and the lady gets three days to herself!"

"I have no intention of keeping a, a—lady friend," Claude says, cursing himself for flushing. "I don't go for that sort of thing." His voice trails to a rapid mumble.

"Of course not!" Jack says smoothly. "How old are you? Fifteen? Ah yes, seventeen! Still a mere boy! I shouldn't be corrupting the young!" He smacks his forehead tragicomically.

A girl in a pair of creaking, pink thong-slippers brings a plate of barbequed roast pork and a small bowl of sauce for dipping. She places them between the two of them and runs back to the stall, returning with two plates of rice. "What's this?" Jack asks, looking at the metal spoon and fork she has deposited in front of him. It occurs to Claude that Jack still doesn't know how to eat the local way.

Ordinarily he would have squirmed at the thought of eating with a spoon and fork in front of an Englishman but tonight he is too distracted by Jack's embarrassing questions and the disquieting back-of-his-head notion that bombs may come raining down from the sky at any moment. "Like this." He pushes the rice into the spoon with his fork, brings the spoon to his mouth, chews deliberately before swallowing. "They also have chopsticks if you like. And the Malays and Indians use their hands, so it's quite acceptable here." Cool, collected, the unruffled tour-guide. At least on the outside.

"Oh no, the fork and spoon will do fine," Jack says, proceeding to dig in. Claude ends up drinking two beers.

Afterwards, mingling aimlessly with the crowd, hardly saying anything to each other, he is tired. The sky overhead is heavily padded with clouds. There is a crescent moon somewhere but its sliver of light is undetectable right now. It's a Tuesday night. Even without the usual crowd there are enough people at the Great World to get lost amongst. Claude wonders how each person seems to know where he's going, how sure everyone is of his destination. All he can see are the Indian girls with their thick braids and the scattering of

petals in their hair, so pungent with coconut oil that he can't separate them from the taste of fried *roti canai* that he sometimes eats for
breakfast, the flat, flaky bread warm in his mouth. Then there are
the Chinese girls in their fitted cheongsams, the long slits up one leg
revealing tantalisingly smooth-skinned snakes that flash slyly,
golden and tan with each stride.

The fruit stalls laden with mango, guava, carambola, pomelo,
lychee, rambutan, durian. The open-air restaurants serving Peking
duck with skin so crisp that it would snap in one's mouth, the bands
striking up a *jongget* or a cha-cha. The taxi-girls with their slender
cigarettes, and the gloves which they peel off so deliciously. The
sailors flushed red from drinking and dancing, their epaulettes
falling off as the night progresses. And everywhere, voices calling
out, in Tamil, Malay, Thai, Tagalog, Hokkien, Cantonese, Hindi,
Farsi, Nepalese, Hainanese. Even though Claude doesn't understand the voices, their rhythms are familiar, their song melodious if
mysterious. And then, of course, there's English—in comparison,
hard, sometimes guttural, quite monotonous in tone, if he allows
himself to be honest, if he allows those two beers to loosen his usual
rigidity.

A woman is singing "O Danny Boy." Boys. That's what the British
call young male natives. If you're not white, you immediately
became the generic to them: boy. The beers sizzle and hiss.

Jack has wandered over to watch a slightly risqué puppet show.
"Still a mere boy!"

The woman is still singing, reaching for the high notes. Claude is
strangely limp, passive—the beers, he thinks again, and allows himself to be gently shoved into the flow of human traffic. The whole
lot: yellow, black, brown-skinned. Against the wash of colours, Jack
recedes. Russet, beige, sienna.

The populace, the common people, natives. Boys.

Another story—to pass time while they manipulate the Body, to
define, if you can, the beginning. You know the legend: He was
Sumatran, a prince—Sang Nila Utama from Palembang. In 1299, he

went on a sea voyage, and one night, a storm broke out. The waves threatened to overturn and smash the ship. Everything had been thrown overboard in order to appease the forces of nature—chests of gold, vestments smouldering with encrusted diamond fires, ivory-handled daggers, spell-laden *kris* swords. But there was still one thing left. "Your Highness," the terrified sailors begged their prince. "Your crown—you must surrender your crown."

Without hesitation, Sang Nila Utama flung his crown into the knotted ocean, and immediately the winds subsided. The furrowed surface of the sea smoothed out into a shimmering satin sheen of moonlight. The rains ceased. They were saved. At dawn, they landed at the nearest island.

"This is Temasek," Sang Nila's advisers told him as he stepped into a squelch of mud. "Only a few small fishing villages around. Nothing impressive."

The bushes shook. Suddenly, a creature darted in front of the prince and raced into the depths of island jungle. It was the colour of mahogany. Its locks blazed about its head. The prince sprang to the hunt. He chased the creature to a river. Cornered, it opened its mouth and sang at the prince, and then plunged into the slow-moving water. Before their eyes, it grew a fishtail, and swam off.

He was told the creature's name: *Singa*. Lion.

He knew then that he was meant to found a new city here. For this island he had given up his crown, his allegiance to his past, his motherland. A new name for Temasek—*Singa-pura*. The Lion City.

Ling-li had asked once, if you would have done the same. Given up your crown for the chance of forging a new country. You had thought long and hard about it. Jungle weeds, salt bogs at the edges, gnat-speckled villages. No certainties. The singular blessing of a fine, natural harbour. It would have been a poor bet.

"They feel the same way," she said, jutting her chin out at a rowdy band of half-uniformed, half-soaked white soldiers stealing coconuts from a shop. The air held the unbearable smell of burning corpses. Prayers were being sung from a minaret. The mullah's nasal voice swelled and thinned, powerful and yet frail in the afternoon sky.

Sang Nila Utama's name swam in your head, his face being unimaginable to you. Despite this, he had a striking solidity about him, a forcefulness and decisiveness that fortified his hazy image. Legends have a way of enlarging in wartime, of acquiring a vividness that makes them somehow more important than they would normally be. Inspired suddenly by this man, you sometimes find yourself almost believing that you too, in a similar situation, might have given up your crown. But then, legends are often deceiving, especially in wartime.

Patrick Heenan has been a busy man. It's no mean feat to sort out the different flight schedules of all the north-western airfields and to transmit them, in his rare lone moments, to the Japanese. But Patrick, when put to the test, can be quite focused and efficient. Even to him, however, the rapidity of the Japanese attacks is a little shocking.

"I swear it's as if the buggers had eyes down here," says one of the pilots. "They've been attacking like clockwork whenever we've had to refuel."

"None of the locals knows our operations," says another. "I'm pretty sure there aren't any Fifth Columnists around here, even though I've heard rumours that they've brought a Chinese in for questioning. They think he might have helped in the Japanese landing at Kota Bahru. It's a good thing we're all the same here. No bloody Indians or Chinese to worry about."

"No, indeed," says the lieutenant, frowning. His eyes follow Heenan, who is loitering around the hangars. "No Chinese around here, but I wouldn't go so far as to say that there're no spies around."

Patrick prays several times a day now. But the unnerving effect of air-raids overhead would turn anyone's mind to God, especially a good Catholic like Heenan, so nobody thinks too much of it when he mutters that he's off to the chapel again. "You might spare us a few words," a young flight sergeant says to him in a low voice.

He doesn't spend too much time there, just long enough to do his duty, enough to send his message to the skies, and then he is back in

action, helping Major France deal with the chaos in the airfields.
There is a spring in his step despite the air-raid sirens. He looks at
the skies warmly. He is a man who is sure his prayers have been heard.

They have begun the dangerous game of mapping out the Body
with knives. Two soldiers, their hands somehow delicate and pale,
cut rivers and roads in its skin. The baritone is back. He stops them,
momentarily inspired.

—Wait! Let's not engage ourselves in a senseless act. Let's try to
educate our young friend here. Yes, let's teach him something.

He sneers at Claude, paces a full circle around him, eyes locked
gravitationally on the Body, the weak, limited Body, measuring,
surveying as a road engineer would. He holds out his hand—a flowing, effeminate gesture—and one of his men places a knife in it,
bowing deeply in that exaggerated way. He approaches.

—A brief history of the Japanese liberation of Malaya, he declares
to the room. A little refresher course for you, my friend. Let us say
this is Kota Bharu . . . He places the knife in the narrow pass
between the right temple and earlobe. When the Body flinches, he
uses his other hand to grasp its chin. A pair of hands clamps down
on the sides of its head.

—December eighth, 1941, he drones on. There are two other
landings that day, in Thailand, at Singora and Patani.

The knife marks the crown of the head, where the soft spot grew
in after birth, and then another point beside it, to the right.

—The troops at Singora then advance down the peninsula
through Jitra.

His knife carves a line from Singora, the crown of the head, down
the forehead, veering—just—towards the outside of the left eye to
rest on the high ridge of the cheekbone. Blood stings the eye and
obscures its vision.

—Meanwhile the troops from Kota Bahru move westwards towards
Kroh. We are met by British troops—codename Krohcol, I believe.

He has carved downwards from above the right ear and has
reached the nose.

—December tenth, Japanese Fifth Division, with tanks, versus Krohcol. A quick battle, he adds before slicing the tip of the nose.

Screams, a terrible wailing. Whose voice?

—The sounds of battle are just beginning to grow, he says. Onward, Fifth Division, to Jitra.

The knife moves again to the left cheekbone.

—Are you following me? he asks, mock concern in his voice. You'll stay with me, won't you, as I work my way down the Jitra line on the west, down your very, very good British road, the spine of Malaya, down to Singapore?

But the Body is young, it is still early in the game, and besides, he's a slow learner. It is too much for you to bear, too much to stay and watch the destruction. So you refuse to stay west, refusing for now to head down the Jitra line. You return east instead, a small useless act of defiance, but nonetheless it is yours. You go east to Kuantan. You will stay as long as you can away from the knifelines at Jitra.

There is panic at Kuantan airfield; no other word will describe it. The ground staff hailing—no, *way-laying*—buses, taxis, bicycles, even a donkey cart and a trishaw, so that they can reach the train station at Jerantut one hundred miles away and ride in to Singapore, the impregnable fortress. Fear, like a poison, leaks noxious gases into the atmosphere, the safety valve released by unseen Fifth Columnist hands. The young British officers inhale it and rush forth into town shooting the door-locks of cars to make a quick escape, hijacking post office buses, contemplating a ride on fat water buffaloes—contemplating, mind you, but not actually having the nerve; those buffaloes are eyeing them back very nastily.

Everywhere the unspoken chant: The Japanese are coming, the Japanese are coming. Yet no-one has actually seen a single yellow-faced Samurai. True, the airfield had been raided that morning, but there had been no casualties and the fires had sputtered out so quickly that no extra work was created for the staff. On top of that, the skies have clouded over since, and even Japanese pilots must surely bow to the monsoon gods. Still, the leak of fear persists,

staining the neatly pressed uniforms of the Australian No. 8
Squadron as they dump the bombs from their aircraft, load up with
men and take off, leaving the British CO stewing.

The Malay villagers are cheerful and happy to assist in any way.
They help pile men into their own cars and lorries, revelling in
thoughts of having the airfield closed and their town back to them-
selves. The Indians and Chinese are astonished. White men fleeing!
Afraid of Asiatics, yellow-skinned men who don't speak a word of
English! What is the world coming to!

And so, an airfield abandoned, evacuated by panicking, fear-
diseased men a full twenty-two days before the Japanese even make
an appearance.

✿

Two days after the landing, Humphrey sits in his study trying to
decide if he should go in to work or not. He has called his office several times and no-one has picked up the phone, making him wonder if the bank was hit during the air-raid. A call to the Winchesters'
home yesterday had yielded the message from their housekeeper that
they were out and Mr. Winchester would return his call sometime
soon. The news has been contradictory—a radio report indicated
that parts of Collyer Quay had been bombed while the newspapers
have only mentioned Chinatown in the attack. It is almost noon,
and Humphrey's headache, present since he awoke that morning, is
growing.

For a brief, ridiculous moment he wonders if the Winchesters
have left the island, a thought he banishes as soon as it appears, a little ashamed of his irrationality. Sinking back into his armchair, he
clamps his hands to his temples. He doesn't want to be unfair, nervous, uncertain, everything he's feeling now, but he can't help it. Not
having news from his office has unnerved him, and besides, he has
always suspected a kind of moral laxity in himself. It's one reason
he's admired the British implacable resolve in the line of duty and
their determined, unruffled sense of decorum. He can't imagine an
Englishman shaking, as he is now, over the declaration of war, or
worrying over the future.

Of course the British have the upper hand, he tells himself. The

Japanese must be crazy to even attempt an invasion. But why can't he settle down and shake this headache? And should Claude and Lucy have gone to school today? It's the last week before the Christmas holidays—surely it would have made no difference if they had skipped classes? He wishes he had had enough presence of mind to collect his family and make a decision as to what they should do—another failure on his part.

The shuffling of slippers alerts him to Grandma Siok's presence in the corridor. He shrinks inwardly, willing her to turn and head towards the sitting room, but undaunted by his telepathic orders she continues down the corridor towards the study. "Oh, hello, Humphrey," she says when she spots him in his chair.

Damn, he thinks miserably. He should have known the old fart's will would overwhelm his anytime. She is dressed in a sarong that she has wrapped around her and an improvised turban over her wet hair. "You're dripping on the rug," he says, unable to help himself.

"I'll just be a moment—I'm looking for a book," she says, heading for the built-in bookshelves. "You look terrible. Were you up all night?"

"Well, yes, sort of. I mean I don't think I slept very deeply at all. I kept waking up and then dozing off again. And I've a devil of a headache now," he says, trying to focus on her face which has somehow split into two floating white discs. He is surprised by her concern and wants to be civil in return. "Take your time—with the book, I mean. What are you looking for?"

"Clausewitz's *On War*," she replies, coming closer and frowning. Both faces bending down towards him as if trying to read his.

"Never heard of it. I didn't know we had it."

"I bought it some time ago. Haven't read it yet, but I thought now would be a good time, just to see how it compares with *The Art of War*. Humphrey, perhaps you should lie down." She places a cool, sun-freckled hand on his forehead to feel his temperature. "You're very flushed."

"It's this headache—" He allows her to kick aside his newspaper and pull him to his feet.

"Upstairs and into bed," she says, leading him as if he were a child.

"Where's Cynthia?"

Temple, she thinks, but keeps it to herself. It's not the right time to get him upset. "Committee meeting."

"Young Orphans," he says automatically, wincing as he takes the stairs. When they get to his room, she helps him into bed, draws the blinds and gets Amah to bring up some cold compresses.

"Get some rest, Humphrey," she says after he has cooled down a little and she turns to leave.

For some reason, Humphrey is reluctant to see her go. "Wait," he tells her. His vision is better and there is only one Grandma Siok face to deal with now. "I—I feel a lot better, thank you."

She acknowledges this with a curt nod but comes back into the room, as if aware that there is more that he wants to say. They stare at each other, he on his bed, a wet towel draped across his forehead and almost covering one eye, she in her sarong, no longer dripping. "I—perhaps I shouldn't have let the children and Cynthia go out today."

"I expect there are relief efforts to be coordinated, that kind of thing," Grandma Siok says smoothly. "And the children will be fine—the Tams have let their twins go as well, so they must feel pretty confident about their safety."

"Yes, I suppose. I just thought—you know, I haven't been able to reach anyone at the office. It's a little unnerving," he says, pushing away the compress and shading his eyes as he looks up at her.

Grandma Siok says nothing for a moment, merely pulls at her lower lip while she taps her foot on the parquet floor. Observing her, Humphrey wishes he had let her leave earlier. He should have known better than to confide in Grandma Siok, of all people. "Probably just taking a few days off—it's silly of me to worry," he mutters, embarrassed now.

"Oh, I don't know," she says. "You might be right about them taking a few days off. I heard on the news that the streets are filled with debris in Chinatown and most of them are closed to traffic. It's been a bit of a mess for people trying to get to work in the financial district."

Humphrey clears his throat, hardly able to believe his ears. "Ah—

thank you, yes, I should have thought of that. I'll, er, get some rest now, if you don't mind, Siok."

She moves back to the door. "I'll tell Cynthia when she gets back so she won't disturb you—oh, and Humphrey?"

He props himself up on one arm despite the white spots spinning in his field of vision. "Hmmm?"

"You know I don't think too much of the British Army—all those men running around in their khaki shorts exposing their hairy legs—" She makes a little grimace. "But I really think it will be all right, you know. Despite everything."

Humphrey listens to her shuffling down the corridor and thinks: She sounds like a wild boar in the woods when she walks. And yet her presence today has soothed him, and for this he is grateful.

❁

Miles away, shortly past noon that December 10th, 1941, *The Prince of Wales* and *Repulse* are sunk by Japanese air torpedoes. Sent to investigate a mysterious message relaying news of a Japanese landing at Kuantan, they divert without the benefit of any air cover—Kota Bahru and other north-eastern airfields gone, Kuantan shamefully abandoned just a day before.

There, in full view of high ground, manned by dengue-ridden British regiments, the battleships are sunk. How neatly and callously history disposes of warships, hope, pride, tradition. History and the sea: One has the sneaking suspicion they are in league with each other, each flowing in waves, eroding empires, crashing down on shiny metals—medals, guns, dental gold fillings—and burying them for future expeditions. And how pathetically naïve for one to believe history to be dormant as a sleeping volcano, the sea to be a mere paddling playground of puddles. How much, yet, to learn.

❁

How the English in Singapore had reviled Somerset Maugham for his portrayal of them, for making fun of his own. He was unperturbed by their malcontent. "A work of fiction . . . is an arrangement which the author makes of his experience with the idiosyncrasies of his own personality." In other words, if someone messed with him, he'd write him into a story.

George and Janet Winchester have been whispering around the house since they returned from the Swiss Club where they had spent the day discussing the war with their fellow Europeans. Katherine has been sent to her room in disgrace, for snooping on her parents from under their bed. "I was just playing house by myself," she says sulkily to anyone who will listen. "Uncle Jack, I was just using their bed because it's bigger than mine."

Jack nods, but doesn't hear her. He is trying hard to catch the muffled phrases of his brother and sister-in-law floating up from the living room. "They were talking about England—going home," Katherine fills in helpfully, slowly edging out of her room. "Father says the *Prince of Wales* has been sunk. It's an omen," she adds solemnly. "Do you think the Queen is sad?"

"You stay in your room," Irene the nanny says, coming up the stairs. "I heard you've been snooping. Terribly rude! Good morning, Jack." She shoos the girl back into her room and closes the door behind them, leaving Jack in the corridor. He heads downstairs.

" . . . I was just calling to confirm the reports . . . Really? At what time, did you say? . . . But how? . . ." George is on the telephone, pacing on the gleaming parquet floors, his footsteps studding his conversation.

"Oh, Jack, have you heard?" Janet says *sotto voce* as he enters the living room. "Both the *Prince of Wales* and the *Repulse*—off the northeastern coast of Malaya! Just three days ago!" She is distracted, trying to listen in on George's conversation at the same time.

"What do you think we should be doing now? . . . Yes, yes, of course we're all praying for the families, but I meant . . ."

"Sunk!" Janet continues, her voice weaving in and out of George's conversation. "Who would have thought the Japanese could do that? They're a scrappy lot, barely civilised."

Jack considers this. He hasn't met many Japanese but the occasional Nippon rice merchant he's seen on the fringes of Chinatown has been generally well-behaved and respectful, always bowing and looking at the ground, even more so than the Chinese ones, who, he has decided, tend to be a querulous lot. "It must have been a fluke, really, for them to hit our ships like that, I imagine. That or some totally unsporting trick they've sprung on our forces," Janet concludes, her mouth set firmly. The veins in her neck look bluer than usual, patterned like tattoos, and she is trembling more with anger than fear.

George puts down the phone at last, leaning heavily on the receiver as he replaces it in its cradle. For a moment he just stands there, spine drooping, his whole weight on that telephone. "George?" asks Janet. "You all right?"

He creaks back to life at his wife's voice. Shakes his head, plops down in his armchair so that the cushions give off a soft sigh and Jack feels the air he's displaced waft around his face. "How," he says finally.

"What did Derrick say? Did you get any more news?" Janet presses, leaning forward in her own chair. "Derrick is George's colleague at the bank," she explains to Jack. "He knows a lot of officers at the Malaya Command Headquarters. Come on, George, don't leave us in suspense!"

When he speaks, it's as if he's trying to convince himself of all that has happened. "The reports are entirely true. Our ships have been sunk by the Japanese, and what's worse, it seems we've lost all our northern airfields."

"But how?" Janet's fingers question the air. "I don't get it. The newspapers only mentioned some skirmishes in the jungle, nothing to worry about."

"Derrick's sources seem to think otherwise. These Japanese fellows are oilier than we know," George says, tapping his knees. "After all, who would have expected them to land in the middle of a bloody monsoon? And they've dared to bomb the Americans as well."

"It was just bad luck with our ships, that's all, it won't happen again." Jack notices how thin his sister-in-law's lips are, and how they disappear when she purses them. He is taken off-guard when she faces him. "I give those Japanese a week at the most. Didn't the

Straits Times run an article yesterday about how outdated their
weaponry is, and about how they're practically starving at home? I
don't think we need to worry about going back to England just yet.
Don't you agree, Jack?"

"What?" He is reluctant to make any predictions.

"Just the same, dear, we'll need to keep our eyes open from now
on," says George. "Derrick seems to think things might worsen and
he's pretty sure the newspapers are making light of things to keep the
public from panicking. Which brings me to the next thing—not a
word." He throws a meaningful look at his wife. "The locals are
unpredictable enough as it is. We don't want a mêlée on our hands."
A pause in which all three adults stare at their shoes. "I say we should
head down to the Cricket Club and see if we can get any more news,"
George proposes at last. "Times like these we should stick together
and present a united, calming presence to the city. We certainly can't
rely on the French to do that. They're too damned emotional to be
any kind of example!"

Katherine's voice drifts down into the living room. "Is the Queen
crying a lot? Will they have a funeral for the Prince of Wales and
burn all sorts of paper things like the Chinese do?"

Irene the nanny: "Don't be silly, Katherine—not *that* Prince of
Wales! It's a battleship they're talking about, that's all!"

Jack thinks: A battleship, that's all. The pride and symbol of an
Empire, that's all.

"Can we have a funeral anyway? I want one of those Chinese doll-
houses, but I won't burn it. We can borrow Cook's pots and bang
them and make lots of noise like they do on the streets," says an
excited Katherine.

"That child," says her mother, "is too morbid for my liking."

❋

The truth is, Prince Sang Nila Utama was a loafer, a fop, a first-
rate playboy gambler of the South China Seas. He had nothing better to do than to spend his days gallivanting around the islands and
picking up native girls for his pleasure boat. "Get a job," his father
told him, "stop this philandering. It's giving the family a bad

name." But what was there for a prince to do except wait for a position to open up in the family household, for the king to die at a convenient and reasonable age and then to ascend the throne and womanise at home in peace and quiet?

And so the boat cruises with the wild dinner parties on board, the lecherous after-hours entertainment, the day hunts and picnics—at least he wasn't plotting to kill off the old man or to overthrow him for the throne. He wasn't that kind of son, didn't quite have the energy and passion for intrigue and betrayal. The old bugger should be thankful and hold off his complaining. It wasn't that he, Sang Nila, didn't have ambitions. It was just that he preferred to have things drop into his lap instead of pursuing them actively. He had that kind of efficiency about him.

The day of the storm, he had been sleeping on deck in a hammock strung out for him between two men (labour was cheap) and he had given strict orders not to be roused until he woke up himself. Four women stood with their arms above their heads, holding a canopy over him (women were cheap) and every half hour or so, when their arms were shaking with fatigue and pain, an alternate team would take over to ensure that the regent was constantly shaded from the sun.

When the storm began, the boat's rocking caused the prince's men to raise their eyebrows and fidget, but nobody dared to wake Sang Nila. The rocking was actually soothing to Sang Nila, who nestled down further in his hammock and sang to himself in his sleep. This would lead to later charges of cowardice and testimonials that the prince had "whined and cried" throughout the storm.

By all standards, discipline was admirable and sustained among the prince's subjects. After all, they held the bloody hammock and canopy until the waves crashed onto the deck and one elderly man shouted, "What are you waiting for? Start baling, and throw off any unnecessary cargo." Everyone save the hammock and canopy holders ran about lightening the ship by dumping supplies, luxury teak wood furniture, several sacks of gold.

One particularly rambunctious wave bumped the ship hard and tossed the prince off his hammock. "Ooomph," he said, rolling over onto his feet. "Who pushed me?"

"Your Highness," the elder said. "The boat's still too heavy."

"Oh, a storm! Listen to that ruckus!" Sang Nila skipped around the deck dodging the waves. "Ha! Missed!"

"Your Highness! The ship is sinking, and we're baling as fast as we can. Help us lighten the ship, please! Sir!" the elder said, grabbing Sang Nila by the shoulders and propelling him towards the cargo hold.

"Ooops," said the prince, slipping on the wet deck and sliding towards the edge. His chest hit the wooden rails, bringing him to an abrupt and sore stop, but the crown over his head, the intricate jewelled nest that gave him a crick in the neck by the end of the day, the symbol of his lineage and promise of future sovereignty—it flew in an elliptical arc, winking and sparking in its worked gold. When it entered the sea, the waves were already so high that it made no noticeable splash.

"Oh, now," said the prince, rubbing his bruised chest. "Father will make a fuss!" But the storm was dying down, and no-one heard him for all the cheering that was going on.

❀

No. 627 Government House. 1609 hrs 13th Dec.
Not for Publication

Penang has been raided several times by daylight and damage to Asiatic quarters has been extensive. So far as is known fatal casualties 200 wounded about 1000 all Asiatic. Owing to destruction of aerodromes in the north air defence has been impossible and the Asiatic morale in consequence bad. Military authorities in collaboration with the Resident Councillor are arranging to control the town. European women and children will be evacuated as soon as practicable.

❀

—Jitra

The knife plays at the cheekbone.

—Not an easy front. Fourteen miles wide, traversing jungle, hills, swamps, paddy-fields, rubber plantations, two major roads and, of course, the railway.

Sun Tzu:

When the army traverses mountains, forests, precipitous country, or marches

*through defiles, marshlands, or swamps, or any place where the going is hard, it is in
difficult ground.*

—So you see, your Major-General Murray-Lyon had some decisions to make. Thick or thin, deep or wide?

The knife draws lazy circles around the left eye, loop-de-loops.

—Spread the army out over the miles, covering every piece of
ground, at the expense of thinning out the troops, or concentrate
on certain key points—the roads, the railway—and fortify those areas
with layers and layers of fighting men? What would you do, Claude,
which would you choose?

How to choose between widespread destruction of one's face and
the gouging out of one's eye? Are these, then, the quandaries of
war? He clicks his tongue. Time's up.

—Well, we'll just stick with Major Murray-Lyon then, he says. The
knife travels. Fourteen miles wide. Jungles, rain-swollen rice fields,
miasmic swamps. Nose, cheeks, mouth.

***

The importance of diversions, denials:

Even in those last days, people persist in clinging to the old ways.
The Chinese continue to barter, to buy and sell, to hawk food in
their wooden carts, pushing them from one burnt-out street to
another, to set up shop and load their charcoal burners. When the
burners are in place and blue flames ring the bottoms of the enormous cast-iron woks, they ladle in lard and begin in earnest, stir-
frying flat noodles in a sweet, dark sauce, little square cakes of white
turnip, fish in a bed of bean sprouts, rice mixed with salted fish and
vegetables. Some have huge cauldrons simmering with broth into
which they drop pork and water chestnut dumplings wrapped in
papery white skins that soften and billow in the broth to blossom
into what are poetically called *wontons*—a swallow of clouds.

The Malays and Tamils pray in their mosques and temples, draw
closer in their *kampongs* and homes, hold elaborate weddings in
pockmarked streets where wedding guests and refugees from up-
country blur and everyone gets a little rice, chicken, sweets.

The English and other Europeans hunker down in the Cricket

Club working their way through stocks of previously hoarded cigars and wine, now in danger of being stolen or confiscated as part of the denial effort. They cling to their teas and tennis games, the business talk of Shenton Way, the concerts at Victoria Theatre. The parties grow more raucous, the laughter more shrill, the dancing more scandalous and the gossipmongers are grateful for the diversion. The topic of the war rotates through the conversation after the horse races, the cricket scores, recollections of holidays on the peninsula. "I say, we'll hold out like Malta," they say to each other as if some big adventure is in store. "Impregnable, quite impregnable, our little island. Did you hear the bombs last night? Quite a show, weren't they?"

Diversions, denials. The frailest defences, and yet so necessary in times of war.

Patrick Heenan knows they know. But he goes on pretending, as they do, that everything is as before, that there *is* no knowing.

He has moments of panic, followed by bravado. Both call for whisky, and by midafternoon, he is suitably relaxed, to the point where he is dancing a jig to a slow waltz that plays in his head. Swirling around, hopping clumsily onto one foot and then the other, he manages to change into civilian clothes. Life in the *kampongs* for a few months won't be bad, he reasons with himself. The women have always had a soft spot for him and he could use a rest. The stress of the past several months has been getting to him. He's done almost everything that's been required of him; with his help, the Japanese have decimated most of the British air forces by now. They'll just have to finish up the war on their own.

Hands in his pockets, he starts walking randomly, then stops to orient himself. North, he finally decides, swaying on his legs, and changes direction.

All those questions, never-ending questions, always wanting to know this and that. Can't they see he is in no shape to answer? That even if he does, his answers are suspect? That the Body is shutting down, losing control? Exhaustion breeds holes, carelessness, skips.

Syntax unwinds, details are missed, coherence wavers. It's not deliberate. It's just the best he can do, and, for the most part, harmless.

❁

"This is for shooting coconuts," Hong-Seng says in whispered Hokkien to his neighbour. He wipes the rust from the rifle off his hand. "They must be joking."

The English officer is explaining something to the interpreter, wasting time in Hong-Seng's opinion. In a very short while, the sun will be out in full force and it seems a pity not to make use of the time now to train before the heat hits them. But the officer is intent on talking about the necessity and importance of having this volunteer group of Chinese men—the Dalforce Irregulars—join the British forces in fighting the Japanese. As if any of them would be here today if they didn't already know this.

They are seated cross-legged on the playing fields of Kum Loong Secondary School. Many have not had breakfast and he can hear stomachs rumbling through the rows of men like a bowling ball. Now, bowling! There's something Hong-Seng can think about all day! He loves the sport. At the Katong Alley where he bowled regularly five nights a week before the war, even the local gangsters asked him to play for their sides.

It was all done very respectfully and formally, though his niece was not too pleased about it. The men, in their white Western suits and hats, would approach him with nods and carefully controlled smiles—not too broad or friendly, not too reserved—and their lackeys would at once begin to pour him tea, whisky, ply him with nuts, fruit and chocolate wrapped like little gold ingots. "Brother Han," one of them would say, his voice low, his eyes welcoming but slightly challenging. "Come, come, how about gracing our team with your superior skills?"

"No, no, I wouldn't want to put your team at a disadvantage," Hong-Seng would say modestly, accepting a chocolate ingot.

"Hardly, hardly. We would be honoured to learn from you tonight," the gang member would say with a little bow. And already the lackeys were off to get Hong-Seng's shoes, which the gang reserved specially for him.

Sometimes Hong-Seng would demur a little more, but not too much. He was not stupid enough to push his luck. All the same, it gave him pleasure to know they were all waiting for his answer, that they had need of him, he was important to them, at least for the night. When he lowered his eyes and bowed to accept, they had already laid out the booth with the plate of preserved olives and plums that he always sucked on while he played.

He made it a point to alternate sides, playing for the Iron Mask Brothers one week, the Laughing Shaolins the next. This way, even though the gangs were generally cordial to each other, he felt less vulnerable. He could be seen as openly neutral, just a hotshot bowler who took no sides except for a temporary game.

"Everybody stand!" The interpreter's shout brings Hong-Seng back to the present.

"What now?"

"They want us to line up and do some kind of drill."

The English officer walks down the line, beaming at all the volunteers. When he passes, Hong-Seng steals a look at the man's red, hairy legs. *Rambutan,* he thinks suddenly, recalling the red round fruit the size of a ping-pong ball, covered with thick hairy processes on the surface—*rambutan* is Malay for "hairy fruit"—but inside the flesh is white and sweet.

"Helmets on," the interpreter calls and there is a flurry as little tin helmets appear on everyone's head. Hong-Seng squirms. The sun, even at this hour, is unpleasant. Almost immediately after he fastens on his chin strap he feels the sweat drops fattening along the curve of his ears.

"We're just joining to help," one man says in Cantonese. "Why do we have to dress like them?"

"It's pressing against my ears," says another in Mandarin. "I can't hear very well."

The interpreter glares at them. "Hold your tongue," he says, using Hokkien, which most of the men know. The officer is looking on, a polite, inquiring smile on his face.

"Look," says Hong-Seng, his precise, staccato Hokkien cutting cleanly between them. "It's to protect our heads. Do you want to be hit by shrapnel? Just let it be."

"Basic drill routine," the interpreter calls out shrilly, turning to the officer, who, realizing that he's on, straightens his shoulders and takes over. All orders are to be learnt in English. It will keep the interpreter busy for the rest of the morning.

After the drill sessions, Hong-Seng is sent to dig trenches with the other volunteers. The Dalforce Irregulars are told to hop onto army jeeps that take them to the northern perimeter of Singapore town where they are divided into smaller groups.

Though it's now past the heat of noon, the sun is still unforgiving and most of the men bypass the chicken porridge that is being distributed for lunch in favour of the sweetened iced tea that is also circulating. Their faces pucker as they taste the sickly solution but there is no wind that afternoon and no-one can afford to refuse a drink.

Lucky they didn't add milk, Hong-Seng thinks. Milk and other dairy products upset his bowels terribly. Instead, he lives off the wonderfully rich soya bean milk that's sold fresh in the marketplace. Sometimes he even treats himself to a bowl of bean curd in a solution of melted rock sugar, savouring the bland custard consistency of the curd.

"You," says the white sergeant assigned to the unit. "Your group can start digging here. Make it nice and deep." The mood is informal and the sergeant helps himself to the iced tea, seeming to enjoy its sweetness.

Hong-Seng begins digging. The sun's sting makes him restless. No matter what he does, he can't shake off that burning sensation on his skin. The day is cloudless and there's a rotting smell in the air that unsettles him. It seems to come from the refugees that have swarmed into the city from the mainland in just a few short weeks. After Dalforce training, he also volunteers at the Han Clan Association in Chinatown. Part of that work involves helping to feed and house refugees, and it seems to him that besides these tasks, the Association has forgotten that other necessity—to wash them.

Everywhere he goes the stink of sweat, urine and armpits follow him. He is a practical man and can see the difficulty involved in bathing droves of refugees even as the water supply is being stretched.

Still, there's the river, he thinks. They can do like the Hindus in India and wash in the river. The idea pleases him and he files it away to relate to the Association leader at the next meeting.

"I don't see the point of this, do you?" the man beside him says. "Do you really think this will help?"

There is a general discussion among the men in Hokkien. "It makes sense," says another. "These trenches should be useful for the artillery." He squints his eyes as he looks ahead. "The road is straight ahead. If the Japanese come, they'll fall like ducks when we fire from these trenches."

"Wouldn't it be better from up there?" People nod in agreement.

"Shouldn't they be concentrating on protecting the Causeway?" someone else asks. "I mean, by the time the Japanese get this far, it'll be too late."

Hong-Seng privately agrees but knows that it wouldn't do for them to be defeated before any fighting has gone on. "Too late, too late! Don't talk like an old woman! Early or late I'll fight to the end for our motherland!"

The men fall silent. Each one there has had relatives or friends who have suffered directly under the Japanese in the ongoing Sino-Japanese war. "I lost my whole family," a young man says. "They burnt my entire village. I was sent here by my family to work and make money, so I escaped. When this is over, I want to go home and have a proper funeral and burial for them." He speaks as if they are still alive, as if he's promising to return and build them a new house.

"I've heard that things are very bad up-country," someone from the back says.

"Don't need to hear it. Just look at all the refugees flooding in! I wonder what's going on. Do the English know what they're doing?"

"War council this, war council that! This committee, that meeting! It's a wonder they get anything done. Just look at that one there—chatting again!" They all turn to see the sergeant engrossed in a conversation over the radio. His face is red and stubbled and his squat legs stick out forlornly from his shorts. There is nothing impressive about him.

Years later, when Hong-Seng reminisces about the British in

Singapore, this figure is called up most strongly in his mind, a memory he can't shake. "They were all right, nothing wrong with them fundamentally," he would say of his former superiors. "But they fell apart during the war. It was like watching people who knew the fancy footwork to all the popular dances, could do all the intricate steps and flash about, but when it came to running or walking—the basics—they couldn't take simple, big strides. They lacked a certain greatness."

One benefit of imperial rule: there's always someone else to do your dirty work for you.

Churchill never believed Hong Kong could be saved, but of course, one had to put up *some* kind of show. How the British love the symbolic act, especially when there are ready and easy stand-ins to carry out the hopeless deed. In such times it is good to have men such as the Winnipeg Grenadiers; in such times, one can always depend on Canada.

The Grenadiers, stationed in Jamaica, were classified as "unfit for combat," but that was just what was needed, the English reasoned, for the *symbolic* act. No need to use up skilled men, all that was needed was a body count, really. So off went the Grenadiers, first back to Canada to be joined by the Royal Rifles, also "unfit for combat," and then on to an unknown destination, an unknown mission.

"Oh, it should take about a week," the British war experts said to each other over tea, "for the Japanese to reach our line. It's forty kilometres, after all, from the border."

It took twelve hours.

"The Gin Drinker's line will hold out for several weeks at least," the English experts agreed.

It held for several hours.

Estimates not being a strong point with the British.

Where was he in the midst of these war games? Does he remember? Does he recall what his parents were doing, what they said they were doing? How does he know that everything they told him was not just some story made up to fulfil a heroic version of themselves? And the telling—does he remember—was it in the active or passive voice? Were they doing, or being done to? Does the story weave, or is it being woven? So many questions for Claude the Body, so much struggle to remember. And yet, for you, remembering is effortless. It's you they should be interrogating. You have enough memories for an entire country, a city, a family.

She has a way of focusing entirely on him, concentrating wholly on his pleasure, and yet managing, at the same time, to be distant when she is with him. Jack has never known a woman like her. Buried under that soft skin and the bruised look in her eyes after an afternoon of lovemaking, is the shining solidity of a steel beam that runs through her. On some days this beam holds her like an unbending spine; on other days it is more like a stake on which she is being martyred. The disturbing thing is that he can't figure out either image, no matter how much he lingers over it. He can only lie there, urges satisfied, curiosity unabated, fingering the cold metallic core of her being under the warmth of her flesh.

He shifts his weight, allowing her leg to roll off his as she sleeps. The room is shuttered and dark, and her body glows with the whiteness of the ocean at noon. Even now, he finds it hard to believe that she belongs to the same race that throngs the streets of Chinatown below; even now, when she is patched in shadows and her face buried in her pillow, and he can imagine her to be any woman, anybody he wants. It is only when he sees her face to face, observes the exaggerated kohl-lined slant of her eyes, the slightly blunted nose and the cheekbones that seem to start under her bottom lashes, that he is reassured of her Chinese-ness.

He has been lucky, he knows. Most of his colleagues have harvested the local trees, but these have been mainly low-lying fruit, overly ripe and soft, slowly rotting in the shade. He, on the other hand, has plucked a fruit from the top branches, sun-drenched and firm, sweet with a tartness that bites. Her small frame and deftness please him. After her, all English girls will feel thick and slow, but he puts that thought out of his mind for now. She stirs and heat rushes through him as he watches her uncoil. He slides his hand between her legs, and as quickly as if he were on a steam-liner at sea, England recedes.

At Jitra, the guard for 2/1st Gurkhas is edgy. While his unit mates catch a brief two-hour sleep in the night, their first in almost three days, he is distracted by the unfamiliar silence. After the pounding sounds of battle, this absence of grass rustling, men groaning in their deaths, indiscriminate shouting in the distance, the lone machine gun stutter here and there in the darkness—it's unnerving. All around him is the muffled sound of rain through the thick jungle foliage. He is wet, but not too drenched. The broad leaves of the trees overhead provide excellent shelter.

He sits, hand ready at his rifle, his stocky frame tensed for action, but nothing happens. Even when he lobs a stone in the direction of enemy lines, there is no response. Deliberately he lights a cigarette, waiting for the expected rebuff from the guards of the surrounding units.

Nothing.

He smokes the entire cigarette, inhaling deeply, his ears still pricked for the familiar sounds of encampment. His strained ears pick up the drone and screech of insects, the creaky calls of crickets, the splat of rain on leaves—background noises of nature. But the sounds of men that he has been trained to pick up on are missing, and he is worried. His apprehension, coupled with the rush of nicotine in his blood, helps him stay awake despite his fatigue. Sometimes he squints his eyes to force images into view, but the jungle dark is unrelenting, and he sees only the imprint of black, as thick and sinister as the inside of a coffin.

In a few hours the dawn will crack the dark. In a few hours he and his battalion will look around them in utter disbelief and bewilderment. They will scout the rain-soaked positions adjacent to them, previously manned by other British units, and learn the unpleasant truth: that the army has de-camped and withdrawn without them.

The Gurkhas have gone nearly three days without food and without more than a few scratched-out hours of sleep. They have so far dug two positions, engaged in fighting, marched twenty miles in jungle and swamp terrain. Being Gurkhas however, they will shrug, shouldering their rifles and move out after their retreating army.

Later, Lieutenant-General Sir Lewis Heath will write in a memo to his general: Communications have been down for most of the battle, leading to a most disorganised withdrawal. Our liaison officers are still trying to notify some outlying units about the retreat, but I'm afraid we may have to give them up for lost behind enemy lines.

He does not write: If you'd only given us permission to withdraw earlier, we would have had time to do so in an orderly manner. We would not be scrambling, fatigued, demoralized and short so many men.

He does not write it, but he and his troops think it. They think it all through their long retreat from Jitra.

The RAF officers find Patrick in the middle of a swamp, stinking drunk and half-crying, and escort him back to his tent, where he is put to bed like a spoiled child. The next morning, Patrick wakes up groggy but tries to pull himself together. He'd just obtained all the flight schedules from the Butterworth airfields the day before and decides to pass them on as soon as possible.

He looks around his room for his typewriter. It can only transmit, unlike the more superior two-way radio in the Catholic Communion set he's been carrying around ("the padre wanted me to look after it," he'd told everyone who'd asked) but it's all he needs for now. He ransacks his room, but both radio sets are nowhere to be found. They've searched the place, of course, he tells himself. Thank goodness he kept the flight schedules on his own person. He drinks from his water bottle to try to settle his stomach, finds and eats a half-crushed biscuit in his pocket.

I could pass the schedules on to Hamid and Chan, he thinks, and they can get it to the Japanese. He has to find his local Japanese agents first, of course, and he doesn't have much time. The officers will come and get him any moment. Feeling a little better now that he has some sense of purpose, Patrick puts on his boots. Hamid's paddy fields will be the best bet for finding his contacts. He'll have quite some walking to do.

Outside he is met by Jock, the driver, and a flight-lieutenant whom he knows by sight but not by name. The latter, however, seems to know him. "Hey, Heenan," he calls out. "Where are you off to?"

"Up the road, not very far."

"Hop in, then. I'm headed that way myself. I'll give you a lift." At his signal, Jock climbs into the driver's seat while the flight-lieutenant opens the door for Patrick. "After you."

Patrick hesitates, glancing around him. Then, with a resigned shrug, he gets into the car. I've done all I can, he thinks, as they drive off. He hates the smirk on the flight-lieutenant's face. As if I don't know, he fumes. They think I don't bloody know.

Humphrey borrows the Tams' Bentley, complete with uniformed chauffeur, for the Winchesters' farewell party. The Lims live in a very good section of Bukit Timah, but the house and staff are the smallest in the area. Nevertheless, Humphrey is popular with the neighbours and none of them seems to mind his frequent borrowings of cars, staff, even the occasional antique, for social functions. After all, the venerable Mr. Tam himself has reasoned aloud to Humphrey, there are times in a man's life when he needs to impress in order to move up in the world, and therefore, he needs things with which to impress, things which he has not yet acquired, but undoubtedly will once he has made his mark in the world. Tactfully, he does not mention a certain satisfaction one gets in knowing that one is in a better position than one's neighbour, and therefore one can afford to be generous, as to a poorer relative.

George Winchester is very much surprised to see his Chinese senior clerk arrive at the party in a gleaming Bentley. "Humphrey, how nice to see you! Cynthia! Merry Christmas! Come in, come in," but his eyes are still on the polished car. "I say, where'd you pick that up?"

"Oh, something we've had in the family," Humphrey says vaguely. "We bring it out for a run every now and then." He waves it aside. Whenever it suits him, Humphrey likes to refer to his family as if he is from old money. He often drops hints about family mansions on Hong Kong Island, plantations in Borneo, even a bauxite mine in Australia. These are details he has freely "borrowed," along with cars and chauffeurs, from the Tams.

Claude has always been uncomfortable with this charade. It's mostly because of this that he remains silent throughout most of the social functions that he attends with his parents. He doesn't have Humphrey's skill for making up stories, nor his ease in sliding through sticky questions with the cartilaginous flexibility of a dog-fish. Usually he composes a staid smile and nods blankly, appearing embarrassed to talk about his family fortune, to everyone's approval. "Not a vulgar bone in that family," it is said among their British acquaintances.

The drawing room is already filled with friends of the Winchesters spearing hors d'oeuvres with toothpicks and helpfully clearing out the Winchester wine stock. Humphrey makes for a group of men that includes several members of the board of directors. Before he goes, he whispers, "Try to loosen up, Claude. Tell a joke or two. The British love them and it's a good way to set everyone at ease. I say, you do know some, don't you?"

Cynthia allows herself to be wedged between some well-rounded Englishwomen discussing the various ways of hybridizing orchids. She herself knows nothing about orchids, or indeed plants of any kind, but she manages to nod knowledgeably and brightly at her companions. Such ugly, coarse women, she thinks, and dissects their features as she smiles agreeably. This is what happens when Englishwomen spend too much time in the tropics. Their skins dry out, they grow fat. Should've stayed in England. She knows *she* would have had she been English.

Claude moves to the large French doors overlooking the garden and prepares to stand guard by them for the rest of the evening. He hates mingling. Beside the open door he can feel the humidity building up, and pictures the storm clouds rushing towards the island from Sumatra. By early morning the ground will be soggy with rain and rubbery earthworms, the air sharper and relieved of its load of moisture. But the Sumatras are not here yet. The brief glow in the sky and the low rumble in the distance are not lightning and thunder. He is roughly facing south-west. Again the harbour, he thinks, again Chinatown.

"Hope that one didn't hit the office," says a familiar voice. "We had a close call two days ago. Merry Christmas, by the way."

"Hello, Jack," Claude says, turning around to greet him.

"I wonder how long they're going to keep this up," Jack says, motioning towards the flashes that continue in the south. With the first rumble, conversation in the room thinned, but now it is back in full force, as if the bombing were merely an inconvenient part of the tropical night, on a par with bats, head-ringing crickets, mosquitoes and bullfrogs bellowing for rain.

"So when are you leaving? I heard you're flying out, instead of going by sea," Claude says, still looking into the garden.

"I have a friend who's arranged it—has air force connections, you know. Anyway, it will give me a few extra days to tie up some loose ends."

How many loose ends can one accumulate in a short year? Claude wants to ask. He knows that Jack lives in a spacious flat not too far away and has not had to involve himself much with the moving arrangements of his brother and sister-in-law. The Englishman has a relatively low-level position at Albert and Burroughs that will be easily filled once he is gone; he has no close friends to take leave of, none, of course, except—Claude himself. I've been his closest friend, he thinks, and suddenly the presumption hits him. How is that possible? Why is it that he has no other close friends?

"What is it?" Jack asks. "Did you say something?"

"No, no." Claude shakes his head, turns to face him. "Yes, well, I hope it's safe—to go by air, I mean. What about the bombers?" He waves his hand casually in the direction of the flashes in the south.

Jack shrugs. "By air, by sea—it's all the same. They sank the *Prince of Wales,* didn't they? But I reckon they'll leave civilian craft alone. What about you?"

Claude is confused. "I suppose you're quite right," he manages finally. "It's the military aircraft they'll be going after."

"I meant, where are *you* going? I heard some talk about a farm somewhere."

Humphrey did mumble something the other day about going to Cynthia's cousin's farm in Punggol, where the chances of being hit by a bomb are much slimmer, but nothing definite was decided. Humphrey, as far as Claude knows, has taken a wait-and-see attitude and nobody at home has mentioned it any further. How would Jack have known about this?

"Nothing formal yet," Claude replies.

"Yes, of course."

Something about Jack's entire manner seems fishy right now—his smile, the casual droop of his shoulders, his weight resting on one leg—and Claude is suspicious.

"There you are, Jack! I almost missed my chance to say goodbye. My boat's going tomorrow." A well-built man with reddish hair approaches. "I say—what's this about not going with George and the lot?"

"Jeremy," Jack says warmly, making Claude wonder—is this a close friend? "I will be leaving, but a week after George—flying out."

"God, I'm glad to hear that. I thought I'd have to come here and knock some sense into you. The governor's a stubborn mule! He should be ordering the evacuation of civilians instead of dilly-dallying as usual."

"Well, technically, nothing's really happened yet to call for that kind of action. There's been nothing in the papers or on the radio to suggest—"

"That's just it, Jack! There's been nothing at all. Don't you understand? Our news is being censored! They don't want us to know the truth, but you've got to be the biggest fool if you don't sus-pect something's up." He empties the shot glass in his hand. "Know what I think? If Penang has fallen, we can't be too far behind. That's why I can't understand the bloody governor!"

A breeze blows in through the doors from the garden, reminding Claude of the clear, liquid notes of the clarinet. He can almost feel the instrument in his hands, the fluent reed moistened by his saliva.

"—and then the refugee situation! In the past month we've almost doubled our population, what with all those natives flooding in from the peninsula. I wouldn't mind a few Malay or Indian families here and there—they're quite harmless and easy-going—but the chinks are another matter altogether! They're a noisy, quarrelsome, smelly lot, and there's just too damn many of them."

Jack coughs rather self-consciously, taking a half-step closer to Claude. Jeremy notices at once. "Oh, well, hello. Jeremy Turner. How do you do?"

Claude catches his father's eye from across the room. *Joke,* he seems to be saying, tell them something lively.

"Claude Lim. How do you do?"

They stand awkwardly, regarding first each other then the cinerary night sky.

"I think they're done for the night," Jack says. Jeremy excuses himself to get another drink. After he leaves, Jack sighs. After a pause, he says, "I've been meaning to ask you—let's go by the Great World another time before I leave, indulge my sentimental side."

"As you wish," Claude says and, to his own surprise, walks away.

※

And amidst the merry-making, Hong Kong is lost.

To celebrate, the Japanese commanders give the gift of the Fragrant Harbour to their soldiers. All Chinese women are prostitutes anyway, they say. Now let them pay the price of liberation.

※

Cynthia circles the room, always looking as if she's on her way to join some friends tucked in a corner somewhere, never quite stopping but nodding and smiling, throwing a few passing greetings over her shoulder, manoeuvering round the room like a ship dodging air attacks and torpedoes.

She appears relaxed, carefree, but Claude senses an inexplicable desperation in her smooth elegant walk. She seems to be looking for someone, hunting someone down. "Hello, Mother," he says as she drifts by. "The bombing has stopped."

"Oh," she says, scanning the room, which is now quite full and difficult to navigate.

"Can I get you something?"

"No, no. I'm fine," she says and her smile is suddenly dazzling. "Merry Christmas, dear. Enjoy yourself." And then she is off, the hem of her dress flickering through the crowd. Claude catches sight of his father conversing with a solemn man who looks as if it's impossible for him to smile. Claude starts making his way through the crowd, determined to find Cynthia again and to stick by her in case—in case of what? He's not even sure. It's just that something about her worries him.

When he sees her again, she is walking oddly. Her eyes are fixed directly in front of her and her gait is stiff, almost wooden, as if she is having trouble remembering to bend her knees. Then he realises she is trying to keep herself from breaking into a run. She slips out of the living room and he hurries to catch up, arriving just in time to see her turn into a room at the far end of the foyer. Claude hesitates, not quite at the door, and it slams shut, leaving him poised, weight on one foot, uncertain of why he is there and what he wants to do.

"Claude, old boy, there you are!" George Winchester thumps him on the back. "Listen, lad, I need a favour. There are more people here than I had expected and we're rather short-staffed, what with the servants running off to be with their families and all, during this bombing business. I wonder if you could help Juswan and Anita out—you know, make sure the glasses are full, pass the little hors d'oeuvres around. You're like one of the family, you know."

One of the family.

Claude wonders what to say, opens his mouth in preparation for the words, and then he hears it, and it comes out as it always has, as he has been trained to respond: "Of course. I'd love to help out, sir." And like an obedient puppy he trails George to where the servants are. And no matter how dressed up Claude is, no matter the lack of uniform, that is what he is tonight—a servant.

❈

On the battlefield, a pamphlet drifts from the sky, dropped from a Japanese plane:

> The cruel English without tanks and planes are keeping the Indians here for sacrifice. You may have heard that their whole fleet has been sunk. Think and save yourselves. For your protection a large army has joined us.
>
> Free India Council

❈

Through the geometric rows of rubber trees in the Malayan plantations, the uneven terrain of karst hills,

Time, time, time, throbs Patrick's head. It's slipping away so quickly . . .

the soggy paddy fields down the coast, General Yamashita's troops bicycle forth by the hundreds in

Already the court-martial has been carried out, days after he reached Singapore fortress, having travelled

winding lines, their broad swords swinging on their backs. If one could forget the war, it would be funny,

all the way by train, handcuffed to the listless private who had been his guard at Penang jail. Did the soldier

ludicrous even.

go back to Penang after bringing him here? From the bits of talk around him, Patrick knows that Penang

The Japanese tanks plunge into dense fortifications, levelling the ground before them. The forward

has fallen by now. The Japanese will win the war, but it must happen soon, or it will be too late for him.

troops fly, bicycle-swift, infiltrating British ranks, agitating Indian regiments. The ingenious engineers

Every hour he expects to hear the announcement of his execution date, but so far there has only been the work endlessly like ants, repairing bridges blown up by retreating British forces.

waiting. He sees in his mind the red sun of the Japanese flag and like everything else these days, it reminds

The master says: *Speed is the essence of war.*

him of the passage of yet more time.

Yamashita listens.

In the coming days, he takes to biting his nails.

Such is the art of manoeuvering.

Four days after Christmas, there is a heated discussion in the living room. Grandma Siok keeps interrupting Humphrey. "Well then, we should start packing," she says finally, clicking her tongue in her habitual way. "We should have left yesterday."

"Claude, Claude, we're going to Cousin Eng's farm!" says Lucy when Claude enters the room. "It's all settled. And I'll get to feed the chickens. Mummy promised already!"

"Are we really going after all?" he asks, looking at his father and ignoring Lucy who is doing rather lame cartwheels round the living room. "Are things really that bad?"

"No, no, no. I still have full faith in the British," Humphrey says. "It's just that in the meanwhile—well, I thought it would be safer to be in the country—"

"He *thought!*" Grandma Siok rolls her eyes.

"Your grandma and I both agree," Humphrey continues smoothly, "that the city is the obvious target for the Japanese, and it would be safer for us to live with Cousin Eng for a while."

"Half of Chinatown is gone already," Grandma Siok says, "and there was a hit near Bras Pasah Road when I was shopping the other day! And they hit the Katong district last night. Your British heroes are half-asleep, I tell you!"

Cynthia has a serene look on her face, as if she's in a pleasant dream.

"What about school?" Claude asks, addressing Humphrey. Lucy makes an annoyed face at her brother: Why did you have to bring that up anyway? "School starts in January and I have the Standard

Certificates coming up." Now Lucy is practically trying to run him over with her cartwheels. "Stop it, Lucy—the SCEs are important!" Especially since there is a good chance, Claude believes, that he might be accepted into Cambridge or Oxford. His grades are certainly good enough, if not for a scholarship, at very least an exhibition.

Humphrey tells Lucy to leave Claude alone. "What do you think, Cynthia?" he asks. "Perhaps we should stay after all. I don't think this will go on for very long."

Grandma Siok sighs. "You don't know what you're talking about," she says. "Before long, there won't even be schools for the children to attend, much less Standard Certificate Exams."

Claude jumps in before Humphrey can answer. "Look, why don't you all go ahead to Cousin Eng's farm and I'll stay here? I'll be fine, and I could pop out to visit you every now and then."

"I don't know if that's such a good idea," Humphrey says.

"Why not? You'll know exactly where I am, and Phatcharat and Amah and Rahman will be here too."

"Rahman will be going back to his village in Mersing tomorrow. He wants to be out of range of the bombs, he says."

"I'll be fine," Claude declares. "With or without our gardener."

Humphrey looks undecided. "Cynthia?" he asks.

When she looks him full in the face, she doesn't try to disguise her irritation. "He's almost a man, for goodness' sake, Humphrey." She looks at her son now, her face unexpectedly challenging. "You decide, Claude, what's best for you."

"I'll stay then."

"It will be good to have someone look after the house while we're gone," Grandma Siok adds, in carefully considered tones, and it's settled. Grandma Siok turns the conversation to getting organised for the move. A thrill runs through Claude. It will be exciting to stay here without the family and with a war in full swing, as the man of the house. Suddenly he wishes they were gone already.

—Yes, yes, all very interesting, but now tell me something more, the baritone coaxes, fringed with impatience. Yet the voice insists on this theatrical civility. Would you care for something to drink?

You don't trust it, would prefer to refuse, but the Body betrays, as usual. It nods eagerly, juts its chin out for the glass that is headed its way, relishes the sweet wetness that runs into its mouth. Coconut water! Surely there is nothing more refreshing than this! The Body sucks in its cheeks, willing in the strength that comes with the sweetness, the only sustenance it's had in—hours? Days? Time, defying impossibility, like the three states of water; time in its trinity of pastpresentfuture.

—Tell me, for example, things you heard in Chinatown.

Things the Body has never heard, in tongues and dialects it can't understand, but, unhampered, you tell on.

—Confess, they say. It's so simple, much of this so needless. Certainly, all that they say happened could have happened. Don't try to tell another story. This is the only one they'll accept. Allow it its potential. All stories are *could haves* disguised as *dids*.

So go ahead, do what say they: Confess—

Hayley Bell watches her pick her way through the crowd, hair swinging as she ducks umbrellas, poles slung precariously on shoulders, a bucket sloshing at each end, wheelbarrows and amorphous bundles, rising like fantastic rainbow-hued clouds balanced on fragile heads. She doesn't so much walk as bounce on the narrow strip of asphalt, and when she reaches him, she flashes him a huge smile and throws her arms around him. He reciprocates with a chaste peck on her head, but it is enough to draw some interested stares.

With his arm coiled about her waist, he leads her off to a side alley and into the first of a row of tenement houses facing a large canal. They troop up the stairs, she laughing flirtatiously and chattering nonsense, and he nodding briefly at the owner whose head pops out for a moment from a room along the long ground floor corridor. "Our usual room?" Hayley Bell calls out in Cantonese, even as he climbs the stairs.

"Only until five," the man responds. "You can't stay the night. I've rented it out already."

There are only two rooms on the third and topmost floor. They head for the far room and his arm falls immediately from her as he bolts the door. "Good show," he says in English, turning to look at his companion who has become serious and distinctly un-amorous, her hands primly adjusting the pleats in her skirt. "Though I must say, your Cantonese requires some work. We'd better use Hokkien next time."

She allows a smile, which softens the angular lines of her thin face. She is remarkably severe, Hayley Bell thinks, for one so young. He walks over to the large window. The canal below is a deep green, velvety with algae and flecked with rubbish deposited by the tenement holders. A group of boys is wading knee-deep in the canal, hunting for tadpoles. "We weren't followed, I don't think," he says.

"We're too boring for that—an Englishman and his Chinese trollop, hiding away in their little love nest in Chinatown!" There is a trace of mockery in her voice, something he has come to expect. "So," she continues, "any news?"

"They've captured Heenan. Our suspicions have been confirmed. It seems he controlled all subversive activities from Thailand to Singapore," he says. "They've been trying for days now to get him to talk, but he's pretty stubborn."

"It's a little late for that now. They should have done something earlier, when we warned them." She reaches into her skirt pocket. "Here's a list of Fifth Columnists in the Telok Ayer area—not that it will help much at this point. By the way, the Indian Independence League has increased its activities significantly. They've been holding open-air meetings along Serangoon Road and, according to my sources, have sent members to infiltrate the British Indian Army, urging Indians to join them in their fight for independence. They're portraying the Japanese as defenders of Asia." She sits on the bed, tucking her legs under her long skirt.

Hayley Bell paces the room. "Yes, well, I had expected that. There's not too much we can do about it now. They should have listened to me two years ago. Two years!" He stops at the window, sighing. "Well, it's done, we have to move on. I have your next assignment."

She sits very still, her ears trained on every word. "We're sending our own agents out to Indonesia to ensure their safety. They're mostly Chinese, with a few Malays and Indians scattered here and there, so we'll need you to translate and be the liaison for the pick-up. The whole operation will be done in stages, to avoid arousing any suspicion. The first three agents will leave from Changi Point tomorrow night. They'll have several boxes of documents among them. Make sure these are dumped into the sea before they reach Batam Island. Anil will pick you up at the usual spot on Patterson Road at nine."

The girl nods. "Anything else?" She looks at her watch. "We've only been here for eight minutes. We'll need to stay a few minutes more, for appearances' sake."

"Oh, I don't know. These things can be quick sometimes," he says, walking towards her, but she doesn't blush. Just an arched brow, a cat-like smile.

"Yes, I've heard that Englishmen can be—premature," she says coolly, and it is he who is unable to stop himself from turning red.

"Have you?" he asks. Then, to change the subject, "Do you believe that the Japanese are defenders of Asia? I know how much you dislike us British being here. Do you think there's something in the Greater Eastern Co-Prosperity Sphere the Japanese are going on about?"

She gets up and passes him for her turn to look out the window. She doesn't say anything for a while, weighing her answer. Silhouetted against the bright sunlight, she looks like a stick figure that a child might draw in a jotter book. "Yes, I do want the British out of Malaya, but I also know what the Greater Eastern Co-Prosperity Sphere really offers us Chinese. Until there's a better opportunity, until we have a real chance at independence, I'll take British rule over the Japanese any day. But that doesn't mean I'm not planning the fall of your Empire! Like most Asiatics, I know how to wait."

There is a suggestion of menace in the tilt of her head, the tense line of her shoulders. From the streets, the tinny, shrill sounds of Chinese street opera rise. Even with his excellent Chinese, Hayley Bell has trouble following the libretto, contorted as it is by the performer's stylised singing. The aria is bitter, longing, unmelodic.

❋

A stir. Have you said something to cause it? Have you, perhaps, said too much? What, if anything, come to think of it, have you said to them in all this time? What has been said and what left unsaid?

Ren. 忍 Knife over heart. That word, received from Ling-li in earlier days, that one Chinese word learnt from her and somehow remembered, has become a talisman. It hangs over the Body like a kind of substitute courage. The Body clings to it, afraid to let go, and so do you. With that one word, you can almost believe in hope.

❋

Despite their Anglo ways, the Tams displayed surprisingly little faith in the British and have left, mobilizing as easily and swiftly in the night as any well-trained army unit. Humphrey was unable to suppress the wave of triumph that surged through him when he heard the news from their chauffeur, Muthu. Yes, they may have professed English ways and mixed readily with whites, but it is clear to him now that the Tams lacked moral courage altogether, uprooting at the first sign of trouble.

This knowledge is immensely satisfying to him, but does not render him immune to private moments of aporia. Is he perhaps altogether too sure and trusting of the British? He has read all the papers, and the news so far has been glowingly optimistic, but even he senses by now the hand of the Censor in every carefully worded column. How much can he take seriously? Should he be making arrangements to leave for Australia instead of nearby Punggol?

The bombings have shaken Humphrey more than he cares to admit, and in the end he chooses Punggol and sticks to this decision. He wants so much to believe in the promise of Empire. Perhaps he should not be faulted. He knows no other story but this one. He must tell it to himself over and over, like a refrain, or like an enchantment.

Cousin Eng's pig farm is in Punggol, a mere clearing that struggles each day to hold fast its boundaries against tropical grasses, vines, creepers, trees and ferns. Its location "in the middle of nowhere" used to discourage family visits but is now deemed desirable because there the air-raids are far fewer, the Japanese rage less perceptible.

It takes them three days to pack, and in that time Amah decides she is going back to China. "If not now, maybe never. I not so young, maybe not so much time left, madam," she says.

"But now, Amah? Why the rush?" Cynthia says breathlessly. "We need you here."

Amah colours, but her mind clings to the limestone crags of her beloved Guilin and she won't change her mind. "Madam, I left home because of too many wars and fightings with warlords. Now here also war. No difference I be here or in Guilin. I go home," and on the last three words, she is tearful.

Seeing this, Lucy starts crying too. "I don't want Amah to go," she says, clinging to Amah's loose black trousers. "Amah, please stay! I promise I'll be very good always."

"You always good girl, Lucy, but I must go home." Gently she tries to extricate Lucy's hands from the folds of her trousers.

"Amah, old girl, this wouldn't have anything to do with a raise, would it?" Humphrey asks. Amah looks away, but not before Claude catches the look of humiliation on her face.

"Didn't you hear the woman, Humphrey?" Grandma Siok says. "She's homesick and wants to see her village again before she dies."

"I think Amah has made up her mind," Cynthia says and there is sadness in her voice. "Amah, we'll take care of your passage to China. Claude can go with you to get your ticket tomorrow."

"Thank you, madam," Amah replies in a low voice. "I can pay ticket. I saved money—"

"But I insist," Cynthia jumps in. "It's the least we can do after the wonderful years of service you've given us." A look passes between the two women that the others miss, but there is clearly regret and loss in Cynthia's eyes, and reassurance and fondness in Amah's. "Claude, make sure she goes first-class. Come upstairs with me, Amah, I have something for you."

Upstairs she gives Amah a jade bracelet, gold bangles and delicate ruby earrings. She hands over some of her best Shantung silks and a

hand-painted batik *kebaya*, "to remember your days in Malaya."
Then she lays her head on Amah's lap and weeps, saying over and
over, "What will I do without you?" while Amah strokes her hair;
and finally, "Tell me about your home." And Amah tells her about
the earthy smell of mud-walled cottages, the children flying kites
and singing their songs like noisy geese, the women slapping smooth
rocks with their washing and, best of all, the sense that no matter
what their trials and difficulties, they are the best people on earth,
and the pride of being, after all, Chinese, the Han People.

And yet, the next day when Claude goes to purchase her boat
ticket, he will only manage a third-class seat for her, for she is, Han
blood notwithstanding, only a poor Chinese servant, going home
forever.

⚙

"You're in charge, son. Aside from school, don't go out unless it's
absolutely necessary, and make sure the servants do the same. And
no heroics, stay out of the way of the army, do you hear?" What else?
Humphrey wishes he had made a list, but he had spent the past few
days closing his accounts and transferring money to Australia, a tricky
piece of business, given the war. It had unnerved him to see crowds
of Chinese merchants queuing for hours at banks and lending companies, taking out wads of their long-hoarded Straits dollars.

"Mindless panic," George Winchester said to his overworked and
unusually jumpy staff at the lunch hour. "You won't see any of our
Europeans giving in to illogical fears like that. Even though Janet
and I are going to England for a few months—mind you, I haven't
taken any leave in years, so this is more like a long-overdue holiday
than anything else—we're leaving our money here as a sign of our
confidence in the economy and, of course, our lads. Needless to
say, I expect the same of you. We have to set an example to that mob
outside." And with that, he strode off towards his office with the
assistant manager in tow, checking off last-minute duty transfers to
the mostly local crew that would carry out basic operations until the
war ended.

The staff went back to work, subdued and hungry, yet nobody felt
like eating. Clerks who had begun filling out forms to withdraw

money had quietly stuffed them into their pockets or crumpled them into wastepaper baskets. Out on the teller floor the employees were mainly Eurasian, with a scattering of Indians and Chinese amongst them. But due to the unusual circumstances, English senior staff were out of their second storey offices and milling around their subordinates, helping to process forms and to approve the more complex transactions. They worked with stubborn politeness in the face of fast-growing lines and the lack of adequate ventilation in the lobby. Nobody spoke about the mounting anxiety over the dropping cash reserves.

Humphrey had resisted at first, but the general uneasiness in the queues was contagious, and when he stepped out into the corridor to use the loo, he took a withdrawal chit with him. In the hollow terrazzo-laid gentlemen's room, he filled the chit out carefully over a dry sink, looking over his shoulders a few times when he heard footsteps in the corridor. When he was done he went back out into the lobby and found Lawrence de Silva, one of his Eurasian colleagues. "Will you sign and stamp this?" he said, handing him the withdrawal chit as casually as he could manage.

"What, man? This is for you?" Lawrence's eyes shifted rapidly from side to side in his nervousness. "But the boss—?"

Steady, Humphrey told himself, keep it down. "Look, Lawrence," he said amicably, "I'm just doing what I can to protect my family and myself. The price of rice has gone up three times already, and we're off to Punggol in a few days. I need some cash on hand."

"Some cash! But you're closing all your accounts."

"Yes, well—Lawrence, you and I both know that it's easy for Mr. Winchester and the other bosses to talk about setting an example and so forth. I have faith in the army—you know I do! But I'm going to need cash to last through this war. That's just a fact!"

Lawrence considered this for a moment. "Okay," he said finally. "I'll process your chit, you do mine."

Humphrey sighed in relief. "Certainly. But don't tell anyone. There's no need to create a fuss."

Because of the growing lack of large bills, the problem of how to carry the money home without attracting attention delayed an otherwise smooth transaction, but Lawrence solved it by borrowing the night *jagar*'s sarong—neatly folded in the utility room next to the loo—and knotting the money within its voluminous folds. "I'll stay in the gentlemen's room a little after closing while you wait outside the window and catch it when I throw it down to you. We can stuff it in the boot of your car and count out the money at your house."

But it turned out that they didn't even have to do that. George Winchester appeared by Humphrey's side just minutes before closing time and asked to see him in his office. Humphrey scanned his face, his stomach curling into a tight ball, but George avoided his eyes and seemed to be fastidiously studying his hands as he spoke. Lawrence gave a small shrug behind George's back and began to tally up his records with an unprecedented scholarly interest.

Their feet clipped across the lobby in syncopation—George's in long even strides, Humphrey's as an irregular echo, loping along unhappily. He swore at himself for his impulsive action—what in the world had possessed him?—but when the door closed behind him and he turned to face George's arctic scrutiny, a tiny stubborn nugget of rebellion nested in his throat, causing him to grit his teeth and stare back with a kind of insolence. "What the devil are you playing at, Humphrey? I never thought that you would conspire to embarrass and compromise your own bank in such an underhanded way! And to do it right after my little speech this afternoon, Humphrey, to get the whole lot of tellers and clerks to spite me—to spite the bank—in such a weasel-like manner!"

Humphrey was astonished. He was quite well off, he knew, but surely the amount he had had in his accounts was nothing to the bank? And getting the tellers to—what did George mean by that?

"At least have the decency to answer me, Humphrey! What's all this about?"

"I'm sorry if I disappointed you in any way, George, but I hardly thought my actions would upset you so much or affect the bank so significantly." It occurred to him that they might be overheard and he did his best to keep his tone pleasant, edging towards conciliatory perhaps.

"Disappointed is hardly the word, Humphrey. How could you incite the employees to panic and to close their accounts en masse—"

"*All* the employees? What are you talking about? Aside from Lawrence de Silva, I didn't breathe a word to anyone else . . ." Lawrence! So he had told everyone else, and had stimulated a withdrawal frenzy. Humphrey's hands itched to rap the silly man's skull several times. And he himself had been stupid enough to confide in the little gossip.

"There's been a misunderstanding," Humphrey said, trying a weak smile on George. "I never planned to cause a panic. I needed Lawrence to sign off my chit and he had wanted to do the same thing, but he had to go tell everyone else. I even told him not to."

"I see."

"Yes, I never wanted . . . that is, I only meant . . . It's not anything personal, you understand. I have the greatest faith in our bank and in the British military."

"So much faith that you decided to empty out your accounts." Humphrey might have apologised and been persuaded to reinstate his accounts as he was beginning to feel he should do, but George's mockery nudged up against something hard in him, a vein of resentment he had never suspected in himself.

"Life goes on, as you know," he said now, careful to keep his tone neutral. "Even during a war there are bills to pay, living expenses to cover. Having nowhere else to go I have to make sure that I'll be able to survive here."

George sat down at his desk, rapped his knuckles over the mahogany surface and stood up again. "Damn it, Humphrey, you should have told me! I would have tried to arrange something more—inconspicuous. Instead we have half our employees stuffing their pockets and shirtfronts with Straits dollars while telling our customers that there's no need to panic and their money is safe with us!"

Humphrey kicked himself. Why *hadn't* he gone to George and explained? Or at least considered his actions more carefully. *That's* what George was so upset over, *that's* what he was reprimanding—his emotional response, his inability to see a rational solution.

"Father? Are you all right? I thought you said you had a list for me," Claude says, looking him over with concern.

"Did I?" Humphrey rubs his tired, pink-tinged eyes. "I was

thinking of something else." He reaches into his dresser drawer to pull out an envelope. "You're going to need some money. Six hundred dollars, in the smallest bills I could find—should be enough. I've paid the servants already, so there's no need for you to worry about that."

Claude takes the wad of notes out and begins counting them in front of Humphrey as he's been taught to do since he was a little boy. "That's it, Claude," Humphrey says, smiling. "You'll find it's all there."

It had been fine at the bank in the end. He had apologised to George and admitted it had been foolish of him not to act without talking it over first. George had acknowledged the rising food prices on the black market and the obvious anxiety the people must be feeling. It had been a misunderstanding, they both agreed, and Humphrey would keep a token account at the bank, to reassure the others and their customers that there was nothing to worry about.

"You just keep your nose in your books and if you come across the soldiers, do what they tell you, right, Claude? Pay close attention to the authorities and follow all their instructions, do you hear?"

His son nods, still counting. It occurs to Humphrey that the boy is excited to be on his own now. Soon he'll be off to England himself, if all goes well, to finish his studies. His son is growing up, and this, Humphrey realises, will be the first of a series of separations and departures.

Perhaps the war will be a good thing, Cynthia thinks as she stacks the last of her jewellery boxes together. It will get her out of town for a while, away from her usual routine. She has long since felt the need for change, but so far has not been able to escape her habits. Despite her best intentions, she is unable to control the eerie plasticity of her own face. She feels the treacherous pull of her facial muscles, contorting surfaces this way and that to suit the circumstances. It happens so effortlessly and quickly that it almost seems natural—only she knows it is not. She is always looking at herself, evaluating her performance from a distance, especially when she is

with *him*. Of all her white men, this one has been closest to getting
to her heart. Something she knows should never happen. Too dangerous, asking for trouble.

But perhaps going away will clear all that. Some physical distance
to break the spell. After all, he is not exactly what one would call
"handsome" in the usual sense, what with his slightly splotchy face
and the gawky way he bobs his head with each step, rather like a very
tall chicken strutting across the pen. All this makes her squirm
sometimes, and yet there is something else. A sensual quality. More:
Instinctively, without her having to say a word, he has understood
the game. Plays it with sophistication, a light but sure hand. This is
what holds her.

Yet she knows it will not be wise to let it get out of hand, to
develop any expectations out of their encounters. And so, Cousin
Eng's farm will be helpful and timely. No romantic notions will
brew in a place that stinks of pig swill and turd.

Cynthia smiles to herself. She is almost looking forward to the
farm despite its inconveniences. She has pushed for it so hard pre-
cisely for this reason. Almost another form of degradation. How
apt. How deserving.

General Sir Archibald Wavell knows there will be trouble with
Major-General Gordon Bennett. The Australian general is too
cocky and too slippery for his liking. None of the British generals,
save Barstow, can stand Bennett. "Let the Japs come," the wiry Aussie
says to the barrage of reporters who surround him, enamoured as
they are of his picturesque frame. "They'll soon know my name and
we'll give the little fellows a flogging they won't forget!" This attitude
has trickled down to his men and it is getting tiresome to see the
Aussies in the mess halls, strutting and puffing themselves up.

In tactical meetings, Bennett has only one game plan: Ambush.
"If it were up to Bennett, we'd be setting up ambushes along our
entire front," the British soldiers say amongst themselves. There is
something distasteful about an ambush, a sense of deception and
abandonment of fair play; but it is the lack of imagination in Ben-

nett's strategies that offends them most—in such matters, he is not a man of sophistication. Bennett, however, dodges criticism well and is hard to pin down on specifics. This is Wavell's worry. Vulgar boasting aside, this is a man who cannot be trusted, and Wavell is badly in need of real leaders.

✺

They sit in the half-dug trenches, looking at their hands or just staring at the mud banks. There is an emptiness in their eyes that is relieved only occasionally, when someone randomly starts singing an old pub song, or when they fill their mess tins with boiled rice and lick them clean. The heaviness of the jungle air weighs on them all. It's like snow, Lieutenant-Colonel Cecil Deakin thinks. When the powdery substance covers the earth it has a deadening, dampening effect like this, a muted, muffled listlessness. But at least there's a rousing quality to the bracing cold that comes with snow. Here the heat melts the men like candles and they only want to sit and sit.

In three short, monsoon-driven weeks, the British troops have marched 176 miles. Their rest period: a total of three days. It is a lot to ask of them, many of them barely trained and under-armed. Colonel Deakin's lips twist in frustration as he recalls General A. E. Percival's latest message to the front: "I believe that our young and inexperienced troops are now getting their second wind," Percival wrote.

Speaking of wind, Colonel Deakin decides, the General himself has got altogether too much of it.

✺

It's not a matter of finding out the truth; it's a matter of finding out the lie. All versions are true except one. Has it never occurred to him, this baritone in his imperial uniform and samurai sword, that truth is vague? The truth has countless permutations. The lie, on the other hand, if correctly told, is specific, clearly defined, embedded with details and incidentals. Any good Fifth Columnist should know this.

Ling-li knows if she relaxes that spot between her shoulder blades, if she lets it go and allows herself to hunch, if she gives in, she will wilt. So she grits her teeth, sucks in her breath feeling the air cool her gums and thrusts her chest forward, her back lamppost-straight. The afternoon heat has turned swampish, the taste of sweaty brine in the air, shadows like mangrove roots tangled and gnarled. Even the birdsongs have dampened in the humid wind; they hang low and soggy, the crispness soaked out of them.

You're a bloody *kayu*, that's what you are, she tells herself and then is surprised that she is thinking in English. Probably because she is here to meet a group of Englishmen; her mind and tongue are already anticipating the encounter.

But maybe they won't show, she thinks, scanning the rim of jungle from her spot under a dancing corps of coconut trees. *Wisha-wisha-wisha*, the long fronds frisk, *washa-washa-washa*, the furrowed sea worries. She twists her head one more time and there they are, four figures in front, two behind, sidestepping jungle creepers and prickly nasties to make their way to her.

She waves, even though there is no need. They are aimed at her and come flying. Her pores lay glistening eggs of sweat at her nape. When she moves they crack and the runny yolks slide down her back.

They'd be crazy, she thinks, to attempt an escape in this heat.

"You're the one," says the tall, furry man in the front when he reaches her. "What was it—*Selamat Datang ke Singapura*? Something like that."

Clumsy, clumsy, she thinks. What if I wasn't the one? Aloud she says, "*Huan ying, huan ying.*" Her bit part. They acknowledge with hellos. Only the two in the back bow. They are Chinese.

"Well, shall we get going?" says the furry man. He shields his eyes and looks out to sea. "I don't see our boat."

"Good," she says. "Then maybe no one else will." To the Chinese in the back she exchanges brief greetings in Mandarin. "Don't trust anyone," she tells them.

The bespectacled one smiles. "Right," is all he says. The other wags his goatee at her.

She leads them through the edge of the jungle keeping out of the shark-toothed bite of the sun. The Englishmen pant. No-one in uniform, she notes. The cowards. "What did you expect?" the bespectacled one says. "One would hardly expect them to desert in full uniform."

A little ahead, the call of seagulls and the land angles upwards. The men look startled; she herds them on. Beyond the slight rise, a hut and more men waiting, still crying like seagulls. "We're here," she says in Malay, annoyed. "We can see you." The brown-skinned gulls, all three of them, start speaking at once. "*Nanti, nanti,*" she tells them. "One at a time."

"We're a boat short," says the first one. He wears a singlet and wields a *parang,* which the Englishmen eye warily. "The last group never came back."

"Can't you squeeze them in two boats then?"

"Too heavy," mopes the second Malay. "They're big fellows. Unless, of course, they want to row."

"What's going on?" demands the furry Englishman. "What's the fuss?"

She explains. He looks at the Chinese men. "Don't even think of it," she tells him. "One of them for every two of you. Otherwise, no go." She gives the bespectacled man a warning look. He understands English but doesn't speak it.

"I have a gun," he says calmly in Mandarin, sweeping his gaze from left to right and taking in a gulp of sea air. To the English he looks as if he is admiring the scenery.

"How many can each boat take?" she asks in Malay.

"Three. Four *small* ones."

"Let them do their own rowing. We'll only need one of you as a guide." She asks which one is the best navigator.

The second Malay has a pigeon brain, is apparently faultless with maps, but she decides that the first one would be better at enforcing law and order, especially with the *parang* dangling by his side, its blade black and efficient. She tells the Englishmen and they look at their white hands. "How far is it?" one asks.

"Not a mile," she improvises. "It shouldn't be too bad." It is tiring switching among all these languages. Her tongue gropes at sounds while her brain spins. "Better eat now while you've time," she advises as her brain goes *make hay while the sun shines, gather ye rosebuds, time and tide wait for no man*. Shut up, she tells it. "You'll need it for the rowing," she adds unnecessarily. The Malay men bring out packets wrapped in banana leaves. The fragrant coconut rice and the fried anchovies inside trigger something in everyone and each man falls to eating in silence. Afterwards they drink greedily from green coconuts, waiting for the sun to dip.

When it is dark they move to the boats, hidden under thick brush. The three Malay men lift the boats over their heads, aided by the man with the goatee who says to his colleague before he helps out, "Just keep your hands free for the gun."

None of the Englishmen even offers to help. They stand about, accustomed to being served. Can't even scratch their own bums if their lives depended on it, she thinks.

She wonders what language she is thinking in.

They reach the beach and high tide. There is a soft, unexpected pattering of rain. "Shit," says the furry Englishman. The others bleat in dismay like sick sheep. "Tell them it's easier to row this way," says the man with the *parang*. "It'll be cooler, don't they know?"

She relays the information in English. "Near Batam Island, your boat will be waiting," she adds. "No-one will take you aboard without these two."

"We know, we know," one of the English grumbles. "We've got to get your nasty informers off to safety. Do we bloody well have to row them all the way to China?"

There is a sea-lapping silence. The little rowboats bob and waves smack at rocks. "Our people," she says affably in a while, "—*our nasty informers*—work for your even nastier intelligence unit, or don't you remember? They work on *our* side—unlike your Captain Heenan, may I remind you—and now they've been officially ordered to leave the island. It's odd that two Chinese agents would need *four* British Army escorts, but how convenient for you, isn't it, that you've been asked to see them to safety? Such a noble alternative to just plain ugly desertion!"

"All right, all right," says the furry man. "Let's get a move on, shall we?"

They clamber into the boats unsteadily like old ladies, and organ-ise the rowers. The two Chinese men huddle together in one boat with the Malay navigator and the smallest Englishman, who pulls up his legs like a jockey. In the other boat the remaining three English-men knock knees and elbows, fold gangly limbs into smaller units. "Big, aren't they?" says one of the Malay contacts, enjoying the show.

"They'll slow everything up," the navigator warns from his boat.

"Well," says Ling-li brightly. "You just worry about your cargo. That lot doesn't matter. Come what may, you get the two Chinese ones to the big boat."

"What are you talking about?" the jockey asks, suspicious.

"Priorities," says Ling-li. "Oi, you lot! It'll be daybreak by the time you get ready! Start rowing!"

The two remaining Malay men push. Oars dip and rise; the boats wobble and then set off, coasting the ridge-backed sea. The three on shore watch, their knees shiny with grains of sand. The rain strengthens, flattening their hair. They start running until they reach the thick lip of foliage and then disappear into the jungle.

✦

PERSONAL
Lt. Gen. A. E. Percival, GOC Malaya Cmd. To Gen. Sir Archibald
Wavell, Supreme Cmdr. ABDA
12th January, 1942

Am NOT repeat NOT happy about the state of morale of some Indian units. Believe Garhwalis and Dogras will continue to fight but some others doubtful. On 10 January two coys 2/9th Jats surren-dered without fighting. Believe trouble due to enemy propaganda working on fertile ground resulting from excessive fatigue and enemy complete command of air.

✦

The beast was tawny, its mane matted from the rain and flattened against its skull. They could see its small ear flaps pricked and twitching. It had a bald patch on its back where mould flourished, and its tail hung lifelessly, not even bothering to swat the flies near its haunches. A forlorn creature, not fit for hunting—if it had been killed, there would have been nothing to boast of.

"Shoo!" said Sang Nila, irritated at the distraction. The animal sprang into the rushes next to the rain-loud river. They watched it struggle against the current as it made its way to the other side. Several times its head submerged and it was carried downstream, but each time, it fought back, choking and grunting. When it finally climbed out of the water it had strength enough only to flop on the muddy bank and gasp for air. After a few minutes, it managed to shake itself dry and run off into the jungle scrub.

"Well, you lot! You'd better come up with a good story for my father of how we wrecked his ship and tossed all his furniture and gold overboard—not to mention my crown!" Sang Nila shook off the women who were trying to dry him and paced before his men. "How long will it take to repair the ship?"

"A week at best before we can sail again, especially as we're without any proper tools," his captain ventured.

"Ho! Now *you* explain that to my father! Tell him why we went missing for a whole week!" The prince stamped his foot, but all he managed on the wet ground was a squishy splat, nothing impressive.

"I have an idea, Your Highness," the elder said, taking in the surroundings. "You know how he says you should play a more active role in the affairs of the kingdom"—*and less in the affairs of the heart* was the second part of the king's complaint, but no-one chose to remind the prince of that now. "Maybe we could convince him that you were doing just that on your trip. You know—on official business and all that."

"Right! And when he demands to know what kind of official business—'sign a peace treaty, son? collected taxes?'—what do we say then?"

"We say you founded a city!"

A pause in which everyone took a good look around. Swamp, jungle, mosquitoes, leeches. No city in sight.

"A mighty creature appeared before you and commanded you to name this place after it. Singa-pura, the Lion City," the old man said spreading out his arms. "From this place will spring forth a mighty port."

Sang Nila pinched his nose as he thought about this. Outrageous enough to be true. Dramatic enough to hold interest. Seeded with myth and prophecy.

He laughed as he imagined himself telling it to his father. "It has the makings," he conceded, "of a good story."

From the peninsular side of the Causeway, the island looks less like an impregnable fortress than an idyllic location for much-needed R and R, but the Gordon Highlanders, following on the heels of 3rd Indian Corps, know that there will no such relief after their crossing. Still, it is stirring to hear the two remaining Argyll Pipers sound the drone, dressed in their regalia kilts and resolute in the glare of sun and sea. It's a funny thing with bagpipes, how they can be jaunty and teasing in their nasal songs and yet catch at the heart and set off an indescribable yearning that can bring the most seasoned soldier to tears.

And then they are over, blinking at the strangeness of having crossed a border without really having gone anywhere, the waves of bagpipe music drifting behind them in the wind. It is the turn of the 2nd Battalion Argyll and Sutherland Highlanders, the hardiest of them all. Throughout the fifty-four-day retreat they have protected the army's flanks, prepared to fight to the death in their uncomplaining and spirited way. Their pipers swell their bags, joining the tail end of the retreating column, their commander and his batman taking the rear. They have been let down by their leaders, and they know it, but there is no trace of bitterness in their march.

The sappers have already placed their charges and wait quietly on the narrow, rocky beach. The signal. A boom that isn't as loud as expected, and the Causeway caves in. The jagged edge of the pipeline from the mainland spills precious freshwater into the briny sea. They will have to rely on the reservoirs from now on.

A mile away, a young woman watches, her thin arms wrapped around her body as if to hold in the tingle of fear that has begun to spread from her stomach. Not even her sources have warned her of this and she knows that the tenuous line of communication is fraying. She has not heard from Hayley Bell for days. Soon she will be on her own.

They are tired of toying with him. A pair of hands, large enough to comfortably encircle his throat, chokes the breath from him.

—I'd like to turn in for the day, the baritone says wearily. Once and for all—his tone sharpens—tell me about this Ling-li, your friendship with the Englishman, Jack Winchester. How did he know the girl?

They do nothing even when he remains stubbornly silent. They are bored.

—Come now, we know about the girl, we have other means. But the Englishman . . . what was he to her? What has he told you?

Since the Body is silent, you force yourself to think quickly. What *was* he to her? As far as you know, there is nothing to incriminate him in your story. No, they have made a mistake in believing him to be anything more than an English civilian who stayed on during the war. The only danger he posed was to himself and to the British Empire, for it was in his company that the Body has come to question so many things. That and Ling-li, of course. But you shall try to steer away from her. You make a sound to get their attention and a groan emerges from the Body.

—What is it? the baritone barks.

—He needed a place to stay, you tell them. He was left behind.

And, as if held back for too long, the story gushes out, and you are helpless and too tired to restrain it.

F
O
U
R

Civilians

THE WORLD IS CHANGING. Everywhere the sky is the colour of gunpowder, the sun vague and distant, as if it has already forgotten the earth and is withdrawing into its own core.

Even though he knows he shouldn't, Claude heads for the river. It is an instinct, nothing more than the insistent blood of a young hounded animal returning to its watering-hole for some reassurance, for the lullaby of waters. Staring at the water rests his eyes, the muted blue-green-brown with its quiet shimmers snaking into sun-constricted pupils the size of grape seeds and leaving its cool waves on the retina.

Fire spills into the wind so that when its draughty breath reaches him it is hot, oily from the burning harbour, festering. When he's not careful and walks too close to the fires this hot air squeezes his throat and he chokes; he should know better than to walk into the wind. At least cover his nose and mouth with a damp handkerchief. At least try to angle his face away from the smoke. At least take shallow breaths. He should know better. People walk by in a daze, the older and weaker ones coughing, clutching bundles, calling out names, dashing back into the flames to retrieve something, someone, to give up eventually, and find rest. But *he* should know better. This is not a time for walks by the river, for seeking the wide curve of the Esplanade. Escapes of this kind are irresponsible and foolish in such times.

But he is, he tells himself, irresponsible and foolish even in the best of times, so at least he is consistent in this period of great change, as bombs explode and the atmosphere is ablaze with the alchemy of warfare; at least he lumbers on, dragging his feet, inert as xenon while the foul-tempered nitroglycerin ignites on the streets.

Xenon—inert, slow-moving. Perhaps these infinitesimally small steps he seems to be taking are enveloped in paradox, so that he will never get there. But that was Xeno. The absence of a letter opens the loop of impossibility. He will never get there.

The river. That's where.

Irresponsibly and foolishly headed to the river where he knows he should not go because this is goddamned War, not an evening stroll with his grandmother; but he persists in being consistent, which is why he is doing this, why he is now being stopped by a soldier, standing in his path with arms thrown wide, chest out, head tilted back, singing "Waltzing Matilda." True to form, Claude tells himself, he has walked right into the Australian Arms of Trouble.

"Halt," the soldier says, but he's also laughing hysterically, perhaps at the sky, at the bombers like ridiculous geese laying eggs. Golden eggs, flambé. Claude almost laughs himself.

To his amazement, the soldier holds out his rifle with both hands. "Here, take it." A king handing over his sceptre: *You silly little yellow man, take back your kingdom.*

Claude takes a step back. These days he's not too sure how to behave at all, of what to say to an Australian soldier, a *white* man, handing over his rifle.

The soldier's face is spotted with mud, leaves and resignation. The eye-whites fluoresce in his dirty face. He is unable to keep them still. They roll around in their sockets in a disconcerting way. He struggles to focus his gaze on Claude, and those marble eyes seem to be saying, It's your lousy piece of land, mate. Go shit or die on it if you want!

He makes a thrust with the rifle and when Claude jumps, the soldier swears in disgust.

Something rises up inside Claude, a powerful and hopelessly confused mixture of shame, guilt and anger spiked with pride. He swallows it down again from habit. But today some residue remains of that bilish taste. It comes from the strangeness all around, the fact that the dreamy, despairing people filtering by are white while the practical, busy ones scavenging the cindered debris are yellow, black, shades of cinnamon.

By now, the Australian has given up on Claude. Has thrown his rifle like a javelin onto a heap of rubbish and the remains of a shattered wall. Turns his attention to a colleague who has run up close behind, shod in slippers, uniform in tatters. A soldier in slippers! Claude struggles with the image. What kind of world is this coming to—? There must be some mistake. Never, in the old days . . . But it's too new yet to know.

The latest arrival flings his arms around the first soldier and holds out a voluptuous bottle, its curves a striking form of wholeness amidst the smashed glass and brokenness all around: a triumph of coherence in the Newly Forming World where everything else is coming into being or disintegrating into fragments, transitions; struggle. The wind shifts and Claude smells the soldier's alcohol breath mixed in with grease and sweat.

The first soldier manages to steady his hand around the smooth, glinting bottleneck and lifts it to his mouth, lip to bottle-lip; drinks.

Claude's bunched-up leg muscles uncoil and he springs like a racehorse at the gates, leaps over beams, cracked pipes, jagged windows, charred doors, melted locks. He can hear the Australians hooting with laughter, but keeps running—past the flaming shop houses, the burning death houses with their load of the almost-departed, past the disbelieving maimed, the collapsed tenements. He heads for the broad band at the horizon, the brushed-chrome water, its depths grey now, like everything else. He is running in a world distinguished only by shades of charcoal and light, by flat, dull surfaces or explosive shine, sparkle, *reflection*.

The Causeway still intact, awaiting its fate, Johore still the battle-ground. So many things yet to come. He is rounding the last bend of January 1942.

※

When Claude's family left for Cousin Eng's farm, the household staff disintegrated. Amah left for China two days later, after a simple but delicious meal with Claude, Muthu and Phatcharat, who had really outdone herself with the cooking. "This real Thai food," she had said when Claude praised her. "Now you know."

"What were we eating before?" he'd asked. He was lively that day, buoyed by the anticipation of taking charge as the man of the house.

"English-version Thai food." She giggled. "English-version Indian food, English-version Chinese food, English-version Malay food. All the same: very little spice, salty—look like food left out in the rain." She leaned back as if to get a better look at his face. "I thought you liked it like that."

He had. "Well, it *was* good, despite your description. It's just that Father can't have anything too spicy. But I think this is super! Now that he's not around, let's eat like this everyday."

She turned red and gazed into her bowl. Amah cleared her throat and they exchanged glances. Finally, Amah said, "Say now, Phatcharat."

The cook gave a small cough and a lop-sided smile. "Ah, Master Claude, how to tell you—I won't be working here no more." She put down her chopsticks and placed her hands carefully on her lap. "I go to Indonesia tomorrow night. I have one auntie there—very old. I go to take care of her."

Perhaps Claude had expected this, for he found himself calmly reviewing his cooking skills at Phatcharat's news: Let's see, he could—boil water, yes; fry an egg, yes; make scrambled eggs, yes;

poach eggs, yes; boil eggs, of course; and then there's French toast, yes . . .

"Does—does Father know this?" he asked.

Phatcharat shook her head. "No, I decide today, when I talk to Amah. At first I thought go to Thailand, but they not selling tickets to Thailand because of war, so I go to nearest family. I come back when everything okay, when British win, like your father say."

"Well, good luck then, Phatcharat," he said. "What will you do in Indonesia?"

"Find job in restaurant, or maybe with another family. I know how to make Western food now, you know."

"Or you could make English-version Thai food," he said and they all laughed. "What about you, Muthu? You going anywhere?"

"I'm not intending it, you know, but I've closed up the Tam house and sent along the trunks, and paid off the other servants. There's nothing left for me to do, so I'll move back into my parents' house in Pasir Panjang, for now." He drummed the table-top. "Looks like you all alone, bugger."

"Maybe you come check every week, Muthu," said Amah. "Make sure everything okay."

"I'll be fine, Amah. I can take care of myself. Besides, Father doesn't think the war will go on for very long. Something about reinforcements."

"What about food?" Phatcharat asked.

"I can cook. Eggs, soup, that kind of thing."

"You eat at coffee shop around Sixth Avenue. I know the owner, I tell him to give you good food."

"Thank you, Phatcharat. I'll check it out," Claude assured her. "Meanwhile, a toast!"

"Toast? I don't think it goes well with Thai food," said Phatcharat. She stood up. "But it's my last night. You want toast, I make it."

"No, no, no—I meant this kind of toast—" He raised his glass to her. "*Salut,* that kind of thing."

"*Yum Sing,* Phatcharat, he means *yum sing,*" said Amah, and she raised her glass as well.

The next day they were gone. In their absence, the house was disconcertingly quiet, as if its engine, its core, had been shut off. The mechanical hum that accompanied their efficient housekeeping gave way to the creak of floorboards and the dismal cawing of crows outside.

✿

For a week Claude entertained himself by calling forth his entire egg repertory for breakfast, as well as exhausting his toast-making abilities and his skill at dripping patterns on the warm bread with inky flows of Bovril. Without Muthu to drive him, he had to get up earlier and walk ten minutes to the nearest bus stop to catch the seven o'clock bus to school. He enjoyed a window seat with the cool morning breeze in his face and the exhilarating freedom of doing something entirely on his own.

School itself was half-hearted those days, with the masters and boys gathered eagerly around radio sets between classes to catch the latest news. It always sounded promising. According to the reports, the Japanese were being taught a harsh lesson at the front and would surrender any day now, once they were willing to concede to the awesome and vastly superior force of the British Empire. The glories of Oxford and Cambridge paled beside the heroic romance of Sandhurst. Boys contemplated military careers and joined the band because its marching practise was the closest they could come to military drills. They played field hockey with combative fervour in PE classes, and obstacle courses had never been so popular in the history of the school. Academic interest waned. In the face of peer pressure, Claude passed over Ensemble Practise for the Fire-Fighting Service set up by Mr. Caruthers, the Third Form chemistry master.

This ended up being mostly talk, but as Claude listened to the excited whispers of the other boys, his interest was piqued. Then, when he was presented with the tin helmet that felt like an inverted rice bowl on his head and the fiery red armband denoting his unit, he began to feel less enthusiastic. Nonetheless he'd already signed on, so there was nothing to do but make the best of it. The worst part was knowing that he looked, well, gangly, awkward and ridiculous in his uniform. As Hamzar, a classmate, said, reminding

Claude of Cynthia, "This is so—China." He pronounced it the Malay way: *Chee-nah*.

Claude knew immediately, of course, what he meant. The Chinese-educated and the illiterate had about them a common touch, exemplified by the way they spoke, the way they dressed, their Chinamen haircuts that turned their heads into moon-faced globes, the fringes straight across their foreheads that heightened their dull, coarse looks. That same immigrant, just-off-the-boat look that every Ah Kow from southern China sported throughout the colony, and that his father deplored. Claude tried taking off the helmet, but Mr. Caruthers would not hear of it. "Protective gear. Mandatory, I'm afraid." He wore one himself, but on his crop of red hair it somehow managed to pass as a faintly military-looking piece of equipment.

Practise sessions occurred daily after school, for two hours at a time, and even then it was mostly verbal review for the first hour. Mr. Caruthers held forth on various forms of fire: oil fires, gas fires, wood fires, alcohol-based fires, electric fires, even the properties of lava! (The chemistry teacher couldn't seem to help throwing in that useless piece of information.) How to assess the effects of wind, smoke damage to the lungs. First aid. He discussed the explosive qualities of various chemical mixtures, calculated the amount of heat produced in their combustion and generally produced a unit that would do far better on the Standard Certificate Chemistry exam than in putting out a real fire. For a while Claude secretly considered joining the Medical Unit, whose members looked impressively busy running about with their first-aid kits and immobilizing limbs with tree branches, but the thought of dealing with real blood made him queasy and thankful, in the end, for the Fire-Fighting Service.

The didactic sessions over, Mr. Caruthers had everyone line up in full uniform on the school field. The boys practised, in pairs, how to rescue people from burning buildings, to roll each other on the ground and stamp out flames, practised crawling on their bellies to avoid smoke inhalation, mouth-to-mouth resuscitation (most unpopular with everyone, but Mr. Caruthers was insistent). Later they moved to handling the pumps, how to aim and hold the hoses steady, taking into account the wind again, of course.

Claude walked home after Mr. Caruthers let everyone go, doggedly putting one foot in front of the other while the sun cooked him in his skin. It began that first day on his own, when he decided to walk instead of getting into the crowded afternoon bus. Once the decision was made, he carried it out mindlessly, trudging down dusty paths beside the road, sometimes hopping over small, clogged drains and patches of mud. Sweat welled out of his pores, his black hair crisped, the bottoms of his feet rubbed against the insoles like matchsticks striking stone.

By the time he reached home, he was dizzy with heatstroke and limp as licorice. It took him a long time and many glasses of water to recover. At night, in bed, his calves ached and he fell asleep almost at once, swearing to take the bus home the next day. And yet, when the time came, he couldn't make himself get on that bus, with its load of sweaty, grim-faced labourers, garlicky amahs and evil-breathed old men, their rotting teeth on display. He shook his head at the driver and started walking.

On the third day, somewhat more used to the sun, he paid closer attention to his companions on the road. Going in the opposite direction—towards town—was a constant trickle of men, women, children clutching makeshift bundles, assorted packages wrapped in cloth or newspapers, furniture scraps and small sacks of rice. Groups of uniformed white men wandered dispiritedly among them. Their behaviour was strange. At times they provoked one of the natives with a prod of their rifle butts, or screamed expletives at each other, simultaneously howling with hysterical laughter.

Sometimes there were one or two soldiers on Claude's side of the road and he scurried by, keeping his head low but not missing the unmistakable scent of alcohol emanating from them. On and on he walked, pushing himself till his legs cramped in protest, and even then, he slapped his thighs briskly in a kind of self-flagellation and continued.

It became a habit.

A quarter past noon. A quarter past the time his plane would have taken off, carrying him and the other passengers towards India and,

from there, ever westward back to England. Instead Jack was sitting
at a local coffee shop, a plate of fried noodles before him and a bottle of beer in hand. And reading:

> Something turned over in Flory's heart. It was one of those
> moments when one becomes conscious of a vast change and deteri-
> oration in one's life. For he had realised, suddenly, that in his heart
> he was glad to be coming back. This country which he hated was now
> his native country, his home. He had lived here ten years, and every
> particle of his body was compounded of Burmese soil. Scenes like
> these—the sallow evening light, the old Indian cropping grass, the
> creak of the cartwheels, the streaming egrets—were more native to
> him than England. He had sent out deep roots, perhaps his deepest,
> into a foreign country.

When Jack Winchester appeared at the Lims' front gate, suitcase
in hand, it was late in the day, almost absolute dark. Since the war,
most families in the neighbourhood had left their homes to stay with
relatives or to live, like the Tams, in their other homes in Australia.
There were hardly any lights on in the deserted houses and the street
lamps had been shut off.

Jack's whiteness made him easy to spot in the darkness outside the
living room windows. Even his white shirt looked grey next to the
paleness of his skin as he stood leaning against the gatepost. "Hello,"
he said when Claude went out to unlock the gate. "I say, is there any
room at the inn?"

"I thought you'd left by now," Claude said, trying to insert the key
into the padlock by feel. "What happened?"

"Oh, my little plane ride didn't materialise after all," he said
nonchalantly. "My friend kept postponing it until I finally realised
it probably wasn't going to happen at all. I was going to get a boat
ticket and then I thought—this isn't going to go on for too long now.
Why not just stay put and enjoy the fireworks? I mean, it isn't as if
London isn't getting its fair share of bombs too. At least we'll soon
have things in hand here and get on with our lives." He slipped
through the gate as Claude swung it open in an arc. "And I can laugh

when poor George and Janet reach England only to have to board the next boat back here!"

Claude looked dubiously at Jack's suitcase and couldn't help wondering why the Englishman had to stay here, why he couldn't have stayed on his own at his brother's house. He was reluctant to have his newly won independence disturbed.

"Ah yes," Jack said, following Claude's gaze. "There was a hitch, you see. My flat was re-assigned to another family, so I thought at first I'd just stay at George's place, but that house belongs to his firm, and they've taken it back since his departure. They're actually using it as a makeshift office so the workers can avoid going into Shenton Way where they're much closer to the bombing. So you see"—he tilted his head slightly—"I came to find out if your family could put me up in the meanwhile."

"What about your—other friends?" Claude asked. Surely he must have English friends he could stay with.

He gave an embarrassed laugh. "Oh, I don't know." He coughed and gazed past Claude towards the solid shadows of the house. "I rang earlier but no-one answered. Is everyone out?"

"They're staying at a relative's farm in Punggol."

"Ah yes, the farm," he said with a knowing nod. "I hope I'm not bothering you. I rather consider you a—good friend, which is why I came, you see."

Now it was Claude's turn to be embarrassed at his own rudeness and lack of hospitality. Jack had come in good faith and Claude had only greeted him with blunt questions, and a grudge against him for intruding upon his eked-out little kingdom. "They're just taking precautions, what with the bombing and all," Claude said. "I'm the only one here right now, so there's plenty of room."

Jack followed him into the house without comment. In the living room Claude offered him the tea and hard-boiled eggs he had prepared for himself. Jack ate ravenously and Claude had to go back into the kitchen to boil more eggs and make toast, frowning a little at the problem of food. Two days ago he had tried to buy some groceries at the sundry store on Sixth Avenue where Phatcharat and Amah had shopped, and the selection at the usually overstocked place was discouraging. Furthermore, the shopkeeper had been reluctant to accept money. "Gold—you have gold?" he'd asked. Claude had finally managed to persuade him to accept his money by invoking the names of Phatcharat and Amah, and even then the shopkeeper had said firmly, "I do this only one time. Next time no more—just gold, okay?"

Claude pushed the worry out of his mind for now. There were plenty of stores downtown, and he could check them out with Jack after school the next day. But when Jack heard this, he shook his head.

"Actually, I've had the same problem myself. There's a food shortage in the city. We've got to stock up before it gets worse."

"But what if they ask for gold? I haven't any gold on me—it's quite ridiculous!"

"Well, we'd better come up with some." He dug into his pocket and produced a pair of gold cuff-links. "We could start with these."

"Mother's taken all the jewellery with her, though Father may have some gold cuff-links himself. I'm sure I've seen a pair. I don't feel right going through his things . . ."

"As I said, we'll start with these and see how far we get." Jack shrugged easily. "By the way, your, um, boiled eggs are pretty good. I'm glad one of us knows how to cook."

Claude forced a smile, wondering if he was being teased. Then, smelling burning toast, he ran to the kitchen to rescue the precious bread.

Those first few nights Claude was poised and gracious, his sense of etiquette carefully preserved and self-evaluated: Had Jack been fed enough? Was he thirsty? Had Claude been sympathetic to the inconveniences Jack had faced in being forced to move out of his old quarters? Perhaps the move shouldn't have been mentioned at all. Jack had looked rather uncomfortable at the subject. Perhaps it was too hot and Claude should have turned on the fans.

By the end of the week there were soldiers going by the house everyday—unkempt, alcohol-drenched, surly—and Claude's self-consciousness abated a little, what with the new crisis. The soldiers rattled the front gate and pitched rocks and garbage at the roofline and the shuttered windows. "Chinks," the Australians yelled, not even in formation as they trudged by. From the start Claude had heard rumours at school of their unruliness, their inability to control their sense of entitlement. One day, one of them fired a round of bullets at the teak front door. What affected Claude most was the way the shots cut into the wood, wounding its sturdy surface, the way its dark, resolute grain was marred by the bullet tracks. That was when he decided to move.

"But where will we go?" asked Jack, his voice cracking. By now he was succumbing—most inconveniently, Claude couldn't help thinking—to some kind of tropical dysentery. It began mildly with nausea and vomiting, an evening fever, but it was enough to wear him down.

"I've thought about it. Amah had a hut in Serangoon Road. It belonged to her and a woman who became her sworn sister when she first moved to Singapore. Amah moved out when she came to live with us, but she took me there once or twice to visit Auntie Yeo—that was her sworn sister's name—and then when Auntie Yeo died last year, Amah inherited the place. Sometimes she would go there and spend the night, I suppose to get away from us all."

"So you think that's where we should go." Although it was a statement, Jack managed to infuse it with doubt.

"I know it's only a hut, but it's really not too bad. After school yesterday, I saw many more convoys along Bukit Timah Road, and people beyond Seventh Mile have had to evacuate, so I think it's only a matter of time before we're asked to move. In a few days we could try to go to Cousin Eng's farm, but I'll have to arrange for a car somehow. Anyway, it might be best for you to rest for now."

Jack wasn't any help with the packing. Claude organised the remaining food supplies and bedding while his guest spent the time in the toilet, groaning away. Claude surveyed the house, stopping to check if the drawers in his parents' room were locked, picking up a jade comb on Grandma Siok's dressing table and slipping it into his pocket, gathering some extra clothes. He emptied his school satchel and stuffed it with clothes and sheets. He found Amah's rattan baskets and filled them with food supplies—stale bread, bananas, a dozen eggs, some dried noodles, preserved Chinese sausages, a few cans of condensed milk and several sweet potatoes. He tied up the small sack of rice left in the house and placed it next to the baskets. That night Claude made toast and finished up the butter by spreading it liberally over the bread. To his relief, Jack ate it without complaint, and even shared a banana for dessert.

The next morning, Claude carried Jack's suitcase out to the waiting scooter he had secured, the only transportation he could manage on such short notice. Then he slung his satchel across his chest, took up a basket in each hand and, with the sack of rice tied to his waist, got into the sidecar, ensuring first that the doors and front gate of the house were firmly locked. Jack had thrown up his breakfast of plain toast and banana and was looking grey, slumped in his corner and clutching the satchel with sweaty fingers. "You all right?" Claude asked, knowing it was a stupid question.

Jack grunted in response, shaking his head, his face the colour of pasty dough. The scooter driver slowed down for bumps in the road and tried to keep in the shade of trees, but Jack only seemed to get worse. At Amah's hut that afternoon, Claude had to prop him up on a chair next to the outhouse.

The next day Claude went to school, not because there was even a semblance of classes left, but because he needed help, because Jack needed help. The headmaster, Mr. Hawthorne, listened to Claude's dilemma. "Oh, you've got to get a GP round to see him. What about your own doctor?" he asked. "Surely he'd come around."

"I rang him from a coffee shop last night but there was no answer."

"Well, I do know someone, as a matter of fact, a local chap. He was a Littleton boy himself, six years ago. He trained in Belfast and has been back for a few months now." Mr. Hawthorne flipped through a book on his desk. "Let—me—see— Hello, here we are. Right! I'll get Kim Siong to go out there with you," he said, picking up the phone. "I'm sure he won't refuse."

Maybe not, but Kim Siong had not looked too happy when Claude met him, as arranged, at the Odeon Theatre. "Where are you staying?" he asked once Claude had identified himself. "All the way out there!" Claude reassured him that he would pay for his travel by taxi. At this, Kim Siong sullenly agreed and planted himself in the far end of the cab, only grunting at Claude's attempts at conversation.

Nonetheless, a remarkable transformation came over Kim Siong when he reached Amah's shack and was introduced to Jack, still propped up beside the outhouse, a sheet wrapped around him and a bottle of water cradled between his thighs. The bottle was almost empty, Claude noted with satisfaction. "This is Dr. Tan," he said.

Kim Siong sprang to life, the soul of compassion. He grasped Jack's hand and re-introduced himself. He made Jack tell him all about his symptoms even though Claude had already enlightened him in the taxi. He asked Claude to re-fill the water bottle, then removed the sheet, took Jack's temperature, declared he needed to have his forehead cooled with a compress, gave Jack a tablet of Paracetamol to swallow right there and then. All this in a solicitous voice, his accent more prominent than before.

Afterwards Claude headed off to the nearest dispensary to fill Jack's prescription. And he pressed cool compresses to the Englishman's forehead, tipped the thick bismuth solution Kim Siong had ordered into his mouth, made him soup even, which he drank reluctantly.

In three days the diarrhoea subsided but he was still weak and febrile. "Probably viral," Kim Siong said with a shrug. When he was not in the presence of Europeans he was curt, spitting out his words in staccato, almost a sing-song quality to his tone. At those times, his English sounded, to Claude's ears, almost Chinese.

Now, a week after the doctor's house call, Jack still has a fever. Claude has not seen Kim Siong in three or four days. Someone—a Littleton boy he meets on the street one day—mentions that the doctor has left for Indonesia, hoping to go on to Australia from there. Actually, aside from the Australians, many others are trying to get to Australia.

Claude enters the hut quietly after his walk by the river, endures the silent explosion of light before his eyes—an internal bomb going off—and is initiated into the world of the bat. His eyes adjust quickly, but his ears place everything first according to the rub of sweaty sheets, the cracking of bones as a hip turns out, the sibilant scratching of mosquito bites behind knees.

The ceiling fan whirrs busily, chopping up the cobwebs strung by an industrious spider overnight. It is remarkable that there is still electricity here. Even though the shutters are closed as they were all night and when he left at dawn for his impulsive walk by the Esplanade, the inevitable leak of light spills through louvres and the space under the door. His eyes search out the cot in the far corner, the lanky shape swathed in sheets despite the swelling heat.

"You were gone for a long time," says the shape as it emerges from its white cotton cocoon, a pair of hairy feet at one end and a balding head at the other. "For a moment I thought that I would never see you again."

"That I might be dead?" Claude asks, moving closer.

"That you'd left." Jack swings his legs over the side and places his feet on the floor. "I'm thirsty."

Claude pours from the pitcher on the bookshelf beside the cot. The shelves are filled with canned food, tiffin carriers, mugs, several plates, a small sack of uncooked rice, a huddle of potatoes, nubbly and shooting buds. There is a small figurine of a laughing Buddha next to a doll-sized porcelain Kuan-Yin, the goddess of mercy, and Buddhist prayer beads that Amah left behind, so that the whole tableau assumes the air of an altar. Divine protection against famine. Superstitious locals.

Jack makes gulping grunts as he drinks. Unintentionally—Claude tells himself—only because he is drinking so quickly; the fever's dried him up. Usually, the English are fastidious about suppressing bodily noises and odours, but one has to take the situation into account. Claude finds the bread on the bottom shelf, carefully wrapped to ward off the ants. Next to it is the jar of condensed milk that he dribbles onto a slice of bread, making loopy designs on the white centre. He hands Jack the bread on a plate, pours him another glass of water and goes to sit in the middle of the room directly under the ceiling fan. Its wobbling makes him wonder if it will fall on him one day.

"What's happening out there?" Jack's voice is doughy with bread.

"Same thing. We're losing the war." Why did Jack think Claude had left him to fend for himself? What kind of person did he think Claude was?

"They're not saying that on the radio." Jack squints as he speaks because his spectacles are somewhere on the altar and he can't see well enough to find them. "What have they hit today?"

"They're still aiming at the harbour. They've knocked off large portions of Chinatown." Claude waits until Jack has swallowed. "The Australians are deserting."

Jack's mouth remains open. "That's a serious charge. What exactly do you mean by that?"

"Running away from battle, escaping, turning tail, fleeing, abandoning ship. In place of military manoeuvres they are looting, drinking and creating havoc on the streets."

Jack thinks about this, chewing on his bread and drinking absently from the glass. "Well," he concludes at last, "I never trusted those Australians. A rowdy bunch, no discipline at all."

"There are English deserters as well," Claude says. Jack stops eating. "It's understandable, I suppose. They probably don't feel it's got anything to do with them," Claude continues, remembering the Australian's red-veined eyes near the Esplanade. "They're not fighting for their families and loved ones." Meaning fellow whites. "Not out here anyway."

"But deserters! Where's their sense of decency?"

Ah yes, the famous English decency. Is being English a prerequisite for decency? Despite the fan, Claude is still sweating. He doesn't understand his own agitation. "Melted away in the tropical heat, no doubt," he adds, an unfamiliar edge of sarcasm in his voice.

Jack ignores him, puts the plate down on the floor and swings his legs up onto the bed once more. The fever is back and he is shivering. "Please turn the fan off."

Reluctantly Claude gets up, flips the switch that immediately slows the white blur on the ceiling so that soon individual blades are visible, even countable—one, two, three—and then splayed motionlessly above. When he looks down again, Jack is under his sheets, lumpy, prostrate, indefinite. Heat mounts in the dead air.

There lies the British Empire, Claude thinks, unable to take his eyes off the drenched, soggy shape on the cot, and he is suddenly amazed at all that has happened. It's as if dark glasses have been lifted from the perch on his nose and the real colours of the world are revealed to him for the first time, flat and unfiltered.

Later that day, in the dark of Amah's hut, as Jack tries without success to tune in to the news on the radio, Claude broaches the subject of his return to England. "I don't think I could get you a ticket on my own, but your brother's colleagues may be able to help."

Jack waves him away, sweat streaking his neck, his shoulders. "There've been riots at the harbour. I don't know people who are important enough to ensure me a passage back to England." He lights a match and holds it to the kerosene lamp by his bed. The wick flares as if infected by his fever.

"Someone at the bank, perhaps? Surely one of your brother's friends . . ." Claude's voice trails off at the Englishman's disinterest. Jack is fiddling with the radio again.

"Your servant. Your Amah. This is her place, isn't it?" For an instant, a wheezy melody drifts from the radio, only to be lost in a sea of harsh crackles. "Where is she now?"

"She went back to China, back to her village." Claude now wonders if she's safe. It saddens him to realise that he may never know.

"Surely there must be someone you can speak to. Your brother knew a lot of important people." Claude points out. "You're a British subject."

"So are you," Jack says quietly, his hands still on the radio dials.

Taken off-guard, Claude considers this. "Aren't you?" Jack presses. "Shouldn't you be equally entitled to a passage to England?"

Subject: the person or thing being discussed, the topic. From the *Oxford English Dictionary*, that definer of all things contained in and sanctioned by the Empire. The thought has not occurred to Claude and he is at a loss as to how to respond. Subject: a person under a particular political rule, a person owing obedience to another. Finally, aware that Jack is waiting, he says, "But I'm not English. A British subject indeed, but not English. There is a difference." Subject: to bring under one's control.

"What might that difference be?" Jack's hands are resting now on the top of the old radio. There is an edgy, almost agitated quality to his tone but it is still soft.

"Really, Jack, this isn't the type of thing you should be thinking of right now. You should be working out a plan to secure your passage out of Singapore." The dictionary plays on in Claude's head. Subject: (Philos.) the conscious self as opposed to all that is external to the mind.

"No, really, I want to know. What is the difference?" No such luck—Jack sticks to his question like glue. Claude considers his options: He could brush him off with a laugh, refusing to take him seriously; he could mention the obvious about the colonised vs. the colonisers; he could, perhaps, even mention the differences in their skin colour. None of those options feels comfortable to Claude, so he shakes his head with a little laugh, opens his mouth to say something, can't decide what to say, shuts it again.

But why shut it, after all? he asks himself. He has spent the last few days ministering to this man, sharing this room with him, has listened to him mumble in his dreams, has wrung out his sour-smelling, sweaty compresses. What is it that he can't say to Jack now, after all this?

Claude stands up, pretending he needs to go to the outhouse. It is only when he is outside, the night breeze wafting limply over him, that he realises he left Jack without another word, as he hugged the temperamental radio, the kerosene light carving out chunks of his face into shadow, a face composed of absence and light.

Is it night? Monsoon winds? Baboon cries in the wet trees? The creak of a branch as a slow loris ambles down its length, eyes wide from peering into the nocturnal jungle?

Claude the Body far below, sleeping, left alone with a small bowl of rice so little cooked that it is still crunchy. But he will eat it eagerly enough when he awakes, knowing it will be his only meal for the day. He has no illusions about the hospitality of the Japanese. Meanwhile, you are examining the ceiling with interest, noting the arterial cracks in the concrete. Funny how something that seems so solid and coherent as an all-white high ceiling, the fifth wall of a room, really, come to think of it, can be so prone to injury, to the caprices of a little heat and humidity.

Again, that animal sound from next door. You are drawn there, but you must not go. Must not look.

White, cracked ceiling.

The slow loris, *Bradicebus tardigradus,* of South Asia. A small lemur, without defences or a tail. Arboreal. Distinctive for its huge eyes. A creature that looks into the night. You must not look.

※

There are times when Claude thinks about her, the Squatter Girl. Mostly when he peers down a drain to take a piss, and examines the stagnant larvae-ridden water below. Is she living in some other wide drain on the outskirts of the city? Will the yellow drops of his urine flow around her ankles as the water level rises in the dawn passage of the Sumatras, the drenching monsoons?

She might have gotten married by now. Humphrey's favourite complaint is that the locals breed like rats. She might have her own Rat Mate by now, and a litter of swarming blind rodents. The image of them suckling at her dark nipples arouses Claude. Almost as much as the image of her making love—breeding, as his parents would say—with the blurry outlines of some unspecified male. Although sometimes he *is* specified; sometimes he is Claude.

Strangely enough, he cannot imagine the feel of her touch, the coarse grain of her work-roughened hands that he knows must exist. He can only see her above him, leaning forwards, hair loosened from her plaits and falling untidily over her face. The fascinating skin tag, that nub of extra skin glued to her left nipple, descends. He reaches up and tugs at it with his fingers and the rest of the skin on her breast pouches out with his pull. She winces.

"Sorry," Claude says.

She gives an indifferent shrug. "They all try that," she tells him. "It doesn't come off." It troubles you that there have been others, but then, of course, it's to be expected.

She reaches for him, but he pushes her hands back to herself. "Go on," he says. "Touch—yourself."

She screws up her face, not understanding. Her hands float out towards him again.

"No," he says, directing them back to her breasts. "There. Touch yourself. I like—to watch."

Now she understands. Her fingers draw circles on her chest, move lower. She pinches the skin tag, and the nipple blossoms. Her irregular teeth catch on her lower lip. A bead of saliva hangs in the corner of her mouth.

She allows him to watch everything, holds back nothing. But all the while, Claude realises, she is—carefully, deliberately, almost insolently—watching him back.

The baritone laughs. He too, it seems, has something he wants to share, a similar memory, he says. He removes a Western-style wallet from his pocket, handles the leather with care. Was it a gift? you wonder. Something given in parting by his wife, a sister, a grand-mother? The photograph he is pulling out from its inner sleeve— perhaps it's his mother?

—A postcard from China, he says, smiling, showing the photo-graph to Claude the Body as you hover over them for a look. It is a picture of him raping a girl, a child no more than fourteen. You see, I understand you. We are not so different after all, are we? Skin of the same colour, black hair, similar *preferences* . . . Should we not be working together for the same side?

You find it hard, despite your disgust, to take your eyes off the photograph. And then a gate unlatches, a knot slips and you begin shouting. Bastards, criminals, murderers!

The futility of words.

—It's a souvenir, he says, replacing the photograph.

Claude the Body lunges at him, snarling.

—Artefacts of memory. War pictures and feats to amuse my grandchildren. Why get so upset?

Artefact. From the Latin *arte*, by art; *facio*, make.

The utility of words. The possibilities.

✺

The Fifth Columnist hadn't thought it would be so hard, this work she has set herself to accomplish. Now, however, sitting at her desk and facing the blank pages, she begins to brood. She doesn't want it to get out of hand, this make-believe business. Just so much fiction in that many facts, the art of the blend. But there's a stickiness to the web she's spinning that she hadn't realised before. One imagined tidbit leads to another, to another and another. Soon, she herself will be lost in the strands and pinned against the mesh, prey of her own making.

✺

She has long since learned the art of peripheral seeing. Tiny gestures, flickers of colour, imprints of shapes are funnelled into her vision, to be caught on the retina and memorised. She remembers the face, despite its new beard and blacked-out front teeth. Hayley Bell had shown her a photograph a few months before the outbreak of war. "Lum Boon Chai, alias Lee Ah Seng, alias Kenny Lum. Leader of the Fifth Columnists in Singapore and Johore. Expert in firearms and radio transmission. A highly dangerous man."

"Why haven't we brought him in?" she'd asked, taking in the long face and the dull eyes in the photograph. Nothing to distinguish him from the countless hawkers and money-lenders plying the streets.

"We did once, but he escaped before questioning. He's believed to be hiding out in northern Johore and training Fifth Columnists to infiltrate our naval security codes." Hayley Bell took the photograph back from her. "He's a master of disguises, but I doubt you'll ever come face to face with him. We suspect he may be sent further north soon, to coordinate Japanese spying activities in Thailand."

But now she is sure he is back. Even from the corners of her eye she can make out the long face, the quick drift of his eyes downwards when she suddenly turns her head to look nonchalantly behind her. He is dressed in rags, squatting on his heels and rocking himself contemplatively as he brushes the flies away from his face. Deliberately, she reaches in her basket. She has just been scrounging around the sundry stores and barren open markets for food. What little she could bully the hawkers into selling her in exchange for her gold earrings and her mother's ring hardly fills the basket. Nonetheless she breaks off a chunk of mouldy bread and flings it at his feet.

He raises his head sharply and when he does, she holds his eye steadily for a long moment. Without breaking eye contact he gropes for the piece of bread, puts it in his mouth, chews. She looks down at his feet. The toes peeking out from his slippers are scrupulously clean. He stops rocking.

She nods at him and crosses the street.

On Serangoon Road, Indian men gather in the evenings to walk hand-in-hand up and down the busiest section of the road, weaving in and out of the spice stalls, flower stands curtained with threaded garlands of chrysanthemum. They watch the Indian girls with their long, flowered hair braided into coils that sway with the swish of their hips as they walk to the temple. The air is heavy with the heady scent of perfumes, oils, fried batter and *murtabak*. Even in wartime, the rules of courtship prevail. Claude moves along the streets trying to assess the situation, to decide if he and Jack should make the move to Cousin Eng's farm in Punggol, but the young men and women around him are enamoured of each other and giggle behind shielding hands as they exchange glances.

In the dimming light, shop-owners ignite the wicks of their kerosene lamps and candles. The dusky Indians blend into the dark, their white teeth and betel-stained tongues like little sparks in the night. His pace slows. An Indian man sings in Tamil and is joined by several disembodied voices. A *tabla* picks up the complicated sixteen-count rhythm so that the song becomes almost palpable, a tactile presence in the air. Claude is so engrossed that his feet grow careless and he trips, his body hurtling into space.

"Ooomph!" grunts the small figure in front of him, whipping around as he regains his balance. She says something in Chinese, her voice sharp.

"I'm sorry," Claude pants. "I tripped. Sorry, sorry," he repeats in the fashion of the local English spoken in the marketplace and then winces at the slip, acutely aware of the sing-song lilt he had unconsciously used in the word.

"Next time don't be so careless!" the girl says, her narrow face disapproving. She speaks with a strong local accent. But Claude is distracted by the pull in his right ankle. It hurts to put his weight on it fully. "Okay or not?" she asks bluntly, though he notices concern on her face.

"Yes, I'm fine." For a moment he stands on his left leg, right foot lifted and dangling from the ankle. The pain is not excruciating but it is enough to make him hesitate to walk.

"What!" She spits the word out. "Sprain or something? Better sit down." She tries to put his arm over her shoulder.

"I'm quite all right, I tell you," he says, irritated by her bossy manner and shaking off her help. But the ankle seems to be throbbing now and when he tries to walk on his own, it almost gives way under his weight. He hops about on his left leg, trying to regain his balance and dignity.

She sizes him up scornfully. "Look, you yourself so careless—trip, almost knock me over, sprain your ankle. So just tell me, want help or not?"

"Well, yes, please." he says, feeling ridiculous.

She puts his arm over her shoulder again and instructs him to lean on her. "Over there," she says, making her way to a hawker stall selling Indian *rojak*. There are some tables and stools set around it for customers. "*Tolong, encik,*" she says to the owner, in Malay slow enough for Claude to understand, "*tengok kaki sakit*"—he has a sick leg. The stall-owner waves at Claude, indicating that he should sit, and goes back to stirring the hot chilli sauce for the *rojak*.

"Where you live?" she asks, squatting by his leg, her hair swinging down to cover half her face. She touches his ankle gingerly. "Bad?"

"Not really, but I can't put my weight on it." Her eyes, feline in slant and large in her thin face, shine up at him. Her ears stick out like her cheekbones. She has a small dimple on her pointed chin. If not exactly pretty, she is arresting.

She clicks her tongue. "Well, better take a trishaw home." Everything so matter-of-factly practical. She gets up and walks to the edge of the street where she expertly waves down a trishaw. Not one wasted gesture about her.

The trishaw parts the human traffic and pulls up beside the two of them. The trishaw-man says something and she taps Claude on the arm. "Okay, put your arm here again and get in." When Claude rests his arm on her, her bones feel fragile, as if they could be torn from her as easily as the bones of a well-cooked chicken. The trishaw wobbles slightly as he hops in on his good foot. She climbs in after him, sits herself down on the cracked plastic seat and looks at him expectantly.

"Just down the road, past the Tian Shan Building. There's a small lane on the left." She translates into rapid Chinese and the trishaw-man sets off slowly, the resistance of his load high at first, but then settling into a moderate pace as the wheels gain momentum. A childish thrill passes over Claude at his first trishaw ride and he is careful to suppress it from the young woman sitting beside him. Nonetheless, when he turns his face away from her and savours the wind in his face, wafting deliciously about his neck, he allows a small smile. There is an exhilaration he hasn't felt in a long time.

"Never been in a trishaw, huh?" She doesn't blink when Claude looks at her. "You look like the taxi kind, or Father's-Car-and-Driver."

Claude examines the floor of the trishaw, the fraying straw mat under his feet. The truth is, he has always been uncomfortable around members of the opposite sex and he is not quite sure what he should say or do now. For a wild moment he believes this is even worse than rooming with an Englishman. There had been little need to have an extended conversation with a girl before. Of course, his sister didn't count.

Luckily, the trishaw-man soon passes the Tian Shan Building and turns into the lane where Amah's hut is. "You live here?" Her face is curious as she takes in the narrow wooden shacks and the outlines of the flimsy outhouses behind them. Claude taps the trishaw-man on the shoulder and he slows to a halt, ringing his bell to indicate their arrival. "Anyone home?" she asks. Jack has left a kerosene lamp on, its glow a halo around the closed shutters.

"No, I, ah, just, ah, left a light on. I'll be fine. Thank you for your help." He tries to hop past her legs to get out. She grasps his arm and supports him to the door. "Quite fine on my own now," Claude says hastily, hoping Jack will be quiet and not cough or clear his throat. "Thank you again." He takes her hand and shakes it awkwardly.

"Ling-li. My name. Han Ling-li."

"Yes, well, thank you, Miss Han, and good night." He gives her hand another firm shake and releases it abruptly. She looks bemused, then makes her way back into the waiting trishaw. In the far distance, a bomb goes off. There is the faint tattoo of machine-gun fire, poking holes in the night air where the deep indigo of sky seeps and leaves its impression. Suddenly Claude is aware of how tiny she is.

"Will you be all right on your own?"

She nods, a smile on her lips, and he knows she means to say, I can take care of myself better than you. But she only says, "Katong," to the trishaw-man and as they drive off, asks, "So, have a name or not?"

"Er, yes," he says, needing to raise his voice a little because they are moving away. "It's Claude Lim."

And there is more gunfire in the distance, but he could almost swear he heard her laugh.

Something about him had irritated her. Probably his accent, the out-of-place formality he extended to her, the fastidiousness that had made him glance warily at the trishaw before entering it and lowering himself oh-so-carefully into his seat. She hadn't planned on it but her own street accent had grown thicker severalfold, especially when she noticed the way he winced at it. She had been instructed to blend in, and that meant the most colloquial English, garnished with Hokkien, Malay and, at times, even Tamil phrases—everything that went against her top-of-the-class schoolgirl English, but who cared? She was doing her job and doing it well. If this odd little mother's boy found it hard on his Anglicised ears, it was nothing to her.

"Who was that?" Jack asks sleepily.

Claude hops towards him. "Oh, I sprained my ankle—tripped—and someone helped me home." Even as he speaks he realises he had not offered to pay for the trishaw ride, and suppresses a groan.

"Are you okay?"

"Oh yes. Just a little weak in the ankle. Have you eaten?" Jack is sweating again and Claude automatically reaches for the basin beside him. He wrings out the wet towel and drapes it over Jack's forehead. "I can't figure out why you still have a fever."

"I can." Jack half-raises himself, tries to kick off the sheet covering his body. Claude folds it back to Jack's knees. "Lower," Jack says. Claude pushes the sheet down further as Jack tries to roll up his pyjamas, baring his right shin which looks red, puffy and is weeping a thin yellow fluid. "An infection."

"But how?" Claude asks, taking in the stains on the bed sheets. "Did you cut it or something?"

"I had some kind of insect bite a while ago and I scratched quite a bit. It swelled slightly but really didn't get red and painful like this until I spilled my tea on it two days ago."

"Why didn't you tell me earlier?" The English are supposed to be sensible about such things, aren't they?

"It was just an insect bite, and then a mild burn after that." Jack grimaces as he shifts his weight. "Some penicillin should take care of it."

"Nothing's open tonight, but I could go to hospital."

"It's only a few hours till morning. Wait till tomorrow."

"I don't know, Jack," Claude says. "It looks pretty nasty."

"Quite, but some Paracetamol should help the fever and the pain.

And tomorrow you can find nice Dr. Tan and get him to prescribe some penicillin." A drone vibrates overhead and they both look up. "Too many damn bombers for you to go out tonight, old boy."

Claude nods, feeling even more guilty he had let Ling-li go off alone. "Dr. Tan has gone off to Australia," he says. "But I'll get some penicillin tomorrow."

Claude unfolds the cot behind the door, sets it on the far wall from Jack and turns his back to the Englishman as he undresses. He is still self-conscious about changing in front of someone else, even though he knows that Jack isn't paying attention. Once Claude is in his pyjamas, he puts out the kerosene lamp, blinding himself temporarily, until his eyes can pick out subtle shadows in the dark. He pads carefully to his cot.

"Good night, Jack."

"Good night." Jack's bed creaks as he settles onto his side. Then, when all is quiet again: "Thank you."

Claude lies awake for a long time. His thoughts turn to the girl he had met earlier. He recalls her bony wrists resting on her lap, the way her hair curved behind her ears, her severe chin. When he leaned on her, his arm draped over her shoulder, he could feel her collar-bones through her thin blouse. They might have looked like lovers huddled against each other as they walked down Serangoon Road, he thinks, then censors further thoughts on the subject by biting his lip. In the dark Jack's breathing fills the room, like parentheses embracing the silence between them.

The screams are inhuman. No longer a high-pitched woman's scream, but a hoarse cry, like the sound an animal would make while gnawing away at its own limb in a trap. The boy had seen this once, in the highlands of Malaya when he was ten and his family holidayed there to get away from the June heat.

He had gone for a walk with Grandma Siok. Just off the road he heard the cry and had frozen on the spot. "A tiger," he whimpered. They had caught one in the village two weeks earlier and the boy had gone with the rest of the family to see the hide.

"Nonsense, what do they teach you at school? That doesn't sound like a tiger at all." Grandma Siok shook his arm. "Too bad," she added.

He followed her into the bush. It was a wild dog, caught in one of the hunting traps laid out by the tea plantation owners. It growled when Grandma Siok got too close, but soon lost interest and returned to chewing its leg. Every now and then it would give off a tired yelp of pain. In the jungle, the cry didn't amount to much, but oddly, the rhythmic sound of teeth grinding bone was loud and unmuted.

She told him to go back to the road and wait. He heard her puffing, heard the determined thud of stone on skull, heard the thrashing of a tail in the brush, the same jungle-dampened yelp. This went on for a long time. The cold highland winds made him shiver.

Grandma Siok appeared, sweating, dishevelled, exhausted. Neither of them spoke on the walk back to the hotel, and she hurried into her room to wash and change before the boy's parents could see her. Two days later, on another walk, grandmother and grandson passed the same spot by the road. It smelled, but not terribly, because of the cool highland temperatures.

"It takes a lot of energy, you know," she said quietly, "to kill something." It was her only comment on the episode.

Dr. Sushil Singh's clinic on Serangoon Road is the closest medical facility to Amah's hut.

As he walks in, Claude takes in the smell of Dettol and urine from the numerous infants and toddlers in the waiting room. On one wall is a poster on the life-cycle of the roundworm, *Ascaris lumbricoides*. There are faded violet mercury stains on the floor, which several toddlers grasp at ineffectually and then sit back on their swaddled backsides, puzzled at the mottled floor. "Change nappy," the broad-faced receptionist orders an Indian mother with twins, oblivious to the harried mother's pleading look.

The wait for Dr. Singh lasts two and a half hours because he has to finish his hospital rounds before attending to his clinic. Claude realises he should have come earlier, at dawn when the mothers arrived with their slumbering children clutched to their drool-wet chests to queue up in front of the locked doors of the clinic. But when he awoke at first light, he had basked in the penumbra of sleep, forgetting it was wartime, that doctors were scarce and sickness common. Now, even when Dr. Singh finally arrives, Claude will be sixteenth in line.

At nine Ling-li walks into the clinic in a fiercely starched white uniform, a cap on her head like a napkin at a formal dinner setting. "Oh," she says when she sees Claude. "I told you it's only a sprain. No need to see the doctor." And she stands, arms akimbo, shaking her head in disapproval.

"I'd like a word with him." Claude draws himself up to his full height, several inches above the top of her head, and uses his most official voice. "It'll only be a moment, I promise."

There is a steely glint in her eye, as if something he said has displeased her. "The clinic is so busy already, everybody so sick. Small things don't need doctor, lah."

That "lah" at the end of her sentence, typical of local English—she doesn't need to do that, Claude thinks. Just trying to be annoying. And indeed he catches a tiny smile of satisfaction on her face.

"I didn't know you were a nurse. I'm here on behalf of a friend," he says, half-wishing he could roll down his socks and show her the size of his swollen ankle. It looks worse than it feels, though he's still unable to place his full weight on it.

"Doctor can't treat without seeing the patient directly," she says, sweeping past Claude to join the receptionist behind the counter. She picks up the first chart. "Mrs. Eswar. Come and let me take your temperature."

Claude goes to the counter, hovering uncomfortably on his left foot. "Now look here, my friend is too sick to come see the doctor. He has an infection on his leg and he's running a fever. Won't the doctor just let me have some penicillin?"

"Ninety-eight point four. *Baik*, Mrs. Eswar." Ling-li beams at the plump Indian woman in her lavender-coloured sari. "Now come sit here so I can take your blood pressure and pulse." She tosses a look at Claude over her shoulder, her eyes travelling meaningfully to his ankle. "Shouldn't stand so much. No, Dr. Singh can't give medicine to a patient he hasn't seen."

"But that's ridiculous! He has a bad infection. He needs some medicine. Some penicillin!" He resists the urge to grab her by the arm and shake her. To think that all this woman is bothered about is some stupid protocol. In wartime too! "Some penicillin, that's all!" he repeats, to get her attention.

She turns around to face him. Deliberately: "You doctor or what?" she asks in her crude English. The crowd in the waiting room, composed mostly of Indians who understand English, sniggers.

Obviously he'll waste less time trying another clinic rather than continuing to argue with her. It's a challenge to maintain his dignity when he has to hop about on one leg. Still, Claude manages quite admirably as he makes his way past the whining children sprawled on the floor and their laughing, whispering mothers. Out on the street he tries to decide what to do next. The General Hospital will probably be packed, but it's worth a try.

Serangoon Road has already come alive with the smell of hawkers making their flat crepe-like *roti* and the aromatic coffee being brewed in the shade. No taxi in sight. Better to head down towards Orchard Road where he can perhaps catch a bus if he's lucky. He pants as he alternates between hopping and limping down the road. At this rate he'll be no use to the fire-fighting team, so he might as well go by the school on his way to hospital and let them know.

"Claude, wait!" Her again. "No, really, please wait." She catches up to him, not having a sprained ankle to contend with herself.

"Well, what is it?" Claude asks impatiently as she stands before him, short of breath, for once a little unsure of herself.

"Your friend," she begins. "Sounds like he's quite *sakit,* eh?" Her tone is conciliatory, but he is in no mood to be amiable.

"What's it to you? You've already told me not to waste my time with your Dr. Singh."

"I said he needs to see the patient first."

"And I said he's too sick to come!"

"And I *was* going to say he can see him this evening on his house calls, but you ran out like a spoiled child!"

Long silence. It's hard to maintain a Look of Righteous Indignation under those quick, knowing eyes. Actually, they're quite beady, lizard-like, come to think of it. Claude wonders how he could have missed this before.

"Well?"

"Could he come around at four?"

"Six at the earliest." Definitely a reptilian quality to those eyes. Claude nods, unable to bring himself to to thank her, and moves on. "Should really stay off your feet," she can't seem to resist adding.

Bossy little lizard.

Dr. Singh calls at six exactly, his promptness pleasing, his manner serious but kind. If he is surprised that Claude's friend is English, he does not show it. He takes his time getting the patient's history, folds his large Sikh hands on his lap as he listens to Jack relate his symptoms. Even though Claude has placed two kerosene lamps by Jack's bed, Dr. Singh says the light is not enough for him to examine his patient and flicks on his torch with a decisive twist of his wrist.

Claude gasps. It is hard to believe that the infection has progressed so much in just one day. The leg is as red as raw liver, and twice the size it was yesterday; the ankle has lost its definition and the leg seems to end in a stump. The thin liquid seeping through the pores leaves a waxy sheen on the skin.

Dr. Singh gingerly feels the swollen limb. Jack swears, the thermometer still in his mouth. Dr. Singh removes it, eyes the delicate mercury column under the direct light of his torch. "Hmmm. When did you last take your Paracetamol?"

"Not more than an hour ago." Jack looks at Claude for confirmation. "Right then, think I'll live?"

"Well, Mr. Winchester, under normal circumstances I would recommend that you stay in hospital."

"But?" Claude asks.

Dr. Singh sighs. "There have been so many bombings. The bed situation, even for Europeans . . . you understand . . ."

"They can't turn him away!"

"Oh no, no, no, Mr. Lim. I'm sure they won't turn anyone away, but the care he'll get won't be very good, I'm afraid." He shakes his neatly turbaned head. "We're short-staffed as it is and the nurses are only attending to the sickest. I think that if you're agreeable, Mr. Lim, he'll get much better care here, with you."

This Dr. Singh is really handling this quite poorly, Claude thinks. Why in heaven's name raise the possibility of having Jack in hospital and then undermine that by saying he'd be better off here? Look, he's sick and you'll have to take care of him, this is what you do, is what the doctor should have come right out and said in the beginning, instead of leaving it to Claude. As if there really is a choice.

"Of course he'll stay," Claude says, hoping he sounds appropriately enthusiastic. "What do I have to do?"

Dr. Singh shows Claude how to lightly bandage the leg, to keep it clean and to elevate it above the level of Jack's chest. Claude is to take Jack's temperature every three hours and to bathe him in lukewarm water if he is febrile above one hundred and three Fahrenheit. "And then, you must give him his injection daily, for I'm afraid I won't be able to come everyday."

"Injection?" Already Claude is nervous. "Can't he just swallow a pill?"

"No, no, no. Not a pill for this." Dr. Singh waves his hands and Claude feels the draught he generates. "He needs very large doses of antibiotics. I'm afraid he'll require injections."

"It's okay, Claude, I don't mind," Jack says from his corner. Of course—the British sporting spirit.

"It's very easy, Mr. Lim, nothing to it. Come, I'll show you." So reassuring, this calm, deep-voiced man who has been doctoring all his life: pumping stomachs, administering enemas, changing dressings, sewing up gashes. He can afford to be so serene, with experience and nerves of steel on his side.

"Are you paying attention, Mr. Lim?" Dr. Singh holds up a small vial. In it is a clear liquid with a thick white slurry at the bottom. "You have to mix it up. Shake it." He demonstrates. "Then you draw it up." Now he produces a rather large needle and draws up the solution into a syringe. "Come on over here. Mr. Winchester, turn over onto your side, if you don't mind. Tap the syringe like this—listening, Mr. Lim? We're eliminating air bubbles this way."

Not only is it getting bloody hot, but Claude is also feeling slightly light-headed as he moves to Jack's bedside. Stiff upper lip and all that, he tells himself. Dr. Singh pulls Jack's pyjamas down so that his strangely small and pale buttocks show. "I'll leave you this bottle of alcohol. Soak some cotton wool like this, clean the site." He scrubs Jack's right buttock. "Feel the bone here, come on, put your finger here."

Claude holds out his hand and Dr. Singh takes it firmly, placing it over Jack's hip bone. "Move down two inches, here." He rubs some more alcohol onto the spot, picks up the needle lying on the bed beside Jack. "Take it."

The syringe feels heavy to Claude, the glass surface cool and smooth as his hands are not. "What should I do now?" At least his voice reveals none of his dread.

Dr. Singh clamps his hands over Claude's and directs the needle to the spot he selected. "Nice and easy, not too hard." The doctor exerts pressure and the needle sinks into Jack's flesh, which feels surprisingly springy. "Go through the fat, then—" He pushes the plunger so that the white suspension is forced into Jack's bottom. When he and Claude jointly pull out the needle, a single drop of blood bubbles out of the injection site.

"That's all there is to it." Dr. Singh beams at Claude.

Images float about Claude's head and he has the sensation of stepping off an unusually high kerb, the moment just before his front foot hits the ground, only this moment stretches indefinitely, and he is suddenly particularly aware of the swarthiness of Dr. Singh's complexion, the darkness of his skin, the stiff ebony hairs along his jaw, his black, black eyes, and yes, yes, all dark.

❀

"Er, Mr. Lim."

"Claude. You all right?"

"There, there, he's coming round. There's a good fellow. Let's sit you up." Dr. Singh is squatting beside Claude, propping him up, his knee kneading the curve in Claude's back.

"I'm fine," Claude says, surprised at the sweat dripping down his face. Dr. Singh pulls him up onto the chair and pours him a glass of water. Jack's face is concerned. Claude notices how thin he has become; his frown emphasizes his facial bones, the jutting chin. Claude wipes his own face with the towel Dr. Singh hands him. The doctor packs his things, making small talk as he works.

At the door he stops. "I'll, ah, send Miss Han here tomorrow. It's on her way home. I don't think she'll mind."

Jack joins Claude in his thanks. When the door shuts after Dr. Singh, he asks who the hell Miss Han is.

"The doctor's nurse," Claude says, thinking gloomily: All I need now. Great. Haven't I enough things to worry about, what with a war, the fire-fighting unit, an Englishman with a rotten leg and my own sprained ankle?

Guess not.

How to control a character with a mind of her own? How to rein her in and keep her on track, without having her stray down extraneous pathways, complicating everything.

A good Fifth Columnist sticks to the evidence provided by extensive snooping. But no amount of investigative work could yield information of this nature. A useful report has only to mention names, dates, places, she reminds herself. It doesn't need anything more and to provide excessive detail would be to invite suspicion. Therein lies the work.

Of course it has to be the first thing Ling-li mentions when she gets through the door. "Fainted, huh?" Not even, Good morning.

Claude decides to ignore her remark, take the high road. "Ah, thank you for coming. So sorry to inconvenience you."

"Actually I was curious. So!" She takes in her surroundings. "Live like this and speaking like a pommy. You a banana or what?" She makes it hard even to see the high road sometimes, much less take it. "Understand banana?"

Claude shakes his head cautiously. "Yellow on outside, white inside!" she informs him with relish and suddenly finds this very funny, breaking out into peals of laughter. His throat constricts as shame, anger and something else—something heavy, sad almost, but not quite, something ancient—washes over him so that he is neither yellow nor white but quite definitely red in the face. "Joke only, lah!" she says, watching him, mildly alarmed. "Don't be so serious!"

"Miss Han, let me introduce you to your patient." High road, high road, Claude mutters to himself, even as things appear to be plunging steadily downhill.

Ling-li, apparently only now aware that it is a one-room hut and that Jack has probably overheard her teasing, sobers up immediately and, taking a deep breath, strides towards Jack.

"This is my friend, Jack Winchester. Jack, Miss Han Ling-li. She's Dr. Singh's nurse." The way he says the last sentence makes Jack raise one eyebrow, but he merely lifts his hand up to Ling-li, who grasps it firmly. A moment later, she begins to rummage in her black bag.

"Jack's fever hasn't subsided," Claude says, determined to remain as businesslike as possible. "This is a schedule of the times I gave him Paracetamol, and I've been using compresses all night. How soon should we expect the medicine to work?"

"Two or three days before we see any change," she says, taking a quick glance at Jack's leg.

"It's the pain that bothers me most," Jack says. "Is there anything you could give me for that?"

She shakes her head. "Not with me right now, and anything I give you must be cleared with Dr. Singh first." She strips the blanket from Jack. "Not good for the fever, see?" The glance she throws Claude adds, What in the world are you thinking, boiling him under a blanket while he has a fever? It doesn't take long for her to resume her superior air.

In spite of himself, Claude is forced to admit that Ling-li is a good nurse. Her hands are gentle as she wraps a tape measure around Jack's calf to track the extent of the swelling. She speaks in a soothing voice he didn't even think she had in her, and when she gives Jack the injection, the Englishman hardly notices it. "Over yet?" he says and is amazed when she nods. "I thought you were still cleaning with the alcohol. You're good."

Claude takes his eyes from the ceiling fan—he had stared at it throughout Jack's injection—and catches her blushing. "How's your appetite?" she asks.

"Lousy. He had two pieces of bread and soup yesterday and nothing today," Claude informs her.

"I'm more thirsty than hungry. I can't seem to get enough water in me."

"Shee-shee?" she asks and Claude is embarrassed for her, but Jack is unfazed.

"Not yet today. I went once yesterday, I think. Claude had to practically haul me to the outhouse, poor man, what with his ankle and all." He throws Claude an apologetic look. "So it's probably not a bad thing that I'm not having to go every hour."

"Oh no. It's very bad! It means you're de-hy-dra-ted," she says, enunciating every syllable. "Start drinking now." She pours him some water. He meekly accepts the first and second glass but protests the third. "Drink." Something in her tone, like an air-raid siren: warning. Jack wisely drinks.

"And if you need to shee-shee, use a bottle. Keep the leg up and don't try to walk around too much."

When it's time for her to leave, Jack reminds her to ask Dr. Singh for some pain medication. "I'll see what I can do. Maybe some morphia," she muses. "But we don't have much left in the clinic. We have to be very careful with it. Last week we had to use a lot for three gunshot wounds he treated."

"Air fire?" Claude asks.

"Stupid drunk Australian adolescents carrying guns and playing soldiers! Went shooting each other after too much whisky," she says. "Why we even have them here?"

There is a small silence in the room.

Then Jack speaks. "They're here," he says sternly, "to help protect Singapore. These young men are prepared to give up their lives defending the island. We should all be more grateful, perhaps, and less critical of their shortcomings. These lads are far from home and I expect the bombings are enough to unnerve even the best of us. If they have to let off steam, we should be more understanding. They're no more than boys, Miss Han, likely Claude's age, and they are defending your people."

Ling-li seems to draw herself up to her full five feet. "Have you been outside in the past week, Mr. Winchester? Have you seen what is going on in the streets? Those Australian lads are nothing more than hooligans! They have been stealing, shooting at civilians, demanding preferential treatment at clinics for scratches and cuts they've gotten from their own little war games! They don't *want* to be here. They don't *want* to defend my people. Not that I would trust them to defend me! I'd rather have Claude here with his lousy ankle. My uncle is with Dalforce, the Chinese fighting unit—the *only* Chinese fighting unit, come to think of it, that the British will *allow*— and there are also Malay and Eurasian units that are defending the island, but so far, what I have seen of the European forces has been *pathetic*! And you, Judge Claude! What do you think of soldiers defying their commanding officers? Deserting? So you, Mr. Winchester, stop your mumbo-jumbo please, just concentrate on your rotting leg"—surely she means rotten? Claude muses—"and when it's all better, why don't you take the next boat back to England?"

She flings the door open before the men can recover. "Oh, by the way, why don't you send your houseboy here to get you some opium to take away the pain in your leg, Mr. Winchester? You British have always been so eager to sell it to the Chinese. I'm sure you'll find some Chinese *samseng* who will be happy to return the favour!" She slams the door and they hear the gravel crunch as she runs back towards the main road.

Claude busies himself with clearing up Jack's old bandages. They will have to be washed. He clears his throat. "Maybe you should drink some more water," he says, bustling about.

"I've had enough," says Jack and turns his face to the wall. A pause.

"Think I'll go out for a walk," Claude says, slipping outside for a reprieve. The oily smell of fires fills his nostrils but something else bothers him. Only as he returns to the hut does he know what it is: Hardly an accent. She hardly had an accent when she spoke.

Perhaps he is getting bored. The baritone has asked a philosophical question. Suppose the past were to come alive and march into the present. What would happen then?

Nothing, you say through the Body, the lips moving with your words. The past is not different from the future. It's constantly coming into being, constantly forged by circumstances and beliefs. It cannot rise up whole and walk. It is always created, always prophesied.

—At least, he says, you are mildly entertaining.

Ling-li is tight-lipped when she returns the next day. "I owe you an apology," she says right away to Jack. "I behaved badly and I'm sorry."

Jack bobs his head. "Accepted," he says without hesitation. He too is tense, formal.

Ling-li draws up his injection and gives it to him. She checks on his leg, measuring the calf circumference again. "I think the swelling is down," she says. "But you still have to keep the leg up." Again, no local accent, Claude notes.

She tucks a pile of blankets and towels under Jack's leg, so that the whole leg sticks up at an angle in the air, as if to make her point. Jack had pushed the blankets away last night, rolling his leg off the heap because it was too hot.

After she leaves, Claude makes porridge. In a pot over an old charcoal stove, he stirs a thin gruel of water and rice. He has hardly cooked anything since he moved in here with Jack, but Amah had always preached the nutritive virtues of porridge in times of illness. Too late, Claude realises that without meat, chopped scallions, sesame oil, preserved salted duck's eggs and bean sprouts, the meal is sadly lacking. Still, food is food, he tells himself, adding a dash of salt to make the porridge bearable. The thin rod-shaped rice grains grow plump, soften; their dull yellow coats seem to shed, take on a white glistening as they sputter and froth. The mixture thickens. "Time for lunch," he announces.

But Jack, exhausted from his restless night, lies on his bed, eyeing the ceiling. Despite the injections, the leg looks the same as before, and the strain of the past few days has taken its toll on him. Claude pours some of the porridge into a crude porcelain bowl and brings it over to Jack, determined to make him eat. "Here." He holds out the bowl but Jack makes no move to take it. "Come on, Jack, you've got to have something. You haven't even been drinking as much water as you should."

Claude's fingertips tingle from the heat of the bowl. Finally he puts it down on the shelf next to the laughing Buddha and pulls the chair up to Jack's bedside. "Let's get you up," Claude says, slipping his hands under Jack's armpits and hoisting him to a sitting position. Claude slips his pillow and some rolled-up sheets in the small of Jack's back to prop him up.

"I can't," Jack whispers, his lips cracked.

"Well, ready or not, you've got to eat to keep your strength up. Come on, Jack, pull yourself together." Claude picks up the bowl, making sure to have an insulating rag between it and his fingers, then blows on the porridge.

Spoonful after spoonful Claude feeds him, digging into the slushy rice mixture, feeling the clink of Jack's teeth against the edges of the spoon, the topography of his mouth, the high hard palate, the teeth ridges, the weight and pull of his tongue resisting the spoon. It is strangely sensual. "Eat up," Claude says when Jack pauses to swallow again, just to say something, to shake free from that odd intimacy.

To distract himself, Claude thinks about the Japanese. He has seen them in films at Cathay Cinema. They're short and yellow, slit-eyed, unintelligible. They eat rice, like the Chinese, like the Englishman being fed rice now by a Chinese who isn't particularly Chinese, but who also eats rice like the other Chinese. All this circular thinking—it makes him dizzy.

✺

The Indian girl is not more than twelve. On seeing the soldiers across the street, she hesitates. Her mother has often warned her of the dangers of white men, of white men in uniform in particular. She is smart and obedient. Usually she does what her mother tells her; usually there are no ambiguities. But today, those white men lie between her and her home. She has just been in the temple court-yard with her aunt and her cousins to hear the noisy speeches of the Free India men. The police arrived and tried to break up the crowd. The Free India men threw rocks and an altercation started out. One of the police, in wrestling with a Free India man, knocked down a shrine to Ganesha, and then the whole temple erupted into chaos.

"See how the white men abuse our beloved Ganesha!" the Free India men shouted through their megaphones. She had looked for her aunt and cousins in panic but could not find them. A moment later she was almost trampled by the crowd. Just in time, a woman who wore a bindi but trousers and shirt like the whites, saw her and pushed her aside. "Go home," she yelled, though her voice was swal-lowed up by the roar of megaphones, police whistles and screaming. "Get away from here. Go home!" The woman pushed her in the direction of the gateway before being herself obstructed from view by the crowd.

The little girl saw the police pushing on the heavy iron gates to swing them shut and she knew that now was her only chance. She sprinted for the gates and slipped out just as they gathered momen-tum and slammed shut. Without stopping, she ran all the way back to her block, all the way back here. Now only the white soldiers stand in the way of home, and her parents. She must cross the street, get past them, turn the corner and run to the end of the lane. There is no way to avoid them. She goes.

They see her before she even steps off the kerb. They point at her pink sari and laugh. She can tell from their unsteady voices that they have been drinking. She must not look them in the face. She must keep walking . . .

✺

Chinatown smells of burning sulphur and singed flesh. Everywhere buildings are hollowed out, caving in, and streets are blocked
with debris. Mr. Caruthers looks unfamiliar to Claude in a white
singlet and khaki shorts. He is shod in thick military boots and wears
the dreadful tin helmet. "All right, boys, we'll start here and work
our way down the street. Those who aren't using the hose can use
their shovels and buckets of sand. No-one is to go beyond the end
of the street, do you hear? We'll let the main fire-fighting units
handle that, boys. Remember, we're just the auxiliary unit. No foolish heroics please!"

The group disperses. There are only seven of them, eight if Mr.
Caruthers is included. Some boys have actually taken time to change
into Littleton uniforms before reporting for Fire-Fighting Service
duty. Four of the others have already positioned themselves next to
the two hoses, so Claude picks up a bucket and heads towards the
lorry carrying what appears to be a small mountain of sand. "From
Changi Beach," Mr. Caruthers had said.

The fire has been raging for six hours already. The central fire-
fighting unit has been at work since the early hours of dawn. The
school's auxiliary unit was hastily assembled less than two hours earlier by word of mouth. Almost nobody lives at home these days;
most have evacuated their districts and headed to the city, staying
with whatever relatives and friends can be found, in shelters,
churches, temples and even in frail makeshift tents in the smaller
alleys. Claude was informed of the fire when he bumped into his
classmate, Hugh Chung, along Clemenceau Boulevard. Hugh was
on his bicycle.

"Claude, old boy, where have you been? We thought you'd left the
island, or been killed by a bomb!" He had surveyed Claude's still-
healthy body in apparent disappointment. "You've missed all our
fire-fighting practises. What's been going on?"

"I've been taking care of a sick friend. He's had rotten luck. I was
on my way to General Hospital for more penicillin. All the chemists
are out of the stuff." Claude looked at the bicycle longingly. It was
at least another hour's walk to the hospital, unless the bus came
along, but that was unlikely. He had waited for it for a good hour

and a half before he even began walking. "I say, can I borrow your bicycle? Or get a lift from you?"

Hugh shook his head. "Sorry, can't. There's a huge fire in Chinatown and I'm rounding up the boys to help fight it. You really should come along. We've only five people so far—I can't seem to find the rest—and apparently it's quite a blaze. They need help desperately." He fixed an accusing gaze at Claude.

"Well, I don't think I'd be much use. I haven't been to practise in such a long—"

"Oh, nonsense! It's not as if we're in the bloody ballet! All you have to do is to aim the damn hose at the fire. Surely you can manage that! Come on, I don't have all day!" He began pedalling in a tight circle around Claude. "Look, when we're done I'll give you a lift to the hospital and you can get your penicillin. You don't need it at once, do you?"

"No," Claude admitted. "We do still have one vial left." He looked towards Chinatown, noting the thick funnel of smoke rising from its centre. Inadvertently he thought of Ling-li.

"Look," Hugh said, his voice lowered. "It's shameful enough that so many people have dropped out of the regular practise sessions. Now that there's a real fire, we have to show Mr. Caruthers that we're made of sterner stuff. What if the boys from Hwa Ming School appear?"

"This isn't a school hockey match, Hugh," Claude said quietly. "There won't be a trophy for showing up the Hwa Ming boys."

Hugh frowned. "You think I'm just making a game of it all?" he asked. "You're one to talk! Why don't *you* get off your high horse, roll up your sleeves and get to work then?"

"I'll come," Claude said. Everything felt so pointless all of a sudden—the fire, Jack, the penicillin, Ling-li and her clinic of patients. An odd feeling washed over him, the yearning to be swept along with whatever was going on, to surrender to the events of the moment. He didn't want to think; he just wanted to keep busy. Nothing would make a difference anyway—better numb diligence at some mechanical task than brooding over unanswerable questions in the hut with a languishing Jack.

Hugh stopped his bicycle long enough for Claude to hop on behind and then headed for Chinatown. Throughout the ride, the Eurasian said nothing more to Claude than an occasional "Hang on" or "Big bump ahead." When they passed General Hospital, Claude hardly glanced at it. *Put out fire, put out fire,* was all he allowed himself to think.

"Move it along now," Mr. Caruthers says now to the three boys throwing sand at flaming tongues. The central fire-fighting unit has passed this way a few hours ago and suppressed the biggest fires and is now pushing on in the direction of the river. The job of the auxiliary units is to follow in their wake, putting out any leftover flames. Mr. Caruthers is taking this seriously. "I don't want you to miss a spot, lads," he says, his eyes lingering on Claude as he works. Claude responds by throwing sand indiscriminately all around, concentrating only on working as quickly as possible. He tries to hold his breath against the smell of smoke as long as possible—not very successfully, since shovelling is hard work.

Hugh, who has been energetically damping down fires, nudges Claude. "Look, the Hwa Ming unit's finally arrived. One hour behind us, and there's only four of them." The Hwa Ming boys, dressed in their all-white school uniforms, are at the other end of the street. They spend a few moments talking and then get to work. They have one hose among them and the rest use their spades to beat down flames as the Littleton unit has been doing, only much more efficiently and rapidly. Seeing this, Hugh settles back to work with renewed vigour. Together, Claude and Hugh smother an angry burning vein that stretches across the street.

Over the next half-hour, more Hwa Ming boys arrive. They seem to have organised themselves in teams and have spread out over the area, putting out fires so quickly that in another quarter of an hour they will reach Littleton's end of the street. "They're quite fantastic," Claude says to Hugh. "There must be about fifteen of them now. And there doesn't seem to be a teacher or anyone else supervising them."

"Show-offs," Hugh says. "We got here first. Now they're trying to get over to our end so Caruthers will notice them."

"You really think that?" Claude asks. "Why would they care what Caruthers thinks? They don't even know him."

"But he's white. He's English. They're trying to show him they're better than us." Hugh whacks at a small fire with his spade, stunning it into a dizzy hiss of smoke.

"But they *are* better than us," Claude points out. "And who cares what Caruthers thinks anyway?" He is tired and the smoke is making him tear.

The Hwa Ming unit is within earshot now, but they are speaking in Chinese. They seem to be surveying the area and making plans for the next stage of the job. Their practicality makes Claude think of Ling-li.

One of the Hwa Ming boys approaches. "Hello," he says, holding out his hand formally and shaking Claude's and Hugh's in turn. "I'm Quah Boon Liew, from Hwa Ming School." His speech is slightly stilted and he has a definite Chinese accent but there is no trace of pidgin in it. "The wind is picking up and our sources have told us that the fire is spreading very quickly along the river. We are going to divide our unit into two. Half will stay here to work with you and the other half will help the central unit along the river." He stops. After a moment Claude realises Boon Liew is waiting for them to speak.

"Oh," Claude says stupidly. "I'm Claude Lim and this is Hugh Chung. You're right—about the wind, I mean."

"You think it's a good plan? Or perhaps you have another idea?" Boon Liew asks, making a small bow.

"Er, not really," Claude says. Hugh's mouth is set in a grim line. "Why don't you come over and talk to Mr. Caruthers? He's in charge of our unit."

"Yes, of course," Boon Liew says, looking around for the chemistry teacher.

"He's behind the lorry," Claude says. "This way."

The three fire-fighters troop over to the lorry where Mr. Caruthers is directing two boys who are using the hose. Claude introduces Boon Liew and lets the Hwa Ming boy explain the situation. "Good idea!" says Caruthers, looking over his shoulder at the rest of the Hwa Ming unit. "I say, what a splendid turn-out you have!"

"We're expecting a few more in an hour. We're going to work in shifts," Boon Liew explains.

Mr. Caruthers is impressed. "Nice planning," he says. "All right then, boys! We're about finished here, so let's move ahead."

Boon Liew makes another small bow. "I'll tell my unit," he says and walks away.

An unexpected admiration washes over Claude as he watches Boon Liew pick his way through the fallen buildings and cinders.

✵

Claude the Body is eating. The rice is giving him strength, even though it's excruciating for him to open his mouth. Every time he attempts it, the cuts on his face re-open and bleed. He has taken off his shirt, and with his good hand is stanching the flow of blood from his nose. This way he can manage to breathe without clogging his air passages with blood. He learns it is impossible to chew without moving the muscles of his face and ends up half-grinding the hard grains between clenched teeth.

You force yourself to concentrate on him, to watch his every move in order to avoid letting yourself stray—to murky territory, an unknown, monstrous terrain—next door. No, you must keep away, keep denying yourself sight of what is so tantalisingly close.

Sounds of teeth grinding bone. Or yelps. You hover anxiously at the ceiling cracks.

Slow loris, you chant to yourself, slow loris.

Slow loris, large eyes. Beady eyes, lizard eyes. Whatever happens, do not look.

✵

Dr. Singh is nowhere to be found, and the receptionist has given her notice. "Too far for me to walk from my house, especially with the planes overhead," she said. Ling-li has been holding the fort for the past three days, her energy indefatigable, her manner soothing and sensible to her patients. Each time that Claude has stopped by for bandages and supplies for Jack's wound, she has been cordial but distracted. She has been sleeping at the clinic, she tells him. "Safer," she says, eyeing the iron grilles that are on every window and in front of the door. "Now that the bombings are almost routine, I prefer not having to travel to work."

"What about your uncle?"

"He's volunteered, so he's not at home either." She shrugs, then slumps into a chair, one hand to her face. "I hope he's okay. They didn't give them much training, you know. And hardly any weapons. Lucky if they can even pop balloons with those rifles the British gave them." There is no bitterness in her voice this time, just acceptance, and something else. Some other undefined emotion lurking under that hand still covering her face. For a wild moment, it occurs to Claude that she might be afraid, but he dismisses the thought. The sight of her shielding her face disturbs him, but he says nothing, unwilling to risk her scorn. The moment lengthens, and several times Claude wonders if she is waiting for something. For what? *To be comforted.* The thought is so unexpected that Claude almost laughs aloud. And yet there is something about that forward hunch to her back that seems to be calling out for comfort, making him want to put his arms around her. He sits on his hands, confused about the vague emotions swirling about in his mind.

Finally, she uncovers her face and asks about Jack's leg.

"That's really what I came to see you about," Claude says in a rush. "There's been no change, even with the medicine I got from hospital. He is so weak, and Dr. Singh is still missing . . ." The floor of the clinic is littered with paper, rolls of dirty bandages, bits of old scabs, a splash of iodine in a corner like a miniature sun. "I . . ." Something in the set of her jaw stops him and he searches for words. " . . . don't know what else to do," he ends lamely.

"Hospital," she says firmly. "Get him there."

"How? He's too weak to move. I have to do everything for him."

"Show some initiative," she says. "This is wartime, understand or not? Grow up a little."

Strangely he is not at all resentful, perhaps even a little grateful. Her words force him to stay above the rush of craziness and fear that has overtaken the city. Again the alarming urge to hug her, which he resists, but his eyes spill a sudden warmth.

She is puzzled by this, then is distracted by a rattling of the iron grille at the front door. She opens one panel of frosted louvres to peek outside. "Sick child," she says, snapping the louvres closed and busying herself with the padlock at the door. She lets in a Chinese woman in a stained *samfoo* carrying a young boy. He is half-conscious, drooling at the mouth, limp in his mother's arms. The woman assails Ling-li with a torrent of Chinese—it sounds like Hokkien, but Claude can't be sure—and she responds with placating little noises, stroking the boy, propping open his eyelids to examine his pupils.

"You'll be all right?" Claude asks, realising he should let Ling-li return to work. She barely nods. "Lock up behind me." He suspects she doesn't hear this, but once he is out of the clinic, the door closes behind him and he hears the padlock clicking shut.

He runs to Amah's hut. Everywhere he meets bewildered, frightened people running like him, clinging to their children, crying. Some have bloodstained clothes but he cannot pause to consider them too closely. Always now at the threshold of his mind are questions, terrifying thoughts, complicated conjectures. He refuses to give in to them. Instead he concentrates on Ling-li's injunction: *Show some initiative, grow up*. It becomes a mantra as he runs, somehow makes it easier for him to breathe, to push his legs a little faster and further.

A man crosses the street in front of him, cradling a small body burnt so crisp it's shedding cinders from the man's tight embrace. They disappear behind the shop houses across the street. Claude pushes aside the rising nausea and keeps running. It's become a song now, strident but necessary—*Show some initiative, grow up*, words that fit easily into the rhythms of a march, an anthem for running.

Okay, getting Jack out of the hut was the easy part. What the hell to do now? Claude's initiative is shrinking to the size of a pea and now that he is out on Serangoon Road, practically hauling Jack, he

is angry at Ling-li again. Easy for her to say, he'd like to see her have
to deal with this—

Jack's grip is urgent, anxiety-ridden. Claude stops and looks
down at his face, paler now, and for a wild, heart-stopping moment
he wonders if Jack is haemorrhaging to death. But the Englishman
is trying to say something. "They're here! They're here, in the city!"
There is panic in his voice and Claude has to remind himself that
Jack has not been out in days, all this chaos must be new to him.

"Let's get you to hospital." Claude helps him sit down on the
kerb. Jack's bandaged leg smells less out here in the open, but the
green and yellow stains that are still oozing through the gauze make
Claude uneasy. "It'll be hard to find a cab," he says, attempting a wry
smile.

Jack is confused, rambling on about "them" entering the city, the
impregnable fortress, how could this be happening? "Just leave me
here to die," he ends flatly. "We'll never find a cab, and even if we
do, it'll be no use."

At this declaration from Jack, Claude jumps to his feet. "Tell you
what! I'll take you on my back." He squats in front of Jack, hunch-
ing forward. "Come on, arms round the shoulders," he coaxes, but
Jack doesn't budge, just sits there like a lost man, all spirit gone
from him. "Come on, Jack—move! We don't have all day!" Claude
says, deliberately harsh. "Now put your arms around my shoulders
and stop whimpering." Encouraged by the authoritative edge in his
own voice, Claude twists to look behind, takes Jack's limp arms,
drops them over his own shoulders. "Now hang on, will you!"

With a grunt Claude thrusts his hips forward, straightening his
legs at the same time, inducing a strange crackling in his knees—
pops of air—and then he is upright, with Jack shrugged over his
shoulders like the ragged hide of some scrawny animal. Luckily he is
lighter than Claude expected. It's more the awkwardness of Jack's
perch rather than his weight that hinders Claude as he makes his way
down Serangoon Road. If only Jack would straighten a little, not stay
so slumped.

"Jack, how's the view?" Claude cries out, wanting to assure himself that Jack has not passed out.

"I hate to tell you this, Claude, but don't you think we're going

the wrong way? Everyone else is running in the opposite direction."
Jack's voice is weak but at least he is trying, and there is a twinge of
sarcasm in it that cheers Claude. His steps quicken, even as Jack's legs
bang against the sides of his ribs. The wail of klaxons surges around
them. Claude settles into a clumsy march, panting hard, but the physical exertion is exhilarating after days of sitting around in the hut.

"Leave it to me," he says, almost jaunty now. In another block
they should be going by Dr. Singh's clinic. A troupe of grimy soldiers in the distance makes Claude glad Ling-li had locked the clinic
door after him. "We'll stop to say hello to Ling-li. I want to make
sure she's okay."

"Should have given her my gun," Jack manages from above, a
slight wheeze in his voice, as if he were the one doing the running.

Claude's steps falter. "I don't think she knows how to shoot." He
has a gun? How come Claude had never known? Did he have it with
him on all those sight-seeing trips? Where does he keep it now?

"Nevertheless, I think she, among the three of us, would be the
one who could really use it when necessary." Jack gives a small laugh.
"If she'd had a gun she'd have shot me when we first met!"

Claude likes the growing strength in Jack's voice, wants to keep
him talking, to keep him from noticing the woman across the street
with the blood in her hair and the man encased in burns, his livid
skin bubbling up in furious blisters. "I always thought she was a little crazy," Claude says.

"Why?"

"Well." Claude pauses, props Jack up a little higher on his back,
leans forward more. "I suppose it's because of her behaviour.
She's—volatile." He recalls the way she pounced on Jack over the
issue of deserters. "She reacts too quickly sometimes, doesn't think
first. Just her nature, I guess."

Jack is quiet for a moment. "Maybe. But it's also something else.
Upbringing, education, I don't know."

Why does Jack sound so uncomfortable? "She's a woman,"
Claude says. "What do you expect?" When Hugh says this at fire-
fighting practice, the boys all snigger and nudge each other. It
sounds so worldly, so knowing.

Jack chuckles. "No, I don't think that's all of it. Some of it, yes, but not all." He feels around for the right words. "She's—been raised differently. Sees the world differently."

"How so?" Claude persists. This isn't a free ride, if that's what Jack's thinking.

"She's, well—her manner, well . . . She's Chinese-educated."

"What does that mean?" What *does* that mean? Claude thinks of Humphrey, all his views on the "locals": "No need to think too much about such things. Has nothing to do with you and the way you've been brought up."

"Just what I said—she's Chinese-educated. Different from you."

"In what way?"

"She's more—aggressive. Difficult. Unpredictable."

Is Claude, then, pacific, easy, predictable? He decides not to ask but the thought remains with him until they arrive at Dr. Singh's clinic. With Jack still on his back, Claude slips his hand through the iron grille and knocks on the door. A face appears at the window, reappears at the door.

"We're on our way to the hospital," Claude says, thinking: *unpredictable*. He almost dares her to be difficult.

"Like *that*?" She opens the door wide. Claude sees movement inside.

"Initiative," Claude says.

She mutters, "Idiot," under her breath, but loud enough for Claude and Jack to hear. "What you think this is, Sports Day at school? You crazy or what?"

Claude's temper rises and and he makes an impatient noise. "Look here—"

But she brushes him off: "Okay, okay, shut up now. No time to talk. Stay here with Jack and the boy." She turns briefly towards the dark of the clinic.

"Why? Where are you going?" But she is gone already, always a step ahead. Claude goes inside, locking the grille and the door behind him, and squats to let Jack down. He slides to the floor in a heap. The woman with the boy is still there; the boy who is lying stiffly on a bench, a funny, unnatural arch to his neck. Claude nods to the woman and smiles, says hello in Cantonese, which is all the Chinese he can manage. She says something back in Hokkien. Jack's head is drooping so that his chin touches his chest. Claude helps him up to a chair, leans him against the wall.

The woman speaks again, her tone more insistent this time. "Sorry,"' Claude says sheepishly, showing her his palms. She doesn't stop. "Look, I have no idea what you're saying." The problem is, of course, mutual. Finally she walks over to Claude, pulls on his arm, gestures towards her boy.

"Loc-tor, loc-tor," she says, mimes driving a car. "Go loc-tor, loctor."

"No—no taxis," Claude tells her. "No car."

"Go loc-tor," she says desperately.

Jack is falling asleep on the bench. He catches himself each time his chin dips, and struggles to get into a more upright position. Claude looks at the little boy again, estimating his weight. No, too heavy for him to carry both the boy and Jack all the way to hospital. He shakes his head decisively at the mother. "No. No, sorry." Distraught, she returns to her son, strokes his hair, tries to hold her hand like a pillow under his head to massage away the pronounced arch of his neck.

They sit for a half-hour before Ling-li returns. Claude lets her in but she beckons him to leave the clinic instead. "Quick, quick, bring the boy and then Jack."

"I can't possibly carry both," he begins but she cuts him off.

"Just hurry, okay?" She leaves the door ajar for him to follow. Swallowing his irritation at her bossiness, he goes to the woman, who gets up immediately, smiles as he picks up her son.

"Yiss, yiss. Go loc-tor." She beams. Claude takes the boy outside, where Ling-li is trying to bring a run-down, almost derelict trishaw closer to the kerb. The seat is too high for her and she has to stand on the pedals, her weight and body going back and forth from right foot to left as she cycles slowly.

He places the boy carefully on the seat. The mother catches his hand to thank him but he shakes it off and goes back to bring Jack out. "Lock up!" Ling-li shouts after him.

By the time he puts Jack in the trishaw, it's a tight squeeze. "Okay, hero," Ling-li orders, "start cycling!"

"Aren't you coming?" Claude asks, struggling to turn the pedals with his legs.

"Yah, but don't overestimate yourself, okay? I'll walk."

The humiliating thing is that even with his greatest exertion, he is pedalling about as fast as Ling-li's brisk walk. He wonders if he will make it to hospital, but then banishes the thought. For her part, Ling-li pushes the trishaw whenever the road rises gently uphill. Luckily, for most of the way, it's a flat road.

"Come on, old boy," Jack manages every now and then. "That's the spirit!" Now that they're really on their way to hospital he seems to have pulled himself together more and is even trying to be encouraging. Somehow it helps, that clipped British voice behind Claude, calling out encouragement. He pedals, not thinking about his quivering thighs, the effort at breathing. He has to get Jack and the boy to hospital; the heroic swells up in him. He feels the best of everything English lift him that day on the trishaw, war peeling around them like cracked paint and settling on the city in crumbling flakes, a skin shed, revealing the raw surfaces underneath.

At the Punggol farm, Grandma Siok is trying to ignore the voices on the other side of the thin walls of her room. After all, it's *their* business, she thinks. Cynthia's voice is low, but it has a whining, malicious quality. I wish she wouldn't do that, Grandma Siok thinks. Humphrey is a fool, but even he doesn't deserve her contempt. Not so much of it anyway.

The voices become more agitated and there is a thud. Cynthia, Grandma Siok sighs. She can't have a disagreement without throwing things around, damaging something. At least Humphrey, for all that he's ridiculous, is sure of himself in his own unquestioning way. The trouble with Cynthia is that she can't make up her mind who she is, what she wants. She doesn't trust her own judgments and keeps cutting off her own nose to spite herself.

The wind changes and the odour of pig drifts into the room. "For God's sake, I can't stand that smell any longer!" Cynthia shouts at the top of her voice.

"But dear, this was your idea after all, *and* your cousin's farm," Humphrey says in a bewildered tone.

Dolt, thinks Grandma Siok, two seconds before a crash and tinkling of glass comes from the next room. He should know better by now than to suggest that Cynthia is at fault. Ever.

"Get out!" screams Cynthia. Humphrey makes soothing noises. "*Out,* I said!"

Afterwards, he walks towards the fishing ponds where he will sit for hours trying to unscramble the enigma that is his wife. In the evening he will go to Grandma Siok and throw up his hands: "I give up."

Grandma Siok will say what she's long suspected and muttered to herself: "I don't think she's quite all together. Mentally, do you know what I mean? When you're dealing with Cynthia, it helps to remember that."

And Humphrey, amazed at his mother-in-law's pronouncement about her own daughter's mental instability, will suspect that such labile behaviour no doubt runs in the family.

Lucy, playing with newborn piglets in the mud pen outside, squeals with delight. At least one of us is happy, Grandma Siok thinks. She opens Sun Tzu's manual and reads:

There are five qualities which are dangerous in the character of a general.

If reckless, he can be killed; if cowardly, captured; if quick-tempered you can make a fool of him; if he has too delicate a sense of honour you can calumniate him; if he is of a compassionate nature you can harass him. Now these five traits of character are serious faults in a general and in military operations are calamitous. The ruin of the army and the death of the general are inevitable results of these shortcomings. They must be deeply pondered.

Next door, Cynthia, who has no appreciation for war strategies—much to Grandma Siok's disgust—is sobbing.

⁂

Ling-li and the boy's mother sit for six hours at the hospital in the wing for natives while he has three epileptic fits, and gets progressively worse. Meanwhile, Jack is admitted to the European wing where he is washed and fed within four hours, all without having once seen a doctor. There is a power outage at the hospital, and the nurses scurry about in shadowed halls with torches looped around their wrists to help them look for supplies in unlit cabinets and boxes.

When the doctor finally arrives, he introduces himself and speaks directly to Jack, telling him he has to stay in hospital for a few days. "You came at the right time," he says about the leg. "Another day or so and we would've had a raging infection on our hands. I see Sister Joan has admitted you already, so I'll write some orders for antibiotics."

"How many days?" Jack asks, wincing as the doctor begins debriding the open sore in the middle of his wound.

"We'll have to see," the doctor says. "We'll have to rely on your houseboy here to clean and provide for your needs, I'm afraid. We're terribly short-staffed right now, as you can tell."

There is a strained silence as the doctor writes in Jack's chart. "This is Claude Lim, Dr. Richards. My friend," Jack says.

"Oh yes," Dr. Richards says smoothly, holding out a hand to Claude as if it were the most natural thing in the world. "How do you do? You'll need to help your—um—friend out for a while. You know, change his sheets, get him his food from the kitchen, maybe even clean his wound. Sister Joan will show you how. You up to it, young man?"

"Of course," Claude says, forcing a smile.

"You don't have to, you know," Jack says awkwardly after Dr. Richards leaves. "I can manage on my own. You've done splendidly as it is."

"I'll stay. You'd do the same for me," Claude says and though he tries to believe it himself, it is hard to imagine Jack changing his clothes for him or helping him to the toilet.

"Thank you," Jack says simply, lifting a hand to wave at Sister Joan who is making her way through the ward towards his bed. It bothers Claude that Jack neither confirms nor denies his statement.

Sister Joan gives chatty instructions on Jack's medical regimen. Unlike Dr. Richards, she looks Claude straight in the face when she talks to him and doesn't slow her speech.

No matter how much Jack explains otherwise, everyone at Ward A thinks that Claude is his houseboy. The patient in the next bed even asks to borrow him for a shave; his own houseboy had disappeared right after the war began. "He's a spy, I'm convinced of it. You can't trust any of these Chinamen," the patient says in a lowered voice.

Jack insists once more that Claude is his friend, not a servant, that the services Claude renders to him are done out of kindness, not obligation.

Claude scans the room. How could they not see this? The other Asiatics in Ward A—the janitorial staff—are mainly Chinese, their English crude and rudimentary, their manners boorish. Their broad faces take on a deliberately stupid look when they are reprimanded and they work sullenly, hardly speaking. How could the Europeans here think that Claude is like them?

To stop himself from brooding on this further, Claude decides to look for Ling-li. He finds her back at the building for locals, filling in a sheaf of forms. The woman and her boy are nowhere to be seen. "What's happened, Ling-li? Is the boy okay?"

"They were going to put him in quarantine—that was about an hour ago. Most of the doctors are in the Accidents department—the last bomb at the harbour was a direct hit on an oil tanker, so they have their hands full. Anyway, the boy had a third epileptic fit and then seemed to settle down a bit, so we laid him on a bench and I went to help some of the other nurses. When I got back, his mother was fast asleep and he had stopped breathing." She doesn't look up, keeps on writing in her precise, square hand.

Claude watches her, his mind on the little boy. How old was he? What was his name?

"Khong Wei," she says. "Six years three months."

"What's that?" Claude asks, his eyes following her pen-marks on the page.

"I'm filling out information for their records. You know the British and their *records*. How's Jack?"

He tells her, leaving out the details of his duties, making small talk, not mentioning the cleanliness and order of Ward A compared to the natives' wing. But she must know this already. Didn't she say that she trained here? All the local staff in Ward A were nursing amahs, consigned to emptying bedpans, scrubbing floors and feeding patients. Was she a housegirl then, when she worked in Ward A, or did she have real nursing duties like Sister Joan? Wisely, he says nothing.

"Are you ready to go?" she asks, finishing the last form. "The boy's mother won't be coming back with us. She's going to stay at her brother's flat. He's picking her up in a while."

Unable to avoid it any longer, he tells her the arrangements, how it's necessary for him to stay and help Jack. She shrugs, tells him it's all the same to her. Actually, she looks relieved, and he doesn't blame her. She could do a lot better without having him and Jack on her hands. "Thank you. You've been wonderful," he tells her, impulsively reaching forwards to give her a hug. The act startles him as much as it does her, and he lets go suddenly.

She stiffens, arches her back and begins to fall backwards, catching hold of the back of a chair to steady herself just in time. "Sorry," Claude mutters.

"I'll see you at the clinic," she says, gathering up the forms with exaggerated flourish. "Good luck with Jack." She leaves in a rush, keeping her eyes averted from his.

The three days at the hospital probably save Jack's leg. Claude, it turns out, is more useful as the ward's odd-job boy than as Jack's caretaker. The nurses shoo him away whenever he tries to tend to Jack. "We can do that," they say good-naturedly. "If you really want to give us a hand, you can unload our supplies from the lorry." At other times they have him mopping the floor when someone's spilled a urine bottle or thrown up, and on another occasion, they instruct him to nail boards across the windows to block out the lights at night during the air-raids. "It works both ways," Sister Joan tells him. "We don't see them and they don't see us. At least, that's what we hope."

The other patients are anxious to chat, bored as they are, but they rarely address Claude, so aside from a few words with Sister Joan, he hardly speaks, not even to Jack, who sleeps all day. The swelling in

his leg recedes and when he is awake, he sits staring at it, as if willing the taut, shiny blisters of infection to deflate and reveal, finally,
a loose, crepe-like healing skin. By his last day, the leg is almost back
to its normal size.

While in hospital, both Jack and Claude are reasonably well fed.
Claude is given less rice than Jack and doesn't receive any milk—but
then, neither, it seems, do the nurses. Milk is reserved for infants
and the sick only, but when Jack doesn't touch his share, Claude
drinks it to avoid wasting it. Sometimes he thinks of Ling-li. In fact,
he thinks of Ling-li much too often for his peace of mind. Why this
craziness? he asks himself. What is she to him?

That time that he hugged her: Had she really been *stiff*? Had she
actually pulled away, or had he, anticipating it, just let go? He had
felt no curves in her body, no softness, it was true, but there was a
pliancy that belied the word "stiff." The unexpected discovery
brought an odd rush to his head and made him feel like leaping. He
had had to force himself to walk back towards Ward A.

That's not what happened. Before he let go, she had yielded
slightly—the smallest gesture, brought on, perhaps, by a softening of
the spine, a transfer of weight. She had *leaned* on him before he let
go. He waited until she was gone and then he went out onto the
grounds, began a lope that broke into a frantic run that exploded
into a jump. He remembered the sensation of Up, the glide through
the air as his legs kicked under him as if he were treading water, the
extra lift from his raised shoulders. He didn't remember his feet
touching the ground. He had to force himself to walk back towards
Ward A.

Now back at the ward, he reminds himself to sneak out some powdered milk and a packet of biscuits for her.

With supplies and food dwindling, Dr. Richards is eager to clear
out the overcrowded wards and on the morning of the fourth day,
he discharges Jack. "He still needs antibiotics, but he can take pills
now." He peers at Jack's leg. "Good work, boy, it looks marvellous.
You've done wonders, and Sister Joan appreciates the help you've
been. I'm sure she'll tell you herself before you leave."

Jack grins from his bed. "Oh, Claude? He's been brilliant. He kept me alive—no offence, Doctor." Maybe there is satisfaction in service, in a job well done, after all, Claude thinks. The glow lasts until he realises that he has to get Jack back to the hut by himself.

On Outram Road there are no trishaws, no taxis anywhere. Not knowing what else to do, Claude keeps walking. For the hundredth time, he curses himself for not taking Rahman's bicycle when he first moved to Serangoon Road with Jack. There are no bombers in the air today, but everywhere he looks there are looters, most of them in military uniform. Bars and hotels have been broken into, their windows smashed and chairs thrown out onto the pavement. People on the streets are avoiding the soldiers, the women and children scattering in panic when they see them. Claude manages to walk on unhindered by stepping briskly and not looking anyone in the eye. He decides to head towards the clinic. Maybe Ling-li still has that ridiculous trishaw.

At the clinic, Ling-li is with a man unfamiliar to Claude. "My uncle, Hong-Seng," she says.

The man ruffles her hair fondly, says something in Hokkien. She grins and replies rapidly, and then the two of them break into loud guffaws as Claude stands there uncomfortably, his shirt sticking to his back and neck. "Sorry," Ling-li offers, still laughing. "My uncle said he was worried about me being on my own. He's been so busy with Dalforce—I told him that I was okay, that I was safe here with—er—you!" So this is funny to them?

"Dr. Richards thought I was a great help at the hospital." The moment the words are out, Claude is embarrassed at his childish need for her approval.

"Yes." She draws out the one syllable. "Yes, I'm sure that they were glad to have you." He wonders if she knows that he was praised for his houseboy skills, and braces for more acerbic remarks from her, but her uncle is talking again—this time very seriously.

"My uncle says things are getting worse. They've lost Johore." At this, her face changes. "They've lost Johore, which means—they've lost Malaya then."

Something, quick, across her face. A glimpse of fear?

"What now?" Claude asks.

She plunges into rapid Hokkien with her uncle, who seems to be disagreeing with her. Claude is too tired from his long walk to pay close attention, happy just to sit down and let the curious rough sounds of Hokkien wash over him while he rests. Finally, Hong-Seng makes a move towards the door. Ling-li's voice is reassuring now, gentler, concerned.

"Goodbye, Clau-de," Hong-Seng says, managing to make the name bi-syllabic.

"Er, goodbye, sir. Nice meeting you," Claude says mechanically, getting to his feet.

Hong-Seng holds Claude's eye for a second, fixes him with an intent look. Claude has the odd feeling that Ling-li's uncle is trying to memorise his face. But then Hong-Seng is looking away and giving Ling-li a fond pat on her shoulder.

When he is gone, Ling-li asks, "Is Jack back at the hut with you?"

"Well, they've discharged him, but I couldn't get a trishaw. I wonder—"

"It's in the back alley," she says quickly. "I covered it with gunny-sacks. When you get back, I'll need help here myself. Now that you've had some nursing training! . . ."

"I'll be back," he says.

"You know, Claude," she says unexpectedly when he reaches the door. "They'll be retreating across the Causeway in a day or two."

He stops to think about this. "Did your uncle tell you that?" he asks. She is rolling bandages, freshly washed in Dettol and dried in the office. Her hair falls forwards past her ears, hiding her face from him.

"Yes, he did—though it's supposed to be a secret." Hong-Seng told her and she is telling him. Why? Claude can understand her uncle confiding in her—she is family, after all—but why is she confiding in him? She starts on the used, washed latex gloves, sprinkling talc over them before rolling them up in brown paper for re-use later. She hardly ever throws anything from the clinic away.

"Should we be doing something?" Claude asks.

She shakes her head. "I wanted to tell someone, that's all. There's nothing else to do but what we're doing now."

"Okay," he says, watching for a long moment. Her hands are steady and she moves with her usual calm efficiency, but there is something in her bearing that unsettles him.

"I'll go get Jack," he says at last.

"Yes, go to Jack," she says. "And hurry back—I've lots of work for you." She carries the supplies into the consultation room.

Claude lets himself out into the noisy street.

✦

At night when Jack is asleep, his face half-submerged in his pillow, his mouth open, the hairs in his nostrils stirring with each soft whistling snore, Claude studies him. What makes Jack different from him? How can the Englishman fall into unconsciousness so easily, so naturally, when it takes Claude so long to arrange himself on his own little cot, his legs stretched out stiffly, his arms neatly folded on his chest? Why does being with Jack involve so many complicated layers, a series of selves melding into an awkward collage, not so much artfully arranged as painfully contrived?

What does Jack really think of him? He has introduced Claude as his friend several times, and once, when Claude lunched with him, Jack paid for them both, saying as Claude began to protest, "Oh come now, what's a few shillings here and there between us?" What had that meant, *between us*? So seemingly close, yet what chasms implied in those words, *between us*?

Another time in the past year, Claude met him outside of St. Andrew's Cathedral. Jack was on his way to the Cricket Club for lunch and invited Claude along. "Why not?" he asked when Claude declined politely.

"Why not?" he pressed. Such a benign question: *Why not?* Didn't he know that Asiatics were prohibited from entering the Cricket Club except under special conditions? By then, he'd been here several months already. Why was this not common knowledge to him as it was to everyone else on the island? It occurred to Claude that Jack might be toying with him, indulging in some strange version of schoolboy hazing.

"I can't," Claude said, wishing he could slink away. "I'm . . . I'm, well . . . not Caucasian."

"Oh." It was now Jack's turn to let his eyes wander, keeping Claude's face out of focus as the latter had done with him earlier. "I see," he said finally. "Well, I can bring a guest. As a member I am entitled to signing in guests for tiffin." The way he said this—as if to another audience, as if to convince himself, as if Claude weren't there—made Claude shake his head.

"No, no. I'm not that hungry anyway. Another time, perhaps."

"I insist, Claude. Let me take you to tiffin at the Cricket Club." He put his hand on Claude's shoulder. "It's something I want to do."

So Claude agreed. Better to go along and get a free meal and to puzzle things out later. When Claude said yes, Jack had smiled very oddly. A baring of teeth, as if he were readying himself for a fight, but then he was moving off towards the Cricket Club and Claude followed.

At the entrance, the *jagar* looked Claude over but said nothing. When they entered the building, a man came after Jack and said, "Sir, the syces have their own mess hall in the back."

"He is not my syce," Jack said, sounding almost as if he were enjoying himself. "He is my guest. We'd like to be seated in the tiffin room now, if you please."

"Yes, indeed." No fuss.

But it felt surprisingly good to Claude to walk into the tiffin room overlooking the cricket field and sit down amongst the ornamental urns of potted banana plants and palms. Maybe it was the music from the piano at the end of the room, or the air-conditioning, or the low, civilised hum of conversation in the room. Something sparked off the promise of Oxford in his mind, and a rare mood of gaiety came over him. When the Chinese boy poured their water, Claude said to Jack, "Well, what shall we have today?" What shall *we* have today! The Malay waiter who served their table came over and handed Jack the menu.

"And one for my friend, please."

"Oh, there's a standard menu for Asiatics," the waiter said with a little bow towards Claude. "Quite, quite good. Rice with yam, *achar*, cucumber salad, fried fish."

"No, that won't do. He'll order from the menu." Jack spoke more loudly than was necessary and several people looked up from their meals.

The Chinese boy eyed Claude from the corner where he was standing with his pitcher of water, supposedly on the lookout to fill an empty glass. The challenge was unmistakable. "Quite right, I'd like the menu please," Claude said even though he'd lost his appetite by now.

"But it's not our policy—"

"There are no specific rules forbidding a member's guest to order his own meal, are there?" Jack asked.

"No sir, but we've always—"

"Here, Claude, take this. It seems they've run out of menus. The chicken dish looks good."

Claude took the menu and flipped the pages. "Hmmm, not bad. I think I'll go for the roast beef though." He steadied his voice just enough to stop himself from stammering.

"I'll have the same. Good choice."

Claude handed the menu back to the disconcerted waiter and kept his eyes on Jack. "And how has work been? Is it what you expected? Or are you bored already?" As if he were Jack's confessor, as if he'd known Jack for ages. For once, small talk flowed smoothly from Claude's lips and he had a stream of easy, chatty topics at his disposal.

He ordered dessert as a flamboyant gesture—"watch this!"—to the waiter and the Chinese water boy. It was an over-sweet custard, which somehow suited Claude's mood perfectly.

It was at this point that Jack quoted something to Claude. Nodding at the tiffin room with its subdued members sinking fast into soporific reverie, he said, "Singapore is a first-rate place for second-rate people. Noel Coward."

Claude glanced around the room in mild confusion, avoiding his cynical smile. Should he laugh? Was Jack being facetious?

"That includes me," Jack said, tapping a cigarette out from the box. Claude never asked if it included him.

⁂

On that last morning, Ling-li woke Claude. He picked up on her face immediately, primed by the darkness of sleep. Her hair seemed slicked down on her skull and against her temples: She hadn't washed it in days.

"There's something I have to do," she said. "It won't take too long. I should be back in two hours or so."

"Couldn't it wait until daylight?" he asked, thinking: Why can't she just stop for a minute? "I mean, what's so important now? Why don't you go back to sleep and I'll give you a hand later?"

"No, this can't wait. If I'm not back here by daybreak, come look for me." She had a bundle tucked under one arm. It was a jacket of some sort, with its sleeves and ends knotted together to form an impromptu sling. Inside were her maps, some papers, small objects he couldn't guess at.

"Where are you going?"

She laughed. "You and your questions!" She seemed uneasy, as if she wanted to linger and was gathering strength to go.

She stood up. "See you later," she said and slipped out the door. Claude turned to check the time on the clock by Jack's bed. The luminescent paint on the dials had faded and it took him a while to figure out that it was just past two o'clock. She should be back by four.

Guilt and a vague anxiety began to build as he lay there staring at the ceiling. Why had he let her go off alone? True, she could probably take care of herself, but this wasn't a time to be wandering the streets after midnight. He must have fallen asleep because when he opened his eyes again, bright shards of sunlight were slipping in through the cracks. Jack had covered his face with his pillow to shut out the light.

The clock read eight-twenty. No Ling-li. And then it hit him that he had no idea where he should start looking for her.

Jack sits up in bed more often, which must mean he is feeling better.

On evenings when the heat and humidity become insupportable— even for the bombers, it seems—Claude makes tea and takes him outside, settling him in the chair while he himself hovers at the door, waiting for the tea to cool. The streets still manage, in between bombings, to exude a semblance of normalcy. Then the movements and the swinging kerosene lamps of Serangoon Road revive Jack somewhat and he manages a comment or two on passers-by that catch his eye.

He seems particularly drawn to the young women who ride by in trishaws or bustle down the busy road in their saris, kebayas and cheongsams. "Lovely," he uttered once at a Chinese girl in European dress. She had a short bob, her eyes slanted up towards her temples, and her skin had a glowing smoothness on her round face. Nothing that impressed Claude, but Jack was so taken by her that he leaned forward in his chair to watch her progress down Serangoon Road until she was out of view. "I think Chinese eyes are the most beautiful in the world," he said.

Claude didn't agree but, as usual, kept his opinion to himself. On the contrary, he was brought up to find Chinese features rather coarse. The button noses, the teardrop eyes, the moon faces—his mother had always expressed distaste for these, priding her family line for their average nose bridges, the bigger and wider-set eyes, the pointed chins that averted—just—the disaster of full moon faces. Claude had strict instructions never to get involved with anyone whose looks might dilute these genetic traits. "Of course, the most important thing is the voice," his father added. "These local women have such loud, shrill voices, and they're always shouting. Then again, Chinese is such a noisy, harsh-sounding language."

Claude wonders what Jack thinks of the sound of Chinese. "Jack, what do you think—" But then he changes his mind. Jack looks up. "What do you think is going on up-country?" Claude improvises. "I mean, the Japanese can't possibly keep this up. Wasn't there a report on the radio about how they're short on ammunition already?"

"I think so," Jack says, wrinkling his forehead to remember. "I didn't expect them to get as far as this. You've heard, I suppose, about the traitor?"

"Just rumours." How did *he* hear? Confined to his bed, he hasn't been out by himself since he moved into Amah's hut.

"They're true, I'm afraid," Jack says grimly. "He's a traitor. Ling-li told me herself. Delivered us right into Japanese hands. He helped plan the Kuantan landing. What kind of man would do something so low?"

One of your own, Claude wants to say, someone for whom this island means nothing, whose dead will never mix their dust with the earth to fertilize the soil here. Ever since he met the Australian soldiers he has not been able to get this out of his mind. "It's got nothing to do with me," the Australian had said. And the English? Has it anything to do with them? Is that why the English captain had found it so easy to sell out to the enemy—pure trade, the buying and selling of commodities, a colony here and there, like a car, a house, a dog?

"Is something the matter? You look like you're wrestling with some huge burden," says Jack.

"Oh no, not at all," Claude says and then finds himself asking the question he was trying to avoid. "I was just wondering what you think of the Chinese language. It must sound very strange to you."

"Which dialect?"

"I beg your pardon?"

"Which dialect are you referring to? They're quite different, as you know."

"Oh." Of course, Claude thinks, but he hadn't even considered this before he brought it up. "I meant—in general, I suppose," he says.

"Though perhaps 'dialect' isn't the most accurate word to use in this case," Jack continues smoothly, as if Claude hadn't spoken. "More like cognate languages, as Carstairs Douglas calls them, with a common written form." He reaches into his pocket for a cigarette.

"Hokkien seems to be the most commonly used dialect here, from what I gather. It's got something of the Cockney in it, don't you think?—that jaunty feel, you know, a certain brazen quality. Many of the Chinese at Albert and Burroughs, where I worked, were Hokkien, I believe—a hardworking group."

Sea pirates, Humphrey had called them, hawks, playing on their name rather wittily, for the Hokkiens had preyed throughout the South-East Asian seas from their home ports in Amoy in the 1800s.

"Cantonese, now, quite different—more stately, formal even. An old, old, language. And there're quite a few true dialect forms of Cantonese, aren't there, like Toishan and Sam Yap?"

"You really can hear these differences?" Claude asks, knowing Jack is trying to impress, enjoying his reaction.

"I have no idea what's being said, but yes, I can pretty much tell one dialect from the other, as I'm sure you can as well." He pauses to contemplate the smoke mushrooming out of his mouth. "My favourite is Mandarin though. It's softer than the other dialects, more sibilant, more elegant, despite it being the youngest."

Jack grins suddenly. "J. Dyer Ball."

"Beg pardon?" Claude leans forward to catch his words.

"*Things Chinese* by J. Dyer Ball. Don't tell me you haven't heard of it? I've used it quite often as a reference since I arrived. I'll show it to you later. It's in my suitcase, along with a few other books." He chuckles. "I've come a long way since my sight-seeing days!"

Humphrey had said once how much he admired the English for their curiosity and careful documentation of the world around them. "Books—volumes upon volumes—about various breeds of orchids, the reproductive cycles of earthworms and tropical birds, local festivals and customs. The impulse to classify and study their surroundings—truly a scholarly race!" It's disconcerting to think that Jack has had more interest in such things than Claude himself.

Jack smacks his left arm, leaving behind a dull red smear on his skin. "These damn mosquitoes! Let's hope that one didn't have any malaria in it. Last thing I need now." He gets up to go inside, instinctively reaches for Claude's arm to balance and support himself as he lifts up from his chair.

Inside the hut the air buzzes with more mosquitoes, and the long-legged insects brush against Claude's face, choosing a nice fleshy spot to land and insert their proboscis. Jack lights a mosquito coil and places it in the centre of the room. "We'll smoke the buggers out," he says almost gleefully.

"Jack." In the dark Claude's voice sounds louder than usual. "Really, reference books aside, what do you think? Chinese must sound awful to you."

"Awful?" Jack sounds surprised. "I wouldn't say that, although they're quite capable of making a din when they've a mind to. No, I wouldn't say it's *awful*—unusual, exotic, and of course quite, quite foreign to my ears."

"I see." The no-nonsense smell of smoke from the mosquito coil wraps itself round the room.

"What do _you_ think?" Jack asks, startling Claude slightly.

"What do you mean?"

"Well, I know you don't speak Chinese and I wondered what the language must sound like to you. You must've grown up hearing Chinese all round you and it is, after all, your native tongue." He sits down on his bed.

"I'm—not sure," Claude says. "It's—it's not very pretty. The sound, I mean." Cacophony, the tongue of the marketplace, the language of barterers and peddlers.

"Perhaps not," Jack agrees, "but it sounds amazingly complicated, all those tones and minute inflections. I imagine it would be the perfect language for a singer who needs to warm up her voice."

Claude thinks of the high-pitched shrieks of Chinese opera and shudders. "I suppose you're right," he says. "Our teas must have cooled by now, don't you think?"

Claude brings their tea in the dark and then sits to drink his own cup. It's mildly bitter and astringent. Somehow it suits his mood perfectly.

"My turn now," Jack says. "What do you think of Ling-li?"

"Ling-li? Why do you ask?" Claude suppresses the urge to get up.

"Pretty, in her own way. A bit too thin, but spirited enough. What? Never thought of turning on the charm for her?"

Ling-li? If he did, he would have no idea where to start. "Um, not really." Yes, quite pretty, lovely eyes. _Chinese eyes,_ but lovely all the same.

"Maybe you should. The two of you would make a jolly pair."

Perhaps Jack is teasing, but the thought is unexpectedly appealing. Claude finds himself imagining her in his arms, burying his face in her hair. She would be quite nice to hold if she could be—softer somehow, less caustic.

"Go ahead, make a move," Jack says. "She won't bite—and even if she does, you might find yourself liking it!"

Claude forces himself not to rise to Jack's baiting. "Not very likely."

And yet, he finds himself wondering, perhaps . . .

She recognises it for what it is—a warning. The bottle smashed against the clinic door with its message scrawled on toilet paper—图穷匕首见. The map unrolled, the knife revealed: The game is up. The Chinese characters are clumsily formed, imbalanced and smudged in places, as if the writer had rested his brush too long on certain strokes and the paper had soaked up the excess ink.

"Hooligans," she tells the patients, sweeping the glass into a neat pile. "Get back inside. I'll be there in a minute." She takes the time to scan the street. A stream of people, no identifiable cuplrit. It's just past six and she should be closing up the clinic. She goes inside and tends to the remaining patients. By the time she sends the last one off, it's seven and she has a headache.

Her hands shake as she tries to tidy up and she stops. What is wrong with her? She has been threatened before, has always been aware of the dangers involved in her role. She reaches into a cupboard and pulls out the bottle of brandy Dr. Singh kept there for fainting women, wound debridement cases and other such emergencies. This is an emergency. She *cannot* fall apart, there is too much riding on her. There are still five more agents to send off to Indonesia and it is getting trickier as the Japanese advance. What is hard is working alone, without any supervision. The only contact she has left is Anil, who introduces the agents to her and deposits them in her care. He knows even less than she does, and looks to her for support.

Her uncle has dropped by on and off, never staying too long, and she cannot tell him too much for fear of involving him. She keeps up her steel exterior in order to get through the day, to relieve her uncle's worries, to do her duty.

But she is afraid, her nerves fraying with every bomb, every crackle of gunfire. At night she has disturbing dreams of being captured by the Japanese, dreams she forces out of her mind in daylight. But they are always there, buried, waiting for nightfall. She wishes she had a friend to talk to, a confidante, someone to hold her at night so that she could sleep deeply, giving herself over completely to the dark. But there is no-one.

And yet she keeps thinking of someone, someone even worse prepared than she is for what might come under the Japanese. How could he be of any help, how could he be any comfort? A ridiculous thought, but stubbornly, the feeling that he could be a comfort in his own naïve way persists.

She swirls the brandy in her mouth and swallows, feeling its warmth slide down her throat. It is time for dinner at the hut. She has taken to eating there ever since the men returned from hospital; it made sense to share their food. She holds her hands up in front of her and is pleased that they have stopped shaking. Her rational side reasserts itself: she has every reason to feel so poorly; she has been starving for days, overworked, lacking sleep. It's a normal, purely physiological response.

But there's more work to be done: now that so many roads have been blocked by the army, she needs to plot another route to Changi Point. The bandages and bloodstains on the floor depress her. The fluorescent lights overhead flicker, causing her eyes to tear. A wave of self-pity threatens to overwhelm her and she slams her shot glass on the reception counter. That's it, she decides. She gathers her maps and heads to the hut. She can plot just as well over there.

She lifts her head and glances at Claude, studying him without embarrassment. Her frown deepens. "That Percival," she says and he marvels at how she can make a man sound an utter fool just by the way she pronounces his name. "He can make a grown woman cry."

Not you, Claude thinks.

"He's convinced the Japanese will try to land in the north-east."

She seems to be expecting some sort of response. Claude makes a noncommittal grunt since he has no idea what the appropriate response is. There's been a lull in the bombing, Jack is finally asleep after a restless day of trying not to scratch his itching, regenerating skin. The healing is slow, according to Ling-li, probably because of his poor nutrition, but overall, she is satisfied with his progress. The night is quiet, almost peaceful, and she has come for dinner. Claude doesn't want to spoil the mood.

"North-east! Nothing there but those useless guns!" She's refer-ring to the famous big guns "guaranteed," according to pre-war newspaper reports, to keep Singapore Island "an impregnable fortress." "North-west, north-west, Percival, you idiot! West where Tengah Air Base lies. West through the mangrove swamps." She is pacing the room, talking agitatedly to herself.

Where is this information coming from? Claude wants to ask.

"A fine mess he's making, moving all defence equipment to Changi and Seletar!" Her hands are clenched by her sides and she is almost snarling. It's a good thing for General Percival that he's not in the room.

"How do you know all this?" Claude asks. "I mean, it isn't as if that information is being broadcast all over the island."

"Well, I keep my ears open," she says hastily. "There's always a certain amount of substance behind the rumours on the streets."

"Are you a spy?" Claude surprises himself with his directness.

"What rubbish! Of course not!" she says, flicking her fingers at him. "Really, you're quite *gilah* at times!" The sing-song quality back in her words. He knows she wants to distract him.

"Why all the maps? *Relief* maps! Are you planning to hike around the island?" He's cocky now. It feels good to have the upper hand.

"My uncle has been involved in the Dalforce volunteer effort," she says. "He knows these things. These are *his* maps. I borrowed them, out of curiousity. As for spying"—she rolls her eyes—"I think your imagination is running wild."

That seals it. She's lying, Claude decides, and smiles. "Whatever you say. It might be more interesting if you were a spy. Give your personality a little—you know, pep."

"Poor Claude," she sighs. "You must have such a boring life to invent such a crazy thing!"

If she's truly a spy, whose side is she on? She doesn't like the British, but he can't see her siding with the Japanese either. She's not a traitor, whatever else she may be. China then. It must be China. That's not great either, because it would mean that standing before him is one Han Ling-li, Communist.

Not a good thing at all.

It's the survival of the most vivid out here. Jack has seen how the tropical light can burn out the brightest colours on a washing line, till they're nothing but muted versions of vermilion, saffron, turquoise, chartreuse. Funny how these colours pale while the skin darkens in response to the same sun. Under such light, only the most stubbornly flamboyant can claim the eye; only the relief of deepening pigment can prevent the white body from disappearing into the surroundings. In the black and white world of his camera, white faces are dependent entirely on shadow and depth for definition. For this reason, he prefers the coloured face.

In wartime, the locals have taken to wearing their loudest colours. Everywhere, pinks and violets bruise the eye; everywhere, yellows and greens are in profusion. It's a pity he can't capture all these hues, but something of their vibrancy is stained on their faces, reflected in their eyes. He still can't quite tell them apart, but his black and white photographs contain a tangible radiance translated from this real-life clash of pigments.

In his mind, the exotic is an excess of colour. He can't stop himself from looking.

And Ling-li is not the sort of girl one usually finds in the backwaters of the Empire, the kind who acts coy beneath her calculating merchant's mind, feigns innocence, reluctance and, if he holds out long enough with practised indifference, would throw herself at him. That's what always happens: some version of this scenario, small variations in the endless little plays they make for Jack, with the end game comfortably assured, of course, to all parties involved. Oh yes, it happens as surely as this blasted sun sharpens its blades of light everyday at noon, it happens as predictably as the tides; every white man here will attest to that.

"No more fevers," she says and there's even a congratulatory tone to her voice. She looks at him in a mercantile sort of way, as if he were a frivolous commodity. That's the way she treats him most of the time. She hardly ever looks at him when she's prodding and poking for medical symptoms, or when she wants to make a point about how useless the British really are.

But Claude. She looks at him all the time. She looks at him with all the intensity of light through a magnifying glass. It's not exactly a friendly look—in fact, sometimes it borders on contempt and ridicule, but it's there all the same, the direct gaze. A challenge, a retort, a critique, but also a connection, an invitation for Claude to look back and maybe even to look in. Something she refuses Jack, the burdensome white man.

Perhaps it's that refusal which excites him. Out here, he has grown used to being charmed with deference and tactful coyness. It's part of the fun, sending secret messages, deciphering code. A type of intelligence operation in which he puts together portfolios, behaviours, lives; a mapping of the Eastern female mind in which he sends out deliberate signals, and draws the revealing contours of responding echoes. Call it a hobby. He can't help flirting.

But this one refuses to play the game, simply does not engage. She spits at him in her firecracker Chinese, the syllables blasting out of her mouth like exploding pockets of gunpowder.

What does it matter what it sounds like? he wants to say to Claude. Chinese, with all its euphemisms, nuances and figurative qualities, is as functional as any other language: Stay away. Go to hell. Drop dead. This much Chinese he can understand.

❁

According to Ling-li, the army has begun evacuating people from the periphery of the island. Claude wants to head out to Punggol, but she urges him to check the refugee centres instead. "I have a list," she says. "Keep an eye out for Dr. Singh, will you? I worry about him."

At the nearest refugee centre Claude speaks to the girl in charge at the front desk. She reminds him of Ling-li, only rounder, and though she speaks in broken English, her voice holds a softness that is rare in Ling-li's. He finds himself smiling at everything she says.

"Lim, Lim—here, look." She hands him the register of all the refugees' names. There are six pages of Lims. He works meticulously down the list, squinting at the tiny handwriting.

Nothing.

He knows he should move on, but instead he stays and talks to the girl. Her name is Mei-chun. Her parents are in Alor Star, where she grew up. "I came here for work just before the war," she says.

"Have you heard from your parents?"

"No," she says. "My brother also there."

"At least he'll be able to take care of them," Claude says with a consoling smile.

Her eyes dart around the room. Beyond the foyer is the hall where the refugees have settled, a blur of colour and movement. The windows are lined with washing strung out to dry and little children skip under bloomers, saris, singlets, dungarees while their parents sit in groups discussing the war. The place reeks of urine and sweat and the older folk spit betel leaves and watermelon seeds on the floor. People move in and out, but no-one stops between the hall and the street outside.

"Actually, much, much worse to have him around," Mei-chun says in a lowered voice. "My father sixty-five, my mother fifty-five. They old. No one will care much. My brother, he twenty-eight. I more worried about him."

"But he can look after himself, I'm sure."

"The Japanese." She looks round the room again. "I very scared. I heard from some refugees that they are killing the young men." She chokes up. "I hope my brother found somewhere to hide."

"Hide? But where?"

"In the jungle, in the hills. Maybe they won't find him."

"And what if they do?" he asks, dreading her answer already.

"I heard—" she says and tries to hold back tears. "They just shoot them. Make them take off their clothes and shoot them. And they choose a few to make example—for these, they cut their heads off in front of the people." Tears are running down her cheeks. She wipes them away, embarrassed.

"I say, who's been telling you all this? How do you know it's true?" he asks, hoping to sound reassuring.

"Ask anyone in there." She nods towards the hall. "That's all they talking about. They say the Japanese going to take their revenge on the Chinese here for supporting China." She summons up a wan smile. "They talk a lot, but what else to do? Probably not really so bad. What about you? Is your family up-country also?"

"No, they went to stay with a relative in Punggol. Which reminds me, I must get going." He holds out his hand and shakes hers.

"Good luck," she says. "I hope you find your family."

"I hope you hear from yours."

Outside the world is in turmoil. The city is smothered under heavy smoke still coming from the harbour and the klaxons are going crazy. He knows he should return to the refugee centre straightaway, but decides to run ahead at least another few buildings. Something about being indoors without a glimpse of the sky, without a clue of what is attacking, and waiting for the ceiling to buckle and bury him alive, makes him risk a quick dash outdoors. He hadn't minded so much when he was in Amah's hut, a mere shack at ground level, relatively light and easy to dig out of. He might break a few ribs if the hut collapsed, but probably not give up the ghost. Not easily anyhow.

He runs a zigzag trail over debris and gravel, dodging beams and brick that are coming loose with every explosion from the harbour. This is how a man comes loose, he tells himself, one brick, one beam at a time.

Japanese bombers flock overhead, far above the anti-missile defences, circling lazily, waving ribbons of smoke in their wake. He stops, counts twenty-seven of them—always the same number. Their holding pattern broadens, they head his way. He watches, mesmerised, ignoring the burn of sun in his eye. Then, snug in formation, they growl in the air, a wave of metal rolling over the city. He stands, legs apart, sweating, heart thudding. They charge at him and he steels himself as he would before a blow, an unstoppable curse; he holds his ground. Then, just before they cloud his piece of sky, his insides loosen, slide down to his shoes and he runs. "Help!" he screams, and a longer: "Heeeeelp!" A man coming loose, tripping over burnt trees and bits of plaster.

The planes, high and far away, bank left, heading back out to sea, but he keeps running. They're going, silly, the cold, calm part of his brain tells him. They were never any real danger. His heart steadies but his feet never let up. It's as if something inside has taken off and he can't stop it. It's got nothing to do with willpower. He'll stop when his body decides to, when physics demands it, when, for example, he hits something.

FOOTSTEPS IN THE CORRIDOR: three people. Two in boots, clomping along, heels dragging slightly in a slow march; one with a syncopated limp that disrupts the orderly steps of the others. You believe for a moment they are coming for the Body but the footsteps pass by and move on to the next room.

The key turns and they are in. You are still trying to distract yourself, not looking, but you are drawn by the sounds. You sense movement: a chair is pulled out, a cigarette lit. Someone speaking: that familiar baritone. You strain to hear what he is saying, can almost catch the words, but Claude the Body begins to moan.

Nonsense syllables, a strange gurgling noise in his mouth, like a wild, choked attempt at ululation. Shhh, you want to say. Calm down. But he is writhing in his sleep, his hands clutching his throat, as if to wrestle off a death grip, and then you know:

He is in the dream again. He is trying to save his tongue. Despite all previous mutilations, he must keep this part of him intact. It's only a dream, you want to tell him, but you know that he will fight the imaginary knives in his mouth. Nothing you say will soothe him. The dream must be played out. You can do nothing but let it pass.

Over the next few days, Claude searches every refugee centre in the city. "Any friends they could be staying with?" Ling-li asks.

"Most people we know lived outside the city and would've had to evacuate as well. I saw an old friend of my mother's at one of the refugee centres, but she hasn't seen or heard from my family."

The three of them are hunkered over a meal of porridge and some shredded pork floss. A patient brought the extra rations and Ling-li surprised Jack and Claude when she appeared at the hut with a tiffin carrier of porridge. "No need to cook tonight," she said. "I need to sit down and rest my feet." Claude made a note to help out more at the clinic—easier to do now that Jack was getting better.

Ling-li almost drinks down the soupy porridge, lifting the bowl to her lips and tilting it. "Hospitals," she says, a moustache of gruel on her upper lip. "Did you try those?"

"My next plan," Claude says. "It's pointless going to the police. They have too much on their hands as it is, what with the looters and other havoc going on."

"And not succeeding very well," she says. She's in an unusually mellow mood. In the yellow flickering light of the kerosene lamp, her angular features soften and her face takes on an unusual warmth. It suits her.

"I have another suggestion," says Jack unexpectedly. He's been very quiet in Ling-li's presence, as if he's trying to avoid her displeasure. An insect dives towards his jaw and is lost in the flourishing beard that's taken root there. "Have you tried checking the hotels?"

"No, I haven't," Claude says. "Good idea! There's probably a better chance of finding all of them in a hotel than in hospital."

"We'll make a list, start in Orchard Road."

"Yes—the Roxy, the Eastern Strand, the Parrot Inn . . ."

"A hotel?" Ling-li says. There is real wonder in her voice.

Claude considers his mother, her carefully filed nails, her neat coiffure and rigorous standards of hygiene. For her, no refugee centre would have passed muster. "Definitely," he says, imagining Cynthia's exacting manner as she orders room service and harangues a porter into pressing her clothes. "I wonder why I didn't think of it myself."

Ling-li is shaking her head, still bemused. "A hotel," she says. "In the middle of a war." Claude waits for her usual sarcasm. Instead she grins, catching him by surprise. "It takes all kinds—I hope you find them, Claude."

"Thanks. How's your uncle doing?" He is pleased with the amicable mood that's developed and wants it to go on.

"He's not too happy with having to take orders from the British. Anyone for the last of this porridge?" She holds up the pot.

"No, thank you," says Jack, looking down at his empty bowl. It occurs to Claude that Jack must be hungry still, despite his polite refusal, for Jack is a tall man, recovering from a serious leg infection, and even Claude himself—much more compact in size and in better health—even Claude is hungry.

"You have it." he says to Ling-li. She shrugs, pours the rest of the porridge into her bowl and eats. It seems to take only a minute. Claude has never seen anyone eat so quickly.

"My uncle says the Dalforce unit has been moved three times in two days. Every time they start digging in, they get an order to move along. No one seems to know what's going on." She washes the porridge down with lukewarm tea, two cups in one breath, trying to fill herself up, trying to stop her belly from rumbling. "One thing's for sure," she continues, "discipline hasn't been our strong point in this war."

"They won't take the island," Claude says, repeating sentiments from the newspapers and radio reports.

"Claude," she says, unusually patient. "What do you know? Have you looked at the facts?" She counts them off on her stick-like fingers, one at a time.

"First, Malaya was supposedly 'impenetrable' because of her jungles. Well, no-one mentioned that the best road in Asia runs right down the peninsula like a backbone, just waiting for the Japanese to march down it, on foot and on their bicycles! Second, we have untrained troops—boys! *unruly* boys!—running around in the jungle supposedly trying to defend us. Third, there are plenty of looters on the streets who are pillaging and setting fire to our buildings. Who are these people? Are they the enemy troops, the Japanese? No! They're *our* forces, taking to the streets like hooligans! Would you like me to go on, Claude? Tell me again now—why won't they take the island?"

"Well," he says, feeling foolish, "I just thought—the reports."

"Propaganda, do you understand? You can't believe any of that." She is still patient, like an elder sister tonight, unbearably didactic and conscientious with her charges.

"What will happen?" Claude asks, thinking, Let's see if she knows, let's see what she believes.

"It all depends. It really all depends on what the War Council decides. If I were them"—she shakes her head at the impossibility of the situation and there is regret in her voice—"I would hold out as long as possible at the Causeway. The Japanese are already suffering all sorts of deprivations, they can't play war games forever. I'd make them spend their ammunition, give them false leads, draw out battles. We don't necessarily have to beat them, we just need to use up their shells as much as we can. But we won't do that." She sighs.

"Why not?" Claude asks. "It sounds like a good plan to me."

"Because boys can never wait, can they?" She gives him a bitter smile. "They'll want to win everything, or give up playing altogether, which I think is more likely to happen, given past examples."

"Our troops will fight on."

"Our troops, Claude? But they're not really *ours,* are they? I just hope . . ." She shudders and turns her bowl mouth-down on the crate that they've been using for a table. "I just hope they won't give us away."

"What rubbish!" Jack exclaims. "I know you don't like the British here in Singapore, Ling-li, but that's a rather unfair thing to say.

We might have bungled once or twice up-country but I for one believe the island to be—as they all say—impregnable." He looks at her fiercely but there's a curious softness about him even as he challenges her.

"Jack," she says, "I hope you're right. But this place has never been—and never will be—home to you English. When you talk among yourselves, you refer to this place as if it were a prison to which you've all been exiled. It's always 'when we get home,' or 'back home in England,' isn't it? There's nothing for that lot out there defending this piece of rock, and I can't ever forget that, no matter what you say, no matter the high theatrics the propaganda department lets loose."

"This is our home too, Ling-li," Jack says, not meeting her eyes.

"This is a tactical resource, a commercial treasure, one of the jewels of your Empire," she says. "But we are a prop, an ornament. We are not the body of that Empire, and as such, we are dispensable. If not, Downing Street would have made sure we were properly prepared and armed."

Claude thinks of school, the incessant studying, exam fever, the inane school plays, half-hearted hockey in the afternoons. All of that seems very far away, a different life, observed and unlived.

The ground, a soupy mush, smells of sulphur and decaying plants. Swamp. Digging is impossible. At high tide, catfish swim inland and mudskippers flop about, startling the men with their loud and sudden plops into shallow water. The Australian troops stationed on the island's north-west end have taken to paddling about quietly in borrowed sampans, armed with nets for a decent dinner. The protein revives their spirits a little, but not much.

When the tide rolls out, the mangrove roots are left uncovered, like an intricate network of bridges and arches above the black, briny mud. Boats are useless then, and walking—even in boots—is unpleasant, slow and noisy. Luckily, the Japanese are on the other side of the strait.

At certain times of the day, it's easy for the Australians to see them setting up camp, piling sandbags, digging trenches, patrolling the Johore waterfront. Once, they spot a boat of Japanese soldiers bobbing about on the far side of the strait, but they are only fishing; they are even more desperate than the Commonwealth troops for new food sources. Later that afternoon, the Australians scan the horizon, only to find the Japanese looking back at them. The two sides stand surveying each other, binoculars glinting, and suddenly, on impulse, one of the Australians breaks into a grin. "You bloody Japs!" he says, waving with his free hand. "Hey, you fucking bastards!"

Tentatively, two Japanese soldiers, eyes fixed on their binoculars, wave back. But as soon as they do so, their officer slaps them furiously, and begins beating them with his whip. The Australians watch, transfixed. "God," says one, "I'm almost beginning to feel sorry for those blokes." The rest mutter their assent, and then, bored, abandon their posts.

Even when it is possible, in places, to dig, the Australians refuse. "Stuff the trenches!" they tell their officers. "It's too bloody hot! And the Japs are supposed to land on the other side anyway."

Charles March of the Royal Australian Engineers is unconvinced. "Look," he tries to point out. "There's thousands of the buggers over there, right before us."

"All right, Sherlock," the troops mock. "Now give us a break, will you? It's time for a nap!"

Later, Charles will tell his friends and family back home, "They just absolutely refused to dig. Then a shell would come over and there'd be the four of us in a one-foot-deep slit trench. It didn't surprise me that we lost. Didn't surprise me at all. I think all of us knew—well before the end—how things would turn out. Deep down inside, we knew."

Storm clouds growing fat overhead, their enormous weight pressing down on the air below, making it hard to breathe. A week into February, and there is an odd stillness on the streets; the humidity has wrung all the energy out of the remaining few people who are out.

"Life must be so much easier in England," Claude says, throwing open the shutters at Amah's hut for some ventilation. Bombers don't fly during a storm, so the rain will be a welcome relief and might help put out some of the long-burning oil fires at the harbour.

"Hmmm? What did you say?"

"I said it must be a lot easier to live in England than over here."

"Easier . . . Well, I'm not so sure." Jack seems to be thinking about this, which is surprising since, to Claude, it's already a foregone conclusion. "It depends on what you mean by 'easier.'"

"Well, you know, better quality of life, cleaner, less chaotic, that kind of thing," Claude says. "More—civilised?"

Jack is silent for a moment. When he speaks again it is to ask, "Tell me, Claude, how do *you* think I lived in England?"

"Well," Claude says, hedging. "I'm not really sure." But the truth is, he has pictured Jack many times before in a trim bowler and an impeccable suit as he is being chauffeured to work. In the afternoons he has tea with sugary ladies in flower-laden hats, nibbling on thickly buttered scones. On weekends, Claude imagines he must go hunting, splashing into streams on his mount and getting his cherry-red coat dirty.

"I lived in a flat in Charing Cross—a bed-sitter, really. My landlady gave me tea each morning—two teaspoons of sugar, no milk, exactly the way I took it when she first interviewed me as a potential tenant. I'd had a little stomach problem that day and had avoided the milk but she took it as my usual habit, no matter what I told her afterwards. 'You didn't have milk when you first came here,' she'd say to me every time I brought it up. 'I didn't include it in my budget.' I took the bus to work everyday, and I had a desk at Albert and Burroughs' main office in London. My window faced the brick wall of the next building. On weekends I visited George and Janet and went to the pub. Sometimes, to change the routine, I went to church."

"Didn't you have a butler?" Humphrey constantly talked about these marvellous institutions of British civilisation, and has always wanted one. Amah, he said, was a poor, unsatisfying substitute.

Jack laughs. "I'm afraid not, Claude. And neither did George, by the way. He had a maid who helped out, and a nanny, but that was it. He didn't have a butler, and he certainly didn't have a chauffeur. I know it sounds strange to say this, but I didn't have a single servant until I came out here."

None of this is what Claude had expected. "What about hunting?" he asks.

This time Jack laughs harder. "Hunting! Good Lord, Claude, you are priceless! Did you really think I was a huntsman?"

"It was just a question," Claude says. "Didn't you think we lived in trees before you came out here?"

"Oh no," he says, smiling. "Not I. Janet, on the other hand . . ."

It has begun to pour. Outside the window the world is blurred through sheets of rain, and the shutters swing back and forth in the wind, as if marking time to the drumming of raindrops on the zinc roof. Jack laces his hands behind his head as he leans back on his pillows, thinking hard about what he wants to say.

"You know, Claude," he begins finally, "it isn't the way you think at all. Most of the British expats I know here never had it so good in England. That's why they stay on, you know, despite everything. This place has given us a chance to experience the high life—servants, parties, bungalows, country clubs and first-class travel everywhere. Yes, we complain about the heat and the 'poor' service, the provincial mentality, but believe me, this is a long way from bed-sitters and riding the bus to work everyday."

When the sky flashes, light hurls itself onto his face and then evaporates, and the brief impression left on Claude's retina is like a photographic negative. The Jack he has known for over a year now slowly develops before him, the colours and detail filling in to reveal an unfamiliar likeness.

"The local people see us as rich and privileged, as indeed we are—only now, only here," he continues. "Most of us would never have made it at home. This is the last resort for a lot of people, you know. If you can't marry rich or pull enough strings to get you a top-notch job, you set off for the colonies to make your fortune. This doesn't shock you, does it?"

"It's just that I thought—you've always looked—I mean—"

"I know what you mean." He props himself up on his elbows. "Believe me, Claude, we're nothing special."

From the window Claude sees a man and a woman duck under the shelter of the Tian Shan Building. They are short of breath from running and laughing. He has not seen anyone look so happy since the war began. The man whispers something to the woman and she looks over her shoulder as if she's afraid someone will overhear. When he nuzzles her neck, she forgets her caution and giggles. They stand there hugging each other, barely sheltered from the wind and rain, and then he picks her up, runs over to the hut opposite—a hovel really, with its back wall missing so that it's exposed to the elements—and carries her inside.

"What is it, Claude?"

"Nothing. The rain. It's really pouring buckets." For some reason, he doesn't want Jack to know about the couple. "It's all very well for you to say that, but the truth is, you English act as if you *are* special. Take the Cricket Club, for example—no entry to locals. And the hotels and the restaurants where we have to sit in different rooms. And, and, well, your *attitude* towards us . . ." He can't believe he's saying such things to Jack, but something's clicked inside, a trigger of sorts, and everything else just seems to follow. There is no movement from behind the façade of the hut opposite but he can guess what they must be doing inside. Jack stirs and, determined to keep him from the window, Claude bursts out again.

" . . . Yes, your *attitude*—it's so damn condescending and self-righteous! We're not clean enough for you, not bright enough, not civilised enough. You can sit there and smile at me and say in the same breath that you're ordinary folk like us, that you're nothing special, but then you go about making laws that set you apart from us, that give you preferential treatment, laws that in effect *make* you special!"

Jack holds up one hand. "I didn't say we were perfect. It's true we have special rights here, and some of it's very silly, I agree, but it's the kind of compensation that makes coming out here worthwhile—"

"Compensation."

"I know it sounds pretty terrible, Claude, but, well—yes."

The rain must be muffling their cries of passion and their laughter. If Claude had to guess, they were about the age of his parents, and when they smiled at each other, their faces had gleamed with tenderness. They were the most arresting locals he had ever seen. Their happiness and spontaneity had a clarity that defined them with a luminous glow.

"What's so interesting out there?"

"It will rain all night, I think."

He comes to the window and looks out into the alleyway. "I suppose."

"You're getting wet standing there. You might catch cold."

"And what about you?"

"I'm used to it. I was born here. I've known monsoons all my life and I've never caught cold. It's a kind of immunity."

Jack makes a small bow. "Point taken." He hobbles back to his seat and pulls his blanket over his shoulders.

Claude never sees the couple leave, never catches another glimpse of their carefree faces, but it pleases him that Jack never sees them at all. The rain continues to gush from the sky, obliterating everything. Afterwards the air will seem cleaner and cooler for a few hours and the city will glisten with a sheen of newness, but by nightfall, everything will have dried off and the heat and dust returned, everything the same as before. But not quite. *He* has not seen the couple, has not seen the way they laughed away the war. Whatever compensation Jack has received for being here, this is one he will never get. Claude takes in a deep breath, filled with a feeling that is almost like hope.

At dinner that night, Claude presents Ling-li with a gift. He has been saving it since the day before, when he was on his way back to Amah's hut after helping Ling-li all day. She looks at him now as if he's gone off his rocker but he remains adamant. "You must! Of course you must take it," he says. "Don't be silly, it's just what you need, don't you see? I was lucky to find it still wrapped and frozen. Imagine, a bomb wipes out the whole shop-house and leaves the freezer intact, still going. It's perfect."

"Absolutely not," she says, not taking her eyes off the package he's holding out to her. "That is pure lard, Claude. You want me to *take a bite out of that*?"

"Well, I didn't say 'bite.' I'm sure there are ways you could get it down." He racks his brains for a few more appetising suggestions. "You could fry it."

"And drink the oil?" Her face suggests she would rather pour it over him.

"All right, it's not the best idea, but given how you're wasting away, I don't think you have a choice! Our rations would be meagre under any circumstances, but with your, your—natural skinniness . . . Like it or not, you're going to have to *eat* this." At least he's made his point, and pretty forcefully. Now she can chew him to bits and spit him out, but she doesn't.

"What do you know about his cooking skills?" she asks Jack, who has been watching from his cot.

"He can do just about anything with eggs," Jack says and, amazingly, the three of them smile. All together. Laugh, even.

In the end it's Jack who comes up with the idea of making a broth with the lard and scattering a handful of rice into the mix to make it more palatable. With a dash of salt, it becomes quite tasty. Ling-li drinks several bowls and then a few more the next day. Claude watches her slurp down her soup and doubts that she will put on any weight from that, but takes comfort in the five pounds of lard he managed to stir into the soup. Maybe she'll hold her own and not lose any more weight over the next few days.

The ceiling, with its intricate map of cracks, attracts a caravan of ants—myrmidons, Grandma Siok called them. Formica ants are bigger, more distinctive in the jointed coat of chitin dividing their bodies clearly into head, thorax, abdomen. The myrmidons are tiny in comparison, crawling spores that speckle the walls and, from the ground, seem like another line of cracks on the high ceiling.

Twelve feet high, to be precise. And the room dimensions—twelve by sixteen. You are being precise in order to avoid registering too much of what is near you. A pair of footsteps pacing next door, distinctive in its slight hesitation, its irregular hobble. Chair legs skidding the floor with a whine. The chair cushion sighs as someone sits again.

The ant trail meanders diagonally across the ceiling and ends in a hole in the corner. Funny how ants can't seem to walk in a straight line; they follow each other in pointless curves and detours that lengthen their journey needlessly. Diversions, distractions. The Body still sleeping.

In the next room, the baritone speaks.

—And now, for you—a special treat. Something to make you reconsider what you may have to offer us.

A muffled answer, scuffle of feet. A woman's voice heaving out sounds like a cornered beast, bursting into spurts of bitter, erratic laughter. A near-howling that fills your ears.

—Since you aren't being very cooperative, we'll try to help you out. Perhaps seeing her in this . . . position . . . will jog your memory?

You have taken to counting the ants, starting randomly, as is usual when you count something. Counting soothes you. Eleven, twelve, thirteen, fourteen—they file past you so quickly that you really have to focus to keep up.

More muttering, an angry exchange. Fifteen, sixteen.

—But we have ways, you see, of breaking down barriers and extracting information. If you watch carefully, you may even learn something.

The woman hisses. Nervous laughter all round, a ripping sound, a grunt. The baritone speaks a rapid-fire Japanese, no breaks between words, no pause for breathing. A forced cheer picks up. Twenty-eight, twenty-nine, thirty.

—Why won't you look? This is not something you are . . . unfamiliar with.

Stop-and-go, stop-and-go, that funny way of moving that ants have—thirty-four, thirty-five, thirty-six, thirty-seven.

—I said, open your eyes.

A slap. Unclear to whom, because the woman lets out a cry at the same time. Forty? Forty, forty-one, just don't look, you hum to yourself. Stay with the ants, forty-two, forty-three.

An expectant pause, and then more rustling, a buzz of voices.

—Shut up, the baritone says in English, but they understand clearly, quiet down.

Is the woman trying to say something? Forty-nine, fifty, fifty-one, fifty-two, fifty-three, fifty-four, block out scream, block out her panicked voice, fifty-five, fifty-six.

The thing is, these ants can't seem to go very far without touching each other, without caressing their neighbours or pawing them. If you squint, it almost looks as if they are whispering secrets, or petting, or grooming, or passing on an invisible gift—a kind of sacred transmission. Is this how they share news, gossip, joy? Is this how they pass on complaints, suspicions, terror?

Fifty-? Fifty-nine, sixty.

—It's a pity you won't look. It might amuse you.

If he won't look, you decide, then you won't either, whoever the "he" might be that the baritone is addressing in the next room. Sixty-two, sixty-three.

The voices next door become rowdy again, as if they are cheering someone on, as if they are spectators at a sport, or taking bets at the racecourse.

An eerie long moan from the woman, as if she is biting her lips to stop the sound even as it comes out. Sixty-nine, seventy, seventy-one, seventy-two. It occurs to you that you could be doing this forever. The ants are endless, seemingly self-replicating. It's a comforting thought, when one has so few other resources.

Next night. All their nights measured now, it seems, by the meals they share. It's almost ten at night and Ling-li has not yet arrived for dinner. Jack is nervous. "She can't still be working," he says, his hand reaching into his pocket for a cigarette and finding none. "She really shouldn't be at that clinic by herself. Did we ever find out what happened to Dr. Singh?"

"Ling-li's tried to call him at home, but no-one answers. She thinks he might have been wounded in one of the raids."

"Well, she can't bloody well be expected to take over his practise," he says roughly. "This is the latest she's ever been."

All day, the air-raid klaxons have been going off, to the point where they've become background noise, along with the frequent gunshots and explosions. "Well, knowing Ling-li, she might have decided to go without dinner tonight." It would be the smart thing to do too. The clinic has a tiny cellar that would work well as a bomb shelter.

Claude talked to Jack earlier about moving out of Amah's hut to one of the refugee centres. It's pure luck that the hut is still standing. The Tian Shan Building just off the alleyway was bombed that morning. There was a tremendous explosion and rocking, as if an enormous train were just pulling out of the station, and then the Tian Shan Building was in flames, its pagoda roof and half of its walls blown off, an entire staircase hanging out like entrails. The alleyway was remarkably untouched.

When Claude approached Jack about moving, he merely shrugged, as if such matters held no interest for him. "You're probably right," he said and then asked about breakfast. It occurred to Claude that Jack was leaving everything up to him as he had when he was sick. However, a strange passivity had overtaken Claude as well, and he was reluctant to move into one of the overcrowded and unhygienic refugee centres. He recalled the centres he had visited in the past days: people squatting on the floor, pressed up against each other and spilling out the doors and windows. The odour of human secretions and unwashed feet was unbearable, lingering in his nostrils until he ran outside and crossed the road.

So he hadn't pushed moving that morning—a certain fatalism had set in. If they were going to die, then so be it. There was no guarantee that a bomb wouldn't land on the refugee centres. Better to be taken out in Amah's spartan but livable hut with Jack than in a packed building with the rest of humanity. Even so, as night lengthens, Claude begins to have second thoughts. There is something about a crowd that simulates a kind of courage and boldness that quickly dissipates when one is alone. Well, Jack is there, but it's not the same. Jack is a responsibility, a burden, and, Claude realises guiltily, he has been thinking of the Englishman as a liability from the start. Had Jack not been here, Claude would have found it easy enough to persuade himself to move to the Bras Pasah refugee centre. With Jack, he has a hundred-and-seventy-pound piece of luggage he must lug along.

Ling-li's presence, on the other hand, would have bolstered Claude. He walks to the window. There are no lights on Serangoon Road, only two or three kerosene lamps throwing an underworld of shadows on the cracked and torn street. The Tian Shan Building is still smoking. A lean dog passes through the alleyway, its eyes like red lanterns; everything is cloaked with danger and hostility. There is too much to brood over and having Ling-li here would have helped dispel the sense of futility.

"Maybe one of us should go over to the clinic," Jack says. He pushes off the bed with a determined effort and hobbles clumsily to the door. Although he has gained mobility in the last few days he still has limited strength. It will take weeks to rebuild that, more without adequate nutrition.

"You should keep that elevated. You can't go out, Jack. Be sensible." All that limping about has brought Claude's guilt out in full force and he resigns himself to being responsible for tracking down Ling-li. But Jack is opening the door. "Where are you going? Listen, I'll do it, come back inside," Claude says.

"You've been running all the risks while I've been ill. Both you and Ling-li. I'm better now. It'll be all right." He limps outside, panting.

"Don't be silly, Jack. It'll only take me ten minutes to get to her, you'll be gone the whole night. Come in, make us some tea, and I'll have her here by the time the water's boiling."

Jack leans against the door. "Will you go now?" he asks in a tired voice.

"Yes," Claude says, holding out his arm for Jack to lean on. "Straightaway."

"I'm quite dizzy," Jack says, wonder in his voice as he walks slowly back to his bed with Claude.

"What did you expect? You've been in bed for days." They both turn around to see Ling-li at the door. A kerosene lamp is in her hand, lighting her face from below and making her look quite ghastly.

"Put that out," Claude says, shocked by her thinness in the unforgiving light.

She sets the lamp in the middle of the room and blows out the candles instead. She has a small sack with her. "Rice," she says triumphantly, holding it up.

"You're late," Jack says, his tone unusually harsh. "And you shouldn't have walked here alone."

"What do you think I should have done then? Waited for you two to come and get me?"

"Claude was just on his way," Jack says, ignoring her condescension. She runs her eyes over Claude. "I see."

"I'll start cooking the rice," he volunteers, uncomfortable under her scrutiny.

"Tomorrow you must move," Ling-li says. "To the clinic. We can all fit in the cellar—plenty of cots there, I counted four or five at least. I don't think the bombing is going to stop."

"What's happening now?" Claude asks, measuring out a cup of rice. He'd like to use two cups, but knows they need to conserve as much as they can.

She peers out the window and then comes back to the centre of the room. He has never seen her so restless. Her collarbones jut out alarmingly and he can see every flutter of the strong pulse beating at her neck. The hell with it, he thinks, and throws in another half cup of rice when she isn't looking.

"It's pretty bad. They've taken Tengah Air Base." For the first time her voice is shaky.

"You mean they're on the island?" Jack half-stands. "But when—?"

"They landed last night. I heard on the streets that there were two landings, one on the north-west coast and the other at the Causeway. The British, of course, were preparing for a landing on the north-east coast—contrary to advice from their own Supreme Commander and the Dalforce leaders."

It is hard to take it all in. Somewhere in Claude's head he registers the words "Japanese," "the defeat of Singapore," "the end" even though he knows she hasn't said these words. He thinks of his family. Perhaps, despite the evacuations, they're still at Punggol. Aloud he hears himself saying, "We're losing."

And then: "I have to find my family. I need to get to Punggol."

"They must have evacuated by now," she says, her tone softer than before. "Our troops are withdrawing from Tengah. Better not go anywhere—it'll just lead to more confusion. We can check the refugee centres again tomorrow and leave messages there for your family. And you've still a few more hotels to check."

"Withdrawal," says Jack as if he is fascinated by the word. "Has it come to that? We've lost already then." He pounds his fist on his bed.

"I believe the plan is to continue fighting from within the city and to defend the perimeter," says Ling-li sharply. "So don't jump to conclusions."

There is a brief silence as they studiously avoid each other's eyes. Claude goes outside to the barrel beside the door where he's been collecting rainwater. It's half-full. He covers the rice with water and brings it back to the charcoal burner. After he lights the coals, he moves them about with a pair of tongs to get a nice even fire, and sets the pot over it.

They hear the buzz of an airplane. Everyone tenses as its engine throbs louder, until it is directly overhead. Claude hunches his shoulders automatically. Ling-li's eyes are shut fast, he notes with some satisfaction, despite his own growing fear. So she's just like everyone else; she's afraid after all. He doesn't realise he has been gripping the rim of the pot until the airplane veers away.

No-one says anything as the explosions from the harbour reverberate through the city. Against all folk wisdom, the pot, watched by three pairs of eyes, boils.

❁

February 8th: Tengah is flailing. The airfield is flooded with stragglers throwing away their weapons and hijacking all transports to head off for town. One Australian unit is making sure they are not forced to take up their arms again by dumping their guns into the airfield's wells. "Navy let us down. Air force disappeared. Let the *bungs* fight for themselves!" the men complain.

Wing Commander Gregson of the RAF is calling for volunteers from the ground staff for a squad "to help plug the gap" formed by the deserters. He himself is an administrative officer, but this does not stop him and his men from gathering up the tossed-off weapons and organising themselves into a fighting unit. What fuels them? Heroism, duty, character. Also shame. "I was ashamed to see the way some of the troops were behaving," one of Gregson's Grenadiers says years later. "I remember one Malay chap asking me why we were running away from these little yellow men, and I didn't have an answer for him. More than anything, I was ashamed."

⁂

The Fifth Columnist doodles over her reports. Some of the versions have not been satisfactory to her—too staid. The trouble is, like everyone else in real life, Miss Competence has an unexciting existence. Nursing is well and good, but honestly, doesn't one sick patient look like another after a while? All that sniffling and moaning. It's an easy profession to take on in a bid for sainthood, and, of course, *she* would play it up, fussing over mite-infested babies and waddling grannies.

But it is nothing compared to this task of writing, of composing a life out of humdrum instances. No public acts of heroism, no forced compassion or moments of glory. Every word typed out in seclusion like some clandestine birth.

It's a lonely vocation.

⁂

For the first time, Ling-li stays the night at Amah's hut, unwilling to risk the walk back to the clinic. The night sky is filled with metallic stars shaped like crosses unloading their bombs across the entire city. The smoke-scented air is oily against their skin and clings to their hair, reducing it to lank, greasy locks. The radio plays lilting waltzes and love songs, and these light-hearted broadcasts disturb them more than the constant explosions outside, but nobody wants to turn the radio off because it takes away the need for conversation.

Ling-li is up before dawn. "Come on, better get moving, okay," she says, gulping down the tea she has made for them. She catches Claude's glance at the somnolent Jack. "Let him sleep, he's not much good for anything else right now." She runs a practical eye over the shelves and corners of the room. "We take all food items, of course, candles, kerosene."

Claude forces himself to sit up and drink the tea she's set out. While he sips on it, glad for the sugar she's added—he's always hungry these days—she contemplates Jack's suitcase. "His?" she asks. "What's inside?"

"I'm not sure. Books, I think."

Her eyebrows lift, making her eyes look bigger. It seems to Claude that her face is shrinking as the days pass. "Well," she says and is quiet for a moment. "Okay, the library stays, but I need the suitcase."

Jack stirs and opens his eyes, and Claude wonders if he has been faking sleep so as to eavesdrop. "Good," Ling-li says. "*Oi*, awake yet?"

"Hmmm," says Jack, looking as if he can't quite place them. "What time is it?"

"Time to move," Ling-li replies. "We *gilah* to stay here last night. I wasn't really thinking," she adds, as if she's the only one here with that capacity. But Claude's earlier decision to stay on in the hut comes back to haunt him now. Amazingly the alley has remained unscathed overnight, but what he can see of Serangoon Road is even more depressing than it seemed the night before. A charred bus is lying on its side in the street; the wind has picked up the dreadful stench of overflowing sewers. It took Claude a long, long time to fall asleep last night, especially as the ground rocked with explosions that were all much, much too close.

" . . . so is it okay for me to empty it out?" Ling-li is asking, bundling food supplies in an old sheet she's somehow produced.

Jack sits up slowly, his eyes fixed on her. "I'd like to have my suitcase as is," he says evenly. "Everything I own is in it."

Ling-li pauses with a jam jar half-full of strips of beef jerky. She puts the jar down on the sheet and walks over to Jack's battered suitcase. She picks it up with an effort. It is hard to ignore the strain on her; she looks as if she might fall over if she takes a step with the suitcase. She puts it down again. "Who's going to carry this?" she asks.

"I'll manage," Jack says. The sky outside is greying. There are shouts, and then quiet again. Ling-li is impatient to get going, and for once Claude agrees with her. Not only is it safer in the cellar of the clinic, but once he's seen Jack safely installed there he can begin searching for his family.

Ling-li gathers up the rest of the supplies and marches to the door. "I have patients to see," she says pointedly.

Claude has packed the stone charcoal burner in a large gunnysack and the last remaining bag of coals. He puts in the cooking pot and utensils. "Look, Jack," he says, trying to be helpful. "I'll come back later for your suitcase. This is all we can manage for now." He waits. Jack will be reasonable; he must.

"It's everything I have," Jack says. "Pictures, letters, books. When you're a foreigner you try to carry bits of your home around with you. I know it's hard for you both to understand, but then—this is your home. You have everything you need here."

It is the wrong thing to say, it is a terribly stupid and tasteless thing to say. Ling-li's body stiffens and practically points, hound-like, at her prey. Against the background of a rapidly lightening sky Jack actually blushes. Claude has never seen him blush and can't take his eyes off him. Under Claude's gaze Jack reddens even more.

"So sorry you're homesick," Ling-li says, "but nobody asked you to stay."

She turns to Claude. "Let's go." Without looking back at Jack she says, "And if he wants his personal belongings let him take them himself. Bloody refugee centres are filled with people who are glad just to be alive, never mind the homes and possessions they've left behind." She is already out the door and stomping towards Serangoon Road.

An unusually cool breeze blows through the open door and windows. "I should lock everything up," Claude says after an awkward pause and starts to close and bolt down the shutters.

"I deserved that," Jack says as Claude leans over him to get to the window beside his bed. Claude says nothing, keeps his fingers busy. "I've wondered over and over—why is she always so angry at me?"

Why is Jack so affected by what Ling-li thinks of him? Claude wonders. Why does he probe into what she talks about when Claude is alone with her, or need to know how "the Chinese mind" thinks? Why be so concerned that he not appear "too foreign" to her?

"I mean, she seems to be waiting to pounce on me all the time," Jack is saying, looking morose. At the same time, Claude thinks: He *likes* her; he *respects* her.

"She's disliked me from the start. I could feel it when we met," Jack rambles on.

Not that there is anything remarkable in itself about that—despite Claude's reservations, he too holds a grudging respect for her; she is the type to command it. But Jack is English, and she is—well, Chinese. Jack really cares about her opinion and is anxious for her to regard him well. That is the part that stuns Claude.

"She takes everything I say as an offence, when that's the last thing I want to do. What is it, Claude?" He looks quite distressed. Claude has never seen him this way. And why is Jack asking him? What does Claude know about her anyway? "I mean, you're Chinese too, so maybe you can tell me, maybe you can follow her mind better than I can."

"Really, Jack, I've no idea." Claude is astonished at the equation Jack made between him and her. *You're Chinese too*—but doesn't he see how different Claude is from her?

"She's overworked," Claude says, the thought just occurring to him, and seeming a highly useful observation under the circumstances. It allows him to be diplomatic. His situation with each of the two is delicate enough as it is, he doesn't need any added strain. "I think Dr. Singh disappearing like that has unnerved her, plus she's worried about her uncle. I think things will improve when we move over to the clinic. We can help more with the patients and lighten the load a bit."

"Yes, yes, of course," Jack says distractedly.

"Can I take the books out then, and use your suitcase? I'm afraid this sack won't hold our pillows and sheets."

Serangoon Road is coming alive with people bustling about, scavenging the rubble for wood with which to build fires, salvaging any other useful remnants. So this is what it means to literally *pick up the pieces*.

"I hope you don't think I'm being petty, Claude, worrying about my books while we're in the middle of a war. It's just that, well, if I can keep my things with me, I'd be very grateful."

"I'll come back for them, Jack—after I look for my family."

"Of course," Jack says. "Of course." He reaches into his pocket and tosses Claude a key. Claude unlocks the suitcase and removes a folio of letters, a brown packet, a dozen or so books and a carefully wrapped object. "My camera," Jack says as Claude pats the bulky cotton cloth that swathes it.

Yes—the camera from those sight-seeing excursions. How he had admired Jack's image as he walked the streets, snapping pictures of unexciting objects like trishaws and fruit stands displaying durian and mangosteen. Claude remembers the couple and the car with the flat tyre in Penang, but not as clearly as he would have liked to. No matter how much he strains to recapture the white dazzle of the man's suit and the woman's face as his thumb brushed her brow, it is all indistinct and blurred. Instead he recalls the three coolies holding up the side of the car while a fourth knelt on the ground to change the flat tyre. Around them strolled Indians, Malays, Chinese in the powdery sunlight, all seemingly unaware of the dust particles they were inhaling. It was as if Claude were viewing them on a screen in the cinema. They talked, chewed betel, carried their bundles, smoked, on a celluloid strip while he watched the show, not participating. There was something alien about their world, something that threatened him though he couldn't define what it was.

Claude pushes the contents of Jack's suitcase under his bed and stands up. "Ready?"

Jack gets up slowly, bounces gently so that his knees and hips click. "Rheumatism," he says, massaging his thighs. Claude swings the gunnysack over his left shoulder. "You'll have to take the suitcase, I'm afraid," he says, wondering if Jack will manage. But it's light enough and he seems encouragingly energetic this morning.

Jack puts his hand on Claude's free shoulder and they make their way to the door. When Claude takes his first step over the threshold he estimates that at this pace it will take them over half an hour to reach the clinic.

The air cracks. Both of them jump, but it's only a child playing with firecrackers. His mother rushes out, wild-eyed, from one of the other huts in the alley. When she gets to him she scolds him harshly and spanks him with a panicked hand. It will be the Chinese New Year soon, Claude remembers. This year there will be no celebrations but more fireworks than anyone will care for.

In the space of a hiccough, time skips. In that unruly interruption to breathing, you are so inwardly focused that the world is missed. You don't see anything, you don't hear much. Just a sharp inhalation that results in a squeak.

You force yourself back to the ants. One hundred and ninety-three, one hundred and ninety-four. You know that you are trying to live within the span of a hiccough, in a prolonged time skip that will protect you from what is happening on the other side of the wall.

All the big hotels are full of Europeans and there's still no sign of Claude's family anywhere. At the Parrot Inn he sees several Asiatic families huddled together in the courtyard where they have been allowed to sleep. "Any of those belong to you?" the American manager asks. "You can't sleep here otherwise. It's only on account of the war that I let them stay. Only the better sort, of course, not riff-raff."

Claude searches the faces and his heart skips a beat when he spots a shape that reminds him of Grandma Siok, but on closer examination she is smaller and has nothing of his grandmother's hardiness. One family is passing around a teacup and dipping unbuttered lumps of bread into it, and he feels a quick pang of longing for Humphrey's sacred tea hour: his dutiful recounting of his day at the office, his mother's determined sips, Lucy's fidgeting, Grandma Siok's obstinate absence on the grounds that teatime interferes with her nap. Images of his family under burning debris or blown apart by bombs play in his head and he feels the quickening pulse of panic in his chest.

"Find them?" the manager asks, as Claude heads for the lobby entrance. He can't bring himself to answer and merely shakes his head. "Better luck elsewhere," says the manager.

Outside the wind churns up dust and ashes, making it difficult to breathe. To avoid choking, Claude pulls out his handkerchief and ties it bandit-style around his face. In the broken glass window of a shop he looks almost debonair, if a trifle bleary-eyed. For some reason, the sight cheers him and he laughs. That's better, he thinks, breaking into a trot. He is at the point of checking out the hospitals when he remembers some of the smaller and more modest hotels tucked along Bencoolen Street. No harm, he tells himself. Fresh ash-tinged air and sunshine at the very least, and some bloody strong calf muscles from all the walking he's done lately.

At the second hotel he tries, one called the Dragon Pavilion, he bumps straight into Lucy. "Claude!" she squeals in delight, jumping into his arms even though she is too heavy for this. "Mummy, I found him, I found Claude!" she shouts into the depths of the empty lobby.

At the far end is a flight of stairs and he hears hurried footsteps descending. His mother's voice floats down even before he sees her. "What? What?" she is saying, as if she can't believe her ears. When she appears, Claude hardly has time to notice the unfamiliar flat way her hair is combed before she's crushed him to her chest.

Humphrey arrives as Claude is catching his breath and he pumps Claude's hand up and down so hard that his shoulder hurts. "We've been looking for you," Humphrey says. "No-one at any of the refugee centres has seen you."

"Yes, well, I can say the same about you. I've been staying in Amah's old hut," Claude tells them. Lucy is still tugging at his arm.

"Amah's place?" Cynthia says. She's never been there, doesn't even know where it is.

"Right around the corner," Claude says. "But at the moment, I'm staying at a medical clinic on Serangoon Road."

"Good God," says Cynthia with feeling. Her eyes rove over him anxiously. "You're not sick, are you, or in some sort of nasty quarantine? With all these refugees about, you don't know what you might catch."

"Nothing like that, Mother. I'm staying with—some friends, and besides, it's better than on the floor at a refugee camp."

"Well, why on earth didn't you book yourself a room at a hotel?" she asks. "It would have saved us a lot of trouble if you'd had a room already. As it was, we had to stay here because all the nicer hotels were full by the time we got to the city."

"I didn't think of it," Claude admits.

"The house," Humphrey says urgently. "I've been trying to get to it, but the blockades have made it impossible."

"I don't know. The soldiers were at the gates all day, and I think they were getting ready to loot the entire neighbourhood." Claude sees the strain on Humphrey's face and decides not to mention the bullet holes in the door.

"Father," he says instead, "Jack Winchester is with me at the clinic."

For a moment there is a blank look on Humphrey's face, as if the name isn't registering. "Didn't he leave with George and Janet? How is he?"

"He had a leg infection. It was quite nasty but he's better now."

"Well, he must come and stay with us then," Cynthia says. "We can persuade the manager to clear out that storage room at the end of the hall, and you and Jack can share it. Our room's packed at the moment, I'm afraid." She smiles at him and ruffles his hair.

"Oh," Claude says, unaccustomed to her caress. "There's no need, Mum, we're fine at the clinic."

"Claude," she begins.

"It's an easy walk from here. I'll take you there if you like, and you can see for yourself."

"Claude."

"Mother, it's fine."

"Humphrey?" Her voice is higher, shrill.

"Son—"

"I don't think Jack would want to move, Father. He's comfortable at the clinic. And the nurse is there to check on his leg." He knows this is his best chance of getting them to agree with him.

"I'll talk to him when I see him," Humphrey says noncommittally. Claude wonders if he can sneak a word in with Jack before his family descends.

"Grandma Siok!" says Lucy, jumping up and down. "We have to tell Grandma that Claude is here!" She races up the stairs, with Claude following behind more sedately.

When he enters his family's room he finds Grandma Siok sitting on the bed nearest the door, with Lucy bouncing on her lap. "Get off, you little bugger," she says. "You're cracking my bones! You're too heavy for me, so clear off." She looks up at him expectantly. "Hello, Claude."

"Grandma," he says, bending to kiss her powdered face. She smells musty, like an old chest.

"What a pong!" she complains, waving a hand over her abused nose. "When was the last time you took a bath?"

"It's been a good two weeks, Grandma." He laughs as he counts off the days in his head. "Maybe a little more!"

Lucy is prancing round the room holding her nose and chanting, "Claude has a pong! Claude has a pong!" She skips over to him. "I thought you did, but I was so happy to see you I closed up my nose to give you a hug."

"I wonder how Mother could stand it," he says, smiling.

"Hummmph," is all Grandma Siok says to this. "Well, boy, what's been going on? A big mess, isn't it? When are these British troops going to give the Japanese the boot? I'm tired of all these hysterics—people losing their homes and having to evacuate, fires everywhere, that detestable bombing. I can't even have a decent nap anymore."

"Grandma, the commotion here has been getting worse by the day. Ling-li—my friend—says they've taken over Tengah Air Base already."

She raises an eyebrow at this. "Worse than I thought."

"We'll be okay, Grandma. The British will rally round." The words sound forced even to his ears. "They've been digging trenches for weeks. They have a plan, I'm sure."

"We shall see, we shall see," is all she says.

Minutes later, he heads back to the clinic, feeling guilty for leaving Jack and Ling-li to manage without him. It must be swamped by now, he thinks, glancing at the afternoon sky. Humphrey has insisted on going along. "When did you move to Amah's hut?" he asks as he follows Claude down Bencoolen Street.

"About a month ago." Has it been only been that? It feels much longer, and the house in Bukit Timah seems like a place he visited a long time ago.

"I rang a few times—it was hard getting to a telephone in Punggol, believe me—and we began to worry when we never heard from you. I was planning to get a lift back to the house to see what was going on, but then the evacuations started and I never got a chance."

Humphrey stumbles often, as if he can't believe the rubble and debris littering the streets and is ploughing straight through them to prove to himself they don't exist. "Father, you'll hurt yourself," Claude says. "Why don't you follow me and I'll find a clear path for us both?"

"I don't understand," Humphrey pants as he clambers over a fallen beam. "How could things have gotten so bad? Decency can only go so far, you know."

"Decency?" This is a new one. Claude turns to get a good look at his father hitching up his trousers so that the cuffs don't pick up the ash and soot on the road. "What in heaven's name do you mean, Father?"

They eye each other in surprise. It's the first time Claude has ever spoken to his father in this way, with a certain impatience and irreverence. "Haven't you been reading the papers? Gerald Tibbats' column or the editorials?" Humphrey says, looking away. "The British are deliberately holding off finishing those blasted Japs! The war was weighted on our side from the very beginning, you know. We're playing with a handicap right now, to square things off, you see. But I say we've taken enough of their nonsense and should get down to business."

"Handicap?" Claude can't believe his ears. Ling-li was right about the propaganda. To think that his own father believes it— "Really, Father! Do you mean to say that the British have allowed the bombing of Singapore Island, have sacrificed their prized harbour, not to mention all their public works, for the sake of honouring some sort of self-established handicap system? So they can uphold their famous sense of *decency*? It's absurd!"

"Watch your tongue, boy." Humphrey snaps. "Don't try to be too smart. You should read Gerald Tibbats before you go shooting your mouth off."

They walk on for several blocks without saying anything to each other. In front of a burnt restaurant, Humphrey stops to rest, coughing as he catches his breath. The smoke is getting to him. "You all right?" Claude asks.

Humphrey nods, still coughing, then clears his throat. When he speaks, his voice is so soft that Claude almost misses it. "You've got to believe in something to keep yourself going," he says. "Might as well be Gerald Tibbats."

He moves past Claude and takes the lead. Claude watches him trip over an abandoned tyre, almost falling, but at the last minute, some shift of his weight—a twist in his body—reasserts his balance and he totters upright again. He looks older now; there is a slowness to his movements, and a hesitancy that Claude has never noticed before. How old is he—fifty, fifty-one maybe? Claude has never kept count.

Humphrey stops, turns back to Claude, holds his arms out to his sides. "Where to?"

"Just another two streets down," Claude says and hurries to catch up with his father.

✦

Most of the time, Jack and Ling-li by-pass each other in the corridor with polite smiles and rush on to complete their work. Jack has been washing sheets and bandages, and sterilizing needles. He moves about slowly, panting and stopping often to rest, putting his feet up on a stool to keep them from swelling. Ling-li has lost two patients already—a young man and his two-year-old brother. They were fleeing bombers on Orchard Road, the elder brother carrying the younger, but the young man tripped and both sustained severe burns in the street explosions. Somehow they managed to crawl to Serangoon Road, where a kind Indian found them, bundled them up in the sidecar of his scooter and brought them to the clinic.

One look from the door was enough for Ling-li to say, "No, no. Take to hospital." The Indian gentleman tried to start up his scooter again when the young man, misunderstanding, spoke.

"No, take us, please," he begged in Hokkien, half-hanging out of the sidecar. "Don't send us away. Save us, please."

Ling-li hesitated. The young man, thinking she would dismiss him from the clinic, spoke up again. "At least take my brother, at least show him some mercy. Whatever time we have left," he added.

They were both severely burnt over their entire bodies. There was very little chance they would make it, and even if they were brought to hospital, it would be a while before they were attended to. Ling-li nodded at the Indian gentleman. "Too late for hospital. Help me take them inside?" she asked in English. He jumped off his scooter and carried the younger boy in while she struggled to help the older one half-climb, half-roll out of the sidecar. Leaning on Ling-li and the Indian man, he managed to move inside.

She made a bed of old towels and gunnysacks in the office area, covered the boys with wet bed sheets and tried to get the little boy to drink water. Once inside the clinic, both of them seemed to lose their will to live. They curled into tight balls, one next to the other, and closed their eyes, refusing to open them even when spoken to. Ling-li, still needing to attend to a packed clinic, called for Jack.

"Bloody hell!" he said when he came upon the pair. "Shouldn't they be in hospital?" She explained briefly. "But even if they had to wait at General Hospital, they would have a better chance of surviving there than here. What can we do for them here?"

"Nothing but make them comfortable," she said. "I think they know—at least the older one does—that they're dying. And I think all they want is a place to die with some decency."

"But in hospital—"

"They can do nothing for them," she cut in. "Look—they're dying. We need to, to . . ."

"Comfort them? Hold their hands and read to them from the Good Book? This is ridiculous, Ling-li. We should send them off to hospital." He eyed the brothers. "I think they'll make the journey. When Claude gets back he can take them over."

"He will do no such thing," she said, clenching her fists. "I called you over to fix up some kind of a makeshift curtain so they can have a little privacy. If you can't—or won't—do that, I'll do it myself, but it would help the patients if you were willing to do it."

They glared at each other until the little boy made a small shuddering movement and died. Ling-li knelt to take his pulse and to feel for a breath. The young man opened his eyes, looked at his dead brother, then reached out to touch her. "Gone?" he asked, his eyes strangely bright. She nodded. He closed his eyes again and turned to face the wall. She covered the boy's face with the sheet.

When she stood up, she began to arrange the furniture to cordon off the area where the two bomb victims lay. "Stop," said Jack. "I'll take care of it." She looked at the dead boy, gave a curt nod and went back to the other patients. After that she stopped by the office periodically to check up on the remaining brother.

The young man refused to let Jack take his brother away. Miming as best he could, he told Jack that he wanted his brother beside him for as long as possible. Jack gave him water, wet his sheets again when they dried out and uncovered the face of the dead boy so that the young man could look at it from behind his fog of pain. The last time Ling-li checked the office area, she managed to look reasonably satisfied. The young man was sleeping lightly, and Jack had placed a small wet towel on his eyelids.

Just before noon, he let out a long sigh, whispered something and stopped breathing. His face seemed to relax in death and he looked almost happy, despite his ghastly burns. Jack signalled to Ling-li.

After one look she went into the waiting room to direct two men with minor injuries to move the bodies. They went through the back door of the clinic into the alleyway and left the bodies, neatly wrapped in sheets, a few feet from the back door. "We'll bury them later," she told them.

Now Jack is boiling water. "I thought you'd finished disinfecting the needles," Ling-li says as she passes.

"I'm making tea," he says. "And boiling some rice. You have to stop for lunch."

"The patients—"

"Can wait," he says. "Here." He hands her a cup and waits until she takes a long sip. "You must be starving." An involuntary smile escapes from her, but she catches herself and stops. "Surely it's okay to smile at me. It won't corrupt you in any way, I promise."

She turns away, but he reaches for her elbow and stops her. "You don't like me at all, do you?" he asks.

"Like," she says, lingering over the word. "No, I don't *like* you. I don't really *dislike* you either." She shakes her elbow loose of his hold.

"What *do* you think of me then?"

"I don't," she says.

"I beg your pardon?"

"I don't think of you at all," she says without antagonism. "Not much anyway. It's really not so different from the way you treat us."

"How so?" He is unprepared for her calm appraisal.

"You see, Jack, most of the time, I don't see you. You're like part of the furniture to me, I forget you're around. Same way you whites treat us, your native servants, your amahs and chauffeurs."

"I know we've behaved insufferably at times, I won't pretend we haven't been biased against the locals—I'm sorry if I've been insensitive or biased myself—"

"Don't be," she says, with a small smile. "I, for one, make no apologies for being biased." She laughs at the look on his face. "Come now, Jack, I'm Chinese—the most intolerant race in history! We consider all non-Chinese to be barbarians. We even built the longest wall in the world to keep everyone else out of the Central Kingdom."

"Ah." He is unsure how to take this.

"So you see, I can identify with your white sense of superiority. Really," she says, folding her arms across her chest as she leans against the wall.

"In that case, why be so anxious to chase us out?"

"You're not listening, Jack," she says. "You're barbarians. We do not want to be ruled by barbarians."

He wonders if she is teasing him, but her face is perfectly serious. "I see," he says. "Well then, any chance you could be friends with a barbarian?"

"No," she says simply, without malice.

"No?"

"Never."

Disappointed, he walks away. Why did he even bother? How could this scrap of a girl's opinion possibly mean anything to him? When the rice is cooked, he brings it to her in a bowl. She takes it from him without a word, without any thanks, as if she were claiming a right instead of receiving a favour, and his disappointment gives way to anger. He realises she has been completely honest—he is nothing more than a piece of furniture to her. Her fingers brush against his in the transfer. They are cool—almost cold—against the hot bowl. Much later, this is what he thinks about when he keeps his eyes resolutely closed, despite orders to watch what he has heard called "acts of barbarity."

✸

One thousand six hundred and ninety-two myrmidons, give or take a few. Scream, groan, cry—she has exhausted the language of pain. Still, he—that unidentifed one in the next room—will not look. He has squeezed his eyes shut and refused to see what is happening directly before him. Even when taunted and goaded, he has remained steadfast. Some things are not for the eyes. Some things are better off ignored. You can't change the world, but you can choose to see what you want of it. Disregard the rest.

Surely it must end soon. Surely they will tire and let her be, as they have done with Claude the Body. Tomorrow is another day. With some rest, she may regain her strength and spirit. And yet, you know: How could they allow her that?

✸

Humphrey is looking at Jack with a mixture of relief and nervousness. "You're positively gaunt," he says. Jack's height and baldness seem to emphasise the lack of flesh on his body. At least he can get up and walk about now, even if it has to be with crutches. "I'm sorry Claude couldn't find better accommodations for you. The silly boy didn't even think of getting a room at a hotel." Humphrey gives a short laugh.

"To be honest, I did think of it," Jack says, surprising Claude. "But neither of us had a way of paying for a room. I mean, we've been living off my gold cuff-links for the past few weeks."

This is sounding worse and worse, Claude thinks. "Not really," he says. "Ling-li sold her mother's ring for food while you were sick."

"Yes, of course," Jack concedes. "I remember her pawning something or other."

"Sold," Claude says.

"Pardon?"

"Sold," he repeats, his voice hardening, and Humphrey looks at him in alarm. "She didn't pawn it, she sold it."

"Ah." Jack scratches the back of his neck. "Technically, yes. But you know as well as I do that it can be redeemed after the war." He pushes himself up from his chair. "Humphrey, do you want a look-around? I'll be your tour-guide."

"Yes, yes. Lead the way," Humphrey says quickly.

Jack gives a low bow before turning to the clinic. "The waiting room and reception desk," he says, walking past the counter where the patients register. People are staring and whispering. "And next to it, the dispensary." He indicates the window where patients collect their lotions and pills. He lifts the countertop, allowing Claude and Humphrey to slip through the opening after him. "The office—where all the paperwork gets dumped." Somehow it looks worse today. Patients' charts and pill bottles are sliding off the desk and cabinet tops. A large, half-empty bottle of brandy sits in the middle of the desk.

"For medicinal use," Claude says hastily, taking in his father's disapproval. "We ran out of anaesthetics."

"The toilet." Jack places his hand on a doorknob and turns it. The WC is narrow and long. At the end is a raised tiled platform, in the middle of which is a hole. Claude has noticed the small square tiles ringing the bowl; apparently the tile-layer had difficulty spacing them. Several tiles have been cut to make them fit around the long elliptical hole. "No sit-down affair, I'm afraid," Jack says. "It's squat and go over here."

"In a clinic?" Humphrey is aghast, as if Claude had personally planned the WC.

"It's clean, and there's a flush system." Claude points to the long chain dangling from the water tank suspended above the hole. "It works, and Ling-li scrubs it out everyday with Dettol. There's nothing wrong with it." He catches Jack's eye and sees the glint of amusement in it—that and something else. A touch of malevolence, perhaps, as if he's determined to prove to Humphrey how shabby the clinic is.

Jack continues down the corridor, pointing out storage cupboards, the makeshift infirmary where three patients are lying on
the floor in the large alcove area across from the broom closet. He
stops at the room at the end of the hallway, from which a bluish fluorescent light spills. "And here we have our resident heroine," he
says. Claude and Humphrey look into the room where Ling-li is
stitching a wound on a young man's foot, Dr. Singh's magnifying
goggles perched ridiculously on her face and distorting her eyes
when she looks up.

"Dedicated nurse, Han Ling-li. See with what care she places each
stitch, keeping the sutures firm but not too tight. The end result is
neat and pleasing to the eye, not unlike embroidery. Notice the
skilled flick of her wrist as she ties little French knots. It is said that
the local women are particularly skilled in delicate needlework, and
watching our Ling-li here, I must agree."

Ling-li's eyes flash, but she says nothing, merely pours some
iodine on a pad of cotton wool and paints the wound with long yellow stripes.

"This is Claude's father, Humphrey Lim." Jack shifts his body to
allow Humphrey a half-step forward.

"Hello, Mr. Lim. Please excuse me, I'm quite busy now, as you
can see. If you don't mind, perhaps we can meet later, in the waiting room?" Her voice is unperturbed, but Claude is angry for her.

"Er, yes, later." Humphrey backs out of the room but not before
taking in the blackened windows and the weathered equipment.
When the door is closed behind him, he turns to Claude with an
accusing eye. "I must say, I expected more of your Dr. Singh. How
did you find this place?"

"This is the closest clinic to Amah's hut," Claude says, following
Jack on the way back to the waiting room.

"And by the way, where on earth *is* the doctor? Don't tell me *she's*
in charge?"

Without warning, Claude stops, tired of all this. Humphrey, directly
behind him, walks into his back. "Yes, Father. Ling-li is charge of
the clinic and she's doing a damn good job too. Now if you'll excuse
me, I have some things to sterilize. I'll let Jack finish up the 'tour'
with you—" He moves past them and heads to the office.

His father's voice sputters from the corridor. "Claude, Claude—come back here and apologise at once!" But already the new stream of patients waiting outside the clinic has swelled. Claude unlocks the door and lets them in and then busies himself with getting them sorted out according to Ling-li's classification system. "Sick, Very Sick, Dying," she said in her usual terse way. "For Very Sick and Dying, you get the trishaw and start pedalling to the hospital. The rest I'll take care of." In reality, the Dying have never made it out the door, so he has ended up ferrying only the Very Sick to hospital in his improvised ambulance service. Thankfully, no one has yet died in transit.

The new patients include a man with a large, draining boil on his neck, another who has cut his hand and a child who has been bitten by a dog, not too badly—there are clear teeth-marks on her arm, but no open wound. Last in line is a woman with blood staining her *samfoo* trousers. "That one," says Ling-li at his ear. She has finished suturing her patient. "Get her to lie down. She's aborting."

Swiftly he helps the woman to the infirmary and covers her with a sheet. "I'll take it from here," Ling-li says.

Humphrey and Jack are in the office. Humphrey laughs as he accepts a shot of brandy and thumps Jack familiarly on the back—a deliberate gesture, Claude thinks, calculated to impress the natives with his closeness to this white man. Claude searches the patients' grim faces, so absorbed in their own pain and suffering. They have no energy to be impressed. Even the few who are well enough to pay attention to the conversation in the office look away, as if slightly insulted.

"The Good Father," Claude says aloud, recalling the tableau at Haw Par Villa, and lets out a small laugh. "Let's clean you up," he tells the man with the draining neck wound, who doesn't understand what he is saying. The boil deflates under the pressure of Claude's fingers. With a wet towel, he wipes the greenish, sticky muck off the man's neck.

"Good work," Ling-li says as she brings in another patient. She says something in Chinese to the man. When she is gone, he is quiet for a moment and then, unexpectedly, he catches Claude's eye and breaks into a grin. Claude grins back. He doesn't want to know what she said. The joke is at his expense, he realises, but right now he doesn't really care.

At Seletar Reservoir just outside the city, the British chief water-works engineer pauses to take his lunch. It is rice cooked in coconut milk, taken with some spicy chilli paste and a small portion of cucumber, and then wrapped in a large banana leaf. Fortunately for him, the local Malays in the nearby *kampong* have taken pity on him and have been feeding him. He would not have had the time to cook for himself, let alone hunt down the few grains of rice available on the black market. The little boy who has brought him his meal watches him with unabashed curiosity.

"Do you want some?" the engineer asks, knowing the boy does not understand English. He motions to the food while trying to recall the Malay word for rice. "*Nasi,* yes?"

The little boy shakes his head. He is probably about six years old. He keeps his eye on the engineer as his feet edge towards the boiler room. The engineer laughs. "Ah, the pumps, eh? I bet you're dying to have a look, aren't you, sonny?"

The boy rocks on his heels and leans his back against the wall. "I'll tell you, sonny, they're a sight. And working perfectly too, when we get some regular electricity around here. I've been keeping the pumps going despite the blackouts. I use the old boiler system—stoke it by hand. Someone has to, though I tell you, I didn't think *I* would end up with the job!" He scoops up the coconut rice with his hand. He has learned to eat like the Malays, without utensils.

"I wish I knew what was happening. The radio's not much use, and I haven't seen anybody but you and your family in weeks." He licks rice from his hand, folds up the empty leaf and tosses it out the window. It lands on the banks of the reservoir, tangled in tall weeds and undulating in the water like a soggy flag. The ground beside the reservoir is damp and wet and the surrounding jungle area is thick with insects and worms. It is a place of rich rot. The air smells of loam and overripe wild papaya. Since the war began the engineer has not gone back to his flat in Tanglin but has lived in his office, sleeping on a thin mat he got from the *kampong* folk. They have also given him a small bolster, which he places under his head, and a cotton sheet for cool rainy nights. He has lived there for four weeks now. He has grown used to it and, to be honest, is glad to be away from everyone else. In the distance he can hear the harbour bombings and the klaxons going off in town. The trees rise so far overhead that he can see nothing except black, smoke-filled patches of sky. At night, looking at the rippled surface of the reservoir under moonlight, he feels the urge to run his hand over it, as if to feel the numerous skin folds of some immense aquatic animal. Lately, he has come to think of this place as home.

"All right, back to work." He gets up, rinses his hands in the WC and heads for the engine room. "Come on then, sonny, I know you want to see this." He holds the door open invitingly. The boy is through it in a second, and finds himself gazing at a large pump situated in the midst of a tangled coil of pipes. He longs to touch it, but is afraid the engineer will not approve. The furnace of the boiler is already dying down. The engineer gives a sigh. "It's a never-ending job. I spend my entire day throwing coal into the damn thing."

Outside, the boy's mother calls. He stands for a moment, unable to decide what to do. Then, without warning, he slaps the side of a pipe, and races out of the room, out of the office and the engineer's makeshift home, into the cloistered jungle. The engineer laughs to himself and keeps hurling coal into the furnace.

❁

Perhaps it has become more important for you to know than for the interrogators. Perhaps it is information you long to possess so that when he—the Body—comes to, when he is no longer half-unconscious, you will be able to tell him everything. What happened? What is the truth? So much hinges on the answer:

On that last morning, Ling-li woke him. The cracks under the door and windows revealed no light and the lack of gunfire and bombs after the surrender was still new enough for him to want to pop his ears to make sure he wasn't deaf. Crouched beside him, she said she had to leave. The light was so poor it took him a while to figure out that she had done something to her hair. Pinned it up, straightened out all the tendrils at her temples. She wore a dark jacket.

"Why?" He whispered because she had. Jack's breathing, barely discernible, divided time into biphasic cycles.

"Do you see this?" she asked, turning around and holding her jacket close to him. It smelled of sandalwood. It was a deep indigo and had a faint sheen to it. Even in the dark he could make out the high Mandarin collar and the quilted surface.

"Your jacket?"

"On the back. Don't you see?"

Eventually, he made out the embroidered floral design on her back. The threads used were only slightly lighter than the jacket. He reached out and touched it, feeling the raised pattern, silk over silk, under his fingertips like some kind of elegant, brushwork Braille: 忍

"Do you see it?"

"It's nice." And he is so tired he wants to put his head down on that soft jacket and fall asleep once again. "It's nice." Perhaps he'd already said that.

Her eyes seemed to collect and intensify the darkness in the room, black onyx stones from a deep mine. "My mother told me the story. In my mind, my mother told it to me."

He waited, listening to Jack's pendulous breath rise and fall. Surrender, surrender, surrender. His eyelids closed.

"Maybe that's why the jacket meant so much to me. I felt it was something she had passed on to me directly, like an heirloom. An inheritance of words. I could sell her ring because as long as I had these words, I would have her with me always."

"It's nice," he said, snuggling up to her feet and clasping her ankles. Such delicate ankles, the bones like yarrow sticks used for divining oracles at the temples he had visited with Jack. Both of them had had their fortunes told for fun, and Claude's hexagram had read *Brightness Hiding*, according to an English-speaking monk at one temple. On that last night, Claude felt a hand brush his hair, his face. It lingered there and he nuzzled into it, fitting his cheek into the palm, thinking: *Ling-li, Brightness Hiding.*

"Claude? Are you asleep?" Sleep or trance, what is the difference?

He turned and pressed his lips into her hand, ran his tongue over her life line. Her hand stiffened but didn't pull away. "Claude."

There might have been a pause. There might have been a sigh, or a small, plaintive sound. There might have been a few more words.

"Goodbye," she said and was gone.

The point of convergence: of history and fiction, of one mind and another, of what's real and what's imagined, of Fifth Columnist and—

It is strange to feel at nineteen that time is running out, and there's nothing he can do about it. The buildings keep toppling, the city burns on, the roads eviscerate across town, bringing up earth and long-buried debris. The signs of defeat are clear and nobody seems to be trying to do anything to change course.

Among the civilian population, a deep resignation has set in. People move about like drugged animals being led to the abattoir, a drowsy, numbed sweetness in their eyes. This, more than the bombs and the endless sirens, is what frightens him. Every time he sees that look he struggles to contain billowing waves of panic that hit him. Slow down, he tells himself. It's a relief to throw himself into the tasks that Ling-li has set out for him—sterilizing equipment, scouting for supplies, cleaning and disinfecting the clinic, cooking. These are routines he is grateful for, has come to depend on to get through the haze of each day.

Though he shares the same tasks, he and Jack have little to say to each other. Jack does try once to apologise for his behaviour during Humphrey's visit. "Remember now, I was stuck here with Ling-li while you were hunting down your family. You know how bossy she can get." He attempts to draw Claude in with a conspiratorial smile but the latter refuses to join him. "I guess I was just trying to take out my frustration on her."

Since then Jack has tried to help out as much as possible. He is good at calming the children, stopping them in mid-scream and making them laugh. They are astonished by his pallor, more pronounced after his illness, and the length of him. Sometimes, with his crutches, he performs a funny bow-legged dance, bouncing on his rubbery legs and then stomping pigeon-toed until the kids are in hysterics, or until the pain disarms him. At those times he keeps smiling, a trifle grimly but never letting up. He sits down heavily and starts singing, watched in fascinated silence by the children and their parents. He doesn't seem to notice that he sings off-key, although on one occasion an elderly Indian woman is moved to stick her fingers in her ears until the recital is over.

"Good morning, sir," the parents say respectfully at their visits. When Ling-li orders something for them or their children they inevitably confer with Jack before going along. "You think it's okay, sir?" they ask, as Ling-li waits, fuming and clicking her tongue. "You think it's the right treatment?"

At first Jack tells them he isn't a doctor, has no medical experience whatsoever, but it makes no difference. The consultations come anyway, holding up the queue, so now he nods gravely at the patients, agreeing with Ling-li's instructions. "Just what I would recommend myself," he says reassuringly, or, "I was just about to suggest that."

The parents smile in relief, and submit their squirming children to Ling-li's capable hands, saying to the children, "Sir here says this will make you better." Claude winces each time this happens, knowing exactly why it happens. And who can blame them in these last days? Yet it is such a ridiculous assumption that he wants to give them a good shake.

Once Ling-li diagnoses appendicitis in a nine-year-old boy and wants his parents to take him to the General Hospital for surgery. The couple refuse to budge until they have heard from Jack, who is at that moment in the cellar hunting down some precious iodine for Ling-li. "I'll get him," she says, heading for the cellar without protest. She has learnt it would be a waste of time.

He hobbles into the consultation room leaning partly on his crutches and partly on Ling-li, takes one look at the child lying still on his side and announces, "This child needs to go to hospital for surgery."

The wife whispers something to her husband who straightens to attention and addresses Jack. "Sir," he says, wagging his head in his Indian way, "my wife thinks perhaps you should give him some medicine and he will be all better. Hospital will be a long wait."

"I'll write a note you can give to the nurse on duty in Accidents. That way they won't make him wait," says Ling-li, already on her way to get some paper.

"Perhaps Sir can write the note," the Indian man says at once.

Jack and Ling-li exchange the briefest of glances. "Of course," says Jack, "but you must take him there immediately and not wait, do you understand?"

"Yes, sir," the man and woman reply together, bowing their heads gratefully.

Ling-li goes out to the waiting room while Jack composes a note indicating that the boy has been examined by a trained nurse and diagnosed with appendicitis, requiring surgical care at once. Leaving him mumbling aloud as he writes, Claude follows Ling-li to the waiting room. It's the end of the day and the streets have emptied out. Only one young woman is left in the waiting room. Ling-li had seen her the day before and had instructed her to return to have her burn wound cleaned and her dressing changed. She takes the patient back to the consultation room, sits her down and begins to unravel her bandages. "Scissors, please," she says to Claude.

He brings her a pair and positions himself carefully behind the young woman in order not to see her wound. He has done pretty well with some ghastly cases recently, but there's no need to upset his stomach unnecessarily. "You see," Ling-li says, "it's quite hopeless. How can we expect to gain any respect if we don't stop behaving as if the English were gods here?"

She begins irrigating the wound vigorously.

"Ouch!" says the young woman. A rather plump lady, in Claude's opinion, and appearing even more so beside Ling-li.

"Sorry," she says, not pausing for one moment. "It's as if we now truly believe that we're inherently inferior to the whites, that we can't think as well or lead as well as they can." From where Claude stands, her hands seem to be scrubbing out the wound.

"*Aiyo*," the woman groans and he can't help feeling sorry for her.

"That looks painful," he says. Ling-li ignores him.

"I guess it's not unlike pickling," she goes on. "You put whatever fruit or vegetable you want in vinegar long enough and it ends up shrivelling and being sour, no matter how sweet it was before. Our confidence has dried up and we've come to see ourselves as the British see us—slow, stupid, loud, dirty. They think the place will collapse without them. We'd be much better off on our own, is what I say!"

"Is there anything else that you *can* say?"

He hurries on before she can open her mouth again. "You've made it very clear what you think of the British and our situation here. And maybe you have a point. But they've done *some* things right, you have to admit that too. This is what we have for now. We can't change it all in one day."

She wraps clean bandages on the patient, speaking to her—relaying instructions perhaps—in Hokkien. When the woman has left, Ling-li washes her hands and begins tidying up the room. Claude observes her, then asks, "Still thinking about what to say?"

She slams a drawer shut and moves to the sink. "No, we can't change it in one day, but if we let one day go by, if we let one second slip by without remembering that we *need* to change, that we *must,* then we're lost." She still refuses to face him and continues to busy herself with the cleaning, filling the sink with water and collecting used instruments in order to soak them in a Dettol bath.

"Is that what you do then—think about it everyday, every second?"

"Every half-second, every fiftieth of a second." She tries to raise a smile with this, but the severity in her voice is absolute, as if she's issuing a command to herself.

He senses she's about to say more, to open up to him, perhaps. If he can only find the right thing to say, a way to urge her on—

"I've sent them on their way," says Jack, his voice appearing before he does. When he limps into the room Ling-li moves away, down the corridor towards the toilet. They hear her shut the door and secure the latch. "And I also let the young lady out—the one with the burn. Funny thing, I could have sworn she was trying to listen in on your conversation with Ling-li. You must've been talking about something very interesting—my ears were burning."

"Then you must be getting an ear infection. We weren't talking about you at all." Claude still can't bring himself to forget Jack's behaviour towards Ling-li during Humphrey's visit.

"Oh no?"

"No, we have better things to discuss."

Jack says nothing to this and moves around the room as Ling-li had, tidying up. When he picks up the needle tray, balancing on his crutches, Claude says, "I can take that."

"That's quite all right," Jack says, pivoting on one foot to avoid Claude. "I've sterilized before." He begins arranging the dirty needles and instruments in a small toaster-like machine.

It's irrational, not wanting him to touch Ling-li's instruments, not wanting him to be in the room. Claude hears her coming out of the toilet. "I've got to go out tonight," she says. "Don't wait up for me—I have the key."

"Where are you going?" It's generally not a good idea to be walking the streets at night, and Ling-li, more than anyone, should be aware of this. She seldom does anything risky without a very good reason.

"Oh, I promised to see some of the people at the refugee centre on Bras Pasah Road," she says.

"Do you want any help? I could help you carry your equipment there," Claude offers.

"Equipment? . . . Oh, I don't think I'll be needing much. If anyone's too sick I'll send him along to hospital." She is almost at the door when she seems to change her mind about something and she returns to the rear of the clinic. When she emerges she has changed from the white uniform she wears whenever the clinic is open—how does she keep it so clean? does she have spares?—to a pair of black slacks and a black top. Jack, having set the sterilizer, looks up. "Quite a change from the angel all dressed in white."

Claude opens his mouth before he can stop himself. "I don't know—they might mistake you for the Angel of Death."

"Shut up," she says with a laugh, and it makes him feel good to be able to joke around with her like that. Even Jack seems more relaxed. "Lock up," she says and is gone.

"Well," says Jack after a long pause. "We could fix dinner."

"Good idea."

◈

The light bulb in the toilet had been removed to replace a blown one in the office but she still flipped the switch from habit, still expected the flood of light. When none came, she remembered and leaned against the door, glad for the cool dimness. She had simply wanted to get away from Jack and, perhaps more importantly, from Claude. His questions had not only taken her by surprise but also placed her on the defensive, an unusual position for her.

She had been so close to blurting out everything, so close to telling him about General Yue Fei and her mother. She must be getting soft, overly sentimental. Perhaps it was fatigue setting in from the incessant work at the clinic, the harrowing trips she made at night to meet Anil who was becoming unpredictable, appearing sporadiacally, sometimes without documents or any of the agents. She wished she could confide in her uncle, or at least see him more often. He had always given her good advice and cheered her up at her worst moments. He was the closest to family to her. Of her parents, she remembered almost nothing. A flicker of faces, too brief to capture; a smudge of colours, shapes. On some rare days, her mother's features would snap into focus and immediately blur again; she could never hold the image long enough for it to register. An old photograph had a curious effect on her. The most concrete evidence of her parents, it somehow left the least impression of all. She would stare and stare, and the couple in the photograph would become stranger and stranger, until they were totally foreign and completely familiar at the same time, faces she had never seen before and faces she had known her entire life.

But she remembered her mother's voice—the low tones, its hoarseness at the end of the day, the way it would crack when it sang. And the stories it told. That story. The one Ling-li lived out everyday as a way—the only way she knew—to remember her mother by.

It didn't help that she felt herself a coward, afraid all the time of
what would happen if a bomb wiped them all out at the clinic, if the
Japanese won. Her fear was a hump she carried on her back, something she fought against each moment. It should have been a scar
that would drive her on to battle, it should have been a mother's
wound. She was unworthy of her parents' memory.

"Your parents were patriots," Uncle Hong-Seng had told her.
"Half of what they earned every month went back to China. They
donated a school to our village, you know, before they died. They
had both wanted to be buried there."

Instead they had been buried next to a mangrove in their Katong
farm, just out of reach of tidal seepage. Every year, at Ching Ming,
she and Uncle Hong-Seng had gone to pay their respects, bringing
flowers, pouring out rice wine at the grave site. In a few weeks it
would be Ching Ming again, time to pay respects to ancestors and
worship at their graves, and yet she couldn't help feeling it was a long
way off. Now that the vendors had lost their livelihood, she wondered where she would find flowers. If the jungle yielded nothing,
she would probably have to make do without.

What a spot of luck, getting access to Miss Competence like that.
She had worried at first that she would be recognised from the rallies they had attended together back in the old days, but that didn't
happen, and the Fifth Columnist relaxed after their first meeting.
Her wound had been cleaned and she had been given instructions
to return the next day. What luck too, in finding the Englishman
there. He had seemed harmless, but what did it matter? It suited her
purpose and provided material for the report.

The aloof, dreamy-eyed Chinese boy was more puzzling. Miss
Competence made fun of him but seemed to enjoy his company. He
did whatever she told him and needed everything to be translated,
just like the Englishman. The Fifth Columnist put him in her files.
He was boring and unappealing—just the thing to keep her records
realistic and balanced. It was such a pity that the war would end
soon, by all accounts. She was just getting the hang of this.

❀

An army depends upon the Imperative mood. Without it, all is chaos; discipline wanes. But more and more, the Australians are ignoring the Imperative, simply walking away from their posts, leaving gaps between battalions along the front line that the Japanese walk through without much fuss. More and more the commanders and officers are relying on the Subjunctive: All plans are conditional, all orders wishful thinking.

❀

When Ling-li returns to the clinic it is past midnight. The cellar is enormous. Jack is fast asleep in his cot at the far end where his snores are less bothersome, but Claude is a light sleeper. His bed is right under the wooden stairs and when the cellar door cracks open, letting in the light of a small candle, he is already awake.

She places each foot carefully on the stairs to minimise creaks and is almost at the bottom step when Claude hisses out her name. She gives a little jump. "Idiot! You gave me a fright."

"Where've you been?" He sits up in bed, noting the mud on her clothes. She has washed her face and it glistens.

"Oh, this!" She brushes off mud from her shirt. "I fell—tripped over some posts in the road." She places the candle on the floor beside his bed and shakes out her hair. Dry leaves flake off. He is sceptical.

"Why aren't you asleep?" she asks.

"I was worried about you."

"That's nice," she says, seemingly amused. "Sometimes I worry about myself too! Still, I've been pretty good at taking care of myself so far, don't you think? I would say my track record is quite a bit better than yours."

"By a mile," he allows, smiling. It's a relief to have her here. "Are you hungry?"

"Always!"

He reaches under his bed for a small package of beef jerky—something a patient had given him in exchange for washing out his shoulder wound—tears off a strip and holds it out to her. She tosses it in her mouth and wolfs it down with two chomps of her jaw. "God, you're something," he says, giving up the rest of the package. She sits down on the edge of his bed to finish it off.

When she catches him staring, she laughs again. "Can't help it," she says, licking her fingers. "I'm starving. And thank you. You're always making sure I eat." When she laughs the skin on her face tightens, stretches across the bones with greater tension and the angles of her cheekbones become much more pronounced. The candlelight emphasises her thinness and an ethereal quality that isn't evident under the harsh fluorescent lights in the clinic, or in daylight.

"Have you always been so thin?" he asks.

She sighs. "All my life. I ate like a pig in my schooldays, but nothing seemed to help, although, I have to say, I was on to something before the war got quite so bad. I ate lots of *chapatis* and *murtabaks*, loaded with ghee of course. It was disgusting to watch the hawkers make them, but they tasted so good once they were in my mouth! I was actually beginning to put on some curves." She glances down ruefully at her flat chest. "Really!" she giggles without warning. She's very pretty when she's like this, he thinks. He has never seen her so light-hearted.

"You're different tonight," he tells her.

She considers this. "Maybe," she concedes. "I don't know what it is either. I think it was just being outside in the night air—it's cool tonight, with a good breeze. No bombers around after about ten. I could almost imagine that everything was back to normal as I walked back here. I've always hated being stuck indoors. If the Japanese don't drop a bomb on my head, I'd go bonkers from being cooped up inside—either way they'd get me."

"Ah, an outdoors kind of girl," he teases.

"Yes. I lived on a farm in Katong—that was when my parents were alive."

Claude thinks of Cousin Eng's pig farm, the bedraggled chickens in their hen houses, the occasional goat driving everyone crazy with its nasal complaining. In his mind he can see Ling-li filling the pig troughs and collecting eggs in the evenings. On market day she'd try to persuade her father against separating the sows from the piglets.

"My mother's cousin has a farm in Punggol. I used to go during our school holidays. My sister, Lucy, loves it. She gets soft-hearted over all the baby animals and always begs to take them home with us. But you actually lived with them! Lucy would be so jealous."

"Well, maybe," Ling-li says. "It was a crocodile farm."

"Oh."

"They're the only animals I know, really. I've hatched the little ones and watched them grow to the size of logs. It was my job to feed them. In the beginning we had to give them cut-up pieces of meat, but when they were older we could just toss in a chicken or two and they'd swallow the whole thing live.

"On days when someone left the gates open," she went on, "I had to skip school to help round up the crocs. Very convenient around exams!"

He can't imagine her wrestling crocodiles. "Oh, but I did!" she insists. "Up to three feet long, I could manage. I didn't touch anything bigger than that. The key is to get up from behind, get a good grip on the jaws and keep your balance."

Perhaps she is pulling his leg but there she is, staring serenely into a corner of the cellar, lost in her memories. "Where did you go to school?" he asks.

"St. Anne's until Primary Six, and then I went to Chung Hwa."

So she was English-educated in the first six years. It accounts for her fluency. "Was it hard, changing schools like that, and languages?"

"Oddly enough, no," she says, arching her back and extending her arms over her head. "God, I'm stiff. No, not at all. When I went to Chung Hwa it was like going home—I felt such a relief. I didn't have to filter my thoughts any longer—you know, through the English Sieve." She notices his quizzical look and continues, "All my thoughts would tumble out in Chinese and I felt like I had to put them through a sieve—The English Sieve, I called it—and what came through on the other side would be those thoughts translated into English. It was a lot of work."

"Did you find your classmates different at Chung Hwa?"

"At St. Anne's almost everyone I knew spoke English at home. They made fun of me all the time because of my accent. I worked really hard at it, threw myself into my books, won all the English prizes every year—just to spite them." She gives a small smile of satisfaction. "But the truth is, they never accepted me and I never felt comfortable with them. They were always so, so—smug, so . . . complacent. They acted as if they owned the world."

She looks down, a flush on her cheeks. "My parents thought that if I learnt English I'd have a better future. They wanted me to be in the civil service, have a chance to move up."

"That's what my father believes," Claude says. "And if you think about it, it's true. How else could we have a chance at power and success?"

"Power? Oh, Claude! Power indeed! You'd be the poor fellow doing all the work while your English boss calls the shots. Don't you get it, Claude, you'd be the labour, not the power, never the power—not this way anyhow."

"We have to agree to disagree," he says with false cheer, not wanting the truce to end. She takes a breath, puffs out her cheeks and blows a windy whistle as she shakes her head.

"All right," she says. "For now, anyway. I'm too tired for another round."

"And I, for one, am too smart to fight someone who used to wrestle crocodiles! Though I'm still not convinced you haven't been pulling my leg."

Ling-li gets up. "I'll prove it to you another time." She picks up her candle and heads to her corner of the cellar. When she gets there she blows it out and he hears her removing her clothes, combing out her hair. Then there is the rustle of sheets and the creak of her bed as she gets in it.

Despite knowing she is safe, he can't sleep. He is wondering, against his best intentions, if she is totally naked in her bed. If he walked over while she slept would he see the dark stain of her nipples against the threadbare sheets, the faint curves of her breasts? And if he waited, would she shift carelessly in the night, revealing a thigh, a hip? He recalls the smell of her at the foot of his bed—sweaty, slightly sweet, disturbingly urgent. It brings on a tightness and warmth in his lower belly, a tickle between his legs. He closes his eyes, tries to blank out his mind.

The next thing he knows it is morning and the ceiling is caving in.

It's happened. The clinic's been hit. Ling-li is hovering in the air above Claude as if dangling from the ceiling—whatever's left of it. But then he realises that she is standing on two large boxes, allowing her to stick her head out through a hole to the ground floor. The wooden stairs have collapsed like a flattened accordion. "Jack?" he calls out.

"Over here," comes the weak reply behind a mass of rubble. Claude scrambles to his feet and starts digging away. When he tugs at a piece of wood near the bottom, the entire heap crumbles. Dust spirals above him.

"It's okay," says Ling-li, coughing. "I don't think any major structural units are badly damaged—except maybe the entire east wall of our clinic. But I think we'll be able to dig him out easily. Just make sure you start from the top." She is dressed in her black clothes, Claude notes irrelevantly. Did she have to jump into them at the first rumble? She climbs down from the boxes to join him. "If you move these over there you can reach the top of the pile and start clearing the stuff away."

Obediently Claude pushes the boxes over to the rubble and starts work. "You're not hurt, are you, Jack?" He throws off planks, scraps of plaster, loose chunks of concrete, pipes.

"No, thank God. I got lucky, I suppose. I just can't see too much." His voice is slightly muffled but steady.

Claude works until the pile of rubble reaches the top of Ling-li's head, and then she joins in, coughing and sneezing from the dust. Soon, Jack's dirty face appears and Claude is able to help him climb out of the mess. The three of them take turns climbing onto the boxes and out of the cellar into the gaping hole that is the clinic. The smell of smoke is mixed in with the bitter scent of pills and

Dettol. "Clinic closed," Ling-li mutters and here, above ground, Claude notices how pale she is.

"Seems like the opposite," he says, waving one hand at the empty space where the east wall once stood. "The clinic is open, I would say." And catching her eye, he giggles, and then, unexpectedly, she giggles too, rocking on her heels, her arms crossed over her belly. Something has unlatched itself and they can't stop giggling, even though nothing is funny. They ride the wave of hilarity willingly because if they fight it, they will go under and be lost. It lifts them so high that it feels like flying. On and on it goes, both of them riding it, so light and buoyant, on and on until Claude wonders if it will end, and then slowly, it flattens out, gently depositing them on the far shore.

"Yes, the clinic is wide open," Ling-li says finally, very breathless. There's a tear at the corner of one eye and, as she wipes it, he sees her hand shaking, but she is smiling. And then she sees something beyond Claude and the smile stiffens, causing him to turn around. Jack is staring down into the hole they've just climbed out of, his face a mask.

"Jack?" Claude says. He looks up.

"I think," he says, "I would like to go home."

So it has come, finally. He has had enough. He wants to go home now. And why not? He has the option and it would be stupid to let it pass. If Claude had the opportunity, he would go himself, most likely. He does't blame Jack for anything, no need for the Englishman to avoid his eyes. Or is it Ling-li's eyes he is avoiding?

But there is no triumph on her face. Instead, she clears her throat, inhales deeply, her hands still trembling. "It won't be easy at this point," she says. "I'm not sure there are tickets left."

"I could ask George's friends," Jack says hesitantly. "If I find them." He turns his back to Claude. "I'll need help."

"First things first," says Ling-li with a sigh. "Back to the hut. We can't stay here."

"I'll get our things," Claude says, eager to move.

"Oh, Claude!" She throws him a surprisingly fond look. "There's nothing to take! Just whatever rice and food supplies we have left."

"At least it'll be a light load," he says. Jack stumbles outside, his hands held out slightly in front of him, his shoulders hunched forward. He looks like a blind man afraid to fall. In the smoky sunlight he is ragged in his scruffy clothes, smaller, older, almost pathetic.

Claude has to repeat his news slowly, in bits, making sure his parents follow him at every step before proceeding. When he finishes, Humphrey says, "I can see why Jack wants to go, and I don't blame him. I should have insisted that the two of you move in here."

"It was stupid, taking that sort of risk." Cynthia's voice is shaky, and Claude is sorry to have put her through this.

"You're right, Mother, we should have moved out." She has turned to face the window, and looks tired and worn-out. He tries to think of something to say that might comfort her. "Anyway, if there's still room, perhaps Ling-li and I could move in after Jack's gone."

"There's no telling if and when we might be hit too," Grandma Siok says. "Just being in a hotel is no guarantee of avoiding a shell. It makes more sense to me that we're spread out, rather than cooped up in the same place where the entire family line could disappear with one well-aimed bomb."

"How is he going to manage this?" Cynthia asks, still looking outside. "Surely there can't be tickets left?"

"Only on the black market, as far as I know. But I'm going to ask Mr. Hawthorne if he has any ideas. All of Jack's contacts seem to have left the island already, or can't be found."

Humphrey taps his forehead as he thinks. "Yes, you're right, son. Try Hawthorne—he's a good sort—and I'll ask the manager if we can squeeze you and your friend in here."

At the door, Grandma Siok pats Claude's shoulder. "You seem to have grown taller, for some reason." She takes a step back to look at him. "Maybe you're skinnier, and it makes you look longer."

He considers this. In the last two days, he has walked around feel-

ing strangely tall himself, and as if his feet were barely touching the
ground. His head is engulfed in a giddy lightness, especially when
he runs or jumps. He has the ridiculous notion that he might be
healthier and stronger now, despite his meagre rations, than before
the war. Yet everyone else seems to have aged and grown more fragile. Grandma Siok herself is quieter, more restrained, and lately she
has begun to shuffle—something she has never been able to tolerate
in other people.

"All that walking and running around must have done me some
good. Look," he says, wanting to make her laugh. He holds up his
arms, bent at the elbows, and tightens his muscles. There are small
but definite bulges between each shoulder and elbow.

She bursts into a grin. "Good old Claude," she says, giving him a
quick hug. "I knew you'd turn out right in the end."

Closer and closer to the end, and the Fifth Columnist can't stop
writing.

All plans are conditional, all orders wishful thinking. In Chinese,
all statements are coloured by the Subjunctive. Possibilities, suppo-
sitions. It's a language she fully exploits in her reports.

Ling-li is digging. It is painful to watch her emaciated form
struggling with the spade and striking the cord-like roots of the rain
trees growing on the empty site along Serangoon Road.

"Maybe," Claude puffs, resting from his own efforts at shovelling,
"it would be easier to burn them."

"I'd thought about that," she says, not stopping at all. "But with
these winds, we can't risk starting a fire." In other words—though
she doesn't say it aloud—keep digging.

There are at least fifteen bodies to be buried. Hong-Seng and his
friends had collected them in the back of an army jeep and laid them
in a row beside the patch of rain trees. They've gone back now to
scout the streets for more bodies and when they return, the count
could be doubled. There are more trenches to dig along Bukit

Timah Road afterwards, and Hong-Seng will not be able to help with the burials. Claude averts his eyes from the row of decomposing bodies and focuses on making a big hole in the ground, but when the crows start coming round and try to peck out the corpses' eyes, Ling-li sends him over to cover the bodies with a tarpaulin and gunnysacks.

The first body is that of a young man, close to Claude's age. His eyes are wide open and as his face shrivels in the sun, his eyeballs have begun to protrude a little. Both his legs have been blown off, and his crossed arms are rigid on his belly. Claude flings a gunnysack over the corpse, but it lands askew, leaving the face still exposed. He has to lean over to tug at the gunnysack in order to cover him properly, and in doing so, his hand brushes against the dead man. The softness of the corpse's hair undoes him and he turns his head just in time to avoid throwing up on the man's face.

Ling-li is by his side at once. "Wash out your mouth," she tells him after he's done. "I'm tired. You can dig while I cover them up."

Six hours of non-stop digging. Hong-Seng and his friends bring back more bodies, never stopping to talk. Afterwards, Claude and Ling-li carry the covered bodies one by one over to the ditch they've dug. The first few times Claude scrambles carefully down the six-foot-deep hole, with Ling-li following closely behind. It is exhausting work. "We can't go on like this," he says, panting.

"Here," Ling-li says, wiping her mouth. She hands him her water bottle which she has just drunk from, expecting him to take a sip now. She is right, of course. If he doesn't drink he will soon get heatstroke, and there is still so much work to be done. But he has always been squeamish about such things, and can't even share a cup with his sister. He brings the bottle to his lips. It is still wet from hers. With twenty-three dead bodies lying around, the smell twisting his stomach and bringing the bile up at every turn, it is not the time to be too particular about sharing a water bottle. Besides, the water is wonderfully clean, clear and sweet.

"We need to conserve energy," he says when he's finished drinking. "We can't keep climbing in and out of a six-foot ditch twenty-three times. We'll wear ourselves out."

She nods but says nothing, her eyes on the mass grave they've dug.

"If we just toss them in—gently—it will save us a lot of energy," he says. It sounds callous when put like that, but he can't see how they can avoid it.

"Let's go then," she says, heading for the next body. She lifts the legs and waits for Claude to pick the body up under the shoulders.

They carry the body to the ditch, swing it slowly as Claude counts, "One, two, three," under his breath, and toss it into the hole. It lands on top of another corpse with a thud, rolls a short way, dislodging the sheet covering it, and comes to a stop with its face and neck exposed.

"Can't be helped," he says. They work in silence for another half-hour, until all the bodies are in the grave. Then she picks up her spade and starts filling in. Claude follows suit, trying to cover up the faces of the corpses as quickly as possible before settling into a more comfortable pace.

"Are you all right?" he asks, his back to her.

"Yes."

When the ditch is half-filled in, she says, "I buried my parents myself after they died."

"Oh." It is all he can think of to say.

"My uncle did most of the digging, of course, but I had to help him, so he let me."

"How old were you?"

"Six. They died of cholera, something I escaped because they were making me drink boiled milk everyday to fatten me up."

He imagines scrawny, six-year-old Ling-li piling dirt on her parents' grave.

"The funny thing is, it didn't haunt me at all until I was eighteen. I had heard reports about the mass executions in China—you know, Shanghai, Nanking. How the Japanese gathered hundreds of people in one place and then had them dig a mass grave. Afterwards, they'd have them stand on the edge of the hole and gun them down in rows. Those who weren't killed right away were buried alive."

Claude's ignorance seems more evident everyday; he has never heard such stories. Ling-li's gaze is focused on the ground as she works and he can't see her face.

"I kept dreaming of my parents being buried alive in one of those mass graves. I'd see them being gunned down—but not killed—by the Japanese, and then they would try to crawl out of the heap of bodies. But the soldiers start covering the grave with dirt and garbage, and soon they bury my parents completely."

For a while, there is only the rhythmic scrape of shovel and spade. The ground slowly becomes whole again, resumes its smooth surface.

"I'm sorry." By this time the hole is almost entirely filled in.

"It's just a dream," she says, straightening up and leaning on her spade. She lets him throw in the last few scoops of dirt, which she then pats down neatly. "There, it's done. It looks like a vegetable patch, doesn't it?"

It is a twelve-by-sixteen-foot square patch of dark, loamy soil. "It would be a good idea to grow something here later," she says. "The soil will be very fertile." She unscrews the lid of her water bottle and drinks.

"I don't know—it would be like feeding off the dead, wouldn't it?"

"But that's always been the case, Claude, don't you know?" She hands him her water bottle. This time he takes it without hesitation and drinks. Perhaps she's right, it's always been the case—the living feeding off the dead. That afternoon, standing there next to her and all those corpses in the grave, drinking from her bottle, it seems so natural and obvious.

The Fifth Column spies are still hard at work. On February 13th, the morning of General Wavell's last visit to Singapore, a bomb is dropped on the Western Area HQ where he, General Bennett and Lieutenant-General Percival are meeting. Fortunately, it does not explode. Still, the generals are shaken. Bennett is a little pale behind his moustache and for the half-hour or so after the bomb scare, he is not his usual bullying self. A pity, Wavell thinks, it takes a bomb to shut him up.

Aloud, he asks the expected questions about how the war is going and receives the unpleasant but expected answers. Bennett is hopelessly out of touch with the events on the Western Area's front and is evasive when pushed to explain the difficulty in maintaining order among his troops. He has also evidently not prepared any defence of the Kranji-Jurong Line and refuses still to talk about the possibility of withdrawal.

The next day, while making his way to his seaplane, Wavell slips on the quay. He lies on his side with one hand pressed against his sore back until members of his staff help him to a sitting position. "Should we carry you to the plane, sir?" they ask, concerned. The old man is grimacing and swearing under his breath.

"No, no, no, no, no." He leans on his aide and stands up with an effort. "There, that's better. No, I'm fine. Just a little slip." Nothing like the big slip that's been made here, he thinks, looking beyond his staff. His seaplane is bobbing gaily in the water, surrounded by ragtag sampans and watercraft, filled to the edges with armed white men in civilian clothes, sometimes wearing nothing more than shorts.

"You might as well rest here, sir," his aide says, unfolding a canvas-backed chair. "We've been delayed."

"Whatever do you mean?" Wavell asks, irritation in his voice. Can nothing get done here without a major fuss?

"We have to first—ah—clear the take-off path of any stray vessels, sir."

So mere foot soldiers will get off the island before a general—the Supreme Commander, no less—does. Totally against military protocol, but then, desertion is the soldier's rebuttal to military protocol. No use getting upset. General Sir Archibald Wavell rubs his back and settles back in his chair to wait the long hour before his flight is finally cleared for departure.

❄

Claude is glad they started out early. Every taxi in the city seems to be taken, the trishaw that Ling-li found (or hijacked?) has disappeared from the back alley and Jack has had to stop frequently to rest. His suitcase is small and light—his left-behind books useless now that he is going home—containing only several changes of clothes and two precious cartons of cigarettes that Ling-li gave him. They might come in handy if he needs to bribe someone, she said. His passport is in Claude's back pocket, its oblong shape not moulding very well to the curve of his left buttock.

"I'll have to rest again," Jack says, sinking onto a short flight of steps.

"We have time," Claude says, sitting down beside him. "I made some sandwiches. Mostly butter, really, but they'll give you energy."

Jack takes the sandwich from Claude and tears into it. "I still don't know how you managed to get me a ticket," he says.

"Mr. Hawthorne, the principal at my school. He knows a lot of people. He's the one who helped me get your papers to leave. Gave me the bread and butter too."

"And what about him? Will he leave also?"

"He's staying on. He's been here for twenty-three years. He says this is his home."

"And you, what will you do now?"

Claude swallows the last of his sandwich self-consciously. "I don't know, really. Stay and help Ling-li, if she needs me, I suppose. She's setting up a small infirmary at the Bras Pasah refugee centre."

"Doesn't stop, does she?"

Claude nods, a kind of pride welling up. "No," he says. "She doesn't stop."

"I'm feeling funny about this, leaving you and everybody else at the darkest hour." He looks disturbed.

Claude tries to cheer him up. "Don't be silly, Jack. There's nothing for you here now. Besides, everybody's leaving. You're not doing anything out of the ordinary." And he doesn't want Jack around anyway. It would be better without him, just Ling-li and himself at the refugee centre, no Englishman to take care of.

"Well, that's it. Not everybody's leaving. You're not leaving. It doesn't feel right, if you know what I mean." Too late now, Claude thinks, but tries to be magnanimous by telling Jack he's doing the right thing, they'll miss him but everything will be fine. It comes out lamely and unconvincingly, but he doesn't care. He's just going through the motions.

Jack opens up his duffel and brings out a book. "I don't really have anything to give you, Claude," he says, holding the book out. There is no dust jacket and the words on the spine are faded. "It's not much of a gift."

"Thank you. Are you sure?" He remember the fuss Jack made

about his books and wonders why he is parting with one now. He
hadn't expected anything from him. "What's it about?"

"Oh, you'll see."

Finally they both get up and continue the walk to the harbour.
Claude lets Jack carry the duffel while he manages the Englishman's
suitcase. By this time the sun is flattening out at the horizon and the
sky is like a charcoal fire, gold blazing into black. "My last day in
Singapore," Jack says.

The harbour is in chaos. There are cars strewn everywhere,
crowds of whites, Indians, Chinese, everyone trying to get off the
island. "Last boat, last boat," someone cries, as if spurring himself
on as he runs towards the quay. Sheds and godowns all around are
burning. Bombers buzz overhead; the musical whine of falling
bombs is continuous. Machine-guns manned by soldiers around
the harbour's periphery keep the Japanese fliers at bay, but do not
stop them from ringing the area with flames.

"We'll never get through," Jack says. Women and screaming children are being herded towards the *Empire Star,* berthed alongside the
Keppel Wharf.

"That's your boat," Claude points out to Jack as a hail of bullets
pierces the air. "Down!" He pulls Jack to the ground.

"What on earth is that?" Jack is looking up at the gangplank of the
Empire Star. A group of soldiers, dressed in Australian uniform and
wearing the unmistakable slouch hat, is clubbing its way up the
gangplank. On board and below, more Australians are firing into
the crowd to prevent people from approaching. "This is insane!
They should be court-martialled!"

The British military police on the gangplank and on deck are
beating off the Australians with their truncheons as best they can,
while continuing to haul women on board the ship. Claude hauls
Jack to his feet. "Up! Come on!" He leads him into the crowd.

"But, they're deserting!" Jack exclaims in shock.

"Didn't I tell you already?" Claude fights the jostling men and
women on the quay in front of them. "Don't let go of my elbow!"

Jack answers something back, but it's impossible to hear him above the roar of the bombers and the screaming crowd.

They plunge into the frantic mass. Several times they are pushed back and pressed up against a tight wall of bodies, but Claude makes sure that Jack's hand is clamped to his arm. At one point, perhaps encouraged by the nearness of the ship, Jack surges forward, pulling Claude along. Two hundred yards short of the ship gunfire erupts again, this time aimed at the gangplank. The crowd makes a wild dash for cover. Jack stumbles, his hand still tight on Claude's elbow, and they both drop to the ground.

For a terrifying moment all Claude sees are legs and feet. Someone steps on his back and over his legs. Fortunately the stampede does not last long. Jack tries to scramble to his feet. "Stay low," Claude says, yanking him down again. "Head down. They won't keep this up."

Sure enough, the firing ceases abruptly as the Australian soldiers at the foot of the gangplank run up it, dodging the police on their way. "Look!" Jack tugs at Claude's sleeve. Over the side of the ship a naval officer has lowered a rope ladder to two civilians on the wharf. They grab the swinging ladder and climb up, swaying alarmingly in mid-air.

"Okay," Claude says, making up his mind. "Start crawling. If we can get you to the ladder you'll be fine."

Jack hesitates. "It's a long climb."

"It's your best chance. Move! Now! Hurry before the crowd comes back." Despite everything, he can't help thinking: This man has no survival skills.

They crawl on their bellies, Claude dragging the suitcase, Jack with his duffel bag clutched to his chest. Their elbows and knees are sore but they push on. Every now and then a half-hearted shot rings in the air. The fires rage around the harbour and a smoky haze covers the scene. Over the sound of sirens and shouts Claude hears a familiar cranking of pumps and realises that the fire-fighting teams are at work. He wonders if his unit has been called for the night. Probably not. As a school unit it's more likely to be assigned to smaller, discrete fires. It's funny how calm he is, crawling towards the *Empire Star* in the midst of fires, air raids and bullets. So this is war—it feels strangely familiar.

"I can't do this anymore," Jack grunts. The men on the rope ladder already are halfway up.

"Short rest," Claude says. It's not even my boat, he thinks. Jack's the one who's leaving on that blasted ship. "Not too far now," he adds encouragingly, hiding his annoyance.

Gradually the crowd comes back, people heading for the gangplank again, manned now only by the police. "Shouldn't we head there?" Jack asks.

"I think we should try the ladder. The Australians will start shooting again, once another batch decides to storm up the gangplank."

"Well, it's quiet enough now. If we make a run for it, we'll be okay. I'd rather not climb a rope ladder if I can walk up the gangplank."

Claude looks around. No soldiers in sight. "Let's go!" They push themselves up and start running towards the ship. A shout rises. Looking over his shoulder, Claude knows that they've set the others off, and a crowd of men and women surges behind them for the boat. We're storming the boat, he thinks ridiculously, trying to run faster, but Jack is behind so Claude slows for him to catch up.

At the foot of the gangplank they are met by a policeman. "Papers," he says, holding up both hands as if to ward them off.

"He's the one who's going," Claude says, whipping out Jack's passport and his papers tucked neatly inside.

The policeman scans the passport, reads the exit pass. "Now see here," he says. "These are exit passes for Mr. and Mrs. Hawthorne. You're"—he flips back to the front page of the passport—"John Winchester. I'm afraid—"

"Read the letter attached. Mr. and Mrs. Hawthorne are giving up their passage for Mr. Winchester to travel. That's two for one," Claude says urgently. The crowd is already sprinting the last few hundred yards to the ship.

The policeman is joined by his colleague. "What's the matter?" he asks.

"It appears someone has given up his passage to this fellow here, but the papers are still in the original holder's name."

"They're all in order, really," Claude says, one nervous eye on the advancing crowd. "Just take him up and you can examine them there."

"Look." Jack is struggling to catch his breath. "I can assure you I wouldn't have made this mad attempt if there'd been anything fishy about those papers."

And then the crowd is there, pushing up against them, swarming the gangplank, overwhelming the two policemen. Someone breaks through, runs up the gangplank. Another follows before police reinforcements arrive, trying to calm the crowd. "Please have your papers ready," a voice says over a megaphone. "Stop pushing, please! Queue up, queue up! Anyone out of line will not be allowed on the boat." The pushing subsides and people begin to queue up. Jack is now fifth in line.

The policemen begin checking papers. Before they can get to Jack again, three men from behind thrust themselves forward. "Out of my way!" one says in his unmistakable Australian accent.

"Get back in line," a policeman growls.

"I said get out of my way!" the man repeats and without warning lifts the policeman and hurls him into the crowd. People topple like dominoes, and a fistfight starts among the police and the hijackers. Seizing the opportunity, others try to make a run up the gangplank.

"Go, go!" Claude pushes Jack. "Run!"

Jack opens his mouth, his lips forming the word "What?" and then, as if coming to his senses, Jack starts running. Claude makes his move next. Noting that it's a mere four feet to the ground, he vaults over two policemen trying to restrain the Australians, over the panicking crowd, over the rails to land safely on the wharf. He looks up, but it's impossible to see Jack—there's only an angry, frightened mass of people.

He edges around the crowd. It feels odd not to have Jack by his side. He keeps checking over his shoulder to see if he's there. How will the Englishman manage on his own? When Claude squeezes through the crowd to get to the main road, his eyes catch, for the briefest second, a familiar face.

He shakes his head. He must have imagined it. With the poor lighting and incessant noise, it's easy to make a mistake. Why would his mother be here in the crowd tonight? He thinks about how easily the English and other Europeans mistake one Asiatic face for another. There may be something to that after all.

By the time he arrives at the main road, the traffic is so bad that people are climbing over cars to get to the wharf. It's disorienting to make his way against the tide of women and children led by desperate men determined to see their loved ones aboard. He can feel the start of a headache and he's hungry again, which doesn't help. This is the end of the British Empire, he thinks suddenly, and then can't get the words out of his mind. He needs to see his family again. He really should go to the hotel where his mother is probably ordering tea and getting cross at the manager for not having Pouchong leaves, and his father is still listening to the radio reports on how the British are winning the war. Grandma Siok is buried in *The Art of War* while Lucy is hiding from bombers under her bed. When the Japanese get here, who knows what will happen to all of them?

A twist in his stomach makes him admit the feeling he's been trying to hold back: fear.

This is the end of the British Empire. Singed air. Sirens wailing. The harbour, bombed and torched. Godowns razed. People weeping. Brittannia sailing the waves in retreat. In a moment, he too will break down, his reserve crumbling like the world around him. In an attempt to hold on to his emotions, he bites his lip. *Stiff upper lip,* his father's pride—the admirable restraint of the English. And everywhere around, the English are near panic.

It is this thought that finally allows him to release the tears. He keeps walking, back into the heart of the city that the English are trying so hard to leave. It doesn't matter if anyone sees him crying. It is too dark for recognition, it is wartime—and therefore appropriate—and really, in the end, it doesn't matter anyway.

The woman in the next room is saying something now. Words you can't understand. Chinese. Perhaps she is even talking directly to you. She is telling you what she is going through. Perhaps she is calling out to you for help. Perhaps she requires words back, words of comfort and reassurance, spells—like armour—or prayers, to shield her from further harm.

It is a relief to hear her talk, in between her cries of pain. Maybe the Japanese think she is conversing with them—they are answering back in their own language. They are laughing at her, jeering. But she keeps on talking, chattering almost. It is nonsense to you, but you listen carefully to every word, every syllable, every bit of organized sound from her lips.

Claude the Body heaves his broken ribcage to breathe in his sleep. You give up the myrmidons. You are otherwise occupied. Until morning, you can listen to her untiring radio of sounds and stories. You can guess at meanings.

Jack doesn't need the book to remember the words. He has read them over so many times that they are a part of his natural thoughts. He is, after all, no different from Flory who had run out on his friend and proved himself a coward:

> He took the lamp, went into the bedroom and shut the door. The stale scent of dust and cigarette-smoke met him, and in the white, unsteady glare of the lamp he could see the mildewed books and the lizards on the wall. So he was back again to this—to the old, secret life—after everything, back where he had been before.
> Was it possible to endure it? He had endured it before. There were palliatives—books, his garden, drink, work, whoring, shooting, conversations with the doctor.

The truth is, it would have been much, much worse in England.

Claude arrives back at Amah's hut early in the morning. The *Empire Star* should have set sail more than two hours ago. He sits for a while in the dark, listening to the distant rumble from the harbour. Out on the streets he can hear occasional shouts, people running, followed by silence. He goes through the shelves, packs into a gunnysack anything Ling-li might use at the refugee centre: extra candles, matches, some twine. Ling-li has said she will be back the next morning. She needed a change of clothes and to talk to her uncle about the bombed clinic. Claude lies down on his cot and falls asleep.

He is up at six, splashes water on his face, swirls the rest in his mouth and eats some dry bread. When he opens the door, the streets are quiet again, and there's a welcome coolness in the morning air. A breeze brushes his neck and he feels his mood lift. Things will be all right. He'll see his family and Ling-li today and whatever happens with the Japanese, he'll find some way to get through it.

He locks Amah's hut, swings the gunnysack over his left shoulder and starts walking. There's a gold chain around his neck that Grandma Siok gave him at his last visit, before he took Jack to the harbour. Maybe he can exchange it for rice, maybe some lentils and powdered milk for Ling-li.

As he turns onto Serangoon Road, he almost collides with someone. "Watch it," he says and his mouth drops open. "Jack."

Jack's few remaining strands of hair lie flat on his head, his face is haggard. "They didn't accept the papers," he says. "They marched me off the ship. The funny part was that people without any papers were sneaking on board while they were interrogating me. I did manage to get a lift to Serangoon Road. Don't know what I would have done otherwise." He shakes his head, looking spent.

"Come on," Claude says decisively. "Let's get you some breakfast."

Ling-li rounds the corner, her face strained. Somehow, she doesn't seem surprised to see Jack. "You still here? Well, it's too late now. The Japanese have pushed us to the city's perimeter—the Final Perimeter, as Percival calls it. In a day or two, they will get through."

"What will happen then?" Jack asks.

"It will be over," she says simply.

Humphrey cannot believe the news. "A rumour, a stupid rumour," he says angrily, but there is uncertainty in his eyes.

Grandma Siok makes a rude noise, but Claude can tell she is worried.

"Oh, be quiet!" shouts Humphrey.

Cynthia, sitting with Lucy as she colours in her colouring book, calls Claude over with her eyes. "How is Jack?" she asks softly.

"He didn't make the last boat out but he's all right."

"And—do you think it's true? About the Japanese?" She watches Lucy's crayon zigzag across the page to fill in a ballgown in vivid pink.

"Ling-li's usually right, Mother. But it'll be okay. I should go. She says no-one should be out today, but I had to come see you."

"Stay. It's safer here." She lifts a hand to him. The manager told Claude yesterday that the hotel was filled beyond capacity and could not hold any more people. "I'll talk him into it," she says, as if reading his mind.

"I can't leave Ling-li alone at the hut, Mother." He takes her hand. "Grandma Siok is right about spreading out the family. And it's actually safer at the hut. Wood is easier to climb out of than concrete."

"Well, maybe Jack should come over. He's not family." She smiles weakly.

He looks at her, surprised. "I suppose. I can ask him again."

"Only because he's been so ill," she adds.

"I'll ask him," he promises, his mind clicking away. He's missing something.

Claude bends to give her a quick hug and then kisses Lucy on the top of her head. She smiles up at her brother quizzically, and then resumes colouring.

Grandma Siok sees him to the door. "Don't worry about your father," she says. "We'll be all right."

"Take care of everyone, Grandma. You're the best person to be in charge here. Don't let anyone go out."

She reaches over to hug him. "Be careful. Listen to that Ling-li. She sounds sensible."

"Yes," he says. "You would like her."

Once he gets to Orchard Road, he knows that it's all over. Bombers swoop so low it seems as if they're intent on crashing directly on him. The road gapes with craters blasted by the shelling, cars are overturned and burning. Fires flame over puddles like apocalyptic vsions. The odour of burnt rubber hangs in the air. A fallen tree smokes with its upturned roots witnessing, for the first time, the sky, made hazy by explosions.

He starts to run. She's right, he thinks, it's over. It amazes him that he is so cool. Even when he is nearly hit by gunfire from a low-flying plane, he acts mechanically, efficiently, calmly, leaping into a hole in the road that serves as an impromptu trench for several other people.

When the plane turns away, he gets up, keeps running. It is over, he thinks, the only thought in his head. The world bobs as he runs, the road glides beneath his feet. There is an unexpected exhilaration in moving, in pushing through the acrid air and willing his body to go on.

It is over, but Claude, running, running, always running, is not.

※

Patrick Heenan knows from the snippets of gossip and conjecture that he has picked up from conversations in nearby cells, from the whispered talk among the British guards, that the Japanese are tantalisingly close. There is an unconfirmed report circulating that they have landed on the island and are working their way down to Singapore Town. He needs to hold on until they get here. There are moments when he's filled with a surging excitement, a bubbling up of joy he hasn't felt since he was a child. He stamps his feet in his cell, does jumping jacks, marches in place, lifting his knees high—anything to work off that excess energy and to keep his guards from suspecting too much. Of late they have been nervy and snappish, even with each other. The Japanese must be very, very close. When Heenan thinks this, he stands for long periods smiling to himself. And when he comes out of those semi-trances, he is mockingly smug to the guards, making fun of their petty ways, their gambling games and shuffling afternoon listlessness.

But perhaps he has overdone it, perhaps he should have been a little more cowed and deferential. They'd have liked that. It's too late now. He's going to pay one way or another. They have come to take him somewhere, perhaps solitary isolation, perhaps a higher security jail. That would make sense, especially with the Japanese knocking at their door. The one thing he is worried about is whether the British will escort him off the island—to Australia perhaps—before they capitulate to the Japanese. The bastards. But he must collect himself.

"I could use a good walk," he says in a friendly, obliging voice. "Are we going far?"

A sullen silence from the two military policemen at his side. Not encouraging.

"Any mail from home?" he persists, forcing the words out with a dogged brightness.

They prod him in the side to keep him moving at a brisk pace. No reply. The smile remains fixed on his face, but inside he is furious. It has always been like this—ignored, looked down upon, despised. Always, when things were getting good, he would be cut off from the action and his share of the benefits. He can barely manage to prevent himself from throwing a tantrum in front of the guards. Keep your wits about you, Heenan, he tells himself sternly, there's a war going on after all. They turn the corner. It appears to be as he had thought. They have come to a jeep and after being blindfolded, he is told to get in.

"It's only a matter of time, you know," he tells them. They're hardly interested in conversation with him. It's only a matter of time, he repeats to himself, before the Japanese are all over the Pacific, perhaps even the world. Australia will be no exception, so they're wasting their time and efforts shuttling him to different parts of the world in order to play a bit of hide-and-seek with their enemies.

It is not a long trip. The quay is only blocks way, and he can smell the old comforting rot of sea air and hear the waves slapping against the side of the sea wall. They order him out of the jeep and wait for him to stumble around on his feet before pointing him so the breeze is at his back. When they tell him to walk, he does so with uncertain, shortened steps, combined with a few long strides of bravado. He doesn't particularly like sea journeys and it will be much worse if they force him into a hold without windows or light. Again, he nearly throws a tantrum at the thought of the unnecessary ordeal to come. What sods the British, what absolute bloody sods!

He blinks away the rush of lights sparking in his eyes before focusing on the scene in front of him: stretches of sea, gunpowder sky, a diffuse sun, indistinct at the edges, floating above the horizon. It confuses him—no boat. And what of Australia?

But when the military policemen beside him laugh without humour, he understands instantly. "Have a good, long, hard look, Heenan," one of them, a sergeant, says. He has a crooked nose, and a dimple on his chin, as if someone had pressed a thumb into his face and left his impression permanently on display there. "This will be your last sunset."

The other guard is younger, blond, but his eyes are filled with the same revulsion and maddening superiority. He pushes Heenan towards the edge of the quay. Patrick moves without fuss, backing towards the water so that he faces the two policemen. "Okay," he says, as if something has slackened in him. The tension of the past month, of counting the days and nosing for news—all of it is gone, and he is suddenly lighter and nobler than before.

"Last words?" the man with the crooked nose asks in a bored voice, clearly impatient to be done with him.

Patrick thinks about this, his head cocked. The man with the crooked nose gives him ten seconds and then turns him around to face the sea again. He holds a gun to Patrick's head.

"It's wrong to treat them the way we do, as if we were their masters and saving them from themselves," Patrick says. A surge of conviction rises up in him. I shall die a hero's death, he tells himself. An unknown one, but a hero nonetheless. "I believe in justice, that's all," he ends solemnly.

"You're nothing but a half-breed bastard, Heenan," the blond man says, spitting in his face. "Let's get that clear once and for all." For all his earnestness, he is unconvincing in his vehemence.

"Justice," says the man with the crooked nose bitterly.

A shot. Patrick's nose bleeds. His face crumbles. He is pushed into the sea. The sun follows, its reflected rays lingering at the horizon. The wind picks up, and the smell of burning oil from the harbour sweeps through the quay.

When General Percival receives notice of the execution, it hardly registers. Having ordered a withdrawal to the Final Perimeter, he is beset by questions and uncertainties: Hold on or surrender? How to fortify the Final Perimeter? How long will the water supply in the reservoir last? Earliest chance of reinforcements? Heenan dead. Yes, well. How long will Yamashita's supplies last?

Questions still unresolved at the close of day, February 13th, 1942.

You've imagined it so many times:

Jack, with his sharp features and appealing height, taking home the prettiest girl he meets at the Great World. He makes her laugh with his jokes and teases her when she sneezes delicately at the froth of dust that rises from the flurry of taxis picking up and dropping off clients. He holds open the door of a taxi and folds his length into it after her. They sit in relative silence in the back, stubbornly holding hands and allowing their legs to touch under the sardonic gaze of the taxi-driver. He rubs her knee with his free hand, occasionally sliding it down her protruding shinbone. She pretends not to notice, and watches the passing scenery with exaggerated interest.

They avoid his Tanglin flat, where he is too well known and where his liaison with her would make the rounds of the European social circles before breakfast the next morning. He does not want to attract undue attention to his private life, given George's prominence in the banking world and his own reticence. He prefers the rented flat in Chinatown, where all the locals watch under their wide coolie hats or bamboo umbrellas, and yet everyone pretends not to notice.

When they arrive, the driver asks for more money than they have agreed upon. Jack waves him off with irritation, but does add a dollar to the tab. She is already at the door of the flat, studying her shoes to avoid looking up. Inside, he lights the kerosene lamps while she shrugs off her shawl, throws herself down on the plantation chair beside the window and kicks off her shoes. Her feet are surprisingly ugly. But he is not looking at her feet. He is watching her from the door, watching the way the light dances on her face, leaving it in mysterious half-shadow.

She waits until he is undressed and in bed before getting up and casually running a practised hand behind her back. Her sangria-coloured cheongsam slides off effortlessly, to land like a small hoop encircling her ankles. She steps neatly out of the circle of crumpled silk and unhooks her bra. Her movements hold no shyness or uncertainty. Finally, she takes off her panties and slides under the thin cotton sheet. Her skin is smooth and bears the tempting coolness and dryness of marble on a hot, humid day. He reaches for her, but she pushes away his hands to reach across him for a cigarette and a box of matches.

He rests against his pillows. He has learned not to rush her. She settles into a routine of inhaling and then exhaling a thin stream of smoke from her nostrils. Despite her earlier gaiety, she is in one of her inexplicable moods tonight. They lie in silence, watching the moths flutter to the kerosene lamps, then drop onto the floor, wings singed to a grey powder.

She picks up his hand, turns it over to expose the inside of his wrist. Then, deliberately, slowly, giving him plenty of opportunity to stop her, she touches the burning cigarette end beside his pulse. He flinches, lets her hold it there for a second, pulls his hand away. The brand on his skin is neat, precise, a circle of red welting up at the base of his hand. She rubs out the butt on the ashtray beside her with a vicious grinding motion of her wrist. He waits until she has finished, and then he slaps her carefully, with just enough force to turn her head and make her eyes sting. Immediately afterwards, he grabs her chin and forces her to look at him. It is a beautifully made up face. It is a familiar face. It is the face of a mother—*the boy's* mother. She is waiting.

He kisses her. His knees dig into the softness of her thighs. He places his hand on the dip of her belly beneath her ribs—

And then you can't look anymore.

Absence of sound. Of movement. You strain your ears, listen with caution, with fear. As painful as it was to listen to her scream and moan, this is worse. The echo of silence is the end of hope. More than ever before, the heart under knife, 忍. A talisman of endurance, fast fading.

As if to protect himself from too much light, Claude the Body shuts his eyes tight in his sleep. Screws up his face, seals himself against any possibility of seeing. You feel a kinship with him. A person only has a certain amount of courage. A person can only bear so much. Better the physical wounds of the body than those of the mind. You descend. Touch him on the head, the neck. Curl into a ball beside him. Try to rest.

It strikes you that the heart can yield under the knife, that it can be splayed to reveal its tough, fibrous chambers, to give up its insistent pulse. But silence, even at knifepoint, cannot be dissected. When split open, it reveals only further silence, which in turn conceals more worlds of silence. It possesses an armoured will that has its own language and reason and cannot be fragmented. Like a word peeled to its final layer, stripped to its heart, it is ultimately and divinely incomprehensible.

With your ear to his chest, you can hear Claude the Body's heartbeat. Between each thud, a compartment of silence, as if each beat were an interruption of eternity. Ignore the lub-dub lullaby. Listen for the in-between absences. This is the way all time is measured.

⚜

Claude steps out of the hut, unsure of what he will find. Everywhere there is wreckage. People cower from the Japanese soldiers who are trotting around, shouting, cheering, kicking those in their way. Even when he can't see them in the dense fog of smoke and the sting of ash in his eyes, he smells them. Grandma Siok wrinkled her nose at him, but surely that is nothing compared to this awful combination of sweat, mouldy feet, dried blood and festering wounds.

A crowd has gathered near Orchard Road and he elbows his way into its midst. In the centre are three men, all blindfolded, all of them white, their hands tied behind their backs. A Japanese soldier is reading, in his own language, from a piece of paper, and though no-one understands a word, the crowd is mesmerised. There is a sneering quality to the man's voice, an irrepressible burst of venom.

When the speech is over, another soldier is called forward. The

crowd gasps. He is carrying a sword, black, curved, the length of a
tall man. Children scuttle under their parents' feet and grown-ups
back away. The blindfolded men, sensing something, huddle together
and are forced to their knees.

Claude has nightmares later, in which he is one of the blindfolded men. In those last moments, he sees nothing, just feels the
burn of sun through the black blindfold. He smells the scruffy
Japanese, he senses the crowd's fear and agitation and then swiftly,
last of all, he hears a loud swish through the air—

Children and women scream, men too, as the three heads roll
and the decapitated bodies jerk like worms, then flop to the ground,
twitching before they are finally still. The crowd flees. Claude feels
sick but can't stop watching. The soldiers rip off the blindfolds and
the eyes stare, startled at the abrupt end to their vision. One soldier
collects the heads, hands them one at a time to another who is sitting astride a comrade's shoulders. He plants each head onto poles
that his colleagues have stuck into the ground in a semicircle, grinning as if he is playing a game, ignoring the blood on his hands. A
wooden board is nailed to the middle pole and the Japanese, letting
out a volley of victory cries, march away, laughing.

Claude can't take his eyes off the heads wobbling on the stakes,
smelling of blood. He retches, tears streaming down his face as he
shakes uncontrollably. Finally, an arm encircles him, holds him as
he sobs, until he calms down. By this time, the crowd has returned,
gathering to read the sign nailed to the pole. Claude looks up. The
message is composed in Chinese characters, incomprehensible.

"The Japanese borrowed our written language." The person
holding him says this. Claude turns. It is Hong-Seng. "They are
rules," he continues in his halting English. "Warning for what happens if you disobey—you be like them."

"But I can't read those rules, neither can my family," Claude says,
his voice watery.

"Where is Ling-li?" Hong-Seng bends over as if to help support
him.

"She left this morning. She says you know where to find her." Was
she lying?

But Hong-Seng nods, satisfied. "Good day," he says and lets go of Claude.

"Hey," Claude begins, stumbling. When he regains his balance, Hong-Seng is gone, disappeared into the charred ruins.

He walks to the hotel to find his family. A lone soldier knocks down the sign that reads *Bencoolen Street*. Everywhere that Claude looks, English is being dismantled. He begins life under the Japanese.

SIX

Breaking the Tongue

WHEN CLAUDE LOOKS UP, he recognises Hong-Seng, the lanky outlines of his body. His features are blurred, but Claude knows it is he. "I heard," Hong-Seng says enigmatically.

"What?" Claude asks. It is too, too bright.

"I heard," he repeats, as if it's self-explanatory. Then he lifts Claude to his feet and props him up. "We go now."

He half-carries, half-drags Claude towards a trishaw. When Claude tries to haul himself into the trishaw, Hong-Seng restrains him. "I do, you rest." He positions Claude carefully in the seat. "Now we go—fast," he says and the look he throws over his shoulder makes Claude panic.

"Where are we going? What's happened?" It is hard to speak through his lips, but when he licks them, they sting from his saliva.

"You released," Hong-Seng says. "Very lucky. We did not think you make it. You gone for five days—your family very worried. In the end, we get message to pick you up."

It seems as if the trishaw is careening down the street without effort, but Hong-Seng must be bicycling furiously. Not bad for an old man, Claude thinks. He must be—what? Sixty? Ling-li comes from good stock.

He sits up suddenly, rocking the trishaw. "Ling-li," he says. Hong-Seng seems to pedal even more energetically. "Hong-Seng, slow down. Where is Ling-li?"

Hong-Seng mutters something—in Chinese, it must be—and flies on. The smell of vomit infects the air. It is coming from his own shirt, he realises. The rush of air against his body burns and he is immensely tired.

"Things can always wait," Ling-li used to say, "until morning." So he forces himself to relax, dropping down in his seat and loosening his grip against the side rail of the trishaw. He lies on the seat and tucks his knees to his chest. He tries to hold himself very still to make the pain more tolerable. But then his face is awash in tears and the saltiness on his cheeks feels like razor cuts. He doesn't allow himself to think of sharp edges and knives. Things can always wait until morning. She has always been right.

Now it has been six weeks. Enough time for new, tough, fibrous tissue to form and seal old wounds, for his face to lose its puffiness and regain its former shape, for cracked bones to mend. He can do nothing about the scars. But what does it matter? He only wants to lie on the cool floor everyday, waiting for the sun to go down and the night breezes to stir.

At first they mostly left him alone. Only Hong-Seng and Grandma Siok took turns tending to his wounds and feeding him. They let him sleep long hours and crept about trying not to disturb him. Perhaps a doctor had been persuaded to make house visits—Claude has vague memories of injections and pills, a stethoscope pressed to his chest. Once or twice he awoke to see his mother seated at the foot of his bed, staring out the window, smoking. When he called out, she simply said, "You're supposed to rest," and left the room. It was just as well. He wanted no complications to his deep, dreamless sleep.

But one day he could sleep no longer, and found himself asking Grandma Siok, "Where are we?"

She looked pleased at his interest. "Hong-Seng's flat. The Japanese have claimed all hotels and houses for their own use." She handed him a small porcelain spoon. "Here, it's time you got back to doing things for yourself." One of his arms was in a cast. "It should be healed by now," she said. "Is it itchy? The doctor said it would be."

"No," he said. "Just hot." The hand with the spoon shook a little, but when she held the bowl of porridge in front of him, he managed to scoop up a mouthful and feed himself. It made him think of Jack, how he had fed him.

"We've had to register this as our address," Grandma Siok said, watching him eat. "When we had to move out of the hotel, we spent three days at a refugee centre before we met up with Hong-Seng. He was looking for you, but we had lost touch with you after the mass screening and registration of locals. He heard our names at roll call and recognised them. Apparently, his niece had mentioned us to him."

"Ling-li?" he asked, suddenly remembering. A thin line of porridge dripped down his chin. Grandma Siok rubbed it with a face towel.

"Ling-li is dead," she said in her even voice.

"I see," he said calmly, spooning porridge into his mouth. It surprised him that he received this news so matter-of-factly, until he realised that he'd known Ling-li was dead all along, ever since Hong-Seng found him after the interrogation. Yes, ever since then, perhaps even earlier.

"Maybe you should talk to Hong-Seng," Grandma Siok said. "I know only a little about your friend. Hong Seng might be able to tell you more."

"I see," Claude said again. Lucy was chatting with someone outside, his father probably. For the first time, he became aware of his surroundings. There was a bed along one wall, and three rolls of mattresses in one corner, with some pillows and sheets on top. A large cupboard was at the foot of the bed. He was in a small cot pushed behind the door. A faded sarong was strung over the window, its thin weft pierced by pinpricks of light. The entire room was the size of his bathroom back in the Bukit Timah house.

Grandma Siok set about tidying the small table beside his cot and gathered up loose newspaper sheets, the face towel, bowl and spoon. She moved to the door and stopped. "Do you want me to send him in?" she asked.

"Who?" He propped himself up on his free elbow.

"Hong-Seng."

"That won't be necessary," he told her. "I really don't have any questions."

She seemed to think about this. "Shall I send Lucy in? We've kept her away from you so you could rest. She's awfully worried about you."

He flopped back into bed. "Later. In the evening, perhaps."

Night of Silences.

The silence of whistling bombs diving through the air, the silence of booms that were palpable through the thick night, the silence of screams and scattering feet, the silence of Jack's tapping against the side of the cot, the silence of Claude's breathing as he squatted in his corner.

The silence, most of all, of Ling-li, who was soundless, sitting in a corner where even flames and explosions could not light up her face.

The radio hummed a forgettable tune, the volume knob stuck at the lowest level. Claude put his ear to it to drown out the silences. It sputtered, hissed, and then, like some conch shell he'd picked up at the beach, it surrendered to the roar of the ocean.

And when she spoke, he'd already heard it in the sudden static, the shutting down of transmitters. "They have signed the papers," she said. "We are now under Japanese occupation."

After the Surrender, all Europeans were ordered to gather on the Padang. They arrived in forlorn clusters, or alone, clutching hat cases and trunk bags, as if about to embark on a long sea journey. One or two dressed defiantly in their Sunday best, the men in exquisitely cut white suits, the women in ruffled sundresses, determined to prove to the Japanese that their morale was unassailable. But it was only a façade, of course. Every European in his right mind asked how this could be happening, how the Japanese could really have won, how an Asiatic tribe could have defeated British troops.

They stood for hours on the Padang without food or water, enduring the sun and the unintelligible megaphone shouts of easily offended Japanese privates who distributed slaps throughout the crowd as if they were giving out alms. The military personnel had already been marched off to Changi in their sagging units. Only the Gurkhas, the Gordon Highlanders, and the Argyll and Sutherland Highlanders high-stepped all the way in precise formation.

By noon, the white civilians, most of them dazed from sunstroke, were heading first for Katong, and then onward to the internment camp at Changi. It took a long time for them to file off the Padang, and it was at least fifteen minutes after the head of the column moved before a third of the Europeans got on the road.

Claude had come to see Jack off. The two of them walked to the Padang after a brief, insubstantial breakfast of tea and unripe mangoes, plucked from a partially uprooted mango tree across the street from the bombed clinic. The acidity of the mangoes, still green and hard, and the astringent tea seemed to be burning a hole in Claude's stomach. It was probably the same for Jack, though he did not complain. The look on his face and the way he bent over from time to time, massaging his belly with circular motions, was enough. The grip he had on his suitcase was so tight that the muscles bunched up in his hand. He had insisted on bringing along every damn book, but he had not allowed Claude to carry the suitcase.

Claude felt strangely guilty, strolling next to Jack with both hands free while he struggled. But he reminded himself that he had taken care of Jack over the past few weeks—both he and Ling-li had done enough. And Jack would have left earlier if he could have, leaving them to be bombed out and captured. And now here Jack was, himself a prisoner of the Japanese, the very fate he had thought was his birthright to avoid.

"You should go," Jack had said when they arrived at the Padang. They were among some of the earliest there.

"I'll stay until they start moving you off." Claude hovered with him on the edge of the field. "Put your bag down. If you need to rest, you can lie down and use it as a pillow."

"I'm okay," Jack replied, a note of amusement in his voice.

There was nothing else to say to each other. Claude swatted at imaginary flies and when he was done with that, stood with arms akimbo, feet wide apart, head down. Jack seemed to be busy scanning the field to see if he knew anyone. A woman with a young child waved at him and he raised his hand in return. Finally, he cleared his throat.

"Look, Claude, you might as well go. We'll be hours here and if you hang around, the Japanese might drag you along with us to wherever it is we're going." He sounded reasonable, but Claude couldn't help hearing a jibe beneath those words. Never mind, he told himself. There was no point in being angry now.

So he took his leave, extending a hand uncomfortably and letting Jack pump it once or twice. "You've been a sport, Claude. I would have been quite lost without you." His voice was low, but it sounded sincere to Claude's ears. "And when you see Ling-li, tell her I said thank you. I wish I'd had a chance to tell her myself."

Claude backed away from the Padang, keeping his eyes averted from the Japanese soldiers now moving among the crowd. He moved towards the Esplanade and joined a small crowd of Asiatics gathered there. They were all watching the Europeans with interest, some of them jeering and others laughing along. He found a spot where he could keep his eye on Jack. He wasn't sure why he has doing this, but a part of him badly wanted to watch.

At last, the Europeans began moving, and from his spot on the Esplanade they reminded Claude of Grandma Siok's ants. He remembered her telling him how ants went to war with other colonies and took prisoners, captured slaves. Jack was taller than most of the Europeans, and with his bald head—by now shiny with sweat—he was easy to pick out. He didn't talk to anyone as he walked, just looked straight over their heads and towards the road.

In the hallucinogenic heat, it was easy to imagine that Ling-li's wish had come true, that the British and other Europeans were being packed off to a waiting boat that would take them back to Europe. Claude moved to stand in the shade, but even then he felt light-headed. He saw several Europeans topple to the ground, creating a minor disturbance among their neighbours.

A cheer broke out—uncertainly at first, then with more vigour—among the Asiatics on the Esplanade. He looked at their genuinely celebratory faces. The cheer became a chant, perhaps in Malay—he couldn't really make it out—but then he found his own mouth moving and he was repeating those nonsense sounds, fitting the syllables to what he was hearing around him. What do the words mean? he wondered, his lips still moving. The faces fused in a kaleidoscope: Indian, Malay, Chinese—he blended in seamlessly, his mouth uttering sounds in unison with theirs, his hands clapping in a rhythm that sped faster and faster. He lost sight of Jack; the voices grew louder. He revelled in the noise, allowed himself to sink in the sea of sounds and to forget, for a moment, the trail of Europeans winding northwards away from Singapore Town towards Changi.

The Sook Ching—the Purge through Purification—was reserved for the Chinese. After the Europeans were dealt with, an order was given for all Chinese males to register at one of the screening centres. Claude went with Humphrey, glad that Cynthia, Lucy and Grandma Siok could remain behind in their hotel room. Later he heard rumours that some centres were requiring women and children to register as well.

Humphrey had wanted to put on a suit, insisting that it was important "to put up a good show." But when he had walked less than half a block in the heat, he gave in and returned to change into a plain white shirt and cotton trousers. "After all, why wear out a good suit?" he decided.

Still, smelling faintly of cologne and freshly shaven, he looked a lot cleaner than Claude, who had barely had time to wash his face and change into a pair of Humphrey's khakis. When his mother complained that his nails were too long, he had trimmed them with his teeth as he had been doing the past few weeks. "Disgusting," Cynthia had said, catching Lucy's eye. "Don't start getting ideas, young lady."

Only Grandma Siok was nervous. It was so uncharacteristic of her that Claude began to fidget as Humphrey was completing his toilette. "I'm suspicious," she said, drawing Claude near the window. "The Japanese have no fondness for us Chinese, and this whole registration thing is fishy to me. What does your friend, Ling-li, say?"

"I haven't seen her since—since the Surrender," he said, wondering if Ling-li's final instructions not to acknowledge their friendship applied to his grandmother as well. Better to be consistent—that would be Ling-li's way. "Besides, Ling-li's not my friend. She's just a nurse we met at the clinic and she helped take care of Jack when he was sick."

Grandma Siok fixed him with a look. "Ungrateful little beast," she said and moved back to her bed, as if she couldn't bear to be near him. "Coward," she'd said when he had thrown the stone at the Squatter Girl years ago, and now she had misunderstood again. But Ling-li's safety came first, Claude told himself, and kept quiet.

However, when he and Humphrey were setting out, Grandma Siok came down rather anxiously to the hotel lobby and instructed Claude to "mess yourself up a little" on the way to the screening centre. She asked to see his hands and he spread them, palms up, before her. His days at the clinic had roughened them and he noticed that he was several shades darker than his father. Grandma Siok seemed encouraged by this. "Yes, good, good," she said. "Now pick up a little soil on your way there. Make sure there's dirt under your nails. Just in case."

Just in case what? he wanted to ask. Grandma Siok enjoyed being enigmatic, but she was usually pretty sensible, so Claude picked up some soil by the road and rubbed his hands in it.

At the screening centre, they filed into a large compound along with several hundred other men. The atmosphere was tense, sullen and people avoided looking at each other as they talked in low voices among themselves. Humphrey rested his hand on Claude's shoulder; Clearly, he was uncomfortable being around so many locals.

Five hours of standing around without food or water. At least the day was overcast, with a constant wind, so it was tolerable. As the time dragged on, the mood lightened a little, and the voices in the compound became less hushed. When the whistle blew, everyone jumped. An impassive Japanese soldier made an announcement and waited for a translator to relay the message. "Bloody hell," Humphrey complained when the translator began speaking in Chinese.

But Claude walked through the crowd, whispering, "English? English?"

Finally, a young man spoke up. "They want us to get into groups," he said.

"Boon Liew," Claude said, and when the young man looked startled, he explained. "The Littleton fire unit—Claude Lim? We met in Chinatown?"

"Yes," he said, smiling and bowing. "Of course."

Boon Liew followed Claude back to Humphrey and translated for them. "They're calling for *towkays* to step up." He looked at Humphrey with sudden interest. "Are you a *towkay*?"

"What in heaven's name is that?"

"*Towkay*—a big boss. I thought you looked like one."

"Oh." Humphrey thought about this. "Well, maybe. Should I go?"

"*Towkays* over there, hawkers on the left, government servants behind us and students in the front."

"*Towkay*'s the closest thing, I guess," Claude said to his father. "I'll go with Boon Liew." They watched Humphrey detach himself and move to where a tough-looking group of men were standing and glaring at the Japanese. He stood at the edge of the group and pointedly faced away.

Claude went with Boon Liew to the students' group. Two soldiers ordered them into lines and as they took their places, a hush descended upon the students. A soldier arranged a row of chairs in front of the group, and when they were ready, five men dressed in white funeral hoods claimed the seats. The first row of students was called to file slowly past the hooded men.

"Informers," Boon Liew hissed and said something else in Chinese.

At a nod from one of the hooded figures, two students from the front row were escorted out of the compound. The tension mounted as the second row filed past. Some students looked at their feet and were sharply reprimanded. From the corner of his eye, Claude could see the *towkay* group waiting to be fingerprinted. He couldn't see his father.

"Our turn," Boon Liew said as their row began filing past the hooded informers. Claude's stomach churned as he followed. The soles of his shoes felt sticky and he had to peel them off the floor. Every now and then he tried to get a good look at the informers, to peer into the protective cave of their mourning hoods. Not out of any sense of mission, really—a base curiosity that he couldn't resist, despite the danger. Still, no-one in their row was called up, and they went to join the others sitting on the ground, while the remaining eight rows paraded past the informers.

By the time it was over, Claude was famished, but other orders were being given. "They want us to get in the lorry," Boon Liew said after listening intently to the translator. Five lorries had been parked at the end of the compound since the identification parade began, but now three lorries had already filled up with people. "Claude, this is not good. Is your father there?"

"I don't see him," he said, looking around, but it was time for the students to move. Claude climbed into a half-full lorry and squatted beside Boon Liew. "Maybe they let him go," he said to Boon Liew, but he was staring past Claude with a frozen face.

A Japanese soldier motioned for Claude to get off the lorry. The translator was saying something. "They want you for questioning," Boon Liew said and Claude's heart sank, his legs almost giving way as he stood up. Boon Liew grabbed Claude's hand with both of his. "Good luck," he said. "Be strong."

The lorries started off as Claude headed across the compound
with the Japanese soldier. Impulsively, he turned back. Boon Liew
was staring after him. He waved sadly and Claude waved back.

Years later, at the unearthing of a mass grave in Bedok, Claude
realised that Boon Liew must have been one of the many young Chinese men massacred during the Sook Ching, that his own interrogation, though bestial, had saved him from Boon Liew's fate.

On that last morning, Ling-li woke him. It was still dark outside.
"Claude, I have to leave now," she said. He blinked at her, knowing
something was different but unable to locate what it was. He sat up,
wincing as his joints dug into the floorboards. He had given up his
bed to Ling-li and now he was paying for it.

"Claude, I need to go, but we have to talk first, very quickly."

He stared at her. She had somehow lopped off much of her hair.
"Why?" he asked, pointing.

"Listen, just listen! If anyone asks about me, you say that I helped
you take care of Jack at the clinic, but don't say any more than that,
okay?" She was insistent, her grip on his shoulder, which he only
now felt, tightened.

"Are you in trouble?" he said. Of course she was. "I won't say
anything if it'll help you."

"It won't help *me*, Claude, it will help you." She sat back on her
heels. Tufts of hair on her crown stood up, giving her a comical
appearance. She looked like a very skinny boy. "Tell Jack what I told
you. Remember, I was just his nurse at the clinic. I never said much
to him, only looked after his leg. I was the quiet sort." Could anyone believe that, anyone who knew even a tiny bit about her? She's
delusional, Claude thought, or at least mildly hysterical.

"If you meet my uncle, pretend you don't know him," she went
on, her knees creaking as she got up.

"What if he wants to know what happened to you?"

"He'll know where to find me."

He got up from the floor. Jack was immobile in his cot. "How will
I find you?" he asked.

She smiled. "You won't. Not if I've done my work well." She moved to the door and he followed. She stopped, one hand on the knob, listening for a moment. "Claude, good luck. I will see you after—all this mess. When we're all free again. And it *will* happen, you must believe it, no matter how bad it seems. There are people who believe this place is worth fighting for."

He caught hold of her arm. "And I? What can I do in the mean-while?" His voice was urgent. "How can I help fight for this place?"

She said nothing, as if debating with herself. "Blend in. Learn Chinese," she said finally. "It will be useful when the Japanese take over. You understand? English will not help you anymore." She almost sounded sorry for him.

He was still holding on to her arm, unable to let go. How *could* he let her go without knowing how to find her again? He could not imagine life without her.

"I must go," she said, but there was a change in her voice and she made no attempt to shake loose of his hold.

His hand slid up her shoulder in a clumsy caress and then he was drawing her to him, pulling her to his chest, trying to say something to her, trying to tell her he was afraid to let her go. She lay passively in his arms for a moment, her ear pressed against his chest, tufts of her hair tickling his neck, and then encircled her own arms around him. "I am so frightened," she said very softly.

"I know," he said, leaning back to look at her. He let his hand slip from her shoulder, and over her collarbone, lower, to her left breast, marvelling at the softness of the silk fabric. She did not move. His finger began tracing a design on her jacket, the only mutual word of Chinese between them—knife over heart—writing it on her skin as Yue Fei's mother had, writing to bless a general.

Voices in the dark, an unintelligible shouting. She pulled away.

"I must go. Good luck!"

When she slipped out, the embodiment of night in her all-black outfit, she did not turn back.

She never did say goodbye to Jack.

The sitting room of Hong-Seng's flat is tiny. Since Claude's recovery, he has given up his cot to his mother while Grandma Siok and Lucy share the bed. The three men sleep on the mattresses which they roll up and put away every morning so that Claude can sit on the floor, savouring its coolness. Some days, he reads from old magazines Grandma Siok has picked up here and there, and at noon, he boils a small cup of rice, potatoes, yam, whatever is available, and sets the table. It doesn't take long. All Hong-Seng owns are a few pairs of chopsticks, some enamel bowls and cups. Only Cynthia and Lucy lunch with Claude, the former barely eating while the latter relays what she has learned in school. He avoids his mother's eyes, or perhaps she is avoiding his. There is no actual conversation to speak of. When he clears the dishes, Cynthia locks herself in the bedroom for the rest of the day.

After lunch, he spreads himself out on the living room floor and gazes at the top ledge of the window. Lucy has learned to do her homework or amuse herself in her own corner of the room. He never falls asleep in the afternoon, no matter how drowsy he gets. His ears buzz constantly and, throughout the day, faint sounds of static, as if from a distant radio station, drift in and out of his hearing. Sometimes, if he closes his eyes, he has a brief vision of Jack fiddling with the knob of a radio, his bald head bent in introspection. How is he taking to life under the Japanese? Does he ever think about Claude or Ling-li? Does he think about Cynthia?

When the light begins to dim, Grandma Siok, Hong-Seng and Humphrey return. Hong-Seng has been scavenging parts from damaged bicycles, cars, trishaws and fixing up usable vehicles. His most prominent customer is the Japanese army. Payment is unpredictable but, when it comes, is in the form of precious food supplies, and in this way he has significantly increased the rice rations for Claude's family, including the occasional limp but edible vegetable or root plant. The pantry where Hong-Seng used to sleep is filled with carefully preserved rations and scavenged food, the family's suitcases and accumulated odds and ends. Humphrey and Grandma Siok help out at the shop, two blocks away. It is an old foundry that was badly bombed except for a small workroom at the back that Hong-Seng has claimed with permission from the Japanese.

The strangest part about this life is not Humphrey's involvement in the shop, working side by side with a local who speaks a broad, Hokkien-inflected English, nor is it the cramped living conditions in the flat. Stringent rations have ensured that everyone instinctively conserves energy. In the last two weeks, Claude has noticed his hair thinning and a dull, listless cast to his skin, but even this does not trouble him. What distresses him most are the moments of near normalcy that pepper the day: when Lucy practises cartwheels in the sitting room, Cynthia tugs painfully at her hair for no apparent reason and Grandma Siok makes her caustic comments to the radio plays that are still permitted in the evenings.

What catches him unaware is the sudden longing to talk to Ling-li, to ask her opinion about something. He stops in mid-thought and forces himself to remember that she is gone. Seconds later, his heart plummets and he begins to pant until his lips and fingertips tingle. What calms him is the cold-water memory of Ling-li's sharp voice: "Enough! Get a hold of yourself." His chest tightens; he holds his breath. The giddy sensation ceases and he is himself again.

Some days he can't bear it.

❀

He doesn't blame Cynthia—what is there to blame, really? In many ways, he has been just like her. Nevertheless, some days Claude is so furious with his mother that he wants to scream at her, to throw a tantrum and demand a reason for her behaviour.

That night at the Winchesters', the Christmas and farewell party— How he felt like a servant when George Winchester recruited him to help out, how he forced a smile when George declared to his friends, "Oh, Claude here is a guest, of course, but the good lad has offered to help me out. Damn bind I was in—servants quitting at the last minute, without even giving me time to find replacements." All that time, while he was circulating the room with the champagne bottle, his mother must have been with Jack—serving him in an entirely different way.

Jack is a different matter. Claude grits his teeth when he reads it,

Jack's strange book. Is this how he saw *her*? And did she, when she was with him, know this and play up to it?

> Ma Hla May was a woman of twenty-two or -three, and perhaps five feet tall. She was dressed in a *longyi* of pale blue embroidered Chinese satin, and a starched white muslin *ingyi* on which several gold lockets hung. Her hair was coiled in a tight black cylinder like ebony, and decorated with jasmine flowers. Her tiny, straight, slender body was as contourless as a bas relief carved upon a tree. She was like a doll, with her oval, still face the colour of new copper, and her narrow eyes; an outlandish doll and yet a grotesquely beautiful one. A scent of sandalwood and coco-nut oil came into the room with her.

These days, his mother looks smaller, still immaculately preserved, but diminished in some indefinable way. There are times when he feels sorry for her.

❀

Lucy only uses red, yellow, orange, black. No other colours for her as she sits at Hong-Seng's dining table, her legs dangling and swinging from her chair. When asked what she is painting, she says enthusiastically, "This is fire."

She does have a way with fire, seems to understand its essence and movement. In one painting, the brush marks shoot straight upwards, all in one direction; in others, they spiral like tornados or wave about like flags in the wind. Once Claude notices more black in a painting than any other colour and she says helpfully, as he struggles to figure it out, "Smoke is a part of fire." The black smog in those last weeks before the Surrender. How much has she seen and internalised of those days? Another time she paints a roseate design and he assumes she has finally moved on to other subjects. But no. "This is fire from an explosion," she says, pleased with herself. From a distance, it looks like a bud in bloom.

One day there is an intense circle of red painted over many times in thick, undiluted paint. It takes a long while to dry. Lucy refuses to tell him what kind of fire it is, but several times he catches her observing Cynthia and considering her own painting.

On another occasion, he finds Lucy in the kitchen, leaning over the sink and splashing water over a fire painting. "See how the water puts out fire," she says as he peers over her shoulder for a closer look. The blaze of the painting is already diminished by the water running over it. The oranges and reds leak and drain from the brushstrokes, the yellow is already a creamy ivory. She hangs the painting up to dry on Hong-Seng's clothesline. Two days later, it is only a shrivelled-up piece of paper with faint washes of colour on it. From a spot in the left lower corner is a glow of orange.

"It will fade in the sun," Lucy tells him and he wonders again where she has learnt all this. "Embers take time to die out sometimes."

Sure enough, in two weeks, the orange is a mere blush. By that time, their father has had his stroke, and spends hours staring at the barely tinted sheet of paper flapping in the wind on the clothesline. No-one has the heart to take it off until it disintegrates to shreds in the sun and rain.

One of the first things Claude notes after his recovery is the change in Humphrey. Like everyone else he has lost weight, but so much that his temples cave in, the veins throbbing prominently under the fragile, papery skin. His hair has whitened alarmingly in just a few weeks. Not greyed, but whitened so unnaturally that he might have bleached it. Though his gums bleed constantly from poor nutrition, he refuses to suck the small, sour native limes that Hong-Seng taught them all to slice and rub with salt before biting into the clear green pulp.

Hong-Seng jokingly refers to the lime-eating as "eating sorrow," a Chinese phrase that means to suffer, to endure difficulties. "He doesn't know how to 'eat sorrow,' your father," Hong-Seng says, pronouncing each word carefully as he is wont to do in Claude's presence, not because he is self-conscious about his English but because he treats Claude as if he is a mildly retarded child. "If he want survive, he must learn this."

But Humphrey learns nothing. He can't get over the Fall—the incredible, unbearable fact that the British have lost their colony and that an Asiatic race is in power now. "How could this have happened?" he asks every night when Japanese marching music plays over the radio. "It doesn't make any sense, I can't understand it." He looks older than Grandma Siok, moves in stiff jerks.

"Do you know how I escaped the blasted Sook Ching?" he yells when no-one pays any attention. "I told them I have many British friends. I told them that I am a British subject and if they touched me, they would pay for it when the British make their comeback!" Claude's impassive reception only eggs Humphrey on. "They let me go, do you hear? I didn't get mauled and interrogated like you because they recognised me as a British subject!"

The British are in prison, Claude wants to say, but there is no point in angering his father further, and besides, he doesn't have the energy.

On some days Humphrey bursts into tears inexplicably, refusing to talk to anyone, refusing to eat. Hours later, he is sullen but dry-eyed, talking minimally when required. "Stubborn old man," Grandma Siok says. "It's not that he can't believe—he *refuses* to believe that the British lost. Let him sulk. He'll come round when he's ready."

Humphrey resists Grandma Siok's constant pestering to help Lucy with her homework. Lucy studies Japanese at school now and has learned how to bow to her superiors in the Nippon way, what Japanese people eat, the divine nature of the Emperor and the celebration of Japanese festivals. But Grandma Siok insists that her education should be supplemented at home. "History in particular," she says. "The Japanese version has too many gaps."

For some reason, it is Cynthia who takes on this task, sporadically but uncomplainingly. Lucy doesn't rebel. She seems to enjoy the new attention from Cynthia and throws herself into her studies. Some days Claude watches them, their heads almost touching as Cynthia refers to an old, tattered atlas to teach Lucy geography. But all this is only for a brief period. Afterwards—a matter of no more than two weeks—his mother seems to lose interest in the household and sits all day without reading or speaking.

The only time Humphrey talks to Claude now is to correct his accent, which has become careless. It doesn't bother Claude that he has picked up traces of the local accent. His ear searches for Ling-li's cadences, the up-down song of her clear, carefree Chinese-tinged tones. Perhaps he hopes to sound like her. Anyway, his father's admonitions go by without any effect on him.

The light waxes and wanes throughout the day as the clouds shift in the wind. Claude closes his eyes and tries to forget the uncomfortable sticky feel of his skin. His bones ache. Last night, he and Grandma Siok sat together and rubbed salve on their legs and joints. It made him smile—a rare thing these days—to be sharing rheumatic pains with his grandmother. But today, she is out at the shop, hauling metal and learning how to solder with Hong-Seng and Humphrey while he lies spread-eagled on the sitting room floor like some lifeless animal skin. Which animal, he wonders idly behind closed eyelids—a bear? A tiger? A zebra? And then—

A sensation of floating, not at all unfamiliar. The buzzing in your ear thickens like a frantic hive. You find yourself bending over, as if to look down, as if to peer into a well. There is water in the well—you can feel its coolness when you stand at the rim and when your eyes have adjusted, you can see a reflection in it:

Humphrey's face is tight with anger and humiliation. He can't stand it when Hong-Seng gives him orders, especially in that thick, halting Hokkien accent. He makes it a point to pretend he doesn't understand anything the man says even when Grandma Siok tries to explain, as she is doing now.

"I always thought you were a bit thick, but this is too much!" she snaps. "He says that the battery you left in the sun exploded and splashed acid all over the entrance. You should clean up the mess. Surely you can understand *that*?"

"I'm not a common servant—tell him to do it himself!" Humphrey says, his voice rising despite his best intentions.

"In case you haven't noticed, Humphrey—servants aren't that common anymore! Now enough of this churlishness and get to work!"

"Who asked you to get into this? You just stop your meddling—"

"Clean. Up. Mess." Hong-Seng's staccato cuts through Humphrey's tirade.

"I don't need your supercilious airs, you, you backward bung, you!" Humphrey stutters, resorting to Australian slang.

"You bigger backside bum," Hong-Seng says.

"Bung, bung, bung!" Unbelievably, Humphrey stamps his foot. "I said 'bung,' not 'bum'! Tell him, Siok, for goodness' sake, tell him!"

But Grandma Siok is roaring with laughter. "Oh, this is precious!" she says, holding her side.

Claude opens his eyes. Sunlight streaming in, rain glinting in web-like threads. Buzz fading to a pleasant drone.

Some things haven't changed.

When, by chance, he is careless and his gaze slips to the mirror while he is brushing his teeth, the reflection startles and puzzles him. Criss-cross lines and thick healed ridges of skin. There is no trace of youth anywhere in the eyes, only a dull suspicion that emphasises the slightly wild look in the image. It is a face that shuns the world.

But Grandma Siok will have none of it. After a few weeks of his lazing around on the sitting room floor, she insists that he work at the shop. "You can clean up, sort parts—there's plenty for you to do." After breakfast, she follows him about, nagging him to get dressed and practically chasing him out of the house.

Humphrey and Hong-Seng descend the stairs together in silence, and on the street they keep a pointed distance apart. Humphrey is not happy with Grandma Siok for suggesting that Claude work and is avoiding her as well. It has been three months since Claude has been outside and he can't help but notice the frantic rebuilding and scavenging going on. The city is almost as busy as in the pre-war days. "All this activity," he mumbles, his legs aching.

"What's that?" Grandma Siok asks, slowing down to let him catch up.

"I'm tired."

"That's to be expected. But all that loitering about at the flat won't help. A week of this, and you'll be fine. You can rest when we get to the shop."

There is a commotion ahead as a convoy of jeeps makes its way down the street. As the jeeps pass, people on either side stand respectfully at attention and bow. "Here we go again," Grandma Siok mutters, "Just do as I do, Claude."

But before he has a chance to arrange his body into a stiff, bent pole, the first jeep of the convoy stops and a soldier screams orders at no-one in particular. Claude turns his head surreptitiously to see who might be in trouble, and his heart sinks when he sees Humphrey half a block ahead, standing upright, chin jutting into the air. Hong-Seng, standing between Claude and Humphrey, stiffens but does not look up from his bow. "Keep your bloody head down, boy," Grandma Siok says in a fierce whisper. "And stay still. Nothing you do will be of any use."

Claude bends low enough to appear respectful but twists his head to see what is happening. Humphrey, despite shrinking a little when the convoy stops in front of him, stands his ground. A soldier jumps off the first jeep and runs up to him, screaming a harsh volley of unintelligible words. He slaps Humphrey repeatedly until Humphrey, totally unprepared, falls backwards and lands on his bottom, his hands covering his face. The soldier starts kicking at the heap on the ground.

A short bark from the commanding officer on the jeep cuts the beating short. The soldier lands another few well-aimed kicks at Humphrey's groin and stomps back to the convoy, calling out something in Japanese to all those standing around, transfixed in reverently bowed poses. The convoy moves on, and the relief is palpable. Once they go by, Claude unlocks his aching spine and hurries to his father.

Hong-Seng is there already. "Very lucky," he is saying. "You real stupid man, but very lucky."

Grandma Siok bends over Humphrey, feeling for broken bones. "Hmm, bruises, cuts, nothing much. Come on, Humphrey, get up," she says in a kindly voice.

But Humphrey is curled up in a tight ball, his face still behind his hands. He lies there quite still, saying nothing. His chest is jerking and Claude wonders if he is having a small epileptic fit. Then he realises his father is only sobbing very quietly, very discreetly behind his hands. He stands by feeling helpless, weighted by the sight of his father weeping in the dirt like an injured beggar.

"I think we go," Hong-Seng says. "He knows the way."

"Yes," says Grandma Siok. "Come along, Claude."

They walk on and turn the corner. The scuffled-up earth beside Humphrey is darker than the topsoil, and moist. Claude starts walking, breaking into a jog, panting as his heart tries to keep up with this sudden flurry of activity. He takes the corner decisively, without looking back.

At the shop, he spends hours sorting out all usable parts of wreckages. Every screw, every bolt is needed, every scrap metal is adapted for new use. Only what crumbles in his hands gets discarded.

Claude is a good worker because he is so absorbed in his task. He scans the heap of junk at the back of the shop and patiently runs his eye over every surface, removing bicycle bells, wire, dynamo headlights, bumper metal, chains and once even an entire leather car seat from the back of a burnt-out Rolls-Royce. This is a strangely peaceful job, one that does not require much thinking. It's an activity he envisions being useful in a sanatorium, or an old folks' home, calling for visual and manual dexterity, but not much mental exertion.

Ever since Claude's first day here, Humphrey has stopped coming to the shop. That day, Claude, Hong-Seng and Grandma Siok waited for him all day, but he never showed up. Hong-Seng did check at lunch hour to see if Humphrey was still lying where they left him, only to report that he was gone. "Go home, probably," he said thoughtfully.

True enough, Humphrey had gone back to the flat and taken Claude's place on the sitting room floor. He didn't even get up to join the rest of the family for dinner, despite there being radishes and small bits of chicken that night, and, when it was bedtime, simply moved to his mattress beside Cynthia's cot. He spoke to no-one and looked like a stranger with his swollen face and bruised cheeks.

"This family!" Grandma Siok. "When you finally get the son up, the father lies down in his place!" But no one tries to arouse Humphrey from his apathy.

Then one day after work, Claude finds him lying on the sitting room floor, with half his face contorted, drooling out of the corner of his mouth. Claude tries to sit him up while calling for help. Humphrey's left hand flails about and he scratches Claude's arm several times. "Father?" Humphrey's lips move with great effort; a gurgle emerges.

"He's having an apoplectic attack," Grandma Siok says as soon as she reaches them. "We'll have to fetch the doctor." But Claude ends up taking Humphrey to hospital on a scooter with Hong-Seng. The three of them wait four hours in Ward C before being seen by a harried local doctor who tells them flatly that there are no more beds and that they should take Humphrey home and keep him well rested, away from any stimulation.

"Will he be able to walk again?" Claude asks. The doctor shrugs and gives him a bottle of pills to lower Humphrey's blood pressure.

Over the next few days, Humphrey recovers enough to take in food with only a minimal amount of choking when he is fed. He even manages to spit weakly at the Japanese anthem when it is played on the radio, and to mumble angrily when he is being moved roughly. He takes his pills without fuss, although Claude has to crush and dissolve them in a glass of water first. His entire right side remains limp the first two days, but afterwards he can wriggle his fingers and toes and drag his right arm and leg a few inches on the bed. Claude exercises his father every morning, lifting his limbs in wide arcs, flexing his knees, hips and elbows as the doctor showed him, in order to prevent Humphrey from stiffening up and to give him the best chance of recovering his independence.

But Humphrey seems to have decided that he likes having everything done for him. He refuses to cooperate with his exercises and ignores Claude when he tries to get him to comb his own hair or wash his own face. "His left side is quite okay," Grandma Siok says in frustration. "He can do a few things by himself. Leave him alone and he'll buck up, wait and see."

So they leave Humphrey to his own devices for a few days, and it is a disastrous experiment. His stubble sprouts in uneven patches on his lower jaw, his unwashed hair sits in lank, oily strands on his head and when he wets the bed, he sits obstinately in the pungent ammonia pool instead of rolling over onto his side. He makes no attempt to feed himself and will only drink if water is brought to his lips.

Finally, Cynthia puts her foot down. "This is ridiculous," she snaps. "Why are we playing his childish games? If he wants to be treated like an infant, so be it."

"You change him, then, Cynthia," Grandma Siok says. "He could use a good bath as well."

"I refuse to be tied to an, an—an invalid!" she shouts and heads for the door.

"Don't forget the curfew, Mother," Claude says, suddenly worried for her. Curfew starts in another hour and the Japanese will tolerate no excuses for breaking their rules. But her only answer is the slammed door and the sound of her footsteps running down the stairs. Claude knows he could fret or do something useful. He decides to bathe his father.

He carries Humphrey into the bathroom with Hong-Seng's help and sits him down on a low stool, his back propped against the wall. He strips off Humphrey's acrid-smelling pyjamas and pours a scoop of tepid water over him. Hong-Seng helps to keep Humphrey upright on the stool while Claude shampoos his father's hair and lathers up his body. By the time they make up his bed with clean sheets and tuck him in, Cynthia is back, her hair a cloud of cigarette smoke. She watches, leaning against the wall, and when Claude begins to feed his father porridge, she says brusquely, "Give that to me."

He shows her how to tilt the spoon and pour the porridge into Humphrey's mouth. She feeds him the entire bowl, gives him a drink of water with his pill and wipes his chin. Her movements are deft and precise, and every now and then, as she turns over her wrist, Claude can see the fresh cigarette burn beside her pulse point.

Hong-Seng sits by himself on the flat roof-top every evening after dinner. He calls it his garden. In several large urns he has managed to grow small patches of watercress and peanuts, which he waters twice a day. No one else goes up there. The door leading to the roof is padlocked and there's an understanding that the roof-top is his private domain, a small compensation for having his home taken over by an entire family. On particularly hot nights, he even sleeps up there, taking care to stay low behind his urns of watercress in order to keep out of sight of Japanese soldiers enforcing the curfew.

One night, after Claude helps Cynthia bathe his father, Hong-Seng surprises him by asking him up to the roof-top. The view is uninspiring. There are a few lorries making their way down the street and hawkers hurrying home shouldering their long poles strung with leftover wares. When he peeks between several buildings, Claude sees an occasional flash of sea. The air smells of seaweed.

The two of them sit for a long time without saying anything. Hong-Seng seems to be waiting. Finally, Claude asks, "Was Ling-li really a spy?"

"Who knows?" Hong-Seng says, spreading his hands to show his palms. "She was always surprising me. Quick mind, strong girl. I think she would have make a good spy." As with Ling-li, his English is more fluent when he is relaxed and off-guard.

"She was a good nurse too," Claude says, emotion welling up.

"You know, she never believed that," Hong-Seng says softly. "She always said she too, what is it? Im-patient." He somehow manages to give the word five syllables. "Yes, that's it, im-patient." Claude recalls the way she used to scrub out wounds or administer injections and has to smile. "And the sick man is a 'pa-tient', no?" Hong-Seng asks.

"Er, yes," Claude says, trying to follow. "Oh—yes, 'patient.' But when you tell someone to be patient, you mean . . ." He snaps his fingers, trying to find words to explain. There is a bucket of sand in front of him, much like the ones used in Littleton's fire-fighting unit. "Like this." He pulls the bucket between his legs, and, with his index finger, draws the character that Ling-li taught him. The sand scratches his finger. Knife over heart: 忍 . Ren.

Hong-Seng grins at him. "You know Chinese!"

"Hardly! Ling-li showed me this, and it took me forever to memorise it. I—I wish I'd had a chance to learn more from her."

A frail rim of moon begins to show itself.

"Do you still want to learn?" Hong-Seng asks after some time.

The street has cleared out, ready for the long night hours of curfew. Long night hours during which there will be nothing to do, except to read the day's propaganda in the newspapers and to listen to patriotic Japanese songs on the radio. Claude once considered trying to buy used copies of the Standard Certificate texts but then lost interest. His old life, exams, Oxford, all seemed like contingents of an old parade—noisy, ceremonial, completely irrelevant to real life.

Hong-Seng gets up. The last few minutes before curfew, time to go back down into the flat. "Would you teach me?" Claude asks. "I'm a slow learner when it comes to memorising characters and I don't think I'll ever be very good at the tones."

Hong-Seng has already started down, so it takes Claude a moment to grasp what he is saying. "You already know how to 忍 , and for Chinese, that will go a long way."

※

Who knows what goes on in Cynthia's head when she pins the orchid to her bodice and further whitens her lemon-bleached skin with rice powder? There is an efficiency to the movements of her hands, as if she has practised this ritual a million times, and yet, when she carefully sweeps her hair up into a soft bouffant, they hesitate on her nape. A reluctance, perhaps, to continue—she has always hated this particular hairstyle, thinks it rounds out even further her already full moon face.

Lucy watches, Grandma Siok watches, Hong-Seng watches, and Claude. It is impossible not to watch in this tiny flat, where they are all spilling over each other, and Cynthia has made no effort to shut the door to the room, but of course, everyone makes a fuss of pretending to do something else. Only Humphrey, log-like in his bed, his speech gnarled beyond recognition, stares off into nothingness, unmoved by Cynthia's defiant preparations.

The last thing she always does is to step back and smile into the mirror. It's always a startling moment for them. The smile is so natural, so carefree that in that moment they believe her to be happy and at peace with herself. Then it fades into hardness and apathy, and they have to look away. How can she do that? Claude asks himself time and again. It's as if she has learnt the art of shaping her face, arranging it as one would arrange flowers in a vase. Emotion has nothing to do with it, he realises. In this, she is a consummate professional.

Suddenly, the air shifts. Grandma Siok clears her throat and starts washing dishes, banging the cheap enamel bowls about, not hard enough to chip them but enough to induce an orchestral clanging that suggests great industry in the kitchen. Hong-Seng stomps triumphantly on a cockroach he has lured out of hiding from a hole in the wall. Lucy is making yet another one of her fire paintings. Nobody looks out the window, and there is nothing to suggest anything might be out there: no tooting of horns, no rapping of doors. Just the usual street sounds, but everyone knows he is here.

Emerging from the room, Cynthia drapes a silk shawl over her shoulders, sweeps her glance around the room imperiously, skims over Claude with a barely suppressed flinch. She has not been able to focus on his face ever since Hong-Seng brought him back here. When she reaches the door, Lucy asks, "Won't you eat first, Mummy?" Her head is still down, and her hand is moving her brush, but there is a distractedness to her painting.

A pause. "I'll have dinner outside," Cynthia replies. "My God, can't you make something else besides those bloody fire drawings?"

Lucy's hand stops, the brush smudging a deep pool of red in the middle of the paper. The enamel clanging in the kitchen stops, and Hong-Seng squats to wipe up the dead cockroach. Slowly, as if pondering a deep question, Lucy lifts her head. "No," she says quietly and resumes painting.

Cynthia slams the door on her way out.

Claude does not get up from his seat to look out the window. He does not watch her wear her all-natural smile and step over puddles towards the waiting limousine. He does not catch the whimsical salute of the Japanese general inside, in a good mood now that he is away from his office. He doesn't know where they will dine, where they will party tonight.

For this, his family receives an extra portion of rice every week and sometimes even scraps of chicken and pork. Charcoal is delivered to their door on Thursday mornings. They have a pass to speed them through checkpoints. This is all the knowledge that is required for now.

It is like memorising the floor plan of a house, or a map with specific directions. Hong-Seng insists on the slow laborious copying process that he says all Chinese students have followed. Each word must be learnt, its design imprinted on the memory, but more than that, the strokes comprising each character are to be constructed in precise, predetermined ways. "Your hand must know where to go without your brain thinking," Hong-Seng says.

Rather like playing the clarinet, Claude thinks, recalling the way his fingers moved over the keys fluidly, without hesitation. That must be what it feels like when the movements are absorbed into the body, when the hand has learnt the way. Still, it is boring, tedious work, copying each character over and over. The mind can lose sight of what is being written.

But one day, Hong-Seng shows him an exercise book printed with squares. A childish but clear hand has filled in many of the squares with characters copied over and over again, for two-thirds of the book. "Ling-li's writing book, when she was small," he tells Claude.

Claude recognises some of the characters, simple words—tree, flower, fruit. She must have been very young. "Five years old," Hong-Seng says, before Claude can ask.

The words drop off and Claude flicks through pages of blank squares. It's as if young Ling-li had given up her lessons. But on the penultimate page, a dense, compact block of words arises, like a building. He stares at it in admiration. Nothing about these characters is in common with the childish hand of the earlier pages. The brush has been deftly angled and confidently handled. Hong-Seng peers over his shoulder. "Still Ling-li," he confirms with a nod. "Grown-up now."

Claude takes in the flow of ink on the thin paper, the sureness of a hand that announced the proud bearing of a general. It is beautiful, full of a shining he doesn't understand but can feel, its light coming out through the characters and entering his eyes so that it is day—not just day, the height and precision of noon, when one's shadows clings tightest to the body, when matter and spirit cohere and there is a sharp burning lucidity to the world.

"We call this style Grass-Style Calligraphy," Hong-Seng offers. "Here, not strict rules, you see. The lines like grass in the wind. The words come freely, from the heart, from the spirit of the writer. Here, nothing hidden. You can read into her soul."

Ling-li's spirit on paper, in words he cannot read. Typical, he thinks, and smiles to himself. Aloud he asks, "Will you translate it for me?"

Hong-Seng's eyes linger on the page, travelling up and down the columns. When he gets to the end, he looks up at Claude. "For you to find out, when you know enough Chinese," he says.

"Just a hint," Claude presses, curious and impatient. "Come on, Hong-Seng."

But he shakes his head and reads the date to Claude. "November eighth, 1941. She copied this down when on her twenty-third birthday, by English calendar." Then he directs his student back to his copying exercise. "Plenty of time later," he says, "to read poetry."

If he ever could meet her again, he would ask her name. For years she has been Squatter Girl in his mind, and it would be strange to think of her as a Mei-Chin, or a Hwa-Liang—who knows, even a Mary or Jane, since locals have been known to pick up English names on occasion, out of a liking for the exotic.

Initially he thought he'd explain that it wasn't his fault that her shack burnt down, that he hadn't had anything to do with it personally, he'd even wanted her and her family to stay. But now, he knows he'd just ask her if she likes the cinema, if she's ever heard the De Sousa sisters on the radio and if she's ever rented a boat at Changi Beach and seen sharks.

Grandma Siok took him to Changi Beach when he was almost fifteen. It was in the middle of a heat wave, and the sea breezes were like oven blasts in his face. His voice had just begun to squeak and crack, and he had a constant rash on his jaw line from the weekly scraping he gave himself to clear the sparse stubble growing there. He wasn't pleased that his grandmother could row much more powerfully than he, and so he sulked throughout most of the outing. But then the sharks appeared, rubbery grey and streamlined, undulating through the waves. They took away his self-absorption for a moment, and he flashed Grandma Siok an unintentional smile in an unguarded moment. She smirked back in satisfaction, and he ignored it, glad to have made the trip with her after all, but not willing to show it.

Would Squatter Girl have liked the sharks? Would she have skipped school to wrestle crocodiles? Is there anyone else in the world who would?

※

The buzzing in his ear has evolved into a comfortable hum. But on the overcast, humid days before rain, even walking brings on an annoying buzz, a vibration of his tympanic membranes with every move. Unexpectedly, unpredictably, the visions appear—short flashes of illumination mirroring the lightning that forks across the sky, or more drawn-out ones rumbling heavily like thunder.

This same one has occurred several times already, with an insistence that is oddly familiar. Not surprising, since it is one of Ling-li. She is behind a tall bush, near water, he surmises from the occasional splash in the distance. He can't see her, but her voice is unmistakable. "Come on," she is saying with that usual click of impatience, "I need your help."

Sounds of a tussle, the crack of dry twigs and scrub. Heavy breathing from Ling-li, as if she's tiring in a long race. His suspicion holds him back, his heart thudding away. "You wouldn't, by any chance, be anywhere near a crocodile, would you?"

"Of course I am!" she replies, huffing. "Now hurry up! I can't hold on to his jaws any longer."

He makes several attempts to go through the bush, takes two or three faltering steps that inevitably stop. "Oi, Claude Lim! What are you waiting for?"

"It's a crocodile, Ling-li. Be reasonable!"

The sounds of thrashing grow louder. "Are—you—coming?" Ling-li pants.

"Yes, yes," he says, still unable to move beyond those first few steps. "As soon as I can . . ."

Soft pounding on the ground, the bush shivers. Ling-li's energies are entirely focused, he knows, on restraining the crocodile. Just a few seconds more, he promises himself, and then he will go through the bush and help her. A few seconds more—

There is no time. Thunder climaxes in a decisive whack across his eardrums, wiping out the buzz as surely as a sneeze clears his nose. He is back in Hong-Seng's flat, and the rain pours like dirty dishwater from the sky.

❁

"It's nice," he said, snuggling up to her feet. Sleep or trance, what is the difference?

There might have been a pause. There might have been a sigh, or a small, plaintive sound. There might have been a few more words:

"I've tried," she said, "I've tried always to live by those words. *The Ultimate Loyalty Is to Serve Your Country*. These last few days—it hasn't been easy." She sat down and crossed her legs. "It was . . . comforting having you around.

"I've been afraid so often, you know." And yet she sounded so matter-of-fact, so far from fear. "It was nice to have you looking out for me. Making sure I ate and all that." She looked down as she spoke and it occurred to him that she was embarrassed.

"Why do you have to leave? Where are you going?"

She bit her lip, as if trying to decide what to do. "You'd better get some rest."

"No, I want to know. What's going on? Where are you going? Isn't the war over?"

"For some," she said.

He didn't understand this Ling-li. She was so subdued, so lost. He reached out to take her hand. "It'll be all right. Things will look better in the morning. Someone I know once told me that." But this raised no smile of recognition in her. "I can keep a secret."

"What you don't know you can't remember."

"What I know I can forget." He didn't even know what he was saying, what was at stake, why he was holding on to her hand as she tried to get up. "Tell me, Ling-li. Where are you going?"

She squeezed his hand, did not pull away.

"Tell me," he said, and she did.

Past Collyer Quay on the way to Chinatown one day, Claude sees a work team huddled by the river. An animated Japanese shouts out instructions which are then translated by a Chinese youth. His words drift over as Claude approaches: " . . . you will repair these roads leading to the river. First you must clear the way and then spread the gravel over the ground . . ."

Each member of the work team is ragged and weary, each skeletal and strangely disengaged from his surroundings, trance-like. Each one white and immeasurably dirty.

The Japanese soldier motions to a pile of rusty spades and an assortment of unwieldy tools. The work team shuffles dutifully towards it. Each member picks up a tool and sets about clearing the rubbish and rotting debris in his path. Square-faced Japanese soldiers supervise the clean-up with occasional yells and kicks aimed at the white men who scurry about, carrying bags that, when they spill open, reveal sand.

It is strange for Claude to see white Europeans working at menial jobs previously reserved for the natives. Strange, and yet somehow exhilarating, as if some cord inside him has finally worked itself loose. What is it that makes him so sadistic, so glad at another man's suffering?

A white man drops his load of charred rubbish, his knees buckling from exhaustion. He lies there on the ground, eyes fixed at the sky. Then, without warning, he turns his face towards Claude, who stifles a shout. A swift kick to the white man's side sends him rolling. His Japanese tormentor hurls unknown insults as the man struggles to his feet, holding his arm to his side as if it might fall off. And then he is back at work, clearing the road.

Claude's heart is pounding. He is sure the man is Jack, though he did not show any recognition of Claude. Jack, on a prisoner-of-war work team. Suddenly the image of the Englishman in a tuxedo at his brother's bungalow clings to Claude's mind. He can't shake it off.

The Chinese translator winks at him. "Serves them right," he says to Claude in Hokkien, and amazingly, Claude understands. Yes, serves them right, he thinks, not meaning it. In the end, he is sad, nostalgic for an era he has come to distrust. There is no logic in the heart, Ling-li would have said.

Ling-li. If he could write to her, this is what he would draw:

Incomplete circle, 不, travelling 之. Recompense, repay, restore; still, yet, continue. If only she were here still, if only she could continue to be, if she could be restored. All of this contained in one word: 還 Return.

"Tell me," he said.

Of course she didn't. That was wishful thinking. She would never have told him anything like that—she could hardly trust him to rinse out a wound. She just smiled, extricated her hand and said goodbye.

He never saw her again, except through wishful thinking.

⁂

Claude is trying to explain to Hong-Seng. "The thing is, it's a *crocodile*. I'm not even sure I would be strong enough to hold it down, much less be of help to her."

Hong-Seng waves off this excuse. "No good, no good. This not good, what you did in dream." Ling-li's uncle is unaware that it was more a vision than a dream, but how to explain? Anyway, for all intents and purposes, the two can be used interchangeably, Claude decides.

"She is asking for help, and you not giving it—not good," Hong-Seng goes on. "When the dead ask you for something, you must try to give it."

At one time, Humphrey would have called Hong-Seng a superstitious fool, the type of local he would have resisted associating with. And at one time, Claude would have been inclined to agree, would have, perhaps, been embarrassed even, for Hong-Seng's sake. But today he sits quietly, considering his words. They resonate deep within him and a crystal of anxiety begins to form around them.

"What should I do?" he asks.

"Look, dream like this can only mean one thing—she needs your help. You better see what trouble she's in. Next time, you go through the bush, you walk right through and find out." He folds his arms across his chest, his face set, engrossed in his own thoughts. Claude, having just dismantled an axle from a split-open Morris, pours a small amount of turpentine onto a rag and rubs it over his hands. The coolness of the spirit soothes the ache in them. The grease comes off slowly as he massages in more turpentine.

"One thing . . ." Hong-Seng says. "We never put up altar for Ling. No funeral, no burial—" he chokes up suddenly. "We never got her body back for burial, but we never even made altar for her."

An altar? With its garish colours and mess of candles? With smoky incense and grinning gods? Ling-li, Claude realises, would love it. "We could make one now," he says.

"Yes, yes," Hong-Seng agrees. "We must make one." He gathers a few things and closes up the shop. It's almost dinnertime and Claude's stomach is rumbling as they walk back to the flat. Grandma Siok has left early to run some errands. He wonders what she will think of the altar.

Back at the flat, Hong-Seng leads him to a small door beside the kitchen. Claude has always assumed it to be a storage closet. Hong-Seng opens it to reveal a small shrine set in a box-like space no larger than an icebox. The shrine houses a white Kuan-Yin, a small trough of sand, a framed photograph, two white candles on either side, an empty offering tray and two name plaques that read vertically, carved and painted over in gold paint. "Han Kwong Luck, Han Oe Liang—Ling-li's parents," Hong-Seng explains. "Ling-li used to burn joss-sticks for them everyday. We should place her next to them."

Claude peers at the photograph of a young man and woman in an old-fashioned studio. The young man is wearing a traditional dark robe. The woman stands behind him on the right, wearing a plain cheongsam, her left hand resting on his shoulder, a closed fan in her right hand. Despite the faded image, he sees Ling-li's eyes in hers.

Hong-Seng produces a flat piece of wood and begins trimming it.

He instructs Claude to grind the ink and to bring out his brushes. Claude works steadily until there is a pool of black ink in the inkwell. "Not good ink," Hong-Seng complains. "Usually we carve first, then paint over, but I find someone to do later. This just for now."

Slowly, supporting his right hand at the wrist with his left, Hong-Seng writes three Chinese characters from top to bottom of the narrow strip. "Han Ling-li." The characters seem to contain all of Ling-li's angularity and thinness.

Hong-Seng places her name plaque on the shrine beside her parents' names. Grandma Siok walks in just as he is directing Claude to light the candles.

She reads the name plaque silently, her mouth moving. "Joss-sticks?" she asks.

Hong-Seng opens the kitchen cupboard and brings out a cylindrical roll wrapped in cotton cloth. Inside are sandalwood-scented joss-sticks. He selects one and lights it.

"Now we bow." He faces the altar, stands at attention and performs a total of nine bows. "Three to each person," he explains when he is done.

Grandma Siok is next. When she is done, she says that she should set up an altar for her husband soon. Hong-Seng tells her he will help her, and they both turn to Claude expectantly. He positions himself self-consciously at the altar, snapping his heels together and brushing aside an unruly lock of hair. In the glass of the picture frame, he catches a reflection of his face and winces, wondering what Ling-li would think if she saw him now.

He bows three times, eyes fixed on her father's name plaque. Then he bows to her mother's name plaque, and then finally he faces hers. The characters of her name swim before him, seeming to fill his entire visual field. For a moment he wonders if he might be dizzy, until he realises that his eyes are wet and brimming. He bows quickly to hide his face. Once, twice, three times. A large tear lands on his big toe.

When he looks up, Hong-Seng is wiping his face with his handkerchief. "I swear," Grandma Siok says brightly. "Ever since the war, there's been more dust around than any other time I can remember." It is true that for weeks after the Surrender, the burning of corpses and the oil fires dying down slowly made the atmosphere greasy and sooty and it has never cleared up since.

"Very bad air," says Hong-Seng, his voice muffled in his hand-kerchief. "Worst air ever."

❁

"I can keep a secret."
Can he? Has he?

❁

Wishful thinking: Across the street, in a coffee shop, a young woman wolfs down a small portion of yam and when she finishes, she drinks glass after glass of water, trying to fill herself. Her chin, if it had a bit more flesh on it, might have afforded a dimple; her wrists look like a child's. She wears a *samfoo* and only speaks Hokkien.

When she looks his way, there is no pause of recognition. She looks right through him, as if he doesn't exist, as if she doesn't exist, as if this were just sleep, just trance. Is there a difference?

❁

The crocodile is making strange noises, a kind of purring in its throat, ominous in its unexpected domesticity. "Are you all right, Ling-li?" Claude's voice is anxious.

"Hummph." You can almost *hear* the rolling of her eyes. In the distance there is a soft plop of water.

"Well, I take it you still want me to come over," he says, feeling stupid as soon as the words are out of his mouth. On the ground, a trail of ants, tiny myrmidons. From this unobtrusive family sprang a race of warriors. Somehow, it's a comforting thought.

"Anytime you're ready, hero," comes Ling-li's reassuringly teasing retort. She is out of breath, but otherwise sounds quite normal—as normal as one can be, he supposes, when one is wrestling a crocodile.

The tall bush has acquired the solidity of a wall, and though it is green, the sense of it is familiar. All he has to do is walk through. All he has to do is will himself over. What is a mere wall when the will is engaged? He thinks of Ling-li and her no-nonsense courage. She would have walked right through in a matter of seconds had he, or Lucy, or some unknown native child been in need of assistance. If he has gained nothing else from her, he must have acquired one drop of her courage.

"I'm coming," he says with determination. "I'm coming, Ling-li." Eyes closed, he walks through the bush, stepping neatly over the sinuous trail of myrmidons.

✸

"I can keep a secret."
Can you? Have you?

✸

A chill, the immediate instinct to shut your eyes and block everything out. But you have already taken the first step to looking, and there is nothing you can do to reverse that. Nothing can erase the image of Ling-li on the floor, hands and feet shackled to four posts, blindfolded, gagged and stark-naked. No pond, no bushes, no crocodile. A terror rises up in you, and nothing can quell it, nothing except for the clear clarinet voice that speaks in your ear.

"Claude Lim, why do you shut your eyes?" Ling-li's tones, liquid and whole.

"I, I thought you needed help—with the crocodile."

"I do need your help," she says calmly, and her steadiness gives you hope. "Now, more than ever, Claude Lim, I have no-one else I can call on."

"What is happening to you?" you ask, not wanting at all to know, but unable to stop yourself. "What have they done to you?"

"What you've always known, Claude, since the time it happened. What you've always known but have refused to see or acknowledge."

She waits patiently, as if aware of how much you have to force yourself to breathe in order to bear what is ahead. There are other faint sounds, from a faraway place, men's voices and barks, a scream that is at once almost silent and yet indelibly palpable, like the whistle that sets dogs howling in a frenzy. A cold glimmer of logic. "How are you able to talk like this?" you ask, remembering the gag.

"The same way you can cross walls and bushes," she replies, a shrug in her voice. "These are extraordinary times, Claude, requiring extraordinary means."

"But this is the past," you say. Six months since the day you were released, bleeding and disfigured beyond recognition, and Hong-Seng found you—a man who has only met you twice before, but able to identify you by name amidst the deliberate distortions exacted by the Japanese.

"You are dead." An illogical hope arises despite your dread. "Aren't you? Aren't you dead?"

"Chinese," she says, "has no strict sense of tense. It traverses time and history, intrudes upon the present."

History. Time, places, names, dates. "Yes," she continues, reading your mind. "But even more—witness and story."

The silent screaming continues, sending an electric spark through your spine. How much more can you endure? "忍耐," she says, partly in answer, partly in encouragement. "你一定要忍耐."

"Turn to your right," she says. "You are not the only one. Open your eyes, Claude, see who else is here."

You turn your head, your eyes still squeezed shut, but with a burst of impatience at yourself you let your lids fly open. Bewilderment: Jack Winchester, seated on a chair, legs crossed at the knee, his eyes resolutely closed, as if in mid-daydream.

"A terrible mistake. They thought he might have some information about me, that he might be, in some way, related to my white intelligence contact." She laughs, a hard sound. "This was their idea of making him talk—they thought that if he had to watch my torture and humiliation he would yield and beg them to stop in exchange for information."

Jack's lips are pursed, his brows furrowed in his determination to shut out the scene before him. "He is at Brighton Beach," Ling-li says. "That's where he has removed himself, in order to avoid seeing. He does not know what they want from him, cannot give them the information they want because he has none. He can exchange nothing for my release, and so does not even try."

Jack was there all along, the familiar presence you sensed but did not acknowledge. And he sat through—through everything they did to Ling-li? "In much the same way as you counted ants," she says flatly, and shame rushes up inside you. What can you say to her now, how can you even begin to tell of your anguish? But she is not seeking apologies. She is a general through and through, and this, more than anything now, is obvious.

"Claude Lim," she says. "Jack can afford to close his eyes, he can afford to turn away. In a few years, it will be over, and he will return to his country, glad and relieved to be home at last. He will be able to put his memories behind him, especially things he did not see. It will be as if they never existed. He and others like him will be able to convince themselves of that."

Her voice changes, becomes melodious. "但是你就不同了," she says. "You're different. You have no other home but here. 你现在应该知道." To your amazement, you understand her perfectly. No need for translation in your head, no need for the clumsy intermediary of English before understanding glimmers. Back and forth she switches, as if already knowing your capacity to comprehend your native tongue.

"If you won't witness this, who will?" she asks. "If you won't remember and record this, who will? This is how our history starts and is transmitted, Claude. Witness and transmission of Story. 事实的见证和传述是历史."

"我没有太多的时间," she says, continuing to slip amphibiously between English and Chinese. "Claude Lim: 你看不看?"

You nod, swallowing hard to evade the emotions that are swarming through you. "Open your eyes then," she says. "As you can see, I was blindfolded and gagged. They did not want me to see their faces and to speak." Before you, Ling-li on the floor, bound, gagged, blindfolded. She waits until you no longer flinch, until your eyes no longer roll about in order to avoid looking directly at her. "I will tell you, and you will witness it, but you will also tell me what I want to know—their faces, height, distinguishing features. Every bit to erase their anonymity," she instructs steadily when she senses you are ready.

Even as she speaks, a soldier approaches, slightly sheepishly, but his companions begin jeering and laughing, and emboldened by

their festivity, he kicks Ling-li in the side. Her body jerks, a muffled cry comes from the depths of her throat. He throws off his
trousers and sits on top of her thighs. The jeering and laughter grow
louder.

"我知道将会发生什么，而且早就知道了，然而当事情发生
的时候，我依然期望出现奇迹。当我感到他压在我身上时，
我知道我应该放弃所有希望。我必须集中精力，决不泄露丝
毫秘密，用我的全部气力，不告诉他们那些他们想从我这些
知道的名字。在我内心深处，我知道这些名字对他们来说无
关紧要。我是一个中国人，然而，在他们眼里我仅仅是一只
动物。

"第一个男人在强奸我的时候摊开我的两腿，我能够闻到他身
上有一股腐败气味，象烂疮的脓味。他不停地轻轻咳嗽，
发出紧张的声音。与他那矮小的体格相形之下，他的手是相当
大的。在他右手拇指下面有一个疣或硬茧。它是我允许自己
去感觉的一个东西。" She pauses, then says, "Now you, what do
you see?"

"He is brown, small like you described. His hair is badly shaved,
he has a mole on his neck—the right side. He is sweating," you say,
your voice breaking.

"勇气," she tells you, and you are instantly angry at your own
weakness. Her voice takes on a hard edge. "第二个 . . .

"他更残酷。他的目标是施加痛苦。在被他强奸的整段过
程中，我只感到痛苦。他紧捏我的乳头并且扭拧它们，我感到
痛不欲生不停地辗转反侧，之后，他将我翻转，强奸我。
我现在能够闻到不同的气味。它是我自己的血和粪的混合味。
His aim is to inflict pain. He pinched my nipples and twisted them
until I couldn't stop myself from thrashing about, and then he
turned me over and sodomized me. I could smell something different now. It was my own blood." She hides nothing, not even her
own humiliation. It is the way, you suppose, of generals.

You force yourself to speak. "Taller than the first one, maybe five-
foot-ten. Sharp face, long scar behind his left ear, down to his throat.
He laughs all the time, a deliberate laugh, hard and unemotional. Bad
teeth, brown and decaying." You keep his face in mind as clearly as you
can, until she can read it, pick it up, examine it to her satisfaction.

"下一个，是个超重的男人。他首先小心翼翼地试著擦去我身上的血。对他来说，仿佛我极肮脏。但是，指挥官命令他继续向我施暴。他拔出塞在我嘴里的布，然后将他的阳物塞进我的嘴里。我想咬下它。当我咬下它的时候，我想著每一个我绝不能说出的名字。他尖声大叫。我的嘴里满是血，然后我将它吐出。他们开始猛烈地踢我的头。我唯一能做的事是希望他们能将我打倒，失去知觉。他们一定是想到了同样的事，因为他们突然停止猛踢，把塞嘴布换掉，然后继续向我施暴。"

"愚钝的相貌，挺高的额头，强大的下颌，" you intone, biting your lip. "His face completely screwed up in pain. He is the cleanest of the lot so far, 他看起来甚至好象洗过他的脸. After you—bite him, he is slapped by the commanding officer."

"我含糊地记得，" she says. You take a deep breath and wonder how long you can go on. A brief glimpse at Jack. His head is down, his eyes still shut. You sense that his jaw is clenched.

"下一个，就日本人而言他是挺高的。他失去了左手的无名指。在整段强奸过程中他不断地用手打我。他用一条布勒住我的脖子，几乎将我勒死，然后他又改变了主意。"

You are unravelling, spinning out of control. "I can't look," you tell her. "停止，停止，我不能再继续."

"这是战争，" she says. "冷静一下，快要结束了。"

You try to take on her unfailing steadiness. "He has a moustache, and sideburns, unlike the others who are mostly shaved. He is the loudest of them all, 即使他在强奸你的时候，他也在不停地奚落别人并大喊大叫。他满脸都是斑点，长长的鼻子，身高差不多有六英尺。"

"最后，"她说，并且停顿了一下。"接下来是最后一个。"她那突然颤抖的声音使你感到恐惧。"他没有什么明显的特征。"

"普通身高，他头上围著白色头巾。长得相当匀称好看，特徵平平，看起来很年轻。和我年龄一般大小。"他小心翼翼地爬在伶俐身上，好象很对他要做的事感到恐惧。然而，当他开始强奸她的时候，激烈的表情使他面孔扭曲。这不是强烈的感情，也不是性欲。

"憎恨，"你犹豫地说。

"我能感觉到，"她回答。此时，她的声音听起来已经很疲劳。"我能感觉到事情会变得更糟。对不起，柯拉德。勇气。"她觉得透不过气来。

当那年轻人强奸完她之后，始料不及的是，他从身边拿起一把刀，迅速地切开了伶俐的阴部。你听到她的尖叫声，你的嘴里满是胆汁，你透不过气来。房间在倾斜，并且象陀螺一样在旋转著。

"伶俐！"你绝望地呼唤。"伶俐！"

"不要紧，"她说。她坚强冷静的声音再次回响在你身边。"我昏倒了。痛苦已经结束。我流血至死。前后有六个小时，然后，结束了。"

You are crying and shaking. You see the knife flash again and again, the blade cutting through Ling-li's flesh. Over? How can she say that, when the memory of it burns in your mind?

"我是说我"，她轻轻地说。"不是说你。"

"你是我的证人，柯拉德，为此，我感谢你。"

A glissando of white walls, the stop-and-go rhythm of ants. The yellow glint of crocodile teeth, echoed in fire paintings. These are the seeds of memory and song. This is what you have come to know.

Hong-Seng's knife etches brush strokes into the wood. A picture forms.

What is required of generals: to take, to hold; the future, what is not yet here; to nourish; to act; to ask; to escort, convey; to lead; the great toe or thumb. In a word, in that word Hong-Seng has scarred into wood: 将.

In the block of two-storey tenement houses opposite the workshop, some children play in the afternoons, taking care not to stray too far from their front doors and to keep out of the way of passing Japanese soldiers. Most of the time, they organise an imaginary kitchen with broken crockery and spend hours cooking up fantastical feasts. They make mud patties, baking them in make-believe ovens, or roll little mud balls, which they fry in a fraying coolie's hat called into service as a wok. They gather rotten fruit peel, which they set in their broken clay pots and then sit in a circle nibbling, as if they were at a large banquet.

One day, however, as Claude is sweeping the front of the workshop, he observes a break from their usual play. Unlike the kitchen-and-feast scenario, they have divided into two groups—one of five boys, and another of three girls. The boys are giving instructions, each one trying to speak over the words of the others. They are carrying wooden stakes and broken broom handles. One boy wears an overturned pail around his neck and bangs on it erratically, whenever the others cry down his suggestions.

The girls listen for the most part, yawning and looking off into the distance, their hands fidgeting with their usual kitchen "utensils." The boys direct them to cook, while they themselves ride around on imaginary horses, fencing clumsily with their wooden stakes. The drummer beats out an enthusiastic unsteady rhythm while making crude trumpet sounds through his pursed lips. The girls, squatting around the "wok," half-heartedly mime the motions of cooking while watching the boys in their new game.

Finally, one girl stands up and walks up to the boys. She demands a wooden stake and a role in the war game. The boys jeer at her, telling her that she can't join in—her role is in the kitchen. In clear, childish Hokkien that even Claude can understand, she says she's tired of playing in the kitchen, she wants to join them on the horses.

The boys are mulish in their refusal. "You're a girl," they tell her. "You do girl things."

Frustrated, she grabs a stake from an unsuspecting boy's hand. "Come on," she says, waving it at them. "I'll fight all of you."

They stare at her uneasily, not knowing what to do. She slashes the air, making impressive whooshing sounds, and whacks one of the boys across his buttocks. He stands for a moment, stunned. Then, with a furious shriek, he pounces on her. The other boys join in gleefully, bringing their stakes down on her shoulders, her arms, the backs of her knees until she buckles and falls. Claude starts running in his uneven lope towards them, waving his broom. "Stop it, stop, you bastards," he yells.

The sight of his face startles them and they cower. He uses his scars to his advantage, scowling hard to disfigure his face even more. "Clear off, do you hear me? Leave her alone." His Hokkien is clumsy, but it is enough for them to understand and to back away. He opens his mouth and lets out a nasty roar. They scatter, throwing their stakes behind, screaming.

The girl sits up, her face dirty and slightly bruised from a whack she must have sustained across her right cheek. "Are you all right?" he asks, holding out his hand. She scrambles to her feet without touching his hand, picks up her stake and waves him back. "Hey! I'm only trying to help!" But she swings her stake and hits him on the calf. The jagged edges of the wood scrape his skin.

"Okay, okay—I'm leaving," he says, throwing up his hands and backing away. She is a plain child; her little face is set in a murderous frown that makes her all the more unappealing. She is probably no more than eight.

When he has retreated to the workshop, she raises a fist at him and smirks. Then she turns and practically struts back into her house, conscious of the hidden gaze of her playmates. Claude decides he doesn't really like her—there is a pug-like cast to her face.

Later that evening at the flat, he practises writing, at first with a pencil, on a newspaper. Then when his efforts meet Hong-Seng's approval, he picks up his brush, grinds the ink and paints on the back of Ling-li's name plaque: 精忠报国. When it is done, he lights a joss-stick for Ling-li and watches it burn off into formless, sandalwood-scented smoke.

❁

This last time in the dream they are holding you down, your arms forced behind you in a numbing lock. But there is something superhuman in your strength tonight. You shake them off, flexing your muscles, but hardly using your full power. It surprises them as much as it surprises you. For a moment, you stand staring at each other, marvelling at this newfound muscularity, this unexpected physical prowess. And then you are looking at your outstretched hand, unsure yourself of what you are asking for.

But they seem to know, for they have placed a knife in the cup of your palm, its blade light and slightly gritty to the touch. "An animal, when caught in a trap, will chew off its own body parts in order to escape," you tell them, the myriad you's in your crazy dream. No one seems perturbed. There is calmness all around, and nodding heads, as if they have been waiting for this moment.

You open your mouth, slide the knife in, wincing as the point hits your hard palate and scrapes the inside of one cheek. Your free hand reaches in, seizes the root of your tongue, holding it as still as you can while it jerks uncontrollably in epileptic spasms. And then you make a sawing motion, the knife blade tearing through tongue muscle unevenly. The dying tongue, twitching fiercely in your hand, still registers the taste of blood and metal, and the rawness of the wound is exquisite enough to bring tears to your eyes. An involuntary moan squeezes past the vocal cords. You keep cutting. There is no terror, no panic this time. Just a ragged determination to complete your task and to free yourself.

Down to mere fibres, the last strips of tissue. On impulse, you throw down the knife, grasp the dangling cord with your freed-up hand as the other one anchors the root by bracing it against the roof of your mouth. You pull with deliberate steadiness. The jagged edges of tongue muscle separate; the sensation is like pulling a particularly sinewy variety of taffy, or of tearing off a drumstick from the body of an overcooked chicken. And then in a flash, there is a release and you are holding the fleshy red organ in your hand. It is heavy, warm and still quivering. You experience a brief nostalgia, but you shake it off. There is no further use for the tongue, and it will soon rot. You toss it as far as you can, and it lands in a splash of unseen water.

Your mouth is burning. Every so often you spit out blood, but there is a novel lightness and spaciousness within. You test your speech. Only a moaning sound. Louder. A gurgle, a wail. Nonsense syllables, the building blocks of new speech.

When fully healed, you will have only a stub to work with. No

miraculous new tongue will sprout in the old one's place, no regen-
eration of what has been lost. Only a muteness—at best, a stunted
form of speech, that will make children laugh and tease you merci-
lessly. No matter. You will laugh along, knowing that they will not
be contaminated by that old tongue.

In your hand, your clarinet appears. You bring it to your lips and
play a simple melodic line, then stop and hum it. Clarinet and
human voice. Pure instruments. You have ventured past words.

What have you learned? About Chinese opera, this:

The female roles in Chinese opera are harder to fathom. While
the males are old, young or acrobatic, the female is classified by
character. *Qing Yi* is virtuous, submissive and well bred, the perfect
Chinese woman. *Hua Dan* is vivacious, flamboyant, flirtatious—the
sex symbol. *Gui Men Dan* hovers at the threshold of womanhood, mis-
chievous and lively. *Wu Dan* performs acrobatics and *Lao Dan* is old,
wise and resourceful.

And then there is *Dao Ma Dan*: female warrior.

The *Dao Ma Dan* is a role of intrigue, military skill, acumen. Her
role requires singing, acting, acrobatics—she does it all. When she is
a general, she wears the *kao* and four pennants strapped to her back.
She may wield spear and sword and on her horse she is a fury of
flight, flags and pheasant feathers. When she falls in battle, even
male generals cry. There is none like her.

What have you learned? If nothing else, this:

That Ling-li is not dead, not really. Words, history, narrative can
all be manipulated. And if you don't want her dead, then it's time
to resurrect her, time to defy and outdo the construct once again,
but this time you have to be patient. This time you will have to out-
write death, and for that you will require a lifetime. You will require
another language.

Acknowledgments

Many thanks to my mentors, Peter Turchi, Andrea Barrett, CJ Hribal, Kit McIlroy, and Claire Messud for sharing the growing pains of the manuscript.

Thanks also to my agent, Brettne Bloom, for her faith in the book; to Jared Williams for taking a chance on a stranger; to Ike Williams for the same. A big hug and thank you to my editor, Carol Houck Smith, for her hard work, insight, and tolerance for my telephone-shy habits.

Thank you to Dr. David Reines for keeping me afloat in hard times.

Thank you to my family for their support.

Thank you to Sand T and Wang Xianmin for help in the Chinese sections.

A huge thank you to Dr. Leigh Ann Clayton for taking such good care of my bunny, Forró.

And finally, to my "tribe," for believing in me: Sonja Kassuba, Robert Redick, Kiran Asher, Cindy Phoel, Carmelina Luongo, Laura Grego, Jeannie Parkus, Marlo Poras, Aparna Sindhoor, Raju Sivasankaran, Debbie Nicolellis, Ana Ilha, Jeremy Zucker, Og Lim, Dorea D'Agostino, Lucien Zoll, Christine Melchior, Stephen Scully, Tree Mason, Martha McFadden, Roy Jacobstein, Lala Roberts, Maurice Butler, Jeremy Jones, the staff and MDs of RHCI, the staff of HMR (W. Newton), and the Warren Wilson community.

BIBLIOGRAPHY

Elphick, Peter. *Singapore: The Pregnable Fortress—A Study in Deception, Discord and Desertion.* Hodder and Stoughton, London, 1995.

Elphick, Peter, and Michael Smith. *Odd Man Out—The Story of the Singapore Traitor.* Hodder and Stoughton, London, 1993.

Sun Tzu. *The Art of War.* Trans. Samuel B. Griffith. Oxford University Press, 1963.

Orwell, George. *Burmese Days.* Harvest Books, 1974.

Conrad, Joseph. *Youth: A Narrative; Heart of Darkness; The End of the Tether.* Everyman's Classic Library, reprint edition, 1991.

National Archives of Singapore. *The Japanese Occupation 1942–1945: A Pictorial Record of Singapore.* Times Editions (Pte.) Ltd., 1996.